A Curious Cartography

by

Alison Littlewood

BLACK
SHUCK
BOOKS

A Curious Cartography

by

Alison Littlewood

BLACK
SHUCK
BOOKS

A Curious Cartography

Black Shuck Books
www.blackshuckbooks.co.uk

First published in Great Britain in 2023 by
Black Shuck Books
Kent, UK

Versions of the following stories have previously appeared in print:
'The Boggle Hole' in *New Fears* (Titan Books, 2017)
'Jenny Greenteeth' in *The Mammoth Book of Folk Horror* (Skyhorse Publishing, 2021)
'In the Wabe' in *Close to Midnight* (Flame Tree Press, 2022)
'The Headland of Black Rock' in *This Dreaming Isle* (Unsung Stories, 2018)
'The Merrie Dancers' in *Cursed* (Titan Books, 2020)
'Ways to Wake' in *Nightmare #70* (2018)
'The July Girls' in *Echoes* (Saga Press, 2019)
'The Marvellous Talking Machine' in *Phantoms* (Titan Books, 2018)
'Hungry Ghosts' in *Shadows and Tall Trees 8* (Undertow Publications, 2020)
'The Light You Can Hear' in *Songs of the Northern Seas* (Egaeus Press, 2021)
'Black Feathers' in *Black Static #22* (2011)
'White Feathers' in *Five Feathered Tales* (SST Publications, 2016)
'Swanskin' in *After Sundown* (Flame Tree Press, 2020)
'The Adventure of the Avid Pupil' in *Sherlock Holmes's School for Detection*
(Robinson, 2017)
'The Flowering' in *The Flowering* (Black Shuck Books, 2022)
'The Entertainment Arrives' in *Darker Companions* (PS Publishing, 2017)
'The View from the Basement' in *The Hyde Hotel* (Black Shuck Books, 2016)
'The Same as the Air' in *Ten-Word Tragedies* (PS Publishing, 2019)
'Words' in *Bitter Distillations* (Egaeus Press, 2020)

Set in Caslon
Cover art and interior design © WHITEspace, 2023
www.white-space.uk

978-1-913038-86-1

For everyone who dares to dream, and wonder, and yearn a little.

And then picks up a book, or indeed a pen, and begins their journey.

| Contents |

~

Contents

|Here Be Monsters|

|The Boggle Hole|

~

Tim's grandad's house wasn't like a house should be. There were white lacy things on the chair arms, and the wallpaper had knobbly bits in it, and the television was too small and bulged out at the back. The carpet had a texture, pale green ridges Tim could feel through his socks, and the worst thing, the thing he really didn't like, was the silence that hung over it all. It was as if it lived there, that silence, like a creature that had moved in and swelled to occupy the space. Tim didn't know how to banish it. He could only make it retreat, one leg at a time, into some corner or other; but he always knew the effect was temporary, that once he'd finished his game it would stealthily creep back, a bulbous, insidious thing that watched him always, waiting for its chance to pounce.

Tim's house didn't have a Silence in it. Now it didn't have Tim in it either, or his mum; she'd gone on holidays of her own, off to a golden beach with a man Tim scarcely knew. It wasn't even summer. It was late autumn, all the fallen leaves already lying soggy in the gutters. He scowled when he thought of her, miles and miles away and having fun.

'Penny for 'em, lad,' his grandad said, and Tim realised he'd come into the room behind him, padding on silent slippered feet. Grandad's slippers were made of brown checked fabric and had holes in the toes. They were so ugly Tim wondered how he had ever come to buy them, but old people were like that; they didn't seem to care what anything looked like. He scowled again.

'She'll be back soon enough, lad,' Grandad said, and he glanced at the window, where the rain had begun to fall in a steady splutter. Tim couldn't hear it but he could see it spitting against the glass.

'I know you'd rather be in that there Bahaymas.'

Bahamas, thought Tim, but he couldn't be bothered to correct him.

"Appen I'll tek you to a beach,' his grandad said. 'You'll see, it's not ser bad. There's nowt on them furren beaches, son. Just wait – ours has got *treasures*.'

Tim looked up.

'There's fossils, an—'

Tim sighed.

'Aye, well. You'd rather them Bahaymas. Fair do's, son.' Grandad sighed and pulled open a drawer in the sideboard. He took his pipe from it, hiding the curve of it in his hand. 'I'll just pop for a puff, lad. She dun't like it in t'ouse, you know.'

Tim frowned as he watched Grandad shuffle towards the door in his slippers. He knew he wouldn't bother changing into shoes to go outside. He always went in his slippers and he always talked about Grandma when he did it, and Tim didn't know why; his gran had died years ago, before Tim could even form the memories to remember her by, and yet Grandad still tiptoed around her. *She wouldn't like this. She wouldn't like that.* He would whisper, as if she were there, listening and disapproving. Tim had a picture of a stolid woman with her arms folded across her chest; it didn't tally with the photograph which sat in an ornate frame on the mantelpiece, of a slender, dark-haired girl with laughter in her smile.

He looked out of the window to see Grandad settling into his usual seat on the rain-damp bench at the end of the garden, puffing on his pipe. The thumb of his left hand kept turning and turning the wedding ring on his finger, over and over, while he stared into the smoke.

Boggle Hole didn't look like much of a beach. It lay at the bottom of a narrow gully: a small cove of exposed rock with a stream running through it. The cliffs stretched away, the colour of pale sand. The beach was not the colour of sand. Mostly it was black, streaked with the bright green slime of seaweed.

'What d'you think?' asked Grandad.

Tim tried not to scowl. *Boggle Hole,* he thought. *South of Robin Hood's Bay. Near Ravenscar.* Such a thrill he had felt at the sound of the words, and now the reality was grey and bare and boring. He remembered when Grandad first told him about it. *Boggle Oyle*, he'd said. *We'll go to Boggle Oyle*, and Tim had thought *Oil*, and wondered why they should want to go to an oily beach; the image in his head had been something he'd seen on television, blackened seabirds being dunked in washing-up bowls by solemn volunteers. Now he looked out at the dark beach under a dark sky and wondered how far off the mark he had been.

'Aye, well. There's a beach in summer. You can make sandcastles. It gets scoured off, though. Winter's on its way.' Grandad sniffed the air, as if he could smell it coming.

Tim sniffed too, and got only cold briny sharpness. He wondered if that's what winter smelled like. He wondered too what kind of beach was only there for some of the time; that did have a whiff of the magical about it, as though it might appear when he turned his back.

'There were smugglers used this beach,' Grandad said. When Tim looked up at him he winked, his face creasing in a hundred places. 'Smugglers and maybe wreckers, too. And then there's the boggle.'

'The boggle?' Tim had thought it was just a name, a strange one, like lots of other names around here. He hadn't known it was a thing.

Grandad's eyes brightened. 'Come on, lad,' he said. 'I'll show you.'

The cave was a dark focal point the cliff swept towards as if pointing the way. As Tim skipped ahead he found there was some sand on the beach after all; clumps of it clung to his trainers like mud, sticking strands of weed to the white leather. It occurred to him there was noise here too, not like in the house: gulls sounding like scrapping cats; the gritting of his feet; the distant growl of a car on the cliff-top. Beneath it all the sea was shushing, as if telling everything else to shut up and listen.

Inside the cave, though, it was quiet. He could still hear the sea but it was as if the cave had its own Silence inside it, a presence that was trying to keep the noise out. Then Grandad huffed and puffed his way inside, and the thought was gone.

'This is it, lad.'

Tim turned. 'What?' He'd forgotten about the boggle, but he remembered when he saw the wink, the fissures in the old man's face.

'The boggle hole. This is it.' Grandad waved his hand around the pocked grey walls. 'This is where it lives.'

'What's a boggle?'

Grandad put his fingers to his lips. 'All right, I'll tell thee. But quiet, like. They don't like being talked about.' He glanced around as he whispered. 'A boggle is a sort of goblin. Some call 'em brownies, or hobs. This one 'ere's a boggle. Along t' coast there's another bay called Hob Hole. That one – well, some used to take their kids there when they got t' whooping cough. They'd ask the hob to cure 'em, and sometimes it did. It's true, lad.' Grandad winked again.

Tim hadn't heard of the whooping cough, didn't know what it was. He shook his head.

'They say this 'ere boggle started out in Robin Hood's Bay. But they play tricks, see, and this one played a trick so nasty they banished him. So now he lives here.'

Tim cast his eyes around the cave. It wasn't a big cave. There didn't seem to be anywhere a boggle could hide. He looked quizzically at his grandad.

'Oh, you can't see him. Not unless he wants to be seen.' There was laughter in Grandad's voice; Tim was no longer sure if it was a real story or something he'd just made up. 'Unless…' Grandad raised one shaggy white eyebrow. 'They say, if you look in something shiny, you can see t' boggle's face. Here.' He slowly worked the wedding ring from his finger and passed it to Tim. 'Careful, now. Try that.' He opened his eyes wide as if in fear.

The ring was old and heavy in Tim's hand. When he looked closely he could see there were layers of fine scratches in it, but between the blemishes, it still shone. He peered at the surface, then quickly looked at the old man, to see if he was being mocked.

Then, in the surface of the ring, he saw a dark outline against a bright oval. It looked a little like a face. He leaned closer and the shape grew bigger; it was nothing but his own reflection. He frowned.

'Aye, well. Maybe he din't want to come out today. Let's go and look for fossils. We might find some by t' beck.'

The sea was loud again in Tim's ears as he walked by Grandad's side, talking now of boggles, now of smugglers and now of dinosaurs. The coast was Jurassic, Grandad said, and that made Tim think of

T-Rexes; he wondered if one could be buried, now, in the cliff. He looked at the beach with different eyes. When he knew the stories, the place was better. *Boggle Oyle*. He remembered what Grandad had said about his beach: *ours has got treasures*. He slipped his hand into Grandad's dry fingers, and when Grandad smiled at him, Tim grinned back.

~

The 'treasure' was a small grey handful of stone, curled into a tight circle that was roughened at one side where the spiral had broken. It didn't look like treasure, but Grandad said it was a 'hammonite', so Tim supposed it must be. He examined it while Grandad took out his pipe and lit it, sitting on a large smooth rock at the head of the cove.

After a while Tim stopped looking at the fossil and started watching the sea, and after that he watched Grandad.

'Why don't you smoke in the house?' he asked, and then caught himself. *Now Grandma isn't here any more*, he had been about to add, but it struck him that would be cruel, not a nice thing to bring up. When he looked at Grandad, though, he saw the old man knew what Tim had been about to say.

'She never did like it, son,' he said, taking the pipe from his lips and staring down at the damp black stem. 'She didn't like the smell, see. Said it lingered.' His eyes went out of focus. 'And she were right, as usual. Bad habit. So I always went outside.'

'But—'

'Aye, I know.' Grandad's voice was gentle. 'I know she's gone, lad. I could smoke in t' house if I wanted. But – I sorter think her memory might not like it either, know what I mean? And I don't want to do something her memory wouldn't like. Case I chase it away.'

He fell silent, staring into space, and Tim thought he should say something else, but he couldn't think what. And so he fell silent too, as if it were something catching, like whooping cough maybe. As if it had followed them from the house and onto the beach.

'Come on,' said Grandad, tapping out the burnt contents of his pipe. 'We'd best get on. Light's going already, and the tide comes all t' way up this beach. You can get stuck. Best put that fossil back, now.'

'Put it back?'

'Aye, lad.' Grandad's face broke into its steady slow smile. 'You mustn't take anything from this 'ere beach. Din't I tell you that? It'll upset t'boggle, see. Take summat of his and he might just take summat from you. And how'd you like that?' He winked. ''S no lie, lad. Every word of it's God's honest truth.'

~

They went back to the beach the next day. Tim walked up and down the sea front, peering into rock pools. Some had brownish-pink squashy things clinging to the rock, bulging and flexing as clear water washed over them. The rocks were made rougher still by barnacles, some with smaller barnacles clinging to their sides. Tim tried to grip one and pull it from the rock, but it wouldn't budge. He stomped instead on a thick mat of bladderwrack, trying to pop the blisters in its dark green fronds.

He looked back up the beach. By the beck – Stoupe Beck, Grandad had called it – two men were standing at the base of the cliff. One of them bent and slipped something into his pocket. Tim grinned. The man had found a fossil – maybe even the same one Tim had found yesterday – and that made him think of the boggle; the revenge it might take for stealing from its beach.

He turned towards Grandad. The old man wasn't smoking his pipe; he was watching Tim. He grinned and waved and Tim ran towards him, laughing. Grandad put out his hands to catch him when Tim drew close.

'Let's have a look for the boggle.' Tim pointed towards his left hand.

After a moment, the old man understood. He fumbled the ring from his finger and passed it to Tim. 'Careful, now.'

Tim wasn't sure if he meant about the ring or in case he saw the boggle reflected in its surface. He peered into the gold, turning it in his fingers. He could see clouds, and the hazy shape that was him. Nothing else. He frowned. *God's honest truth*, the old man had said.

Grandad tapped the side of his nose before holding out his hand for the ring. 'Only when he wants to be seen, son,' he said. 'Now, how's about I teach you to find something shiny for yourself?'

They walked up and down the beach, but it didn't work. Grandad stopped and bent with a 'pfft' and scraped through the stones with his fingers. There was nothing.

'You have to walk with the sun behind you, see,' he said. He pointed at their shadows, dim and hazy. Tim turned and tried to make out the sun; there was only a place where the clouds were a little brighter.

'It's best at sunrise or sunset. You walk with it behind you and it shines 'em up, see, like they're polished. Sometimes there's agate, or carnelian. You can't see 'em for looking, normally. They're dull, like pebbles. But when the sun's low and shining on 'em – they glow. You can see t' gemstones then. They shine right back at you.' He winked. 'Maybe it's the boggle. They're his treasure too, see. P'raps he won't let 'em go, not today.'

Tim's face lit up. 'Tomorrow, then?' He looked once more over his shoulder at the faint trembling light.

Grandad sighed, then smiled. 'Aye, lad. Tomorrer.'

The next day, Tim fidgeted through games and sandwiches and television programmes. Sometimes Grandad caught him looking at the window, watching anxiously for rain, and each time he did they would share a smile; sometimes, they laughed. It wasn't until later, when they were about to set off, that Tim realised he hadn't thought about the Silence at all. It had retreated, hiding at the back of the airing cupboard or under a bed, somewhere quiet and small and still, until it could come out again. *Maybe tomorrer*, Tim thought, and grinned to himself as they got into the car.

The sun was bright and low, shining straight into Tim's eyes, dazzling him. It was going to work. He knew it even as they pulled into the little car park above the beach and saw the fossil hunters packing up to leave. Their car was grey and looked older even than Grandad's, and when Grandad saw it, he gave a low whistle. 'Look at that,' he said in a low voice. ''Appen t' boggle's nicked their hubcaps.'

Tim grinned even wider. *Take summat of his*, he thought, *and he might just take summat from you.*

At first, Grandad watched while Tim carefully set the sun at his back and walked along the seafront, *crunch, crunch, crunch*, over the pebbles. He said he was keeping an eye on the tide just in case, but Tim knew he was really having a puff on his pipe.

When he'd walked a distance away, he turned and walked back, and then he tried again. This time, the sun seemed… not brighter, but redder. *Readier*, he thought, and he turned towards the boggle's cave and stuck out his tongue.

Soon his shadow was sharper where it lay against the pebbles, each stone sharply delineated with a black crescent. Every fissure and crease in the sand had its own crisp outline. *Now*, Tim thought. He stretched out one foot in a long stride and let it fall again. *Crunch*. Then again. *Crunch*. The sun was at his back. His shadow was long before him. It looked like some kind of giant: *for scaring boggles away*, he thought. *So he can't hide his treasures*. And something shone amid the grey and the murk and the stone. It glowed like living sunset fallen to the beach, a footprint marking the way to the boggle's hoard.

Tim pounced on it. When he straightened and looked at what was in his hand, though, he frowned. It was nothing but a dull pebble about half the size of his thumb, reddish perhaps, but with a surface that was greyed like old skin. It wasn't even a nice pebble, and he drew his hand back ready to throw it into the sea when he had a thought.

He turned and the sun glared into his eyes. He held the stone between thumb and finger, and the light shone through it. It was like something alive, the bright orange-red of carnelian. He turned to his grandad with a look of triumph, but the old man was busy tapping ashes from his pipe onto a rock. Then he stood and raised a hand, half waving, half beckoning.

Tim looked down at his feet as clear frothing water rushed over them, stirring the tiny stones as if in offering: *take one of them instead*. He closed his hand over the gemstone and slipped it into his pocket. Then he started to make his way back up the beach.

It was in the car that Grandad made the sound. It was a little choking cough, way back in his throat. Then he started breathing really loud and patting at his coat, wriggling in his seat to check his trouser pockets.

'What's up, Grandad?' asked Tim.

Grandad didn't answer; he only looked back at the boy with wide open eyes. They were watery at the edges.

'Grandad?'

'It's me ring,' he answered at last, and he held out his left hand, the fingers spread. 'Me ring, see. *Her* ring.' He panted and patted some more. 'I must 'ave dropped it.' He stopped, gripping the steering wheel as if holding on. 'I must 'ave.' He looked down at his hand, at his broad fingers. Tim remembered the way he'd worked the ring off his finger, twisting and pulling until it came loose.

'You looked in it, din't you, lad?' He turned to Tim, his eyes lighting up. 'You did.'

Tim shook his head. 'That was yesterday,' he whispered. 'Yesterday, Grandad, remember?'

But Grandad hardly seemed to hear as he turned away from Tim, staring out of the window. 'It's too late,' he said, breathless. 'Tide's coming in. It's too late to go and look.'

That evening, the Silence was back. It had grown while they were away, stretching itself into corners and around walls and seeping through doorways that should have kept it out. The television was on, but there wasn't any sound. Grandad stared at it without seeming to see. His eyes hadn't dried. He kept nodding to himself, as if listening to something Tim couldn't hear. He kept turning towards the photograph of a grandmother Tim didn't remember, a woman he didn't know. He'd glance at it and then away, quickly, as if he couldn't bear to look any longer.

Tim hunched himself into the chair, trying to make himself smaller. Silence expanded to fill the gap he left behind.

His hand went to his pocket and he found the thing he'd put there. The stone was small and smooth and cold. Tim ran his fingers over it, but it didn't seem to get any warmer. He turned and turned it in his pocket, and he tried not to think, and he closed his eyes.

The next day Grandad didn't talk about the beach. He didn't seem to want to talk about anything. He made breakfast, his hands shaking, and then he switched on the television and sat there without looking at it.

Tim went to his side. 'We'll find it today Grandad, won't we?'

Grandad shifted, but he didn't reply.

'We'll go back to the beach, won't we?'

The old man shot him a quick look and put out a hand and ruffled Tim's hair. It pulled, but Tim didn't protest. He was thinking of the stone in his pocket. *Me*, he was thinking. *You should have taken something from me.* It wasn't right. It wasn't fair.

'Please, Grandad,' he said, and this time his voice got through.

Grandad turned. 'I s'pose. Aye, all right then.' Tim had to lean closer to hear him. 'Come on, lad.'

A short time later, they got out of the car and walked together down the narrow lane towards the sea. The sky was packed with low gathered clouds and the sea gave back the grey in a dull shine. The waves were slow and listless, giving way to the beach in tired little wafts.

Grandad stood where he'd sat the day before, looking at the ground. He gestured to Tim. 'Go and play now, lad.'

Tim nodded and turned away. He knew where he was going; it was all right. Better that he should go alone. He made his way up the beach. When he looked back, Grandad wasn't watching. He was staring down at the ground, at the millions of pebbles, and he wasn't moving.

Tim started to run. He only stopped when he reached the mouth of the boggle hole, listening to the quiet coming from inside; and then he stepped forward and went in, and the cave swallowed him.

His hand was in his pocket. He clutched the stone.

He opened his mouth to speak but his voice was hoarse. He cleared his throat. 'I brought this for you.' He took the carnelian from his pocket and held it out. 'I want you to give the ring back.'

He looked into the corners of the cave. It was no good, it wasn't here. Instead he felt the Silence massing behind him, coming from the sea. He turned and found he could hear it after all, mocking him: *Hush. Hush.*

He stepped out into the light and stared. Had the sea taken the ring? It came right up to the cliffs, Grandad had said. Right into the cave. It would have crept over the beach in the dark, greedily sucking and reaching for any bright thing it could find. His gaze went to the roughened rocks between here and the shore, just as the sun cleared the clouds for an instant; it shone back from a watery surface and was gone.

Tim started to walk towards it, picking his way. It was a rock-pool, a wide one, its bottom lined with dregs of sand and fringed with black fronds like hair in bathwater. The sides were sharp overhangs, no telling what could be hiding beneath. Crabs, maybe. Fish. Fish with teeth. Tim narrowed his eyes as the light caught the surface of the water once more. *Shiny*, he thought, and shuddered.

And then he saw what lay beneath the water. He gasped and rushed towards it, falling to his knees onto the rock. It hurt, but he didn't think about that.

There, lying on the pale sand under the clear water, was a thick gold ring. Tim looked up; his grandad was a small figure standing on the beach, staring into the waves. Maybe it was better that way. Tim could imagine the surprise on his face when he ran to him and held it out. He let out a spurt of air, almost a giggle, and thought he heard an answering sound somewhere behind him.

He tried to turn; there was nothing there. It was an echo, that was all, coming from the cave or the cliff; the sound of water trickling through stone.

When he looked back into the pool, the ring remained. He pushed up one sleeve, gripped a spike of rock and leaned over, pushing his hand into the icy cold. He opened his fingers, grasping for the ring; and they closed on nothing. There was only sand, fine grains of it, the sand he'd wanted to find when he first came here; now he didn't want it. He let it slip through his fingers with a little cry. He withdrew his hand. When the drips and circles on the water subsided the form took shape again: a golden ring sitting on the surface of the sand. No, not on the surface; *above* the surface.

Tim frowned and reached for it again, leaning further this time. He poked at the ring with one finger, meaning to spear it through its heart, but there was nothing there.

He sat back again, letting the water grow still. There: a ring, but nothing he could grasp. Then he understood.

'It's here,' he muttered. 'Here. Have it.' He took the carnelian from his pocket and held it over the water a moment, seeing it dull and lifeless in his hand. He let it drop.

The carnelian fell into the water with a plop, and it vanished.

Tim frowned. He leaned in again. There was no carnelian; he couldn't see it anywhere. He poked at the sand again to see if the stone had been covered in its fall, but there was nothing.

Then he saw a bright glow coming from the other side of the pool; an orange-red glow, something small at the bottom of the water. He shifted his knees, shuffling his way over the rocks. There was something there. He could see it when the sun shone behind him. He glanced at where he'd been. Blinked. He couldn't understand how it had passed from there to here. Perhaps this water was flowing after all, going back to the sea, and had carried the stone with it. Or maybe it was a reflection, something about the nature of the pool and the sun and his eyes. He shook his head; it didn't matter. What mattered was, he could see the carnelian below him. It was deeper here. He'd have to lean all the way out, his face nearly touching the water.

He gripped the rocks tightly with one hand and eased himself out over the pool. He plunged in his other arm almost to the shoulder, grasping below him, raking the surface of the sand. There was something cold and hard and smooth under his fingers. He grabbed it and pulled himself back, cold, dripping. When he saw what was in his hand he nearly dropped it. It was an old scratched ring. It was his grandad's ring.

Tim looked up at the cave mouth and slowly grinned. He gestured with the ring: *Thank you.*

And something caught his eye in the pool as the sun passed overhead: a brief bright shine, and the suggestion of a face, ugly and distorted and fringed with shaggy hair, laughing on the surface of the water. It was there for a moment and then gone. *A reflection*, he thought, *that's all it was.* But he still wasn't sure as he pushed himself up and started to make his way back over the beach to his grandad, who was motionless, staring at the waves as they broke, over and over, against the shore.

~

There was something in Grandad's eyes. At first they had lit up. It had been just as Tim had imagined, him holding out the ring and the fissures appearing, deep lines of joy written into the old man's skin. He hadn't been able to speak. He had only taken the ring and pushed it, trembling, back onto his finger. Then he had opened and closed his hand before wrapping his thin arms around Tim, and they'd looked at each other and they'd laughed.

It was later that the look appeared. A small frown, and a single line between his eyes. It deepened when he looked at Tim. 'Where'd you say you found it?' he asked.

Tim pointed up towards the cave. 'The boggle had it, Grandad,' he said, and the line grew deeper still.

They walked along the beach some more, but it wasn't long before they both turned, as if by some unspoken agreement, towards the car.

'We din't go thee-er,' Grandad muttered as he fumbled the keys from his pocket.

'What, Grandad?'

Pardon, his mother would have said, but his mother wasn't here.

'We din't go up near t' cave yest'day,' said the old man. He didn't meet Tim's eyes. He just looked at the keys in his hand. No: at the wedding ring that nestled beneath them. 'We din't go near it.'

'No,' Tim said.

'Did you see owt?'

Tim swallowed. 'What?'

'When you looked in t' ring.'

Tim looked at him, and this time the old man looked back. The thing in his eyes was still there.

Me, Tim thought. *You should have taken something from me.* Slowly, he shook his head. 'I didn't take it, Grandad. It was the boggle.'

'Aye. Aye, you said.' Grandad heaved a sigh. 'Well, it's back. That's t' main thing. Come on then, Tim. Let's get going, eh.'

Tim, he'd called him, and for the first time it struck him as odd. Grandad never called him Tim. He called him lad, or son; never by his name. It was strange he'd never noticed that before. Now he didn't know what he was supposed to think about it. But there was nothing to be done but get into the car and start heading towards home as the rain, viciously, began to spit.

The Silence was there. This time it wasn't hiding and it wasn't creeping. It was a fat, sullen thing, sitting in the middle of the room so that Tim could almost see it. He stared at the window, watching the rain streak the glass: time passing, outside. Soon, his mother would be home. She would come to fetch him, laughing and tanned from her holiday.

Grandad was doing a crossword in the newspaper, his reading glasses perched on the end of his nose and his wedding ring shining on his finger. They hadn't spoken about it since they came back from the beach. They hadn't been back there, either. They had been here, in this house, with the Silence sitting between them.

Tim drew a deep breath. 'Grandad, about the boggle.'

Grandad buried his nose deeper into the paper.

'If the boggle took summat from you, and you took—'

'That's enough o' that now.' Grandad let the newspaper drop with a loud rustle. 'Enough o' that.' After a moment his look softened and he gave a small smile.

'But, Grandad—'

'It's nowt but a story, Tim,' the old man said. After a moment, he raised the newspaper again, holding it close to his eyes.

Nowt but a story.

Tim thought of the thing he'd seen in the surface of the water: its bright cruel grin; a whisper of laughter heard over his shoulder. He closed his eyes tightly. Grandad was surely right: things like that couldn't be. It was nothing but a story, and Tim had been lucky to find the ring, and that was all.

'S no lie, lad. Every word of it's God's honest truth.

He remembered the way they had laughed together. The way they had winked. It had been different then, when there was the story between them. Something that was for them, and them alone.

He thought of the fossil hunters, trawling their way along the base of the cliff. Them returning to their car and finding their hubcaps gone, being tormented perhaps by whispers and nips and things missing from their pockets, things they'd never get back.

He was forgiven, he knew that. But he also knew the old man would never forget, no more than he could forget his dead wife's face when he stared into his pipe smoke. It was there, an intangible writhing thing.

Me, he'd thought. *You should have taken something from me.*

But as Tim watched the old man intent on the newspaper, that line still there between his eyes, he knew that was exactly what the boggle had done.

|Jenny Greenteeth|

~

The bombs had stopped falling. That was the first thing that struck Alice when the train pulled away, its smoke and roar fading into the distance, and she looked out across nothing but green for miles around.

The silence crept into her, like long fingers snaking down her throat, and she felt she no longer knew how to breathe. The air had no smell in it, not even the taint of coal and steam any longer. Sometimes, at home in London, she hadn't been clear whether the percussion of incendiaries was really still happening or if the sound had lodged in her mind, an endless battle that wouldn't stop. It at once terrified her and awoke a nameless longing that wore the face of her mother, solemn and silent as the fields that stretched away.

She didn't know where she was. She only knew she'd been told to alight here and so here she stood, with her bag at her feet and a cardboard sign hanging around her neck, over the gold cross that had been her mother's. An evacuee.

'Oreet, lass.'

The voice was rough, as was the man who'd spoken. His dark hair was plastered to his sweaty forehead and his chin was rough too, speckled with stubble. He spat out more words she couldn't make sense of, she caught something about a cart, and he picked up her bag and she followed him. He put her things into the back of a wooden wagon, jerking his hand towards the seat, and she stepped up too. He sat in front of her, his back turned, and took up the reins. She stared at the horse's fat chestnut haunches as they rolled and shifted and pulled her away from everything she had known.

Across a cobbled yard, a place of squawking chickens and straw and spattered dirt, she reached the farmhouse. The mother wore an apron that wasn't really white and a distracted expression. Strands of hair hung in her face. She said that Alice was welcome but she didn't smile, and when she said that Alice was their only billet, she pulled a face as if the word had a nasty taste.

Then two girls came rushing into the kitchen.

One was a little taller than Alice, with mousy curls: Olive. The other was rather shorter with plump, unformed features and a gap-toothed smile: Betty.

'Come wi' me,' Olive said. 'I'll show you summat.'

She turned and ran up the stairs before Alice could reply. She was tired and hungry and she could smell bread somewhere in the kitchen but she followed the girl anyway, into a cramped room with two little beds squeezed into it.

'Mam said *you* should share,' Olive announced, 'but we said *we* would. We're together, aren't we, Bet?'

Betty nodded. Alice could already see that nodding was what she did.

'I've got *this*.' Olive went to a drawer and pulled out a little circle of plaited string with deep-green beads threaded onto it.

'It's a bracelet,' she said. 'I've made one for me and one for Bet. You can have this un.'

She held it out. Alice reached for it, giving a little smile in spite of herself. She was almost touching it when Olive snatched it back, shoving it deep into her pocket. She grabbed her sister's arm and they ran, thundering back down the stairs, their laughter still ringing around the low beams.

There was real milk, squirted warm into a pail. Real eggs gathered in a bowl, never reported for the rationing. There were sheep with yellow eyes and the stamping, farting horse and a goose that hissed as loud as a train. There was the father, always doing something, gesturing this way and that to a limping boy who was the farmhand. Their voices confused her. It was hard to follow the accent. They used phrases her parents never had; words were like things stuck in their throats they struggled to expel. They laughed at her: her shoes too dainty for the yard, the way she said *Lancashire* instead of *Lancasheer*, her fear of the old dog with his dripping red tongue.

After she'd fed the chickens and dusted the rooms and kneaded the dough to the mother's satisfaction, Alice was told she may go. Olive and Betty were sitting at the old deal table that was much scarred from a knife, shelling peas, Betty swinging her legs in time with a tune creaking from the wireless.

Olive slipped from her chair, sidled up to Alice and poked her arm. 'We'll show you summat you'll like,' she said.

Their mother smiled as if that's what she wanted to see, and Olive led the way from the kitchen.

They went across the yard and into the lane. Then they climbed a narrow stile and tramped across a field, the path clogged and slippery with mud, towards a little stand of trees. But it wasn't the trees they'd come to see. When they reached their edge, Alice saw the shattered remnants of a drystone wall, a hole in the ground a bit like a crater, and in it, a dank pool surrounded by mossy stones. The water looked slimy. The sun didn't seem to reach it, and when she looked up, the sky was a flat grey; she couldn't see the sun at all.

The whole place was drab and dull and she didn't know why they'd come here. It was cold too, a nip in the air... but then, it always seemed colder here than it had been at home.

Olive spoke as if she was proud of the sight. 'This was part of the river, once. The Dee. Not any more, though.'

That much was obvious to Alice. The pool was stagnant. It didn't flow anywhere, didn't make a sound. There was a smell to it. The water wasn't blue but green, and she couldn't see into it.

'It's where Jenny Greenteeth lives.'

Alice didn't look around. This was it, then, some new trick they wanted to play on her.

'We hear singing here sometimes,' Betty piped up. Had her sister primed her to say the words?

'Oh aye. But we don't see her. She hasn't got a face, not really. She's got long straggly hair and bony arms and claws for hands, and she'll grab you and pull you under if she can. Then she'll soften you up and suck the flesh from your bones.' Olive giggled.

Betty looked afraid. She hung from her sister's arm, standing a little behind her.

'You have to give her stuff.' Olive stared into the water. 'An offering. You don't get owt for nowt, my dad says. Have *you* got a dad, Alice?'

Alice thought of her father, the last time she had seen him. He'd been given a few days' leave for her mother's funeral. He had held her hand but hadn't comforted her. He'd sat her on his knee as he used to do, but it hadn't been the same. *He* wasn't the same. It was as if he'd been replaced by someone who only looked like him, but he didn't play with her hair or tickle her any more. He didn't speak. There were no words inside him. When she twisted on his lap and looked at him, he didn't seem to see her. He was staring out of the window as if it were another country, and he didn't answer when she whispered his name.

She forced herself to focus once more on the pool. The water was greened and slimy with some sort of plant that was growing there, floating just beneath the surface. She imagined ragged hair among the weeds, the discoloured ivory of teeth gleaming from the moss. She frowned. She knew that death came in fire and cracking stone and blackened skies. It hadn't occurred to her that it could also be cold.

'If you give her summat,' Olive went on, ''appen she'll give summat back to you. Summat you lost. Summat you want.'

She pulled something from her pocket. Alice knew, before she caught the girl's sly look, what it was: the macramé bracelet that had been offered to her and snatched away.

Olive's grin broadened as she drew back her hand and threw it out into the pool. The water took it with a low *gloop* and Alice peered, wondering if she could see it there, caught on the pondweed. She took a step forward, trying to make out what it was she saw just beneath the surface, and Olive shrieked in her ear.

'Don't go near! Or Jenny Greenteeth'll pull you in!'

The sisters hugged each other, grinning with delicious fear. Alice didn't move. She didn't feel afraid. There were worse things, she knew, and anyway, she was too busy wondering: what exactly was it that Olive had offered to the spirit of the pool? What was it she had asked for in return?

'Now you,' Olive said.

She stepped in front of Alice, scowling, and Alice saw that the girl's cheeks were too flat, her nose too sharp, her eyes the colour of mud. Is that why she was so mean all the time? Betty lined up next to her, her eyes the same hue as her sister's.

Alice shook her head. What could she offer? What was there that Jenny Greenteeth could possibly want? In spite of herself, her hand stole to her neck and rested on the little gold cross that had been her mother's.

'That.' Olive pointed.

Alice shook her head.

'That's what she wants.'

Again, Alice shook her head, and Olive's expression darkened. 'You're cursed, now,' she spat. 'Jenny Greenteeth is going to get you!'

She ran away with her sister, hand in hand, both of them shrieking and laughing their triumph into the air.

That night, Alice was sent early to her room. She lay in the little bed staring up into the eaves and listened to the raised voices snaking from between the floorboards.

'It's no good skrikin'. Go there again and I'll clout thee one.'

A low wail.

The mother's milder tones. Did she sound half amused? 'That story's supposed to keep you away from watter, not drag you where you don't belong.'

She couldn't hear Olive's reply.

The mother again. 'There's your sister to think on. An' London girls can't swim. I'll want your word on it, now.'

At some point during the softer words that followed, the sound of footsteps on the stairs, Alice closed her eyes, thinking of Jenny Greenteeth: her hair like weeds, her too-long fingers tipped with broken nails, and no face that she could see; but she had eyes, rimmed with baleful yellow, and when she opened her lips...

She shook her head, half asleep and half awake, and felt hands reaching for her, dragging her down. She couldn't breathe. There was a smell; she couldn't get any air. She felt fingers closing on her, bony yet swollen, and she awoke to see a face up close to hers, not green but black.

She let out a shrill sound and it jerked away, just as she saw another face near hers. This one was pale and smudged but she recognised

Olive, still holding the gasmask she'd been pressing against Alice's mouth.

The girl smirked and retreated into the dark and the door closed behind her. Still Alice could barely keep herself from screaming at the memory of the mask; the terrible blankness in its eyes.

She took long gulps of air that smelled of nothing but the rabbit stew they'd had for tea, and she tried to think of anything else. For a long time, she couldn't.

Then, as she started to drift, a memory came.

That night. The air raid. The siren ripping the night apart, shaking their souls. Dragging them all from their beds. Her mother pulling her into the street, wrapping her nightie closer around her, throwing a blanket over her shoulders.

'I have to help Mrs Beattie. Her legs. She can't manage the stairs so fast.'

Alice had heard the words, though half the vowels were lost to the mechanical scream rising into the air. She knew all about Mrs Beattie's legs: fat. Swollen. The veins showing blue-green under the surface of blotched, grey skin.

She felt her mother thrust her hand into that of another neighbour, from the family two doors down.

'Go now,' she said. 'I'll be along soon.'

The last promise she had made to Alice. *I'll be along soon.*

Alice stood at the edge of the pool and touched the cross that hung at her throat and thought about her mother.

Her mother had touched the necklace too, often, without thinking about it. Alice knew she sometimes hadn't even been aware of doing it. It was what her mother did when she wanted to be reminded of God.

Say your prayers, her mother had said, every time she'd kissed Alice goodnight. And Alice had, though they hadn't seemed to help. They didn't stop the bombs from falling or keep the things that were taken away from leaving. They didn't give anything back. Alice had sometimes stopped the whispered words before she'd finished, just to listen to the silence they left behind.

In London, God lived in buildings, not pools of water. There were stone churches for Him everywhere and yet how easily they had toppled, their stones shattered as easily as a promise.

Now she raised her hands and found the clasp at the back of her neck, releasing it. She curled her fingers around the necklace – it had no weight at all – and remembered what it had been like to have someone to tell her to say her prayers. To have arms wrapped around her, a kind face pressed against her own. Someone who smiled at her, who didn't roll the word *billet* around on their tongue.

With one jerking movement, she threw the necklace towards the pool. It made a brief glitter in the air and she pictured the dirty water sucking it in – *gloop* – but it didn't. Her offering fell short. It landed on the banking at the edge of the pool and glinted softly from the grass.

Alice stepped forward. It no longer felt as if she were quite alone, and she leaned towards it. How long were Jenny Greenteeth's arms? Long, she imagined, with fingertips like hooks, ready to catch and pull.

She imagined being held under the slimy surface, her face hidden among the weeds. How long would she feel it on her skin before she stopped being conscious of it? How long before she opened her mouth and tried to breathe the nasty stuff?

A bubble rose to the surface with a soft *glug* and she watched a ripple spread, gradually subsiding amid the pondweed. Then the fronds moved, shifting as if something had stirred beneath, turning restless in the water.

She caught her breath and stepped back. Maybe it wouldn't matter. Jenny would surely find the necklace. Her offering would count after all.

She forced herself to turn her back on the pool, telling herself that it wasn't her mother she'd left at the water's cold edge; just in time to see a small figure sneaking away between the trees.

The next morning Alice was splashing her face in cold water from a ewer when she heard the mother calling Olive's name. The tone wasn't right and in the next moment her door opened.

'Is she in here with you?'

Alice frowned, confused. 'She's with Betty. They share.'

The door closed in her face and she heard footsteps on the narrow landing and raised voices. One of them was Betty's. Then the child started to cry.

Alice dressed and went downstairs to find everyone already in the kitchen, the father stomping in his boots, mud flaking from them to the clean flags. Alice knew, when the mother didn't tell him not to, how worried she was. Only Olive wasn't there and Alice felt her absence in the sharp looks that leaped around the room.

'I'll go and check the sheds,' the father said.

The mother didn't say anything about that either, twisting her hands in her apron as if shoving the words down deep. Betty wrapped her arms around her waist and her mother looked down at the child's head as if she didn't know what she was doing there, alone, not half of a whole any longer.

Alice ran to the corner and got her shoes. She half expected someone to stop her, but no one seemed to notice she was there at all. When the father went out, she followed and ran across the yard. She already knew where Olive would be.

She made her way across the field, surrounded by the long grass and its whispers. The air was cold on her face, but she didn't mind. If she was cold and didn't feel it that would mean she was dead, after all, and that would be awful, like—

An image flashed before her: Mrs Beattie's legs, swollen and mottled and transparent, blue veins pressing upward from beneath. She shook the thought away. She had almost reached the trees and didn't feel alone any longer and she swallowed, hard, before stepping out of the light, under their branches.

Everything was green: the water, the stones, the shadows. She felt the underwater light on her skin like reaching fingers and she shuddered.

Olive was there, floating on the surface like a rag doll cast aside. At first Alice thought her face was black, then realised she was lying face down, looking at – what? Her hair, darkened with water, fanned about her head. Her clothes looked heavy, tainted green, but somehow they hadn't yet dragged her down.

Alice didn't scream, but Betty did. Alice hadn't even known the child had followed until she felt her arms flailing at her. Alice gasped at air that was too warm and heady with growth. She couldn't move as Betty filled the air with her siren sound and then she forced herself to turn.

The others were already running towards them along the path. Even the old dog lolloped by the side of its master, teeth sharply white against its red mouth. When it came, though, it wouldn't go near, staying quite motionless at the edge of the trees, only its nose twitching.

Alice opened her mouth to cry out a warning but the father didn't listen. He waded into the pool, his trespass sending loud splashes into the air, and he grabbed his daughter's arm and pulled her from the water. He ended up kneeling on the banking, his arms around her limp form.

Olive didn't look as if the flesh had been sucked from her bones. Perhaps she hadn't yet been softened enough. She looked as she had before, except that her face was slack. It was still her, though, just the same; only her eyes had changed.

Olive stared at the sky. She couldn't see anything any longer, Alice could tell. What had been her last sight? Perhaps she hadn't seen anything at all – only felt long arms snaking around her, clasping an arm or an ankle before the world tilted. Or perhaps she had. Perhaps she alone knew what Jenny Greenteeth looked like.

Olive's mother knelt at her side, her mouth opening and closing, no sound coming out. Betty's wails had stopped too.

Alice stepped forward. Betty grabbed at her in a new panic but Alice pulled away and took another step towards the pool. She only wanted to see, and she did: the necklace she had left there, her mother's gift, was gone.

It wasn't difficult to sneak out. Alice had feared she wouldn't be able to, but the mother had taken to her room, her eyes wide and shocked-looking, as if she hadn't known that people could die. When Alice slipped across the yard, Betty followed, running after her as if Alice were her sister and it was unthinkable she'd go anywhere alone.

Alice took the little hand. Were they friends now? She supposed they were, and for a moment she wondered if that's what had come in exchange for the necklace. She shook her head.

They climbed the stile and picked their way across the muddy field. Betty hadn't asked where they were going and she didn't say a word, though her grip tightened on Alice's fingers as they drew closer to the trees. Alice could already smell the water, its cool green sourness, and as its taint reached her she thought she heard something too: a soft voice, singing?

She frowned. Betty had spoken of this once, but Betty was only little. She'd probably mistaken the breeze soughing in the branches for the soft lilt of music, like someone humming through a mouth full of water.

She slowed her steps, as did Betty, who pulled back on her arm. Alice dragged her along the last few paces. Stepping beneath the trees it was cooler at once, as if they were being immersed.

Alice kept her gaze on the ground, though she heard a soft splashing, as of the surface being disturbed – *a fish*, she told herself as her heart began to beat faster, though surely no fish lived in such a pool – then came the muted sound of water dripping onto stones sheathed in moss.

When she looked up there was a figure standing under the trees, its form like their branches, dull under the shadows. Was that hair twined about its shoulders? Were those fingers, bent like twigs – and a little plaited bracelet wound about the bone? Were those eyes gleaming from amid the moss?

They blinked and fixed on Betty. The two stared at each other: matching pairs of eyes, the colour of mud.

Alice opened her mouth, but no sound came out. She realised that she had let go of Betty's hand and reached for her with fingers that grasped like claws but closed on nothing. A movement at her side followed by the rustle of long grass told her that Betty was already running away.

It was better to be alone. She had made her offering. The pact was between the two of them.

I'll be along soon.

And she realised that the figure waiting for her wasn't as it had first appeared. It wasn't Olive; it wasn't even pretending to be her any longer.

Alice opened her mouth again, meaning to say all that she needed to say, everything that was inside her. It was too much to encapsulate: the touch of her mother's hand on her hair; the shine in her eyes when she looked at her daughter. All of those things that were tiny and yet everything and wordless. All she had desired. The things she had asked for when she offered up the most precious possession she had, leaving it at the edge of the pool.

If you give her summat, 'appen she'll give summat back to you. Summat you lost. Summat you want.

The spirit of the pool had grown taller than Olive would ever be. Her hair was dark, curling now over her shoulders, water running from it as Alice watched. Her eyes were no longer mud-coloured. And her face—

But Alice knew what her face looked like. Still, she was thin; so very thin.

She reached out with one long arm, long fingers, and beckoned.

Alice imagined what it would be like to have that arm around her and she shivered. She imagined being embraced, not in the warmth of her mother's kitchen, but in the cold pool. Is that what her mother would have wanted for her? Perhaps it was only as Olive had said: Jenny Greenteeth was a wicked creature with no face of her own, none she hadn't borrowed from whatever she could scavenge: a touch. A corpse. A golden necklace.

She thought of the offering she had made. Not just a *thing*, an object treasured and thrown away; but the love she had wrapped around it. The longing for her mother – and something else: the awful wish she had buried beneath the one she had worded in her mind.

She closed her eyes and saw not her mother's face, but her father's. The cold way he'd stared out of the window. The way he had become something she couldn't name, just under the surface of himself; some new creature lurking beneath his arms, his legs, his face.

And she knew what it was she had truly asked of Jenny Greenteeth, besides the need to see her mother once more: the way she had begged her to make it possible that Alice would never have to go home again.

|In the Wabe|

~

My daughter vanished three years ago. I'm no closer to finding her. Every time I think I've found a new clue, it only puts me further away. The more knowledge I gain, the less I can believe in any of it.

She disappeared on May thirteenth from Central Park, a little to the north of the East 72nd Street and Fifth Avenue entrance. Anyone familiar with the Park will tell you that's close to Conservatory Water, where you can rent remote-controlled sailboats any day as long as it's not raining. My daughter wasn't interested in sailboats. She preferred to sit at the north end of the lake, on a giant bronze mushroom: Alice at her back, the white rabbit on one side, the Mad Hatter on the other, patches of their heads and arms and shoulders rubbed shiny by generations of New York children. I always thought that was fitting somehow, since Alice too had left her home in England and eventually found herself here.

One side will make you grow taller, and the other side will make you grow shorter. I think it was the Caterpillar in *Alice's Adventures in Wonderland* who said that. I picture my little girl, Vivian, reaching around and breaking off a piece of mushroom, nibbling it with her front teeth, just like the time I got her to try broccoli. And I picture her shrinking, shrinking, shrinking, until she's as small as Alice in the story, smaller even, just the right size to captain a remote-controlled sailboat and sail away, then smaller, smaller still, until no one can even see her any longer.

That day, I turned around and she'd gone. Every mother's nightmare. There's a rabbit hole that opens inside you, one that never seems to end, blacker and blacker, deeper and deeper. Falling, falling. There was no answer when I shouted her name. No one had seen her. There was no sign my daughter had ever even existed; she'd gone, and I hadn't a clue where to find her.

It was a cop who spotted the bag lady a couple of streets away from the park, wearing – or trying to wear – my five-year-old daughter's clothes. A tiny pink t-shirt with glittery stars, ripped from under the sleeve to the hem, was pulled across her shoulders, a gauzy purple skirt twisted around her leg. The clothes were dirty, half hidden by a ratty old blanket. The woman claimed she'd found the blanket by a dumpster and I always thought that was odd. She could have said she'd found my daughter's clothes, not the blanket that no one cared about, but she didn't.

No: those shiny pink and purple things, she said they were hers.

My husband was a cop too. I met him when he took an extended vacation in England and I moved out here for him, thrilled by the sudden new potential in my life. We separated a few years after Vivian was born; he was killed on duty not long afterwards. And I'd begun to dream of home again, little green lanes, quiet roads, all so familiar, *safe*; then my girl disappeared and I was forced to stay.

It's someone from my husband's old precinct who shares the audio with me. 'Picture it,' he says. 'A grown woman, sitting right there on the Alice statue.'

I don't comment, since I've done that same thing plenty of times myself. It's not illegal. Children – and kids at heart – are welcome to climb, crawl, sit on, touch the statue. It belongs to them, after all. It's their story.

Each time I go there, I'm surprised by the size of the thing. It looks friendly, moulded to a human scale, but that sculpture is eleven feet tall. When you get up close, the mushroom is above your waist. You have to use the smaller mushrooms as steps to get up there, the bronze dormouse on one of them always getting in your way. When you reach her, you realise that Alice is not life-sized. Even adults are like children when they're next to her: that huge face, big eyes, wrong somehow. Central Park's Alice is a giant. She must have been nibbling at the wrong side of the mushroom.

Picture it.

A mom – she says her name is Sandie Gordon – sits down next to Alice. She's watching her daughter play. Her daughter is called Bree-Anne, a stupid name I always thought, but don't say. It wouldn't be right, under the circumstances.

Now imagine Sandie with the squeaky, whiny voice of a little kid. Listen.

I WAS WATCHING HER. SHE'S MY GIRL, OF COURSE I WAS WATCHING HER. I DIDN'T EVEN NOTICE THE KID SITTING NEXT TO ME. I TURN AROUND, DON'T KNOW WHY, AND THERE SHE IS. SURE I WAS SURPRISED. SHE'S RIGHT THERE, A LITTLE GIRL ABOUT THE SAME AGE AS MY BREE-ANNE, SO I SAYS, 'HEY! WHERE'D YOU COME FROM?'

SHE SAYS, 'HERE, SILLY.' AND SHE GIVES THIS LITTLE SMILE, LIKE SHE'S GOT A SECRET, YOU KNOW THE ONE? SO I ASK HER WHERE SHE LIVES AND SHE GIVES ANOTHER SMILE, A WEIRD SMILE, AND SAYS, 'UNDER THE MUSHROOM.'

I WOULDA LAUGHED, BUT RIGHT THEN, BREE – SHE'S RUNNING WITH SOME OTHER KIDS AT THE EDGE OF THE LAKE, AND SHE TRIPS. SO I'M LOOKING AT BREE-ANNE AND THIS KID NEXT TO ME, SHE SAYS, 'SHE WON'T FALL.' I JUST MENTION IT BECAUSE BREE-ANNE DIDN'T, EVEN THOUGH I WAS SURE WE'D HAVE SCABBED KNEES AND TEARS AND WAILING FOR EXTRA ICE-CREAM, BUT THE KID WAS RIGHT, BREE JUST CAUGHT HER BALANCE AND KEPT ON RUNNING.

On the tape, there's a sniff. It kind of sounds like she's being snotty about this kid, knowing better than she did about the girl not falling. But I wonder if she's trying not to cry. I wonder if it's really because she's talking about Bree-Anne and wanting her and missing her and needing her and she can't have her.

SO I SAYS TO THE KID, 'THAT'S A FUNNY PLACE TO LIVE, IN A MUSHROOM. WHADDYA EAT UNDER THERE?' A DUMB QUESTION, I MEAN SHE COULD EAT MUSHROOM, BUT ANYWAYS. AND SHE SAYS, 'YEARS.' JUST LIKE THAT. YEARS. LIKE SHE SITS DOWN WITH A KNIFE AND FORK AND DIGS RIGHT IN.

SO I ASKS HER HOW THEY TASTE.

SHE SAYS, 'THEY TASTE LIKE MILK. CAN I KISS YOU?' JUST LIKE THAT, JUMPING FROM ONE THING TO THE NEXT, LIKE KIDS DO. BREE-ANNE DOES THAT ALL THE TIME.

She sighs. I hear that quite plainly, and I don't think anyone needs to try and explain what it means.

SO I SAYS, 'I GUESS SO,' AND I PAT MY CHEEK TO SHOW HER WHERE, JUST LIKE MY GRAMMA USED TO DO. AND THE KID—

A pause. When she speaks again, her voice falters.

—I GUESS SHE DID KISS MY CHEEK. I THINK SO. ONLY, THERE'S A WORD I CAN'T GET RID OF, THAT GOES ROUND AND ROUND IN MY MIND. LATCHED. THAT'S WHAT IT MADE ME THINK OF – SHE LATCHED ON. LIKE BREE-ANNE USED TO DO WHEN SHE WAS BREAST FEEDING, SOMETHING LIKE THAT, AND THEN I SORT OF WOKE UP.

Another pause, a longer one.

NOW, I WANT TO SEE MY DAUGHTER. I HAVE TO SEE BREE-ANNE. YOU PROMISED ME.

A cop's voice responds. He says she can't, not just now. What he means is, not ever. What he's not saying is, she'll never see Bree-Anne again. She won't even get near her, because she isn't Sandie Gordon; she's not Bree-Anne's mother. That's who she claims she is, who she seems to think she is, even who she believes she is, but it's not her. It can't be.

On the tape, there's shrieking. Screaming. It all gets a bit incoherent, but it's plain enough when she starts yelling at the cops to let her the fuck out of there, she wants her daughter, she has rights, and why don't they just open the fucking door?

They still don't know her real name. But I've seen the photographs, and it's clear that the person claiming to be Sandie Gordon, mom to Bree-Anne, is about six years old.

It's incongruous, even grotesque, hearing her speak, knowing what she looks like. Talking about breast feeding her daughter in that squeaky little-girl voice. Shouting. Swearing. *OPEN THE FUCKING DOOR.*

I picture this little girl in the park, sitting on the mushroom, watching the other kids play. Witnesses said she grabbed Bree-Anne and tried to drag her off, but Bree-Anne wouldn't go. A passing tourist intervened. The unidentified child told him where and how to fuck himself. She said she was Bree-Anne's mommy, and everyone could get out of her damn way. Bree-Anne was crying. It didn't help the situation when no one could find her real mom, nor that this kid – this strange kid – appeared to be wearing her mommy's clothes.

The cops were called, but Sandie Gordon has never been found. Bree-Anne has been sent to live with her father, who was divorced from Sandie last year. The little kid who tried to grab her is with Social Services. They've confirmed she was wearing clothes way too big for her – a T-shirt more like a dress, an adult's miniskirt down past her knees. I wonder where they are now, those clothes. It hasn't been proved that they were Sandie's. Bree-Anne wasn't considered a reliable witness.

I don't know if they ran DNA tests, on the clothes or the kid, but I think I know what the tests would say. I just don't know how, or how to begin to explain. I don't suppose anyone could.

I've seen some freaky stuff in New York. I know about the weirdos of this city. People who follow you, put their faces up close to yours. Kids with too much in their eyes. Adults with too little. A vagrant clutching a toy car like it might save him, or maybe a doll. Someone showing a photograph. *Have you seen her?* A bag lady in a gauzy princess skirt, way too small. Little boys with shaved heads, smoking, drinking, shooting up. Teenagers kicking a tramp to steal a paper cup full of change. Maybe they want to buy drugs. Maybe they're dealing drugs. Thirteen-year-olds living alone, forging parents' signatures, making rent. A geriatric woman in makeup that could have been applied by an infant. A pretty woman who, close up, has skin stretched taut and unnatural over her bones. Who's to say how old anyone is anymore? You can't judge any longer. You can't even guess.

The bag lady wearing my daughter's clothes had grey hair and ugly creases running down her face, her jowls sagging.

Like the kid in the audio, I screamed and swore.

'How did you get Vivian's clothes? How the fuck did you—'

Fear froze her. Her eyes were blank with shock, her mouth hanging open. She seemed unused to being screamed at, but how could she not be, living on the streets? There was something missing in her, I could see that. It wasn't just her expression; it was in the way she kept saying, *I am Vivian, I am, I am.* It was in the way she called me *Mommy, Mommy,* and all the time staring at me, not laughing, not smirking, not even blinking. Not looking away from me for a second.

I told her, 'I'll kill you. You say that again, I fucking will.'

That time they did run DNA tests, but they figured they must have mixed up the results somehow. They took samples from the clothes and from the old woman – under her nails, in her hair, a cheek swab. Every single one of them was an exact match for my daughter.

They admitted they must have contaminated the samples. It was all messed up anyhow, and they had to let her go. Apart from the clothes – which she could have found, same as the blanket – they didn't have much to go on. If she'd snatched Vivian, what had she done with her? There was nowhere she could have kept her or hidden her. And after all, the woman was mad. Mad as a hatter, but harmless as a little child.

These days, I often go to the sculpture. I climb up onto the mushroom – past that damned dormouse – and sit and wonder where my daughter went. Is she lost in the rabbit hole? Sitting by the side of the Red Queen? Playing croquet with flamingos on a smooth lawn under a strange sun? Deep down, I know there are worse things, real things, but I try not to think about those.

Sometimes, when the sculpture is busy with kids crawling over it, mommies and daddies taking their pictures, I sit at the edge of Conservatory Water and simply stare at the bronze figures.

There is Alice, frozen forever in the act of reaching for the white rabbit's pocket watch, the Mad Hatter standing by. The design is based on Tenniel's original illustrations for *Alice's Adventures in Wonderland*, but it never seemed quite right to me, and now I know why. I looked it up. The Mad Hatter is a caricature of George Delacorte, the man who commissioned the sculpture. Alice is actually the image of a girl named Donna, the daughter of José de Creeft, the sculptor.

That seems strange to me, almost sad. What must it have been like for Creeft, knowing that his daughter was always here, yet unreachable? He created this thing in 1959. No matter how she changed or grew, where she went or what she did, even after she died, she would always be here, always caught in the act of reaching for that pocket watch. Always the same, but no matter how many people look at her, they'll see someone else; never who she truly is. Not Donna, but Alice.

But kids – maybe they do see something else.

One day, there's a little boy. He's pulling on his mom's arm, pointing towards the base of the sculpture, showing her something.

'That's funny,' I hear her say. 'I didn't notice her till you said she was there.' She shrugs before pulling her child away, suddenly keen to be gone.

I look at where he pointed. My first thought is of a missing child, but then, I'm always thinking of missing children. And I can't see anything, only the granite base of the sculpture with the words inscribed there: *Twas brillig, and the slithy toves did gyre and gimble in the wabe.* Lines from *Jabberwocky*, Lewis Carroll's poem, but in that second they almost seem to mean something different. Is that where Vivian has gone – into the wabe? It makes as much sense as anything else.

The next time I'm there, a dad is holding up his phone, telling his son, who's sitting almost in Alice's lap, to smile. When the boy clambers down, Dad shows him the screen. His son frowns.

'Where's the girl gone?' he asks. 'Where's the girl who was sitting next to me?'

They walk off, both as confused as each other, perhaps to find the statue of Hans Christian Andersen instead: besuited, benign, civilised. Sane. Or so they probably imagine.

That boy really looked like he was chatting to someone when he was sitting on the mushroom, though. I'd told myself it was the Cheshire Cat, peeking over Alice's shoulder – but was it?

I begin to look at photographs online. Pictures of other people's holidays, their kids sitting in Alice's shadow, posing, grinning. After a while, I begin to notice.

Sometimes there's a little girl lying full stretch under the Alice statue. Sometimes it's a woman. I stare at her face, always obscured by shadow, and feel the intensity of her gaze as she watches the world. She rarely seems to bother anyone else. Their smiles are all the same.

I picture a hazy form materialising at Alice's side, not the Cheshire Cat, but *someone*. First her grin: there's always a grin. White teeth, sharp. *Can I kiss you?*

What do you eat under there?

Years. They taste like milk.

❧

There are billboards on the streets. The latest moisturiser. A miracle diet. Cosmetics. Surgeons. Everyone wants to look younger. Even the oldest of stories knew all about that. The youngest princess, the littlest mermaid. No one cares what happens to the others. Why should they?

Women's voices on the subway.

'Youth: it's wasted on the young.'

'If I could be that age again, knowing what I know now…'

The women never see the little girl who steps off behind them, her hair in ribbons, and skips off towards the park entrance. A little girl who's the exact same age she wishes to be.

But perhaps she isn't a little girl, the youngest, a princess. Perhaps she's really a crone, a hag, a wicked witch: a witch who drinks years.

Maybe, for some, that's a good thing. She gives them another go-round at their lives, knowing what they know now, and still remembering their names, even if no one else can recognise them any longer. She puts things right. She puts things wrong too, but shit happens, and anyway, who can say she doesn't enjoy that just as much, or more?

But sometimes, she might meet with a little child. She can't drink their years. They don't have enough to satisfy her. Instead, she feeds them: she gives them everything all in one go, year after year after year, until they shrivel and the skin droops from their bones.

I wonder how she chooses. Is she punishing the kids who notice her, who see her for what she truly is? Or does she actually think she's making their wishes come true? Kids are different, after all. They always dream of being older. Vivian was always three and a bit, four and a half, five and three quarters, always looking ahead to the next birthday, always longing to grow up.

No one is ever happy with the age they are.

I can see why she chose the statue for her home. She's as nonsensical as the story, as capricious as a child. Or perhaps it's that the Alice sculpture makes people show the age they are, inside. It makes them show her their hearts.

One side will make you grow taller, and the other side will make you grow shorter.

At last, I find her. It's easy, in the end: impossible and easy. I always knew where she lived, after all. I'd searched for her there before, many times. Watched for her. I just hadn't looked for her the right way.

One side to make you taller, the other to make you shorter. I had begun to wonder if, in some way, that applied to her too. I'd often circled the statue, running my hand along the brim of the Mad Hatter's hat, glancing down to read the words *in the wabe*, edging around the back of the mushroom and past the white rabbit's shoulder to the beginning again, and never arriving anywhere.

This time it's different. I look for her in one direction and she isn't there. Then I turn and move gyre-wards, gimble-wards, this time reading the words as they were meant to be read. I look the other way – contrariwise – and there she is.

Or perhaps the witch wanted to be found. Maybe she wanted to find me. She's been here a long time, after all; I can see that in her face. I wonder if she was always here, even though her eyes are shiny and round and blue as a child's. They are also as endless and deep as the rabbit hole. She might be older than the city. Maybe she came on the Mayflower, or maybe she was here before that, just a little girl in a Wonderland, waiting for someone to play with.

After all those years, maybe she needed to talk. Wouldn't you?

She peeks up at me and slowly, she grins. Her teeth are white and very sharp. She pulls herself from under the sculpture and gets to her feet, then walks past me, no taller than my waist. She steps up onto the smallest mushroom, then the next, wrinkling her nose at that inconvenient dormouse, and sits down next to Alice. She smiles at me and indicates the place next to her. After a moment, I haul myself up and sit beside her. Together we look out over Conservatory Water, where miniature sailboats leave long white triangles reflected in the lake.

The witch lets out a long sigh. She's wearing a blue pinafore dress, matching ribbons in her yellow hair, shiny black Mary Jane shoes. She looks about six years old.

'I get tired,' she says. 'Some days, my back hurts. Some days it's my hip. My eyesight comes and it goes. I think I might have cataracts.' She sighs again. 'I really need a fucking drink.'

I feel, rather than see, her glance. She says, 'That's not why you're here.'

I shake my head. 'You know why.'

'You want her back. You want it all to be the same, but it won't be. There's a price.'

I nod. I already know what I might have to do. I picture the cops coming for me, but not my friends, not any longer. I won't even recognise them. I'll be on the ground, looking at concrete, my hands spread wide while they point their guns at my back.

'I'll kill you anyway,' I hear myself say. 'If you don't give her back to me, I'll kill you right here.'

I wonder if I've gone as mad as the Hatter to be sitting here, in the Park, saying these words. The day is cloudy but warm. Families wander the paths around me, eating ice cream, exploring little bridges and tunnels, peering at the skyscrapers reflected like ghosts in the pools. I swallow. She's still a child. She's always a child and here I am considering bashing out her brains on a bronze mushroom, a sculpture that belongs to children, to stories, to fairy tales.

My hands twitch. It's obscene, but I'll do it anyway. I will. I have to.

Then she says, brightly, 'Okay.'

She flashes me a smile so white it seems to hang in the air as she shuffles to her knees and turns to stare up into Alice's giant face. She twists to sight along Alice's right arm, the one reaching for the white rabbit's pocket watch, then turns her head to look at the other.

I'd never thought much about the other, but I do now. What was it that Alice is reaching for with her left hand? Nothing but air? Is she trying to take the hand of a child, to lead them… where?

The witch reaches out as if she'll be the one to take that huge bronze hand. But when she turns back to me, she's holding another pocket watch. This isn't like the other. It's smaller. This one is life-sized, on a human scale. When I glance away it turns insubstantial, nothing but a haze, but when I look at it directly it has a sharp, bright clarity; it's almost too bright. It glows.

She holds it out to me and I take it. The watch is as cold as ice and impossibly heavy.

Then the witch leans back, crosses her arms over her chest and slides off the mushroom. Her Mary Janes grit on the floor as she ducks under its gills and I know I won't find her again, no matter how I search. She's gone, nothing left of her but the memory of her grin.

I don't search for her. I do jump down after her, though. I'm still holding the pocket watch and I can sense all the years it holds, the hours, the minutes, captured within its smooth, cold, curved weight. I heft it higher into the air, then flip it over and bring it down on the bronze dormouse's ears.

I feel more than hear it shatter, although I hear it too: a bass *clang* that starts low then begins to grow, louder, until it resounds in my bones, until the whole bronze sculpture chimes in sympathetic resonance. There comes a higher sound, like sproinging springs, like cogs de-cogging, and then there is silence.

I open my fingers, half expecting to see delicate golden watch parts falling to the floor, but it's gone. My hand is empty.

For days, I wander the streets. My clothes and skin and hair become soiled with dust and disapproval and hostile glances. My skin grows dry, the lines digging in deeper around my eyes and lips. I don't care. I don't long to be younger. I want to be just the age I am, for how else will my daughter recognise me when she sees me again?

Then one day I'm walking along yet another city block, staring at the concrete, and an alleyway opens at my side and I turn and see her.

A little girl about eight years old, just the age she would have been if she'd never gone into the wabe, never passed beyond my reach. Vivian's hair is the same dark brown it always was, although it's ragged and tangled now. Her cheeks still possess the smooth curve of a child's, but her eyes are different. There are things in them and I wonder what my child has seen in the time she's lived alone, out here, fending for herself.

I wonder what words rung in her ears as she scavenged for food, hungry and cold and afraid.

Mommy, mommy, she had said. *It's me, I'm Vivian.*

She'd sounded so scared. And I had only been repulsed by that child's cry emerging from such a worn throat; the pink sparkles wrapped around that ageing body; the little girl's tears springing from her wrinkled eyes.

And I hear again the words I said to her in return, my daughter, my baby.

I'll kill you. You say that again, I fucking will.

I walk towards her. She doesn't run away from me. I don't suppose she has anywhere to run to. Her expression doesn't change as I put my arms around her. She doesn't even move, not to hug me back or hold me or push me away. I rest my chin on her shoulder, ignoring the smell of her, taking in the familiar-strange feel of her. And I tell my daughter I'm sorry. I have nothing else, there isn't anything else, so I keep on saying it, like a spell or an incantation: *I'm sorry, I'm sorry, I'm sorry.* I say it over and over and I don't stop, because how could it ever be enough?

You want it all to be the same, but it won't be, the witch had said. And she hadn't lied to me. I'm not certain she knew how.

There's a price.

And I know that there always will be.

|The Headland of Black Rock|

~

There was a dead seagull at the foot of the cliff. It lay on its back, wings spread, white underbelly exposed and swollen. There was nothing but a bright red hole where its throat had been ripped out. I leaned over it, smelling only the sea, and saw tiny black insects wriggling in the wet. I grimaced. I couldn't guess what creature might have done it – killed it and left it there without taking another bite.

The cove was small and mercifully empty. The sea shattered against the rocks, sending up spume that dampened my skin and booming echoes that resounded around the cliffs. I was about to walk away when a smaller sound, a scraping of stone, drew me back. There on the cliff, its speckled down almost camouflaged against the rock, was a chick. It was large but ungainly, its feathers nothing more than fluff. I searched its bright black eyes for some expression I could recognise, but they were alien to me. As it shuffled along the rocks it revealed a malformed left foot, like a half-melted candle, and I knew then that it would die. It was probably always going to die, yet it peered down at what must have been its mother, no doubt hungering for some vile, half-digested fish. Had the gull died protecting her chick? It didn't seem likely. I imagined them to be cold, ravening creatures, no affection in them.

There wasn't much I could do about it either way. I took one more look around the cove: wild, smelling of brine and seaweed, too rough to swim, too pebbly for tourists to build sandcastles with their kids. Good. I fixed momentarily upon an odd arrangement of rocks just offshore – it looked a little like a seated figure – but there was nothing else to attract visitors. The guidebook had said that Cornwall's tourist hordes kept to Sennen Beach to the north and Land's End to the south, leaving only a few hardy souls venturing along this stretch of coastline, fewer still troubling to scramble down the steep cliff path. I had found what

I sought: isolation; nature; the simplicity of the world. The despoiled gull wasn't quite what I'd had in mind, but I pushed that thought away before I started the climb back up to Trevanann Cottage.

The holiday letting agent was waiting on the step when I arrived. I was gasping for breath, my sweat turning cold in the sea breeze. A few years back I would have jogged up and asked for more, another take maybe; I used to be as fit as my profession required. She smiled, her eyes widening when she took me in – recognition? I sighed. She was grey and worn out and I wanted only to dismiss her, but she fumbled among her papers, found a bunch of keys and jangled them.

'I'm Sheila. Didn't like to go in without you.' She laughed as if she'd made a joke. 'I just called by to see if everything's all right. Brought a few things.'

I unlocked the door with my own key, wondering if she did this for all the guests or if she'd decided I was a special case, and she bustled in, pointing out the hob, the dishwasher, even the sink, as if a man on his own couldn't possibly have found them already. Trevanann was an old fisherman's cottage, retrofitted with everything I'd want for a month's stay – possibly longer, if I needed the time. She pulled a bundle from her bag, draped a fresh dishcloth over the tap, turned to the open-plan living area and withdrew a selection of magazines. I stared at the shiny pictures, the screaming fonts, recognising *Movie Scene*, its lead feature 'Forties and Fab'. The muscles in my jaw went tight. What did she want, an autograph? But she fanned them across the coffee table, a supply of well-thumbed paperbacks nested beneath.

'Anything else you need? You've found the cliff path, I see. Been to see the Irish Lady, have you?'

'The—?'

'It's the name for the rock just off the cove. There's a legend about it. You can read about it in the books.' She gestured towards the paperbacks and I barely glanced at them.

'Course, it can be lonely, too.' Her voice grew warmer, almost sympathetic, and I swallowed down my irritation. 'I'm always here if you need anything – anything at all, mind. If I'm not around I'll be helping at the pub in Sennen. You can find me there too, if you'd like. Any time. The Old Success.'

Again, I clenched my jaw. *The Old Success* – was she taking the piss? But I realised it was the name of the pub just as I took in her coquettish stance, her fingers combing back her wiry hair. *Anything at all*. She didn't imagine…?

Had she not realised who I was? I felt a sudden urge to flip through the magazine and show her, to point out that I'd been in a *movie*, for fuck's sake. How could she think I'd be interested in her? An image rose of my last girlfriend – and I remembered the blank adoration on her pretty face, her tiresome helplessness, all her proclamations of love, and I forced myself to nod and smile as Sheila finally made her exit.

The first thing I did was pick up the magazine, though I'd sworn I was leaving all that behind, at least for now. My PR had said I would be featured and I'd acted like I didn't care. The truth was, I'd been surprised. I hadn't had a decent role in too long, and besides, I'd softened about the middle, lost a little hair.

I found the feature, which had lots of photographs and very little text, and saw that I'd been right: they'd bumped me after all. Then I saw the opposite page and my breath stopped.

'…And Not So Much,' the heading went, followed by more pictures: semi-remembered actresses' faces long since grown puffy, their bulk squeezed into the clothes of summers past, and in the middle, there I was. I'd been in the garden, my shirt off, my belly hanging over my shorts, the unflattering angle giving me multiple chins. *Bastards*. I'd never even seen the pap who took the picture.

I threw the thing across the room, knowing I shouldn't have looked. Should I fire my PR? Call the editor? Anything I did would only make it worse.

Instead, I went to the window and stared out. I looked beyond the cliff edge to the grey sea, the grey sky, all the miles and miles of nothing, and took deep breaths until I calmed.

The annoying woman was right about the book of legends, though it took a while to find it: an ancient, dog-eared thing called, somewhat misleadingly, *Popular Romances of the West of England* by Robert Hunt. The Irish Lady had a section of her own. A ship had foundered off Pedn-Men-Du, the Headland of Black Rock, during a storm. She was the only survivor. Daylight revealed the sight of her clinging to the rocks, but the sea remained too rough to reach her. Days and nights passed during which people could only watch her dying; eventually, her body slipped into the water. Ever after – wasn't there always an ever after? – fishermen would catch glimpses of her when the waves were high: sitting on her rock, a rose in her mouth. They seemed to think the flower was meant to show her indifference to the tempest, though I hadn't heard of such a thing; I always thought that roses meant love.

I imagined the local people watching her die. It must have been quite the story, because Humphrey Davy had written a poem about her, dwelling on her tender age and her beauty. But of course: if she'd been old and ugly, she wouldn't have been worth the ink; she wouldn't even be in the book. The fascination in watching her light go out would have been all the stronger for how brightly it had burned.

I flicked through the pages, pausing on a different legend, struck at once by the similarity. Mermaid's Rock, a little further along the coast, was said to be the haunt of a Cornish mermaiden. She would make her appearance before a storm, singing most plaintively of all before a shipwreck. Young men, lured by her voice, sometimes tried to swim to her, but none of them ever came back.

That seemed a more obvious kind of yarn to tell, and I wondered why they hadn't assumed the Irish Lady to be a mermaid too – appearing when a ship was lost, so many sailors drowned. But what did it matter? It was only a rock, only a story. I tossed the book aside. Later, after lunch, I would go to the cove again. If nothing else, the walk would help me shift a couple of inches from my waistline.

The headland was indeed black, at least where the sea darkened the rocks. Again and again the waves threw a veil of white lace over them, and I blinked, because for a moment it seemed there *was* a woman sitting there: her legs twisted together, her hair long and wild, her face turned away from me, towards the horizon. Then I saw it was only a rock. I was allowing things to get to me, and a series of images – mermaids, girlfriends past, my own ageing self – began to circle around and around in my mind as the gulls circled overhead, their cries like human voices, the sound of the wind and the waves the same.

The birds reminded me of the dying chick and I turned away from the sea, looking for its ledge. The gull was still there, its twisted foot held up and out – was it showing it to me, asking for help? Its eyes held that same blank brightness and I wondered if it would be there again tomorrow, and the next day – like the Irish Lady, growing weaker, thinner, until it was gone.

I couldn't feed it, couldn't save it. I imagined chewing up raw fish, spitting it onto a plate for this ravenous wild thing, and grimaced. I told myself it was impossible; I told myself there could be no fascination in watching it die.

Then I saw I was not alone on the beach after all.

She was caught in the perfect camera angle – a girl walking by the shore, long hair lifted and wrapped around her by the breeze, picking her way barefoot, a single gold thread gleaming about her ankle. She seemed unaware of anyone watching; and she was beautiful. She was the image of holiday romance, of youth, of carefree days filled with laughter and golden light, and she made me feel, suddenly and deeply, that life could be lived; that everything could start again.

I straightened, though she wasn't looking at me. She might have been the only person in the world, needing nothing other than the touch of sea-spray and the sound of the waves. I wished at once that I knew her name; I wondered what her voice would sound like. I wanted to run my hand across that taut young skin – but I felt the distance between us, surely a divide impossible to cross. I wondered if she was real at all, or only another image conjured by my mind.

She turned and saw me. She smiled, and it was a real smile; I'd seen enough fakes in my time to know. Then she simply stood there, as if she was waiting.

The old questions arose – *an autograph hunter? A fan? A headcase?* – and were gone. I no longer cared. She surely wasn't like that. This girl was entirely natural and lovely, and I was walking toward her before I'd consciously decided to do so.

As I drew close she raised her head, revealing eyes that were perfectly blue, and gestured towards the sea. I called out, telling her my name, asking for hers, but she didn't reply. She gestured again – this time a finger-burst from her lips as if to represent sound before shaking her head.

'You can't speak?'

A shrug and another smile, as if a voice wasn't something she needed or even wanted. And maybe she was right; the silence – or rather, the sound of the sea all around us – said all that was needed. She reached out and caught my hand, pulling me towards her, stepping back towards the water.

'Oh – no, I—'

She mimed pulling off my shoes and I let out a sudden laugh. Paddling, at my age? But why the hell not? I tugged off my trainers and let them fall. Her fingers were slender and strong and sure as she led me into the surf.

The pebbles were sucked out from under my feet at once and I sank into them. She was light-footed, drawing ahead, her skirt floating on the water. She didn't fuss over it, didn't seem to care. When she turned to me again her smile was like a gift, beautiful and young but without all the things I'd grown so tired of seeing: the layers of meaning, the blind adoration, the recognition of who I was, and what; the *needing*.

Despite her muteness she spoke to me using her eyes and a twitch of her fingers, drawing me deeper, silently laughing. And I followed her, the water a shock of cold above my knees, gasping as a deeper swell reached my thighs. She kept looking at me, *into* me – and she leaned towards me and kissed my lips. She tasted of iodine and salt, of the sea. I felt the pull of the waves and of her arms and I thought of simply letting go, drifting with her, then slipped and almost fell, one arm plunging into the water, meeting with nothing. I managed to keep my feet and staggered back towards the shore, still keeping hold of her hand. When I saw the state of us both I laughed, though the breeze set me shivering. I gestured towards the cliff top, mimed drinking coffee. I suppose I could have spoken the words, but somehow our silence felt right.

She withdrew her touch and I felt a pang of loss, but she cast a come-hither look over her shoulder as she walked ahead of me towards the path. Was this really happening? It struck me that she was like me, on holiday alone and perhaps a little bored, but I didn't want it to be so prosaic and was glad I couldn't ask. It felt as if a little moment in time had opened, forming a bubble around us where nothing need matter.

She didn't turn again until we reached the top of the cliff. I was trying to gulp in air without letting her see how short of breath I was, but she didn't care. She kissed me again, long and deep, and then we were stumbling in at the door. I was enveloped in her hair; her arms were around me, then her leg wrapped mine, sand gritty against my skin, and I realised she must have left her shoes in the cove. I didn't take my lips from hers while I guided her to the bedroom.

When I awoke, the cottage was empty. The girl seemed as unreal as a dream but the sheets were damp with seawater and rough with sand, and I could still *feel* her, filling the empty spaces inside me, making everything new again.

I swept my hand over the bed as if I could conjure her shape, then pushed myself up and went in search of her. I already knew the cottage was empty. I could sense it in the still air, the silence that was now bleak and unwanted. I opened my mouth to call her name, realising I still didn't know it. But she had left a sign after all: a trail of wet footprints led across the floor from the bedroom, across the living area and towards the door. I couldn't imagine how her feet had remained so wet. I'd surely have heard it if she'd taken a shower; perhaps the moisture had come from her sea-damp skirts.

I tilted my head so that their gleam caught the light and made out the shape of her right foot, slender and elegant. Then I saw the other – oddly shortened, as if her toes melted away into nothing. I wondered why that was, then realised her left foot must have been partially dry. There had been nothing wrong with her form; she was flawless, and I felt the lack of her, the emotion stronger than anything I'd felt in months. I pictured her walking away from me, carrying the trace of my kisses on her salty skin, and something inside me sank.

I shook my head. What the hell was wrong with me? I'd had women throw themselves at me, proclaim their devotion, pursue me, and the only thing I'd felt was contempt. I felt a pang of guilt at that – but those woman had been deluded; they'd *wanted* to be deluded. When they looked at me they saw nothing but their own dreams.

This girl wasn't like that. Innocence like hers couldn't be faked.

A short time later I was on the beach, pacing the shoreline. I kept seeing her in my mind's eye: the turn of her head, the shifting of her hair echoed in the tortured shape of the rocks. Was she a local? A holidaymaker? Would she ever come here again?

I sat on a flat stone and waited, but the cove remained empty save for a rock shaped a little like a woman, its form mocking me now, and a dying seagull perched on the shelf of a cliff.

I spent much of that day at the cove, and the next. What else had I to do? I became used to the salt on my skin, my hair becoming lank with spray. I told myself all the old lines – it was just a moment we had shared, nothing more – but couldn't believe them. I waited and I watched. The Irish Lady bathed in the cold waves. The chick wasted away on the cliff. Nothing changed except the sea. Eventually, I began to see that it held countless colours: ever-changing moods, innumerable faces. I couldn't take my gaze from it. I imagined the myriad fish hidden beneath the waves, their cold bodies, gleaming scales, their viscid, staring eyes. I barely drank or ate and I'm not sure I thought of anything else, didn't care as time began to skip. A crab skittered across my foot and I picked it up without a thought, crushing its shell between my teeth.

At night, when I returned to the cottage, I could settle to nothing until I found the book again and read of mermaids. I learned of the merry-maid of Padstow, who choked its harbour with sand in revenge for some slight; of a man granted three wishes for saving a maid stranded in a rock pool; and I read of Honour Penna's daughter, stolen away as an infant and replaced by a mermaid changeling who lived as a human girl. Wronged by her lover, she pined away, but later she lured the wicked man to his death to repay his sins. Her kisses chilled his heart, keeping him in her spell as he drowned. I found myself whispering the words of her song:

Come away, come away,
o'er the waters wild!
Our earth-born child
died this day, died this day.
Come away, come away!

I wondered again about the Irish Lady. If a woman could turn into stone, why not a mermaid or something else? An image rose before me: the girl walking naked through my cottage, every part of her perfect save her left foot, which ended in the twisted, malformed claw of a gull.

I shook my head. What the hell was wrong with me? I must be having some kind of breakdown. The girl hadn't turned into anything. She was only a girl. She'd got into a car and driven away, or worse, been driven away by someone who actually mattered to her, and I would never see her again. Unless, that was, I looked so hard that I imagined her face everywhere, in the waves, in the rock...

I went into the kitchen and forced myself to eat, my throat gulping and convulsing over the dry mass of bread, and I grabbed my jacket. The girl had been real. That meant I had to be able to find her.

The Old Success was brighter and more modern than I'd imagined. A couple of bearded, grizzled locals sat in the corner exchanging yarns while a family complete with buckets and spades squabbled around a table. Sheila was standing behind the bar and when she saw me she waved with her whole arm, as a child might, and called, 'Yoo-hoo!'

When I went over she stared as if she'd never seen me before, then reached out and brushed at my cheek. I began to pull away, then felt salt flaking from my skin.

She didn't comment, only let out her sputtering laugh, and I thought, with a stab of spite, that no one would ever write a poem about her. I pictured the girl on the beach, her lovely form, her golden hair, and even as I asked after her I wondered if my breakdown was so complete that I'd imagined the whole thing. It didn't help when Sheila's smile faded and she said, 'No, I don't think I know her. Sounds like you've seen a mermaid!' She sputtered again.

I tried not to show my dismay. 'I thought everyone here knew everybody else?'

'Oh, it's not like that now, love,' she replied. 'Not like it used to be. Some of the families go back a ways I suppose, but there's a lot of holiday lets now. A lot of strange faces.' She rambled on, telling me how she'd only moved down here a few years back, that she'd been quite the thing in the city in her day, and I tuned her out and made my escape.

∽

The cottage couldn't hold me. Its walls were closing in, everything too small. I found myself writhing on the bed, burying my face in the sheets, grasping at grains of sand that slipped through my fingers. It had been real. *Real.* I pictured a mermaid on a rock, combing her lovely hair, perhaps even singing. And people watching her from the shore, so close but at an impossible distance; unable to see her for what she really was, seeing only what they imagined her to be. Was she wrecked by the storm or did she raise it? Had the sailors truly perished in the tempest or had they leapt, despairing, into the waves?

Had they ever existed at all?

The words that came back to me were Sheila's: *strange faces.*

I went to the window, seeing my own pale reflection, my features distorted. The sky outside was already dark, gunmetal clouds roiling in from the west. In the far distance came the first flicker of light: a storm was rising.

I thought of all the imagined glimpses of her face I had seen, and of the lonely cove. I thought of the gull trapped there, its leg useless, its body wasting, and it came to me: I had been watching it *die.* It seemed suddenly important, this thing I could have saved, some little good that I could have done with my life, and I started towards the door.

I half scrambled, half slid down the cliff path. The sky was monstrous, alive with movement and noise, as was the sea, as if something stirred within it. I had been warned that storms could whip the spray as high as the cliff top, and found my face damp; I blinked it away. Bright foam marked the meeting of wave and rock; moonlight formed a path into the sea, but all else was dark.

I made my way to the foot of the cliff where the chick had been and squinted up at the ledge. At first I could see nothing but shadows, then lightning flashed and I saw that the gull had gone. Perhaps it had flown after all, or been taken by a predator. I was too late and I felt my eyes sting – salt water?

I cursed myself as a fool for venturing out in this, for climbing down here for nothing, and then I turned and saw the girl, just as she had been, walking by the edge of the sea.

When she turned towards me moonlight limned her hair, her face cast into shadow so that I couldn't make it out. And as I walked towards her I remembered another tale of a mermaid, one I had heard many years before, when I was young. This mermaid was young too, the most beautiful of them all. She had given up her voice, her home in the sea, everything she had, in the hope of gaining love: but her prince had never really seen her. He hadn't understood who she truly *was*.

She waited for me, the sea raging around her, and beneath its roar I heard the more plangent note of its echo resounding from the cliffs. For a moment, I was certain I heard her voice. It was just as it had sounded in my dreams, the ones I'd never wanted to leave: low and sweet, lulling my senses.

I realised she was smiling, holding out a hand towards me. Didn't she see how the waves seethed – wasn't she afraid? A wild comber lashed her to the waist, but she didn't flinch, only waited. I had to reach her. I hurried down the beach, not pausing to remove my shoes, and glanced across the cove – black rock, moon-glitter striking the sea, cliffs etched against the sky – and the Irish Lady, where was she? I glimpsed only a sheet of flat rock, but that must be an illusion; the sea obscured everything.

Blinded by spray and drenched at once, I waded in, reaching for her. She must be deeper in than I realised – but then I caught sight of her, holding out both hands to me. She appeared calm; I made out the shape of her lips, curved into a smile.

The current's deep pull dragged at my legs, my muscles quickly turning cold and leaden. I told myself that if she could stand firm so could I, and I pulled in a breath, tasting the brine. I tried to picture myself as she must see me: young again, strong and vital, full of life.

I took another step, felt the pebbles giving way beneath me, everything roiling and turning in the waves. Nothing was sure, nothing certain. And the words I'd read came back to me, as if carried on the freezing air:

Come away, come away...

I reached for her, flailing, and by some miracle felt the touch of her hand. Her skin was cold and pallid, almost like something dead. I had to get her out, to warm her – and I dragged her towards me and really saw her at last.

It was she – there were the same eyes, the same features – but changed; and I saw that she wasn't young at all. She wasn't even beautiful. Her eyes weren't wide or welcoming; I wasn't sure she was entirely human. She made me think of things deep under the sea: pliant bodies, pale skin, creatures that lived outside humanity, without the knowledge of joy or mercy or love.

I tried to make out the expression in her eyes, hoping I was wrong. I tried to see the love in them. They were unknowable and alien and bright.

Suddenly my arms were without strength and I felt all the passing of years, the way I was failing, and instead of pulling away she drew me in until the sea was up to my waist. She wasn't even looking at me any longer: she was already tired of me. There was no fascination in watching me die, not when my light had already half gone out. I thought of the girls I had dallied with, taking my pleasure and casting them aside, heard their entreaties ringing in my ears. But the words they whispered had changed, becoming lines from a story I'd read in a book: the mermaid's song as she lured the lover who had scorned her into the waves.

His corse shall float

Around the bay, around the bay...

I shook away the words but I couldn't fail to hear as she opened her mouth to speak at last. I saw her white teeth, the red inside of her mouth; her voice was a raw, plaintive cry from the back of her throat. Her laughter was the cry of a gull and in her eyes was not innocence but a terrible knowledge: a hunger as endless as the sea.

|The Merrie Dancers|

~

It was after nightfall when I first saw my new neighbour, though I didn't know when she had decided to go out into the garden. I'd been busy unpacking boxes and telling myself I should be grateful for what I had, and it was dark when I went to draw the curtains across the window. She was in a wheelchair, nothing but a hunched, shadowy shape against the shrubbery. I might not have seen her if it wasn't for the movement of her feet, kicking continually at the blanket covering her legs. I thought of Parkinson's, of restless leg syndrome, other illnesses I couldn't name and knew little of. Had she been taken ill just now, or was it of long duration? Did she need my help?

I felt bad that I didn't know. I'd never met her before, though Mum had lived in this house for some years. I'd left home as soon as I was eighteen, anxious to experience all that London had to offer, and only came back when she got ill. I'd chosen to look after her, though I hadn't wanted it, and by the time I reached her it was already too late. Now I was here, it was as if I couldn't leave again – I couldn't be so ungrateful as to abandon her a second time, even though she was already gone.

The old lady next door tilted back her head to stare up at the stars, shielding her eyes as if they were too bright, and I just made out the smile that touched her lips. It seemed suddenly terribly romantic. She was old, infirm, perhaps couldn't even walk, and yet there she was taking in the night air and dreaming, while I was twenty-four and acting as if my life was already over.

I told myself she was fine and didn't go to check on her after all. I didn't see her again that night, didn't watch to see that she'd gone inside, that she was safe. I slept right through to the next morning, stretched the stiffness from my limbs, brushed my teeth and dressed, and opened the curtains to see her still sitting there, in the place where she had been.

I couldn't breathe. Was she stuck, unable to go inside by herself? Had she fallen asleep – or something worse? She was old and alone and had needed help; help that, once again, I had failed to provide.

Thinking of heart attacks and strokes and other terrors of the elderly, I rushed downstairs and into my own back garden. Our two houses were the only ones set at the top of a leafy lane, separated from each other and the softly rolling hills around us by knee-high fencing. I stepped over it and rushed towards her, calling to see if she was all right, and she turned towards me, her look of astonishment stopping me dead.

'Goodness,' she said. 'Have you seen a ghostie, lass?'

My alarm turned to apologies. I explained my concern and introduced myself, and she told me she was Flora Scollay, that she had just this moment stepped outside again – *wheeled*, I thought but didn't say. Her legs kicked against their blanket, a grey tartan, and the thought came again that she had some kind of illness, a muscular palsy over which she had no control. I tried not to look, though now and again a sharper kick drew my gaze.

'I did come out a wee while last night,' she said. 'I hoped to see the merrie dancers. It was on the news they might be seen this far south, but I didnae spy anything at all. Did you happen to see them, Sophie?'

I said I had not, though I remembered the news item she referred to – I should have thought of it before. If I hadn't been so set on finding a place for everything, I might have tried to see the Northern Lights myself, though despite the newscaster's assurance, it had seemed unlikely they would grace the skies of Lincolnshire. They were meant for wilder climes, more northerly parts of the world.

'It's still oorlich, though,' she said, shivering as if to explain her meaning. 'We had that part of it, at least.' She fumbled under her blanket, pulling another one free; it looked as soft as mohair. She passed it to me and I shook my head – I'd come out here to help her, not the other way around – but she said, 'That shade of brown, it's called a murat. One of the finest you've ever felt about your neck.'

A strange curiosity came over me and I took it, wrapping it around my shoulders, and felt comforted at once. I snuggled into its warmth.

'My father reared the sheep gave that blanket,' she said. 'Shetland sheep, on the isles. That one's from my favourite. Bonxie, I called her, after the Great Skua chicks that lived on the sea cliffs. She was one of the best, the kindly sheep we called them, the ones that gave such wool.'

I couldn't resist rubbing it against my cheek, almost thinking I could smell not the lanolin of sheep but the briny scent of the ocean.

'That's right,' she said, as if I'd spoken. 'There were ponies too of course, our neighbours had them, and I'd see them whenever I could. I'd put on their halters and lead them about like dogs, for they were no bigger.'

'You grew up on the Shetland Islands?' They seemed as unknowable to me as a place in a story. I wasn't certain I could have pointed to them on a map.

'On Foula,' she said, relishing its name on her lips. 'The most westerly of them all, and separate from the rest – divided from them by a nasty reef, the Shaalds, though I always thought of them as the hungry rocks. The loneliest island in Britain.' She said this with a touch of pride.

Lost in her words, I said, 'I thought I detected an accent,' though the truth was that at times I could and at others I couldn't. It seemed to come and go, like something she half remembered.

'Aye, it's still in me, when I think of it,' she said. 'Mostly it's gone. I lost a lot of things when I left. Found some too. That's what happens, I suppose.'

She glanced at me as if she saw right through me and I thought of the way I'd inherited the house, had been handed everything. It had been at once too easy and too hard. I had lost my mother; I had done nothing to help her. I hadn't earned such a home, hadn't *given* enough. But I was helping now, wasn't I? Old people liked to chat about their memories. Flora certainly seemed to want to talk to someone, and Mum might have liked to know that I'd listened – so I asked Flora to tell me about her life on Foula.

I wasn't sure she'd heard. She had focused her gaze on the shrubbery, on a twig that was twitching as if a bird had just flown from it; then she looked away as if it was nothing after all. Her gaze softened, as though she saw again distant places and other times.

'I saw a trow when I was thirteen years old,' she said. 'Is that the sort of tale you like, hen?'

I smiled and nodded, wondering what a trow was – a fish? A bird? – trying not to feel like a child at bedtime, listening to stories at her mother's knee.

'The aurora shone that night,' she said. 'The dancers were merry then, perhaps a little too merry, so in a way it was all their fault, for if they weren't shining, the path would have been too dark to go out. It was approaching winter, and the nights were longer than any you'd imagine, though it was between the weathers: we had gales before and gales after, but that night it was still.

'I'd only been to the Turvelsons'. They had the next croft to ours, and my mother had sent me to borrow a little butter. She was baking biscuits for the wee ones' birthdays, but it was me who had to go.'

Her accent deepened as she remembered. She pronounced mother as *modir*.

'It didnae take long, and the parcel was greasy in my pocket. It's lucky our neighbours were close by. Fewer than forty souls lived on Foula even then, all of us on the easterly plain. Most of the Isles are empty, did you know that? And none can count them. There are said to be a hundred islands and skerries, but no one really knows. Some are said to appear and disappear at the bidding of the selkies.'

I smiled at her whimsicality, but now she'd begun she seemed barely conscious of my presence.

'The sky to the north was all aglow,' she said. 'Every few steps the path shone green at my feet and I saw everything – and nothing, for the shimmering in the sky made the hills darker than ever. The trows are hill-dwellers, did you know that? I looked at the great mound of Hamnafeld, which drops on the other side sheer into the ocean. On its top, that's where they say the door is: the Lum of Liorafeld, an opening that goes straight down to their homes underground. Some have let down lines to try and find the bottom, but no one ever can. Those who seek it rarely even find the door.

'That's what my grandmother told me, and that's what I was thinking of. Perhaps that's why it happened: they were drawn to my thoughts, or perhaps it was only the butter, or they liked the pretty lights. Whatever the reason, I felt their eyes on me.

'That feeling you have sometimes, of being watched – it didnae happen often on Foula. There are more ponies than people and more sheep than ponies and more birds than the rest put together, and ne'er a stranger, especially not in winter. Still, I knew it when it came, that feeling, crawling all over me like dirty fingers.

'I turned about and there he was: a shape where none should be. He stood halfway between their home and mine, as if he'd just then stepped out of the peat bog. One moment he was clear, outlined in the flicker, and the next I could barely make him out. But tall he was, and grey; his clothes were grey and his skin too, his raggedy beard and tatty hair, all of him, and I knew he was looking at me, though I couldnae rightly see his eyes.

'I dinnae know what I would have done, screamed or run or nothing at all, but thanks be, he started to leave me. He didnae walk like ordinary folk, though. He walked like a trow, and that is, backwards – he never so much as glanced behind him to see his way. At least, I dinnae think he did. He came and went in the light, but I still felt him watching me, and I shivered, because I knew I'd seen one of the folk. Some say the trows are like Norwegian trolls, others the English fairies, but I think they're something in between.

'The fear took me then and I ran all the way home. When I let myself in at the door, my mother called out for the butter, my little brother and sister looked up from their game, but Gran took one look at me and shrieked fit to wake the angels in heaven.

'There was uproar then. "What is it? What is it?" My mother cried out, and I couldn't speak for trembling, but Gran grabbed my face and held it to the lamplight, tilting me this way and that way.

'"What did you see?" she said, and I was so frightened I thought to lie, but I knew she'd see it on me. She saw many things, too many perhaps, and so I told her.

'She crowed as if she'd caught a fish. "I knew it!" she said. "It's left its mark on you!"

'Well, my brother grinned and my sister laughed, but my mother sighed and went back to the oat-biscuits, and took the butter with her. Me, I went to the mirror. I stared and stared into it, trying to see whatever Gran had seen. *Left its mark on you*, she'd said, but no matter how I tried, then or after, I ne'er could see a trace of it.'

Flora stirred in her wheelchair, blinking as if she didn't entirely know where she was. I became conscious of her feet constantly shifting against the blankets, the sound seeming suddenly loud. I realised it had been there all the time she spoke, almost like whispering, or perhaps waves breaking on the shore. I realised she was waiting for me to respond and yet I didn't have the first idea what to say.

'There's more to it, of course,' she said. 'I should tell you of the year I turned sixteen – of Yule, and of the thing that happened to the twins – my brother and sister.'

Her whole body twitched in her seat and she gave an especially hard kick. The tartan blanket fell aside and I caught a glimpse, not of some wide-fitting brogues or house-slippers or any such thing, but the most exquisite bright red shoes. She caught her breath and pulled at the blanket to cover them once more.

'I'll tell you of those too,' she said, 'but not now.'

I stepped closer without meaning to, thinking to help her I supposed, for she reached out and grasped my hand, crushing it in her bony fingers.

'I'll go inside,' she said. 'I've said enough, I think.'

She cast glances to left and right before waving me towards my own garden, ignoring my goodbyes and offers of help as she pulled at the wheels of her chair. Her legs were covered once more but I could still picture those shoes: the brightness of them, the perfect red of them; their pointed toes, the tiny, almost invisible stitching, the suppleness of the leather. I realised I hadn't said a word about her story. It wasn't until I got inside that I found her soft woollen blanket was still draped about my shoulders.

As I got on with the task of settling into my mother's house, Flora's tale began to seem more and more outlandish. I didn't know what to think of it, nor of her for telling it. Her words were surely make-believe, perhaps a mingling of her past and the tales she must have heard in childhood.

Still, I kept returning to the blanket where I'd left it on the table, picking it up and touching it to my cheek. Was that scent still there – the harsh, raw wind, carried across the Atlantic? But when I closed my eyes it was those shoes I saw, such pretty shoes for one so old, and I wondered how it must feel to wear them. Was that why she was always fidgeting, as if she longed to dance? Or did her feet simply follow in the wake of her wandering thoughts?

I shook away the idea and decided to look in on her again. It seemed like fate, then, when I looked out of the window and saw her emerging into her garden, into a day that was still struggling to become bright.

I went out and waved to her as I stepped over the fence. I made to hand over the lovely blanket but she gestured for me to hold onto it, so I wrapped it about me and nestled in once again.

'My grandmother had a lot of superstitions,' she began, as if I'd never been away. 'She always said the trows would punish a lass for forgetting to place a little resting peat on a waning flame. They like the fire, you see. They also like to wash their bairns on a Saturday and she would bid me leave out the water for them. If I neglected to do it, or if I did it well, before she'd even thought of it, why, she put it all down to the night I saw the peedie man.

'She'd no let me forget, and anyway, how could I? I thought of him often, standing out there under the dancing sky, watching and watching for me. I dinnae know if I still carried the mark Gran had spoken of. I didnae like to think of it, much less ask – but the longing of it was on me, that's what she always said, and it sent a shiver through me every time, as if I was still out there in the cold and the dark.

'But it's Yule when the trows really wander above the ground. They come out seven days earlier, on Tul-ya's e'en, and so it was, the year I turned sixteen. Gran had me stick knives into the hams to stop the trows getting them, and it was me who had to do the blessing on the little ones.

'I did it to myself first: washed, then dipped hands and feet into the water while my mother dropped the coals in, so the trows couldnae steal away the power in them. Then it came time for me to bless the twins, but they were older then, turned seven, and they pulled faces and fought while they had their bath. They had me drenched, and so I told them they could take their chances.

'Truth be told, I was sick of them by then. I had to feed them, scrub their silly matching faces, comb their matching hair. I had to fetch this, tidy that, while they put out their matching tongues at me behind our mother's back. Besides, that was the year of the red shoes, and after I saw them, I could think of nothing else.'

I realised that her feet were restless still, shifting and rustling under their blanket. I'd almost forgotten their movement; had neglected, somehow, to notice.

'Oh, but I was wild for those shoes. I saw them in a fancy shop on the mainland. Right in the window they were, and after I saw them, that was that. Besides, the dance was coming, and I felt I had to wear them. If I only had those shoes, Alex Galdie might dance with me. If I only had those shoes, I swore I'd never ask for anything else. I'd never even *want* anything else. Have you ever wished for something like that, Sophie – needed it so badly it's like a knot inside of you that'll ne'er come loose?'

She paused and I cast my mind back, but it was her shoes that came to mind, the lovely red of them, their softness, their perfect form, and I thought of dancing; of flying through the air as if I'd never fall to earth again.

'I saved and saved,' she said. 'I dropped one penny after another into a jar to help buy them, though it was never enough. I begged; I wept. I did everything I was asked to do, wiping the bairn's mucky faces before I was told, sweeping the hearth, anything my mother asked of me. And in the end she gave a great sigh and said I must be witched – *in the hill* was how she put it, meaning in the trow's power – but she said they would be mine.

'Maybe she thought me cursed even then, you see, but I didnae see it that way. Why should a girl be dutiful all her days? Why must she think only of work and home and bairns and nothing more? It was a great wide world outside the door – right across the ocean. Every time I looked out I thought of it, and every time the young men looked at me I heard fierce music playing, felt the dance already in my feet.

'On Foula, Auld Yule is still celebrated in January, as it was in the Julian calendar, though all the rest of the world changed that centuries ago. We hung onto things long past anyone else, perhaps because there was so little to go around. And so the dancing was set for the sixth. After that, the grey neighbours would go back inside the hill, their holidays over, but before then they too would dance all they could – even if they had to do it disguised as mortals – and so would I.

'There was rarely any snow on Foula. You may not believe that, since it's so far north, but Atlantic currents keep the climate mild; it only feels so cold because of the wind chasing in from the sea. But it snowed that night – the night of the dancing. A good skim of white, and the wind made it bitter, every flake like a knife driving into your skin. The way they flew all about, it was hard to see your hand before your face.

'The sea was alive as we made our way to Norderhus, near the harbour. I heard its song, deep and fierce. The Atlantic and the North Sea were at war, the sea black, the sky pale as death. That wasn't the lights, though; the only merrie dancers that night were all within. I could hear the fiddles on the wind, loud one moment, the next quiet and quick. I wasn't wearing my red shoes; I carried those under my oil-coat so they wouldn't get wet. There was my mother, grandmother and me. The twins were judged too young, and I wasn't sorry for that.

'Everyone was in the ben, the inner room, and in there, it was roasting. I left my boots with all the rest and slipped on my lovely shoes and the music was in them at once, fast and free and telling of new places, and almost as soon as I set foot in the room I was off – clasped by the hand by Alex Galdie, as close as you like, and he didnae take his eyes from mine a moment. We spun and we twirled. There was a light in his face when he smiled at me, and if I wasn't witched before, I was witched then. I saw my mother watching and my grandmother both, and didnae care a bit. My shoes carried me off, and I was happy to go.

'I never once thought of home, or duties, or the land I was born in or the trows and their ways – not even their love of the dance. That tune ended and another began, wilder than the first, and Alex never let me go. He danced with me again, whirling me by the waist, and my feet went faster and faster till I laughed with joy.

'Trows love the fiddle, did you know that? It's said they stole away the Fiddler of Yell for years and years, though he thought only a night had passed while he played for them. And it seemed they were not the only ones, for after a while, I noticed from the tail of my eye the door opened and the twins glided in, all quiet-like, their eyes wide and their faces two matching smiles. Sneaked by they did, not speaking to anyone before they joined in the dance. I saw them now and again as our paths crossed, touching hands, whirling away. Little knowing looks they gave me, and never a word. I remember thinking they must have longed for it just as I had, and I couldnae blame them for that.

'They danced beautifully. Not a hink nor a kink in it, and them so young.

'It was around midnight when my mother grabbed me by the hand and said we must be off. I looked about for the twins and couldnae see them anywhere, so I asked where they were. I fidgeted all the while because the music played on and Alex was near and I could hardly bear to stand still.

'She shook her head, looked confused. I thought the music had stopped her ears and so I shouted louder, but it was like she still couldnae fathom it. All the time the twins had been dancing, you see, something had stopped her from seeing; she'd never noticed they were there at all. Then Gran said they couldnae have come, not all alone, because when she stepped out of the door she'd made sure to lock it behind her.

'Well, there was uproar then. The dance stopped quick enough and everyone put on their oilskins and sou'westers and went out to look.

'The snow hadn't stopped falling, but the sky was dark again, deeper and blacker by contrast with the lights that danced across it. The merrie dancers had come after all, just as if they were mocking us.

'The bairns were not at the croft. That was quiet, though the door stood wide and snow drifted in across the clean floor. Their beds were empty.

'We found them at the edge of the peat bog, in just the same place I'd seen the peedie man. They were lying in the snow, their eyes open to the sky, and snowflakes drifted into them, not melting. They were dead. They'd been there all night, you see. They never had been dancing, and never would – it was the trows that had come to the sound of the fiddle, borrowing the twins' likenesses so they could join in the revels.

'I dinnae know if the trows had had to take the twins first. Perhaps they needed to steal their breath before they took their shape; or perhaps it was only an accident that they died. Perhaps those little bodies weren't really the twins at all. My real brother and sister might have been stolen away under the hill, and the dead ones were nothing but empty skins that the trows had worn for the night, just like they were puppets.

'I wonder sometimes if the real twins are dancing even now, under great Hamnafeld. I wonder if that's why my feet won't be still – because I must dance with them. When at last my shoes give me peace, maybe I'll know that my brother and sister are dead. But time passes differently under the hill. They might be children yet, or far older than I am; my brother with a beard reaching to his feet, my sister with the light of ages in her eyes.

'My mother wailed and my grandmother wept, and I had no comfort for them. I looked down into my brother's eyes, and my sister's matching ones, and at the snowflakes falling into them, and thought of the way I'd saved for those red shoes, one shiny coin after the next falling into a jar. It was me who'd failed to bless the twins. It was me who'd tired of them. It was me who'd wished to be free; and I *was* free.

'Did the grey folk grant me a wish that night I saw the peedie man, do you think? Or was it a curse – or both together? For I'll tell you this: sometimes, having your dearest wish put into your hands is the most terrible thing of all. And I never can forget it. Not while these shoes keep dancing and dancing.'

Flora stopped speaking but she didn't look at me, just went on staring into the past, and I was glad of that, because I didn't know what to say. Did she really imagine her feet fidgeted because her shoes were bewitched? That was something out of a fairy story, one I'd read myself when I was young: the girl in Hans Christian Andersen's *The Red Shoes* was also punished for thinking too much of her finery. Her new shoes forced her to dance and dance until she was so exhausted a woodcutter had to save her by chopping off her feet. Was that the root of Flora's tale? Perhaps she didn't have a physical illness at all. Perhaps her legs wouldn't be still because she was punishing herself for some accident that happened to her siblings, and her ailment – her curse – was psychosomatic. But why did she not simply take off the shoes? I gazed at her in dismay, realising I might not be able to help her at all, that maybe she needed more than I knew how to give. I had no idea if she was mad, but I didn't think she could be altogether sane.

'Oh, it wasn't like the auld story.' Flora lifted her head and looked at me as if she saw through me, and I fought the urge to squirm.

'You think you know it, but it wasn't the same. Andersen's tale came out of a softer land, and it was naught like mine. There's no woodcutter in my story, nor any wood; there were never any trees grew on Foula. It was a peat-cutter I'd set my heart upon, and he never did chop off my feet. He didnae carry me over the threshold or tie my dancing feet to the kitchen table so I could gut the fish for his dinner. What kind of a man would do that? No: Alex Galdie simply decided he didn't want me. He married a girl from Hametoon and settled on the island. It was me who left, on the very next boat I could. What else was there? I couldnae go home again. I'd been right, you see. After I got those shoes, I never really wanted anything else again.'

I still didn't know what to say, so I took the blanket from my neck and wrapped it around her. She grasped my fingers, gently this time.

'You could help me,' she said. 'Would you help an old lady, dear?'

I told her that of course I would. I asked what it was she needed.

'I cannae take them off,' she said. 'I've tried and tried. But I know that you could – if you were willing. If you knew the story of them and chose to take them anyway, to make them your own instead of mine.'

She kicked away the tartan covering her legs. Her feet kicked freely, her toes pointed, marking out the steps she couldn't take. For an instant, they looked as if they were being worn by someone younger; someone whirling in a young man's arms.

I focused again on her face, which was old and lined, her eyes watery. I reminded myself that hers was a mad, wild tale, with no sense in it. I didn't believe she'd worn those same shoes for so many years. I didn't believe that she couldn't stop dancing.

But Flora did. And I realised that perhaps I could help her after all; I could free an old lady from an unhappy delusion. I may have failed to help my mother, but I could help her neighbour – her friend.

And Flora could rest at last. She could have peace. She could go where she wanted, even home, perhaps. An image rose before me: Flora standing on a rugged hillside, united with her brother and sister at last. And then somehow, in my mind, the three of them began to walk away; but they went backwards, their steps perfectly steady, without a hink or a kink, never taking their gaze from my face.

I looked down at those red shoes and the image fled my mind. Another feeling came over me, one that had been waiting somewhere beneath; a wild longing for something I had left behind, but never really given up. I told myself it would be doing her a favour to take the shoes. Anyway, they were wasted on her. She was *old*. What would be the use of her dancing?

I reached out towards the soft leather and a sound reached my ears: the swift, low rushing of a fiddle. But the memory that came, with sudden sharp clarity, was my life in the city, not so very long ago: flashing lights in the close dark. The insistent beat of music throbbing from tall speakers. The touch of a young man's hand, held in mine, around my waist, in my hair. And I remembered how it had felt to dance; to never want my feet to be still. To be free.

It's only a story, I thought.

Still, I felt that if I took those shoes, Flora would be right; it would be for always. I might never come home again. I reached out and touched the red shoes and I listened to the rhythm of the dance, sensed it beating in my blood. I could smell the sea, feel the cold ocean breeze in my hair. And I looked up, into Flora's eyes, and found that I couldn't move a limb.

|Ways to Wake|

~

I hear the sound while I'm still only half awake. Someone is eating, too loud and too close, although I should be alone in my room. When I open my eyes, I see the cat; the one we're all supposed to adore, the one whose presence is meant to be therapeutic, lowering our blood pressures as we stroke its grey fur. I did try, once. It felt to me as soft as dust, as unpleasant as cobwebs.

The cat is sitting at my feet. My breakfast must have been brought in while I slept, left on a shelf wheeled across the bottom of my bed, and my porridge now drips from the cat's sharp teeth. It pauses only to twist its head and glare at me; its eyes are a dirty yellow and do not blink.

I've asked them to keep the cat out of my room, but they never do. They smile as if mine is the odd whim of a child who'll one day learn better. Now I tense, trying to prepare myself to move quickly. That isn't as easy as it sounds, not these days. My breath has a tendency to rattle. There's stiffness in my spine and hips. It's been worse in recent days, which is why I'm having breakfast in my room, but I can't let it get to me now. The little bastard needs to get what's coming to it.

I lurch forward, but the cat is gone before I even see it move. I was prepared for that too-soft fur, a snaky body, fluid muscles, flexing ribs. My hands close on nothing but the bowl, slopping porridge over my fingers. I hear an odd sound from the door, a half-meow, half-yowl, and a voice says, 'Oh, puss-puss. Did nasty Mr Wescombe scare us again? Did he? *Did* he?'

It's Della, one of the carers. She strokes the smoky shape that's wrapped around her ankles, then picks it up. A rasping engine starts up deep inside it as the cat begins to purr. I try to read the expression in its yellow eyes – reproach? Triumph? But of course there's nothing. It's only a stare.

'Poor Jack.' Della nestles her cheek against his head. Then she sees the bowl and her tone changes. 'Oh, look at your porridge.'

I open my mouth to tell her the cat ate it, then realise it's still all over my fingers. What does she think I've been doing, dabbling in it? I refuse to make excuses, and begin to lick it off – then catch myself. I must look like a child. Anyway, am I sharing the *cat's* food, now?

'I'll get a cloth.' Jack flows out of her hands and away. Her movements become sharp and spiky and I know she won't bring me any more porridge. She doesn't like me; that's why she uses my surname, as if to underline that I don't quite belong. All of them do. I'm the grumpy old sod who doesn't like the cat.

'It stared at me,' I say.

'Well, that's what cats do.' She's gone before I can tell her she's wrong: they do stare, but not like this.

A little later, as I fumble to pull on my socks, remembering the thousand times I'd done it before so easily, and never known that it was easy, I hear it: another of those odd sounds he makes, not like a cat at all. Jack is still outside my door.

He doesn't meow. The noise is raspy and resonant, almost as if multiple voices are emerging from his throat. It sounds a little as if they are talking. This is new. Usually he wails like a wounded woman; or perhaps like a banshee, mourning an imminent death.

And that's what Jack is, though no one says it. No, they call the cat something else: a miracle; a blessing.

I remember the way Patricia, the manager, had smiled when I first came here and she told me about their famous cat. 'He's been in the newspaper,' she said. 'Whenever anyone's *going*, you see. He knows. We call the relatives as soon as Jack curls up with one of our residents. He never gets it wrong.'

I had nodded, wondering if I'd lost my mind or if she had.

'He cares, you see. No one has to be alone, here – they're comforted. By the next morning, they've usually passed. But the cat is with them.' She had beamed with pride. 'Everyone loves our Jack.'

Perhaps they did, until I took up my place in room ten.

The next time I awake, I smell the cat before I see him. He doesn't smell of animal. He smells like he looks; like smoke. The scent seems to come from somewhere far distant, but when I open my eyes he's sitting on my chest. He stares back at me and I see the glimmer of dying coals in his eyes.

It is only then that I feel his weight, surely impossibly heavy on my ribs. I can't think how I hadn't noticed it before. Slowly, Jack flexes his claws until they pierce my thin pyjamas and rest against my skin. I want to swipe at him, but I can't move; any energy I had is gone.

He opens his jaws but no sound emerges. The inside of his mouth is red; his teeth are very white and sharp.

The door opens. It's Della, and a succession of emotions flicker across her features. She's resigned to seeing me; she's pleased to see the cat. Then it occurs to her that the cat is with me, and she warms, thinking I've relented. Then she realises it's *with* me, and sympathy comes. She imagines me slipping away, happy, comforted, and she ends with a gentle smile.

'Oh,' she says, her voice barely audible, 'Mr *Wescombe*.'

Jack jumps down and wraps himself around her.

I find I can push myself up, and I do. Strength flows back into me; that's how it feels, like being filled, and I am suddenly thirsty for life. *Wake*, I will myself, and it occurs to me that the word is also connected with death, with funerals: *Awake. A wake.*

I sit up. Jack is peering between Della's legs, and it sinks into me that he was sleeping on my chest. Does he know something?

Della's eyes are limpid with the beauty of it all. She knows why we're here, of course. We're supposed to accept death, to go into the dark with grace. She thinks we should drink in any comfort we can find along the way, be grateful even. I want to tell her to go fuck herself, but my throat is too dry. I pull in air, count to three, let it go. Repeat. *Wake*.

She sets down my porridge and smiles at Jack, all conspiratorial, before slipping out of the door. Thankfully, the cat goes with her.

They've tried to explain how animals sense things. They say they can smell cancer, or the biochemicals given off by dying cells. I read about it in the newspaper article Patricia showed me. 'It's no time to be alone,' she'd said, before sending me off to the ten foot by twelve foot room where I was supposed to wait to die.

But isn't there an older legend still? Not about what cats sense or know, but what they *do*. Sitting on people's chests, sucking out their souls through their sleeping lips. Feeding on them, like vampires. Not predicting who will die, but *choosing*. Draining them of life until their strength is gone; until nothing remains but a husk.

Later, I sit in the day room opposite another resident, Reenie, who has set her knitting aside so that Jack can lie on her lap. He is limp now, like discarded skin. He doesn't look at me and his eyes don't gleam. He appears to be what they claim, just a cat, happy to be petted, to have somewhere warm to sleep.

Jack. Such a stupid name for a cat.

Reenie has bowel cancer, and even I can smell it on her. She's like a skeleton in a dress and I wonder, uncharitably, if Jack had meant to choose her room instead of mine. But then, he likes Reenie. Maybe he doesn't want her to die.

I shift in my seat, wondering what it will be. Maybe it's my heart that will go, or my liver, or my lungs. Or a stroke; that might be better, after all, than fading in this chair day after day until I *want* to go, am desperate for the end.

For now, I pick up my mobile phone and adjust my glasses. The care home's WiFi is next to useless, but I bring up the web browser and will my clumsy fingers to find the right letters. I hit search, and read:

The chordewa, a being in the form of a cat, will eat a sick man's food. From then on, his fate is sealed.

Its meow is not like that of other cats.

It is difficult to catch, will claw and bite like a demon.

A witch can send her spirit into a cat. If it is caught, the woman whose soul is in the cat will be rendered powerless. If it is injured, matching wounds will appear on her body.

'Mr Wescombe?'

I start as Patricia leans over me, her shadow falling across my phone. I clutch it to my chest, concealing the screen. It isn't her concern. She wouldn't understand. She's say it was senility or dementia. Perhaps she'd be right.

'I wondered how you're feeling?' Her voice is too bright and I know why. She thinks I'm going, today or maybe tomorrow. She's heard that Jack chose me and she's trying to see the death in my eyes.

A sense of weariness weighs me down, but I fight it. 'I'm absolutely fine, Patricia. Is there anything I can do for you?'

Her smile fades. She adopts an *If you don't want my help I shan't give it to you* expression, then says, 'Well, I'll be in the office.' I stare after her as she stalks off, stiff-legged. If anyone here is a witch, sending their soul into a cat, she would be my first choice. Maybe that's why she's so proud of Jack.

Reenie nods in her chair, oblivious to everything. The cat too appears to be sleeping.

It is difficult to catch; it will claw and bite like a demon.

And I wonder.

Slowly, I get up. Reenie doesn't move and the thought strikes me that perhaps she's dead; then her mouth pops open with an audible sound and my heart hammers in my chest. I step quietly towards them. There's no one else in the room. The activities coordinator has them playing whist on the dining room tables and distantly I hear a cheer, followed by laughter. No one's coming. No one will see.

I half fall, half pounce, and Jack's eyes are open in an instant but my fingers are buried in his fur. I feel the skinny body, the fragile bones, and grip tighter. He can't twist far enough to bite but he tries, giving off a rattling hiss like a teakettle or a snake, a sound I can feel through his skin. His scrabbling front claws find nothing but air but his back ones sink into my wrist.

The pain is remarkable. It's sharp and sick-feeling and *wrong*, and I hiss too, but I don't let go. My face is inches from Reenie's. Astonishingly, she hasn't awoken. Her face is slack, the skin sagging, her eyelids looking bruised. She barely seems to be breathing. Was Jack stealing her soul?

The door bangs. Someone has come after all. There are no words but I hear rapid footsteps and then a hand is prising at my fingers, stronger than I am. I see muscular forearms, broad wrists, knuckles gleaming white. It's Patricia.

My fingers snap open before she can break them. The cat leaps; Reenie's eyes snap open too. The hissing stops and everything is suddenly very quiet. Patricia's grip shifts to my injured wrist. She squeezes, as if it's an unconscious act, and the scratches throb in time with my pulse.

Her lips are close to my ear as she says, 'Go to your room.'

I want to protest that she can't speak to me that way, I'm not a child, but I think of what she's just seen and I don't. She releases her grip just as Reenie pulls in a shaky breath. She starts to ask what's wrong, what happened, and Patricia begins to comfort her. I can't see Jack any longer. He might have vanished into the air.

I'm still in my room when Patricia comes looking for me. There's a book open on my lap, but I can't concentrate. I've been thinking of the way Reenie had lain there so still. *If it is caught, the woman whose soul is in the cat will be rendered insensible.*

Was Reenie weak from illness, or was it something else? If I'd injured Jack, would the marks have appeared on her too, like magic – bruised ribs, a limp? But I hadn't managed to hurt him at all.

I tell myself I must be losing my faculties to even consider such things. That I'm just a stupid old man, dying alone in a home where no one likes him. I glance at the photograph of my wife, Helen, on the bedside table, already years dead. Why do I linger? I should welcome the cat, open my arms to it, suffocate myself in its smoke-smelling fur.

That is when Patricia walks in. Her brows are drawn down, her lips narrowed between slab-like cheeks. Her anger hasn't faded, not a bit. I know that even before she says, 'I want a word with you, Mr Wescombe.'

She reaches down to straighten my sheets and I feel them zipping taut under me.

'You know, you chose to be here,' she says. 'We didn't ask for you. We didn't want you.'

I can only stare. Is she supposed to speak to me that way?

'You're afraid,' she goes on. 'I know you are. But is that Jack's fault? He's nothing but an innocent creature. And you – you're a coward, Mr Wescombe.' She pulls on the sheets once more; this time I am lifted slightly from the bed before she lets them go. She leans over me, her breath coffee-sour, her eyes rimmed with red. 'Unless, of course, you just *like* hurting cats.'

I can't or don't reply.

'I know some people are like that. Not nice people. Not *our* kind of people.'

She waits for a reaction, staring into my eyes, but I can't meet her gaze. She straightens. 'Well, there's not much I can do about that. Except to let you know how it feels.'

She reaches out and pats my arm. But she's not patting it; she's lifting it, gently, out of the way. She rests it on the bed next to me. Then one hand pushes down on my shoulder; her other arm bends, her elbow forming a spike, and she places it against my side.

She leans on it.

Pain starts deep inside then bursts outwards, exploding through my body. Lights spark before my eyes; I hear a dry gasping, something desperate, like an animal, and I realise it's me. Patricia lets out a grunt of effort and the pain intensifies. For a moment, I see Helen's face; I can't make out what message is in her eyes.

When Patricia straightens, I am whimpering. My crotch is damp; I don't know if it's sweat or urine. For a moment, she leans her face in close to mine once more. Her eyes are bright and sharp and she looks pleased, even triumphant. She reaches out again and I flinch as she pulls me forward to plump my pillow.

'Good night.' She says the words as if she'd just popped in for a nice chat before bedtime. 'Sleep tight.'

It isn't bedtime, probably not even suppertime, but I can't think; the pain is in me still. Patricia goes to the window and tugs the curtains closed in two sharp whisks. Then, without looking at me or saying anything else, she leaves the room.

I try to take steady breaths. I realise she was right: I won't be going down for supper. I don't feel hungry at all.

Sleep tight.

I don't think I will. And an image comes to me: not of Helen, not this time, but of myself as a child, lying awake in the dark and thinking of monsters. The kind I'd believed in back then hadn't worked in care homes. They had lived under the bed or hid in the wardrobe. I suppose those had been easier to imagine.

After a time, Jack comes for me. The door is closed and he can't get in, but I hear him slinking against the wood, first in one direction, then back again. He's pacing. Waiting. As my eyes begin to close, I hear that peculiar meow. It doesn't sound at all like a cat; it's more akin to a small child's cry of distress.

~

I feel the weight on my chest before I open my eyes. I lash out, but my hands meet with nothing; the cat isn't there. Jack didn't come for me, or at any rate, he couldn't get in. I wonder if he's still waiting for me, just outside the door.

I swing my legs over the side of the bed and wince at the pain in my side. I wait for it to subside a little before pulling on my clothes. I'm going to have breakfast downstairs with the others and I tell myself that's because I refuse to be afraid, refuse to be *shamed*, but in truth it's because I don't want to risk another visit from Patricia.

In the dining room, there's an empty seat next to Reenie, and she looks up at the wrong moment and catches my eye. I force myself to sit next to her.

'Enid's dead,' she says.

'I beg your pardon?'

Reenie scoops cornflakes into her mouth with a large plastic spoon and milk drips from her lips. 'Jack knew. He went to her. He stayed at her side all the time.'

'But Enid was fine. There was nothing wrong with her.' I splutter the words, wondering if it was all my fault, for shutting Jack out. Perhaps he was hungry, and finding nothing – no *sustenance* – he'd gone to someone else instead.

'She wasn't fine. She couldn't have been fine, could she?'

I have no answer to that. And she's right, in a way; there's something wrong with every one of us, after all. That's why we're here.

'They let the soul out. Did you know they still do that, let the soul out?'

I nod, picturing it. The carers would have gathered at Enid's bedside and opened a window, to let her soul go wherever it was bound. It's not something they talk about, though we all know anyway. But I somehow don't think Enid's soul was there. That would have already gone, stolen away while she slept by something that only looked like a cat.

Reenie reaches out. Her silk-soft fingers brush against the scratches on my wrist and the pain pulses, once, under her hand. 'You'd like him,' she says, 'if you got to know him.'

I know who she means and I don't reply.

'Oh, now. You know you would. So warm, he is. And his fur's so soft. It makes you feel better.'

I grimace. How can she think I'd find solace in Jack? She must know what his comfort means, or thinks she does. But it isn't a balm, nor a gift. If anything, it's the opposite: a taking away.

I sit back in my seat. When I was a boy, if I was afraid, I would kneel by my bedside and clasp my hands. *I pray the Lord my soul to take*, I'd say, and I used to believe in that prayer, but belief doesn't last long enough, does it? Like our bodies. Perhaps, if the monsters had taken me then, it would have been better. At least I would have imagined that my soul was going somewhere. Now there's nothing but the dark.

I suppose, if my suspicions about the cat are real, it *would* be a comfort, but not in the way Reenie thinks. It would mean there's *something*, wouldn't it? Something beyond our understanding. If he's only a cat, death is only death. There might not be any such thing as a soul to be stolen through our lips or to fly, on angelic wings, through open windows.

That night I go to bed as usual, but it doesn't feel like usual. I haven't seen Jack all day and now the air feels heavy, as if there's a storm coming. I think of the old words – *I pray the Lord my soul to take* – and it doesn't seem so very long since I knelt by the bed and whispered them. For a fleeting instant, I can smell my mother's perfume: rosewater, the only one she ever wore.

I turn my head towards Helen's photograph. I can't make her out; it's at the wrong angle, and all the dark areas of the picture have turned to mirrors. All I can see is myself, but in fragments: creased skin; white stubble; sagging jowls. My appearance doesn't match the image I carry inside myself. I'm still in here somewhere: the boy I was, the man I have been. What does Patricia see when she looks at me? An old man who hates a cat. Someone who should accept that he's already well on his way to the next place, and should do so without the indignity of clinging on or protesting.

A soft sound comes. Something presses against the door, then there's a single scrape of claws testing wood. Nothing else: no yowling, no mewling in protest. Jack knows he can wait. He has time.

Except, maybe, he doesn't.

Quietly, I get up. The carers have done their rounds – I heard Della's cries of 'Night night', as if to children, some time ago – and I go to the door and pull it open. I expect teeth and claws, but the corridor is empty. Jack has been and gone, but it doesn't matter; it's not the cat I need to find.

I creep along the corridor. Not far away, a glow rises from the stairway. It's always lit, just in case, and someone is on duty all night, though they might be anywhere. They're probably downstairs, though; it's the residents with more severe mobility issues who sleep in the ground floor rooms, and they need more attention. I don't need to go downstairs. I'm going to see Reenie.

Because Jack loves Reenie, doesn't he? But he never spends the night in her room.

Reenie, who lay insensible while I'd held Jack in my hands. Reenie who'd tried so hard to persuade me to let him in. Reenie, whose lap Jack likes best – as if she makes him feel safe. Or as if he's protecting her, while she sleeps.

I pass a series of doors. None of them are locked, in case of emergency. I half expect Jack to come haring down the corridor in a screeching trail of smoke, but he doesn't appear. Reenie's door is number three. The handle is cold in my hand and I turn it until there's the faintest *snick*.

Reenie is lying on her back. That will make it easier, I suppose. Her hair has fallen from her face and her profile is outlined by the moonlight that's spilling through the curtains. Her nose looks sharper than ever, her chin more prominent. She looks like a witch; the kind I'd imagined when I was young.

I reach out and pull one of the pillows from under her head. She stirs, letting out a breath that still smells of the cod fillets we had for dinner. A sense of unreality steals over me. Am I really doing this – for what? A story? A feeling? The dark, twisting path of senility?

I glance over my shoulder – guilt, I suppose – and see Jack.

He's sitting in her wingback chair, which has a paperback romance novel folded over one arm. He must have been there all the time, waiting to see what I would do, and as I look at him I feel suddenly very tired. I'm not even certain it's the cat that's draining me. The sight of Reenie is enough. She's as helpless as a child. The breath going in and out of her even sounds like that of a child. I wonder what it is she's dreaming of. Perhaps she's young again. She's fussing over a puppy she had once, or playing hopscotch in the school playground. Or maybe she's a young woman, kissing someone for the first time.

The cat is here because he likes her. Because Reenie is kind. When I look at Jack, there's no superior knowledge in his yellow eyes; nothing demonic. He's just a cat.

The voice inside me whispers its protests, saying it might be her or me, but it's a small voice and I'm no longer listening. I place the pillow on the floor next to Reenie's bed, where it might have fallen naturally. I reach out as if to pat her hand, but I don't; I go to the door, stumbling a little as I walk away.

Then I get back into bed, pull the sheets over me and shiver. I don't know if I've just failed some test or if I've been saved from something terrible. Helen's photograph isn't visible in the dark, but I can see her eyes looking at me anyway – the way she had looked at me so many times before the end – and I know exactly what she would say.

The next morning, I'm awoken by a cry somewhere outside. My heart thunderclaps in my chest and I flail at the sheets, which seem to have become knotted around me. Footsteps chase along the corridor and I stand, then lean on the bed for balance before I can look out. The corridor is empty now, but one door is open: Reenie's.

I can't breathe. I put the pillow *next* to her bed, didn't I? It couldn't have done any harm.

I walk towards her room as I am, in pyjamas and with bare feet. Della is there, leaning over Reenie, who is lying in the same position as I'd last seen her. She doesn't look the same, though. Her face is grey. Her cheeks are hollow, but she no longer looks like a witch; she only looks dead.

'Open a window.' It's Patricia's voice; I realise she's standing over by the wall. She doesn't look at me, and she doesn't help Della, who struggles with the latch before doing as she's told. I know it's to let the soul out and I try to sense Reenie floating past me, her arms outspread like a child playing aeroplanes, but there's nothing. Whatever was in her body is gone.

Movement calls my gaze to her chair in the corner. Jack is curled in the seat, the image of contentment; as I watch, he rests his head on his paws and licks his lips.

I've barely got back to my room when Patricia bursts in. My door bangs back against the wall and she is suddenly there, her face up close to mine. She smiles, but there's no warmth in it; I'd rather she scowled. I'm sitting on the bed and she leans over me, bending back one arm so that her elbow forms a spike, and I stare at it. I remember the pain and the dampness and the shame; a part of me wants to plead, but I force myself to keep silent.

'Looking for Jack, were you? If you try to hurt that cat again, Mr Wescombe, you and I will *talk*. We'll get closer, you and I. I'll make sure to look after you personally; I'll be sure to give you my special attention.'

Then she draws back and she's gone.

My heart staggers from one beat to the next, like a blind man clawing his way along a corridor. I have a feeling I'm not going to be around for her *special attention*. It will be tonight. I'm suddenly sure of it: a drift of soft fur, ungraspable as smoke; a glimpse of yellow eyes; the smell of dying embers, and I'll be gone.

Later, I see Patricia again. The other residents are at lunch and she's sitting in the staff office, which is like a goldfish bowl, all panes of glass. She's on her own in there. She's sitting very straight, but she isn't looking at the paperwork in front of her. She doesn't move; she doesn't blink at the sight of me. Her mouth is hanging open a little to reveal the tips of crooked and yellowed teeth and I realise that she's asleep – asleep with her eyes open.

Jack jumps up onto the counter. His hiss is audible through the glass.

Patricia still doesn't awake. Her eyelids don't even flicker. Her breathing – *is* she breathing? – goes on like before. I lean in towards the glass and Jack glares back at me, every muscle and limb rigid. He's protecting her. Of course it's her; it always was. If I went into the office now, he'd rip the eyes out of my head.

Patricia stirs. The cat's arched back relaxes. His bristling fur subsides.

I hurry away before Patricia can notice me, though I don't suppose it will be long until I see them both again.

I lie awake, my door ajar. I'm waiting for Jack. My curtains are open but tonight clouds are covering the moon and I can't see any stars. The whole place seems tired. Fatigue hangs in the air, an exhalation I can feel. It's everywhere and inside me, in each scraping joint and strained muscle. I tell myself I am not afraid.

In my hand, I'm clutching one of Reenie's knitting needles. I'd wanted a knife, but it was easier to take this from Reenie's craft box and slip the woollen stitches from its length. Somehow it seemed more appropriate.

I expect to hear Jack when he comes in, but I don't. The first sound comes when his weight lands on my bed; it transfers to my legs, and then there's stillness. I can still feel it, though, and keep perfectly still. The knitting needle is slippery with sweat, and I hope it will be enough.

I feel rather than hear Jack lying down, then shuffling upward along my body. He's almost weightless now; nothing but smoke. I tighten my grip on the weapon but he freezes. Is he sizing me up? Maybe he's smelling for cancer cells or decay or the presence of death. Perhaps he's already begun his work, breathing me in, calling to my soul.

I start to slide my hands from under the covers, and two yellow eyes flicker open.

I feel him growing heavier. No; it's my own body that's doing that. My limbs, withered to sticks, seem to have weight again, like wet sand; like flesh. It's as if I am growing young again, and yet I do not move. I'm no longer certain that I can. It's as if I'm sinking – sinking so deep, and the bed is so soft; soft like dust, like cobwebs. Like fur. All I want to do is sleep.

I think of Helen's face; caught in a picture, the love in her eyes trapped behind glass, a moment in time. And I think again how nothing lasts long enough. Not even, when it comes down to it, love. Some say that couples are reunited in death, that they find each other again, but if I were to admit it to myself, I'm not certain Helen would have wanted that. By the time she died, we'd… drifted apart, isn't that the term? The photograph is an old one. She hadn't looked at me that way in years. We'd been alone even while we were still together, but people didn't separate, not then. We weren't supposed to just give up. But still, she'd looked at me; oh, she'd looked at me.

I wonder now which would be worse: going into the dark alone, or being alone in whatever comes next. Seeing her, or not seeing her. And a voice echoes in my mind. *No one has to be alone, here – they're comforted.*

But I am alone, even though Jack is right in front of me. I stare into those yellow eyes and wonder if that is eternity I see, reflected in their depths. I wonder if that is more terrifying than the dark. I wonder if monsters truly exist, and how many there are; I wonder if, at the very end, one may finally recognise another.

|Here Be Spirits|

|The July Girls|

~

Sophia didn't knock. It was my room – I'd even put a sign on the door – but she seemed to think she owned everything. People who looked like Sophia always did. I was lying on my bed, reading a school textbook by lamplight. Outside its glow the room was dim, but her hair still shone gold. *All that glitters . . .*

She twisted her lip into a sneer, and I wondered what she'd say if I told her it made her look ugly. But then she tossed her head, sending ripples of light along that hair, and I was silenced. Oh, how I loved that hair – though I never would have told her. Mine was dull, average length, and an average colour: mouse. Her name for me.

'Aw, is ickle mousy working? Hasn't ickle mousy any *fwiends?*'

I had no answer, but she didn't wait for one. She crossed to my window and tugged the curtain aside, peering out into the dark. I knew what she was up to. Mine was the room which overlooked the extension. From the window she could run across its flat roof, jump down onto the banking at the back of the house and slip out of the back gate. Someone would be waiting for her. They always were: someone tall with broad shoulders, most likely wearing a leather jacket and holding the keys to a car, or better still, a motorbike. She never was alone. She probably wouldn't know how to be.

She turned. I could have spoiled everything for her then, but I didn't call out. Still, even when she ought to have been nice to me, she couldn't help herself.

'Aw, maybe one day you'll find an ickle boy mouse to play with. Won't that be nice?'

She swung her tanned, shapely leg over the sill, ducked under the window frame and was gone. I heard the scrape of her feet on the flat roof, and then nothing.

I'd like to think I kept silent for her out of some sisterly conspiracy, but I can't pretend. What went through my mind was: *I hope you get pregnant. If you want to ruin your life, I don't give a shit.* And then – I could remember the thought as clearly as if I'd spoken it – *At least this means you're gone.*

~

The house changed after Sophia died. Mum and my stepdad went quiet. The rooms went quiet too, only the dust seeming to move, turning in on itself while time did the same. Familiar objects, tainted by the atmosphere, went stale somehow, as if they belonged to a world that moved more slowly than it should. But the biggest change of all was that I could breathe again.

The same wasn't true of my mum or Sophia's dad, and I hid it from them, though I felt my inner self expanding, uncurling from whatever tight ball I'd been hiding in. Then they told me about the holiday, and I wondered what they thought that could fix; but I smiled at the thought of Cornwall's busy little harbours and the salty taste of chips and the sunlight on skin that would not grow cold like hers, that would not turn grey as hers must have, laid out on a mortuary slab. Whatever skin she'd still possessed, anyway.

It was Sophia's dad who told me we were going. He sidled into my room, as if he was ashamed of being alive when his daughter was dead. He didn't even look into my face, turning instead towards a shelf, running one finger along its edge. 'I have some news,' he said, 'it'll be great,' and his finger stopped moving and he stared and didn't say anything else. He reached out and picked something up from the back of the shelf; it was unwieldy, and he teased it out from behind my old teddy bear.

It was a picture frame. Two girls stared out from a photograph: one of them with sleek blonde hair, beautiful, slender; and me. For a moment, I might have been there again. It was taken on Sports Day at school. She'd been picked for the hundred metre sprint, while I'd have been lucky to do an egg and spoon race. Our smiles looked the same, but we weren't smiling at each other. She'd been making eyes at her current crush, sitting a short distance away, and I was smiling because someone had told me to.

When her dad turned towards me, tears were brimming at his eyes. 'What a lovely picture. I had no idea...'

He smiled, and this time he saw me – really looked at me, I think, for the first time in weeks. And he told me about Cornwall. 'We'll relive some old memories,' he said, 'and – and we'll *enjoy* them. Just the three of us.' He grasped my hand then, squeezing my limp fingers, and he left me to stare at the photograph he'd replaced on my shelf. I didn't have the first idea how it had come to be there.

He obviously thought I'd chosen it, but I never would have and neither would she. I moved to put it under the bed – or in the bin – and I saw again the way he'd lifted his gaze to me, warming to me, and instead I put it back on the shelf. I didn't face it toward the room, though, where I'd have to look at it. I turned it towards the door, where anyone would notice it as they came in.

The long queue of traffic on the A30 gave way to single track lanes, walled in by tall hedges thick with flowers and birdsong. We wound our way along them, hardly seeing anyone; we only had to back up once, to allow a tractor to pass. Most tourists stayed by the coast but my family had always preferred this rural backwater, a drive away from the beaches and cafes and crowds. I preferred it too, though Sophia hadn't. I could almost see her scowling out of the back window in disgust, all the way to the little rose-bound cottage.

Mum came in while I was unpacking, shoving t-shirts into empty drawers, finding space in the wardrobe between an ironing board and spare blankets. She didn't say anything, only sat on the bed and looked at me as if we had just met and she wanted to size me up, and she smiled.

I pulled a hoodie from the top of my suitcase and her smile faded at the sight of what lay beneath. 'What's that?'

She reached into the case and removed something rectangular and heavy, something I hadn't packed, something that didn't belong. I froze as she turned it in her hands. The frame was broad-edged and silver-coloured. I had seen it before; I didn't want to look at it again, but the smiles flashed at me as she tilted it, two girls beaming out. Cold fingers brushed the back of my neck.

'That's so sweet,' Mum said, putting it back. 'Come down when you're ready.'

I think I nodded, but couldn't be certain. My face barely felt like my own any longer. I flipped the photograph over, hiding the picture. How had it got there? Even if I'd wanted some reminder of Sophia – which I hadn't – I'd never have packed something so bulky. It must have been *him*, I decided. For some crazy reason of his own, my stepdad had slipped the picture into my suitcase – but why? Had he thought he was doing something nice?

I went to the door, pushing it closed. Then I grabbed the photograph and hid it in the back of the wardrobe, shoving it in among the blankets. There. I'd have to think about Sophia anyway if we were going to *relive some old memories*, but that must be enough; I didn't have to look at her too.

I found the others ready to go for a walk and we stepped out into evening sunshine and the humming of bees. We strolled, not talking about Sophia, but she was there: I saw where she'd once pressed up against the hedge as a busload of grey-haired trippers squeezed past. I saw where she'd leaned over a fence, her athletic legs swinging. And I saw her walking ahead of me, putting her arms around her dad and my mum, leaving me to follow.

Yet this, if anywhere, was where we'd been the closest. With nothing else to do and no one else to see, we'd actually spent some time together, splashing into crystal clear waves, running our fingers through white sand. We'd been the image of girls on holiday, then: July girls, my mum had called us. And we'd walked along these lanes, complaining of how boring they were, the endless hedges making everywhere look the same.

I thought of the photograph that had followed me from home. Those two smiles, shining out – but we had been like that, hadn't we, when we were here?

And maybe Sophia *was* here. A part of me couldn't believe, even then, that her dad had sneaked the picture into my suitcase. I couldn't shake the thought that she'd brought it here herself; that maybe

Sophia was trying to tell me something. She might have *liked* to smile at me now, to let me know that, despite our arguments and bitchy comments, it was all right.

Then we turned a corner in the lane and I saw the opening in the hedge which led to a path I remembered, and I stopped dead.

'Are you all right, love?' Mum's tone was all concern.

I told her I was just tired and she nodded and walked on, linking arms with my stepdad, but her stride was different, clumsy, and she soon suggested we turn back. I didn't look at the path when we passed it again but I could still see where it led: the nettles and rosebay willowherb, the KEEP OUT sign, the clearing beyond.

By the time we reached the cottage the light was fading, chill shadows clawing their way along the narrow lanes. The glowing lamps and cosy sofas banished it all, as did our laughter and the burble of the television, and I said good night and made my way up the stairs.

I saw the picture as soon as I opened the door. It was on my bedside table, those two smiles shining out, like sunshine; like summer. And I whirled because in the corner something coalesced: a shadow, a little like a figure.

I blinked. Nothing was there, never had been; only the picture, which had no reason to be there either. Had my stepdad come up here, searched my room, moved it from its hiding place and put it by my bed? I tried to picture him rummaging through the depths of the wardrobe and couldn't.

But he must have; it was the only explanation. I went to the picture and gripped it, the frame digging into my hands as I thought of *another* explanation, one that wasn't even possible, and I yanked open a drawer. It was almost empty apart from a Bible, left for the edification of any visitor who cared to read it, and I shoved the picture in underneath, wondering – or hoping, perhaps – it might keep her from coming back again.

Then I sat on the bed and stared into space for a long time. I didn't see the room. I only saw Sophia: her perfect skin, perfect teeth, perfect *life*. What the hell had she ever known about me? She hadn't known what it was like to walk into school and see the stares; to know, every time she looked into other people's faces, that she wasn't good enough.

I shook off the self-pity. I didn't need it. This was my place now, my time. She never had wanted to share anything with me. Now I supposed I had everything after all. I was sleeping in the second biggest room. Our parents were mine. I could have anything I wanted that had once been hers, and there wasn't a damned thing she could do about it.

A photograph was only that. It didn't mean she was still here. I might even have brought it to Cornwall myself, acting on some unconscious impulse. There was nothing unnatural about it – and she wasn't going to scare me.

Later, I awoke in darkness more complete than any I had ever experienced at home. I couldn't see a thing and yet all my reassurances drained from me, because I could feel someone standing in the room. I opened my mouth to whisper, 'Mum?' and closed it again. It wasn't her. I knew that. I could feel it in the silence, heavy and watchful.

I reached out to switch on the lamp and hesitated as an image of my stepsister rose before me. She wasn't smiling. It was Sophia as she truly was: dead. Mutilated, as she had been when her stupid boyfriend turned his motorbike over, skidding along the tarmac, dragging his passenger with it. She hadn't been wearing a helmet. That wasn't her style; I suppose she liked to have that golden hair flying behind her in the breeze.

From the fragments I'd overheard afterwards, she'd been scraped raw.

No one had knocked on the door. No one called out or whispered my name. They simply stood on the other side of that darkness – and I pictured her face flayed and bloody, but still with that lovely hair; still with that look in her eyes.

My hand snapped out and I switched on the lamp. The room was empty.

The picture, though, was back. I might almost have touched it when I reached for the lamp. I peered at it, fearful that it would have changed somehow, showing her as she was after the accident; but Sophia was still there, in all her beauty. I stared into her face, trying to make out what lay beneath.

When I could bring myself to move, I crept into the hall and peeked in at Mum's bedroom door. There lay two covered mounds, so deeply entrenched in sleep I couldn't believe they'd ever woken. It wasn't my stepdad who'd moved the picture. I don't think I'd ever truly believed it was.

I awoke the next morning before anybody else. I wasn't in my bedroom; I hadn't wanted to go back there, and so instead I'd slept on the sofa. Light flooded in through the open curtains and I stretched my stiff limbs before going towards the stairs. Why had I allowed myself to be spooked? I wasn't afraid of a picture. What harm could it do?

Sophia was *gone*.

When I opened my bedroom door I thought the picture had moved again after all, but of course it hadn't; the image was simply blanked out by reflected light. I had to go closer to confirm that the image hadn't changed. There she was, that look in her eyes that said the whole world was hers – and yet it wasn't, not now. It was *mine*. Still, I couldn't dispel the thought that I'd spent the night camping on the sofa, just as if she could take it all away from me any time she wanted.

I cast my mind back to our last holiday in this place. It had been Mum who'd told us to go for a walk, tired perhaps of the sour looks and tension that so often hung between us. I suppose she'd thought we might come back best friends. Adults could be so very unrealistic.

Sophia and I had met Lucy before we'd even gone out of the gate. About our age, her blonde hair was so sun-bleached it was almost white, and her eyebrows stood out palely against her tanned skin. She told us she lived here year-round, in a broken down farmhouse her dad was restoring. 'It's a complete tip,' she'd said, 'and there's nothing to do. Except…'

It was that 'except' that led us along the lane and towards the path, swatting away midges as we went. Sophia and Lucy went in front, talking about their lives, a thinly disguised game of one-upmanship. We didn't pause at the path, just pushed our way along it through waist-high weeds until we reached a copse, low branches barring the way, as did a chain with a KEEP OUT sign hanging from it, the letters roughly painted.

It was Sophia who said, 'Where the hell are we going? This where you hide your wacky baccy or something?'

Lucy grinned, stepping over the sagging chain. She ducked under the branches, pushing the undergrowth aside, and led us towards a clearing. A large mound of earth rose at its centre, covered with tussocks of grass. There was nothing else, no sign saying what it was supposed to be, but it didn't look natural.

'It's a fogou,' Lucy said.

'Oo-ooh.' Sophia was all sarcasm.

'It's a hidden chamber.' Lucy went on as if Sophia hadn't spoken. 'No one comes here; no one's bothered. There's a better one at Carn Euny, and a few others. This one's all ours. If you dare, that is.'

'Dare?' Sophia sounded interested at last. I felt something twist in my stomach.

'No one knows what it was for. I reckon it's a burial chamber.' Lucy didn't quite respond to the question, and yet I thought she'd answered the one in my mind anyway. And I saw that the mound wasn't quite complete, after all. There was a small opening, maybe a foot high, lined with crooked stones like teeth. I imagined lowering myself to the ground and crawling into that hole. I shuddered. That couldn't be what she meant. It was probably dangerous. It looked as she had said, like nobody cared, like nobody had been here in years.

'It's Iron Age.' Lucy went on, as if she'd turned tour guide; as if it mattered. 'Some call them holts, or fuggy holes, or vows. It's not far to the chamber. But first there's the creep.'

Sophia's gaze shot to me, a new kind of amusement in her eyes.

'Some say the little folk still haunt it. Pixies. Piskies.'

'Pigsies,' Sophia said, her gaze still on me, and she giggled.

I looked away, casting my eyes around the lowering branches that hemmed us in, the pure whiteness of the clouds scattered across the sky. The air was so clean here. It had been one of the first things I'd noticed about Cornwall. It felt impossibly distant from cities or factories, and this place felt even more so; as if it existed outside time itself.

'Does she talk?' Lucy nodded towards me and Sophia let out a trill of laughter.

'You don't want her to. Bo-ring. So, what's the dare?'

Lucy didn't say anything, didn't have to. She turned and pointed to the hole.

Sophia fanned out her hair, showing off its clean fineness, as if to say, *Really?*

'It's a squeeze,' Lucy said. 'Some reckon it was a proper passage once, but it's partly filled up with dirt over the years. There's no mortar holding the stones together. There's one bit – the roof comes down. You have to wriggle.'

I still didn't say anything, but I think my eyes opened wider.

'Come on, then.' Sophia's voice was loud. I looked up sharply and realised she was watching me. Of course she was: that was what we did, wasn't it? We watched each other. And I'd been off guard. She had seen my fear. Now she would push at it, see how deep it went.

'The moss inside glows.' Lucy seemed oblivious to our hostility. 'It's phosphorescent. It's not that rare, it's just you don't normally get to see it like that. Like magic.'

Sophia waved a hand, a *who cares* gesture. But I did care. Glowing moss? That was something I would like to see, but there was no way in hell I was getting down on the ground, putting my face in the dirt and wriggling inside.

Sophia didn't pause. She knelt in front of the hole, then turned and looked at me. And yet it wasn't her usual look. There didn't seem to be anything hidden in it, and she smiled – a real smile – and said, 'Come on, sis. Why not? An adventure.'

I didn't answer, partly from surprise, but mainly because I was afraid. I knew that Lucy must have been in the chamber lots of times. But I wasn't her, and I wasn't Sophia. I couldn't do it. I couldn't give up the clean air and the sun for whatever adventure lay inside that hole, not for anything; not even for her, to mend whatever it was between us.

Sophia shrugged before she slid, neat as an eel, into the hole, her legs wriggling as she disappeared. Lucy didn't wait for me either. Looking annoyed that she hadn't led the way, she hurried after and I watched as she too slithered inside and vanished.

I sat on a fallen branch and waited. Above me, the clouds went by; time passing, in another world. Here, there was silence. I couldn't even hear birds singing or insects humming or distant cars in the lane. There was nothing and I was alone, and I wished suddenly I'd gone with Sophia; reached out maybe, and taken her hand.

My seat was becoming uncomfortable, another sign of time passing. And the thought struck me: what if they didn't come out? There was only me who knew where they were. I'd have to go after them. I thought of crawling into that hole, feeling for them blindly in the dark, and finding Sophia's face under my hands; unconscious perhaps, overcome by the stale air. I'd have to get her out. I imagined wriggling backwards, trying to pull her with me, and not being able to move her. I pictured Lucy in the chamber behind Sophia, wedged in, helpless; Sophia – the *body* – between us; and me, stuck in the place where the roof came down, unable to go forward or back.

The sourness of bile rose to the back of my throat. I stood and walked over to the hole in the ground, listening, feeling a breath of cold air on my cheek. There was no light in there – couldn't they have used their mobile phones? – and there were no voices. There was nothing at all, and then, distinctly, I heard the scratch and flare of a match.

Was that a greenish glow, coming from somewhere within? I blinked and speckled light danced in the tunnel, playing tricks on my vision. I thought of Cornish pixies, elusive and mischievous, and I heard laughter, distorted as if coming from a great distance away. It echoed from stone to unmortared stone, until I couldn't be sure how many voices there were. It was like something from a fairy tale and I thought of a little palace inside the rock, lit by glowing moss. But it wasn't a fairy tale. Even if it had been, there was never a stepsister in any of those stories who actually got on with the heroine – with the *real* daughter.

Something moved in there. I started back and they came spilling out, and it was over. They were laughing, out of control, frightened and relieved and together; bonded, the two of them. Like sisters.

'God, that bit…!' Sophia squealed then laughed again, clutching her belly. She leapt to her feet and reached out her hand, and without a second's thought Lucy took it and Sophia pulled her to her feet. They didn't look at me. Sophia didn't talk to me all the way home.

I came to myself sitting on the bed, clutching the photograph in my hands, wondering how things would have been if it was me who'd gone with her, if I'd taken her hand. Another image came: Sophia, sneaking out of my window. If I'd snitched on her then, everything would be different. She wouldn't have been in the accident.

I felt hands close around mine and the picture was lifted from me. I caught my breath and looked up to see my mother's face. By her expression, I knew she believed that I'd brought the picture here myself, that I'd done it out of love for Sophia, and I couldn't bear it.

I blurted, 'She hated me.'

'What, love?'

'I hated her too.'

She sank down onto the bed next to me, cradling the picture as if it were a child. 'Oh, sweetie. I know you didn't always get on, but people don't, and – it doesn't mean they can't find a way to live togeth— it doesn't mean they don't love each other.'

I leaned against her and she rubbed my back, just like she had when I was little. She had to be right, didn't she? Maybe she wasn't so unrealistic after all. It had only been pettiness and jealousy, and we'd have got past it sooner or later. Wasn't Sophia beyond it already?

And she was *dead*. I surely couldn't think so badly of her any longer.

We spent the next day by the sea, every wave glittering, the sands shining so whitely in the sun I had to shield my eyes. It reminded me of Sophia and me at our best – the July girls – and the salt air gave me an appetite and a good kind of tiredness, but I wasn't about to rest. It was still hours until sunset when we got back to the cottage and without telling anybody, I packed a few items into a backpack and crept down the stairs. I could have said I was going for a walk, but it seemed more appropriate to Sophia's memory to sneak out.

I slung the backpack's straps around my arms and hurried along the lane. It was cooler than it had been, and quiet. I didn't know what I'd find at the fogou; the chamber might have been sealed or fenced in since I'd seen it last.

The willowherb grew higher about the path than I remembered and I pushed through it, everything smelling of sap and growth and nectar. When I emerged near the trees the sign was still there, hanging from its chain. The only difference was that its letters were a little more faded than before, but their intention remained clear enough. I didn't pause, just stepped over. I hadn't seen anyone else and I wondered if Lucy still lived here or if she'd moved on, as people did; at least, those who were still alive.

My arms were bare and it was cooler at once under the shadow of the trees. Low branches clawed and scraped and I felt them in my hair, like fingers, trying to make me stay. I tried not to think too much about what I was doing. I told myself it would be all right. Sophia had laughed in the face of this; it had been easy for her. She'd asked me to go with her then, and I'd refused, but I wouldn't refuse now.

The clearing was just as it had been, the same white clouds scudding overhead. It could almost have been that same day, as if it was always summer here; always July.

The hole in the ground was there too. It hadn't been filled in or fenced over or sealed. It looked cold, the grey stones more than ever like teeth. *Hungry*, I thought, and pushed the thought away. It was only a short passage – the creep – and then I'd be in the chamber. I could take the things from my backpack: a candle from the cupboard under the sink, and a box of matches. I was going to light the candle for Sophia, to let her know that, after all, we were family.

Some call them holts, I remembered, *or fuggy holes, or vows*. Well, this would be my vow to Sophia: to remember her as she would have wanted me to.

I knelt and looked into the entrance. There was a steady movement of air, so slight it was like cold breath on my cheek, and then I couldn't feel it any more. I shuddered. I could only see a short way in, an arched passageway lined by more of those stones, then blackness. My breathing sounded as unsteady as it felt, but I couldn't wait or my courage would fail. I'd become that same person again, the one she'd turned her back on. I had to show her – and maybe myself – that I could be different.

I grabbed my mobile phone from my jeans pocket and switched on its torch, the thin beam vanishing in the daylight. Then I ducked into the tunnel and started to crawl.

I realised at once the torch wasn't going to be much use. The roof was lower than I'd expected, and when I raised my head I felt stone brushing against my hair. I bowed lower, seeing only dry-packed earth, hard as rock against my hands. The air in here was a constant cold, chilling my skin. There was a smell too, one I didn't like to think about: a smell like old bones, grave dirt and time. I wondered when Lucy last came here. It felt abandoned, as if no one had been here in centuries. She'd probably lied about the chamber. There was no magical glow; there was nothing fairy-like about it.

I forced myself to take another deep breath. Still, I couldn't help thinking of the weight of earth over my head, nothing but the arrangement of old stones pressing against one another to stop it all coming down.

I shuffled forward, hitting my head on a lower stone that jutted from the roof. The pain was sharp and I rubbed it then held my hand before my face, trying to see if there was blood. But it would be worth it, wouldn't it? Soon I'd be through. I'd spill from the mouth of the tunnel and I might even laugh, never mind if I was alone.

I twisted to see the passageway ahead, shining the light from my mobile into it. The centre of the tunnel was dark, nothing to catch its beam; I saw only fragments of stone, one hanging lower where the roof bulged downward. What had Lucy said?

There's no mortar holding the stones together. There's one bit – the roof comes down. You have to wriggle.

It was nothing unexpected. Sophia had done this and so would I. I'd be back at the cottage within the hour, and this time I'd put the picture away somewhere and she wouldn't bring it back. It would stay where I put it, because I'd laid her to rest; because, if she could see what I was doing, she'd be happy.

Cold air gasped into my lungs and I pushed aside the panic clouding the edges of my vision. I imagined the darkness creeping into me with each breath… *No.*

I knew I wouldn't be able to hold the torch any longer, not until I was through the squeeze, and anyway, it wasn't doing any good. I slipped it into my pocket. Then I lowered myself fully to the earth, feeling it dry and gritty against my arms, hard against my chest. I wriggled as they must have, pushing with my toes, pulling with my forearms, my hands finding the way. I imagined the low stone hanging above me, ducked under where I thought it was, and felt colder air like fingers brushing my scalp. Was that the chamber? The passage hadn't been so very long after all, just like she'd said. Then I felt pressure against my spine as my backpack pressed downward.

I froze. Why hadn't I taken it off? But I'd rushed at this, not stopping to think. I'd almost forgotten about the pack anyway, since it weighed almost nothing. And yet, now, it felt heavier – heavy and unwieldy.

Breathe. It wouldn't help me to panic. An image rose before me of the extra handle jutting from the top of my backpack, designed for carrying it in one hand. It might have snagged on something. Another wriggle would free it. I could even remove the pack here – I tried twisting an arm behind me and the pressure on my back increased, my elbow connecting painfully with the wall of the passage. I decided I'd take it off once I was in the chamber. It wasn't far, after all, and the way out would be easier, the centre of the tunnel shining white instead of dark.

I pressed myself into the ground, shuffled an inch or two backwards, and the straps around my arms tightened.

I let out a little sound, one I was glad no one else could hear, my breath too loud and too fast. Forget Sophia, forget everything; she wouldn't have done this for me – would she?

But she *would* have. She'd have done it because she wasn't scared, wasn't stupid, wasn't like a… like a *mouse*, scurrying through a tunnel.

Slowly, I realised that the sound of breathing wasn't just mine. It was coming from the darkness itself, as if this whole place was alive… But of course, it wasn't. It was only my own breath echoing around me, distorted by the old stones.

I scratched at the earth and tried to pull myself along and couldn't move. There was no give in the straps holding me in place. There was no light, none at all. I closed my eyes and opened them as wide as I could: nothing.

And there was no air. I gasped, my lungs straining as if there wasn't enough to fill them; it felt as if there never would be again. There was only the cold dark, and I was a fool – what had I been thinking? I had to get *out*.

I shuffled backwards once more and the straps around my arms tightened again, compressing my chest. I wriggled as hard as I could.

Grainy light burst around me and I realised my eyes were closed; when I opened them, the dark remained. I couldn't reach my mobile phone to get any light. An image: the strap of my backpack caught on a loose stone. The arch was held in place by the way those stones were arranged, each one doing their part, bearing its share of the load. What would happen if one of them fell?

I took deep breaths. When I moved forwards again, it would be all right. Anything else just wasn't possible. A few hours ago I'd paddled in the pure, clear sea. I'd squinted against the sun shining on white sand, and wished it wasn't so bright.

I wished it was bright now. I wished I was there – but soon, I would be. Tomorrow I would run in mad circles in the water, splashing it high, and Mum would laugh at me, not knowing the reason why.

And the thought came to me that no one knew where I was.

I pictured all the distance between us, the clearing, the trees, the lane. They wouldn't hear me, no matter how loud I shouted. My screams would only fill the chamber, echoing back at me, driving me mad…

I forced my thoughts in a different direction. None of it mattered. I wasn't really stuck. In a few seconds I'd be in the chamber and I'd shrug off the backpack, as easy as it had always been. I wouldn't even stay to light the candle before I was out of here.

I made myself as flat as I could and tried to drag myself forwards, feeling my nails breaking against the ground, and this time something gave. I moved maybe an inch and then I was caught again and there came, as clear as daylight, the sound of breaking glass.

I shifted my weight a little to the side, hearing another glassy sound. I knew what it was. I pictured the photograph, two girls smiling into the dark, their faces obscured by the cracks in the glass holding them in. The photograph that I hadn't kept, hadn't packed, hadn't wanted to see; the one she had brought to me, in case I could forget her, in case I could breathe again. I imagined its frame, square and heavy, jutting from my backpack, because she'd put it there; because she wouldn't be laid to rest, not by me or anybody. Why had I ever thought she would?

Now I wasn't sure it was a strap that had caught against the roof at all. Had that picture frame somehow wedged into a gap between the stones? If I moved, would it prise them loose?

I twisted my head, resting one cheek in the dirt, and without volition, a memory came. It was Sports Day. Sophia had been surrounded by her friends, only coming over to me when called to pose for the camera. I remembered the way she'd been looking over at her boyfriend; and I remembered the way I had.

No. That must be a false memory; it was the kind of thing she would do, not me, never wanting me to have anything—

Could she actually have been jealous of me? Had she hated the way I looked at him – the way I looked at *her*, at her perfect skin, her golden hair, her *life*? Had I wanted it all so very badly?

My mind skipped, loosened, found another memory. Later that same day, Sophia had been waiting for me behind the gym. She hadn't smiled then. She didn't even speak. We weren't the July girls, not then; we never had been. I remembered the feeling of her hands clawing in my hair. Of hitting the ground, my elbow striking the wall, pain flaring. The weight on my chest as she knelt on my back, the way she'd pushed my head into the earth: 'Stay down, bitch. Just stay down, or I swear…'

I'll bury you.

The only kind of vow she'd ever made to me.

Oh, God.

Without thought, without purpose, I struggled. I couldn't lift my head, couldn't get my breath. But I wasn't going to die. I would get out, because I had to; soon, I would get out.

I felt the touch of fingers in my hair, there and then gone. I let out a sob, too loud. It couldn't be her. There was only the chamber ahead of me, and that was empty.

And an answering sound came, slow and insidious: a whisper? The chamber didn't *feel* empty, not any longer.

But of course it wasn't empty. Sophia had come to me and put the picture into my bag, hadn't she? Something to remind me of her, if anything were needed. How could I forget? I'd spent so long thinking of nothing else but her. And now she hadn't forgotten me. She hadn't forgiven. My mother had been wrong: Sophia was here and she hated me. She hated me because I was jealous. She hated me because I wanted everything she had. She hated me because she was dead and I was alive but I didn't know how to live, not really; not without her to show me how.

But I *was* alive. I gasped in a breath, tasting earth and stone and time. And I tried to heave forwards and there was a dull scrape as something gave and I could move. I shot forwards but the sound was growing, a far-off rumbling getting closer and louder, and then the world came down.

I think I screamed but I couldn't hear it because that sound was all around me. I waited for the earth to fill my mouth but it didn't, it was my legs and my back it took, and I waited for the pain to begin. It didn't, not then. It was coming though, I knew, getting closer every second. For now, there was only an awful and intense pressure. I tried to move my legs, to wriggle my toes. I couldn't feel anything at all. I tried to twist my head and couldn't. It felt as if someone was kneeling on my neck.

Stay down, bitch. I'll bury you.

I let everything go limp, tasting despair at the back of my throat. The tunnel must be blocked. No one could look into it, see me there and pull me free. And the air would be sealed out. Soon it would go stale—

I started to shout, inarticulate sounds without words; I think I screamed. And then I felt those fingers again, running through my hair, easing it away from my face, stroking my skin, as if in comfort. It quieted me.

And I realised I could see something after all. There was no light to see by and yet something was glowing, dancing before my eyes, an illusion or a trick. Still it grew brighter, and the breath caught in my throat. I could see a glow, unmistakeable now, but it wasn't moss. It was hair: gleaming, golden, lovely hair.

Sophia did not speak. She had no need of words. She had already said everything she wanted to say. I knew why she was here. It wasn't her who'd wanted to own everything, to take it all; it was me. And there was only one thing left to her now that I didn't have: death. She wanted to share that with me too. There, in the dark and the cold, she had decided to be my sister, after all.

|The Marvellous Talking Machine|

~

It is across a distance of years that I remember the events of 1846, and yet it might have been yesterday that I first heard the voice that haunts my dreams. It is not the words that have troubled me so, ever since I was a boy; it is the way they were spoken – and the fact of their emerging from no human throat.

I was twelve when I first heard of the inventor Professor Joseph Faber. Now my hair is grey, though inwardly I feel much the same. I still remember my father's theatre, the magnificence of its halls; the sense of never knowing what wonders would pass before my eyes; the idea that perhaps, truly, they were not entirely of this world.

My father set me to work early, not because we were in need of funds, but because I begged him to release me from the tyranny of slate and desk. For what were schoolrooms to me, when life itself – and such life – passed daily before my eyes at the Egyptian Hall?

The edifice itself was a curiosity to behold. Part of the row of mansions lining Piccadilly, it was yet a thing apart; for its gargantuan figures, winged globes and lotus motifs would be better suited to an ancient tomb of Egypt than the heart of London. The mysteries continued within. Vast pillars suggested the great avenue at Karnak, while indecipherable hieroglyphics adorned every surface. Its ever-changing displays were equally entrancing, having included extraordinary statuary, dioramic views, historical artefacts – including Napoleon's coach – and indeed human entertainments; we had hosted a family of Laplanders offering sleigh rides, the Anatomic Vivante or Living Skeleton, and a mermaid – this last, alas, sadly pretend.

Indeed, it might be said that I was accustomed to wonders, and yet, when faced with something more remarkable still, I longed only to turn my face away. But I was not alone in that, for Joseph Faber's was one of our most poorly received attractions.

My first sight of the man was not promising. He was a hunched fellow, wearing a frock-coat with too few buttons, and those dulled with time. His beard was untrimmed, his shoes smeared with street-dirt and his features were unprepossessing; his eyes, which were dull likewise, looked askance when he was addressed, even by me, a mere child.

He gave his name softly and with a slight German accent. It was only when he directed the placement of his boxes and crates that his expression became sharp, even mercurial in his assiduousness. I showed him to the chamber wherein his display would appear and he glared about before closing its door in my face, presumably to prepare himself. Later, my father sent me to offer any assistance he may require. I knocked and a voice responded with some phrase that I had no doubt meant 'Go away'.

I did not go away, however, for I was young and curious; or perhaps it was stupidity that made me press my ear to the door and listen.

He was constructing something: that was certain. I decided I must ask my father what it was, for I had been much distracted by the imminent arrival of General Tom Thumb, a fellow celebrated for his diminutive stature and comic scenes, and had paid little attention when he told me of it. I knew only that it was some kind of machine, and so it seemed, for I detected the sound of wood being slotted into place and the clearer sound of metal striking metal. But it was Faber's mutterings that interested me the most.

It did not sound as if he were talking to himself. He would murmur in a low voice and then pause so that I could sense him listening before giving some reply. It sounded as if he were engaged in conversation with someone I could not quite hear.

Suddenly my ear stung as my father cuffed it. He told me to step sharp and see about the scenery flats in the main theatre, in tones so loud that Faber, shut up in his room, must surely have heard. And so I left him in there, alone yet not alone, speaking to whoever would listen; and to prepare for his performance that evening, whatever that may be.

I stared down at the handbill. THE MARVELLOUS TALKING MACHINE, it proclaimed. I had wasted no time, after dressing the stage for the hilarious capers of Tom Thumb, in obtaining a copy from the ticket-seller.

So here was the answer to the sounds I'd heard coming from Professor Faber's room. The bill informed me that not only could his machine speak, but that a full explanation would be given of the means by which the words and sentences were uttered. It said that visitors may examine every part of his Euphonia – that was what he named it – not only demonstrating a wonder of science, but providing a fund of amusement to young and old alike.

All at once, I understood. Examination notwithstanding, it was clear to me that Faber was a cheat; for of course he must have some accomplice who would be concealed within this 'wondrous' machine and speak on its behalf. It had been done before. Almost a hundred years ago, Kempelen's chess-playing Turk was heralded as the most magnificent automaton of its age, until it was discovered that its contests were won by a mere human hiding within its base. Thus it was made plain: it was a feat of wonder for a machine to mimic a man, but a matter of imposture and derision for a man to mimic a machine.

I could not confront Faber or reveal him as a fraud, however, for were we not his hosts, and party to all that passed? Yet I was determined to see for myself how the trick was done, and I confess I longed to lay eyes on whatever little creature may be concealed so cunningly. For, of course, it occurred to me that he or she may prove even tinier than Tom Thumb himself.

My disappointment may only be imagined when my father asked me to sort through a heap of mouldering costumes, to put some aside for repair, others for disassembling and yet others for the ragman. I knew I would never finish in time to take my seat for the start of Faber's demonstration, and it being held in a somewhat small chamber, I could not then disturb those who had paid their shilling by making my entrance.

Still, as the time came for it to end, I could not resist waiting in the passage to glimpse what I may when the doors opened. This time, I could more distinctly make out the sounds from within. People called out in turn, the audience I supposed, and something answered, though in tones the like of which I had never encountered. The voice was flat and dead and empty, and it made me shudder, and then the first notes of music sounded, and the awful voice began to sing. It was the National Anthem, but emotionless and dry, as if the life was missing, or perhaps the soul; as if the voice progressed from the very heart of a tomb. But of course this must be Faber's Talking Machine, his Euphonia, and I grasped the reason at once. For he could not wish it to sound human; if it did, all would guess at its true nature and his imposture would be discovered. It must perforce sound like something long dead – indeed, like something that had never lived. And yet I could not quite shake the chill as I pressed my eye to the keyhole.

But the door suddenly shook and swung open. I started back; a gentleman stood there, with commodious whiskers and a gloriously shining top hat. He gave me a disdainful look before leading the exodus from the room, and I made a hasty bow, gesturing towards the exit as if I'd come especially to point the way.

All the ladies and gentlemen filed past me, and as they went, I realised something odd about them. Usually, our patrons left smiling and laughing, exclaiming over what they had seen. But these did not smile; they did not laugh. They were entirely silent as they moved towards the cabs and carriages that awaited. There was no light in their faces; the only emotion emanating from them was dismay.

I looked away from them and saw Faber, his skin pallid, his eyes as lightless as the rest – and fixed upon mine.

I mouthed an apology, catching a glimpse of the contraption behind him: a wooden frame, through which I could see the back of the stage; an arrangement of keys and levers and bellows; and, affixed to its front, a human face. It was in the form of a woman – or rather, a girl – with bow lips and gleaming ringlets, but with a cold and empty expression. It unnerved me to look upon it, and I knew in that instant there was nowhere for anyone to hide, even if they were half the size of Tom Thumb.

Faber stepped towards me and I turned and closed the door between us. I did not leave, however, but leaned heavily against the wall. Thankfully, he did not follow; after a time I heard shuffling sounds and the scraping of wood against the floor.

Then I heard a soft call of 'Gute nacht'.

I froze, thinking he called out to me, then the light that crept from under the door was extinguished and I was left in near darkness. Faber was to sleep in the chamber, then, with his machine. Whatever his trick, it seemed I would not discover it that evening.

The next day, I asked my father what he knew of the strange inventor who remained ensconced within our chamber. In response, he pulled a face.

'His takings are underwhelming,' he said.

I opened my mouth to enquire further and found myself unsure what it was I sought. However, he went on regardless.

'He's a scientist, not a performer, and a mad one at that. This isn't his first talking machine, did you know? He burned the first one.'

'Why did he do that, Papa? Didn't it work?'

He looked as if he'd like to spit. 'Who knows? Drove himself maniacal with it, I reckon. It's clever – more than clever, some would say – but people don't like it all the same. There's some asked for their money back.'

'It really speaks, then, his machine?'

My father affirmed that it did, and I remained silent, musing on that. It seemed intolerably sad to waste such an effort, if the professor really had somehow made the thing work. But perhaps his first attempt had failed?

I did not realise that I had voiced my feelings until my father replied. 'Sad, you say? There's worse things, boy. Sleeps in the same room with it, he does. Insists he can't leave it by itself. It's not good for a man to become so obsessed – mark that. And—'

'Yes, Papa?'

He hesitated before he spoke and when he did it was with reluctance, as if it were something better left unsaid. 'It's just – I did hear tell he's given that machine his dead sister's face.'

I recoiled, thinking for an instant he meant it was made from flesh and blood; but of course it could not be so. I remembered the Euphonia's visage, her bow lips, her pretty ringlets – her lifeless eyes. And it came to me of a sudden that 'euphonious' meant pleasant, honeyed, bell-like;

agreeable. How could Faber give his deathly sounding machine such a name – and such a face, one that was dear to him? But of course, he could not have meant it to sound as it did. Perhaps that was why he had been driven mad, why he burned his first machine; he must have realised the gulf between what he hoped to achieve and reality. And yet, if his machine could truly speak, he was responsible for a miracle – was he not?

That evening, I witnessed the miracle for myself.

I did not know if Faber saw me as I scuttled inside and took a seat at the back of the room. I did not see him, only his machine, its pale face and shining hair standing out from the shadows. The edges of the room were dimly lit, though the stage was bright with gaslights, hissing and sputtering and highlighting each strut and lever and key – making it abundantly clear to all that no one could be concealed within. Those lights would not be lowered, not for this performance. Everyone could see as much as they wished.

Faber stepped forward. In a halting voice, he begged the liberty of introducing us, one and all, to his Marvellous Talking Machine, his Euphonia. His voice softened when he spoke its name, and he looked upon the immobile face with something like affection. I saw that he had hung a white dress beneath it for this performance; a dress that hung limp and empty almost to the floor, swinging slightly in some unseen draught. The hem, I noticed, was a little frayed, and I wondered where he had come by it. Had this, too, been his sister's?

Faber took his seat at the instrument as at a pianoforte, stretching his hands from his sleeves like a great proficient before placing them above a set of ivory keys.

A noise like a great intake of breath filled the room. It was the only sound; no one moved or spoke. Then the Euphonia opened her mouth. Slowly, so slowly, she said, with a slight German accent, 'Please excuse my slow pronunciation. Good evening, ladies and gentlemen… It is a lovely day… It is a rainy day.'

I realised I was leaning forwards in my seat. Despite the ordinariness of the words, I was repulsed; fascinated. Her lips moved like human lips. Her tongue lolled within her mouth like a human's. She breathed like a human, and yet no one could mistake her voice for a human voice.

I think my feelings were shared, for it was only when she ceased speaking that those around me began to move again as people do, shifting in their seats, rubbing their lips. No one applauded, however. No one cheered.

I looked at Faber, whose mouth was compressed into an unhappy line, his brows drawn down.

He invited the audience to provide words for his machine to copy. One soul, braver than the rest, bid her say, 'Buona sera.'

No doubt he intended it for some trick, but say the words she did, though slowly, sounding each syllable as if she were learning his language. Another called out a line from *The Taming of the Shrew*. She could pass no comment upon it, only copy his words. Another demanded something about the fineness of the summer and this she spoke too, all with the same languor, although sunshine and warmth seemed a long way from this accursed chamber.

Then Faber demonstrated how, with the turn of a screw, the Euphonia could whisper. This was even worse. In this way she gave out the words of a hymn, though such a horror of a hymn I'd never heard. Still, I could not take my eyes from her empty gaze, until I became sensible that someone else was watching; someone standing at the back of the stage.

It was a girl, almost concealed by the curtain. Her hair was shining, her dress white, her face pale. I did not look at her directly but even from the corner of my eye, I could see that her lips were moving. Was this Faber's accomplice after all? I turned my head to better focus on her, and saw that no one was there. It was only a fold in the curtain, nothing more, and I shook my head. I told myself I was unsettled by the dreadful voice and the dismal man operating it. Little wonder he had burned his first effort – would that he had burned the second!

Then everyone around me rose from their seats, and I realised it was time to inspect the machine. I did not wish to go closer, yet I followed, not wishing to remain alone either, and in the jostling of the crowd I found myself standing directly before the Euphonia's face.

Close to, it appeared more lifeless than ever, more like a doll, and I wondered that I could have imagined it to be made of flesh. Faber explained its workings: the replicated throat and vocal organs made of reeds, whistles, resonators, shutters and baffles, and then he showed how the bellows drove air through it all, and the Euphonia opened her lips and let out a long exhalation. It felt like breath on my cheek, but cold – cold as the grave.

I started away from it and, hidden amidst the bustle, slipped from the room. I had heard the Euphonia speak. I had no wish, now, to hear her sing.

I could not keep away, however, for after the crowds had dispersed, I returned to that little room. I did not know what drew me there, only that I had been unable to cast it from my mind. Perhaps it was pity for poor mad Professor Faber. I expected to find him lost in despair at the horror induced by the thing he loved, but no; even from the passage I could hear voices and the clanking of keys.

Quietly, I opened the door and slipped inside. He was seated once more at his infernal machine. He had not seen me enter, for his head was lowered as he played upon it. The Euphonia's mouth gaped and twisted. She was singing after all, but not *God Save the Queen* or any such thing. I had not heard its like before, but I guessed this must be some German nursery song, perhaps even a lullaby.

My gaze went to the place by the curtain where I had imagined seeing a young girl. With those sepulchral tones resounding all about me, I could almost believe I had truly glimpsed the spirit of his dead sister.

Faber suddenly let out a cry of despair and slumped across his machine, folding his arms before his face.

And yet – I can see it still – the Euphonia sang on. Her lips continued to move; her eyes still gazed blankly at me, holding me there until her song was done.

Slowly, Faber began to unwind his arms and lift his head. I did not wait to see his sorrow, or whatever message his expression might hold. I grasped for the door again, pulled it open and I fled.

~

That was many years ago. Faber left us soon afterwards, saying he had an opportunity with Barnum in America, and yet success was never his. I heard sometime later that he had destroyed his beloved Euphonia once more; and he too had then perished, by his own hand. It seemed plain to me, upon receiving the news, that they must always have risen or fallen together.

And could I believe that his was only a machine – that the glimpsed figure was an illusion conjured by my overwrought imagination? Sometimes, perhaps. But more often it seemed to me that he created not a Talking Machine, but a vessel; and that something immeasurably distant yet always close to him had come to reside within it.

I have thought upon it more than ever after my wife, Mary, passed away. Like Faber, we had no children. My father died long before; I was the last of my line. I was grown old and was alone, and lonely. Mary went before me into the dark, and I wondered: what would I not do to bring her back, to have my dear wife speak to me again?

The question would have signified nothing, of course, if it were not for the parcel addressed to me that arrived at the Egyptian Hall, years after Faber's death, but not long after my wife's.

The writing within was in a tongue strange to me, yet I saw its purpose at once. For there were plans and diagrams within: plans with levers and keys and shutters and baffles, and an empty space where a face should be.

Some unknown beneficiary of the professor must have sorted through his sad possessions at last – yet it seemed almost meant to be. It appeared that Faber had not been able to entirely destroy his life's work, but had decided to pass it on, to let some other man decide whether it should live or die. The only name he had bethought himself to write on the stained, torn envelope containing all his wisdom was mine.

And I began to dream of it, that awful, dry, dead voice whispering as I slept. Would it be worth the cost, I wondered, to have my wife speak, but in such a voice – dead – soulless? But perhaps, I told myself, it needn't be so. I pored over the plans with increasing avidity. Could not the arrangement of baffles be improved upon a little? And the whistles and resonators could surely be of finer make than had been available to Faber. If I followed the plans carefully, exactly, yet made my own little improvements here and there, surely the vessel would be perfect. I would hear her the way she was in life, her honeyed tones, her bell-like laughter...

I could only pray it would be so. It took many more months of hearing that voice, of wondering, but eventually I could resist its call no longer. I had the papers translated piecemeal, so that none but I would learn their whole secret. And I started to build, creating lungs, glottis, vocal cords, tongue, lips. I laboured long in closed rooms, my beard becoming unkempt, my clothes as stained as Faber's had been. It consumed me, this thing, and yet still I hoped.

Now it is nearing completion. With his footsteps carved into the earth before me, I have achieved what cost Faber many years of torment. Soon it will be time to take my place at the machine and see what emerges from its waiting lips.

The time has come to try my creation. I sit at its keys, regretting the arrangement that has Mary's face turned outward, so that I cannot see it. I wonder what expression might be revealed upon it? But it is of no matter. If my wife returns to me, I will know. I will feel her presence.

I place my hands so that they are just resting on the ivories, and fill her artificial lungs with air. She takes a breath. We are ready.

I touch my fingers to the keys, and in answer she begins to speak. I press and press and her vowels turn into words that become sentences, and still I cannot stop, though I want to; with my whole heart, I want to. But my fingers betray me. They keep pressing, performing their dance, and I do not know what drives them; perhaps it is horror. Perhaps it is only that I wish, so very badly, that it is not true...

The voice speaks with a German accent. It is unmistakeable, even in its hoarse whisper. And there is so little life in it that I can almost convince myself I am wrong, but as it speaks to me, I know: the voice is not a woman's, but a man's. It is Faber's voice I hear.

I sense a presence, though not hers, not the one I longed for so badly. I can picture the dishevelled, hunched figure standing at my back, watching me with narrowed eyes. I feel his sorrow, his yearning, his unfathomable despair, and still, I play. I make my machine whisper. I make it sing, but even then, the truth does not change.

I press my hands to the keys more firmly than ever. I am driven onward by something – madness, perhaps; yes, it is likely that. And yet there is fascination too, with the terrible miracle that is before me. Most of all, I realise it is fear. For what would happen if I ceased giving it these words – my words? The thing might not stop speaking. It might keep opening its lips – and what might I hear then?

I keep feeding it, and as I do, I feel my own humanity slipping from me. I do not mourn it as it goes. I think of Faber shutting himself in a room, setting fire to his machine, to himself. I can almost sense the flames that await me, that are waiting to consume us both.

|Hungry Ghosts|

~

When I stepped out of my hotel, the old quarter of Hanoi had metamorphosed into something entirely new. The maze of narrow streets full of tiny shop fronts, bars and street sellers was now filled with low plastic stools covering the pavements, distorted with flashing coloured lights, and heady with the scent of *pho* noodles and alcohol. Dance beats spilled from anonymous-looking doorways, along with cries of 'You come.'

It was a puzzle I couldn't solve or begin to understand. I thought I'd done as Mai had told me: turned left from the hotel, followed the road to the top and turned right by the ATM. It had sounded simple, but the eatery she'd named wasn't here and neither was my friend. She hadn't replied to my texts and hadn't called.

I couldn't see any signs and the narrow ways all looked the same. A harsh cry made me step aside, making way for a bicycle laden with conical Vietnamese hats for sale. A farm worker was right behind, unwieldy with panniers full of guava yoked over her shoulders. I dodged again; I'd stepped into the path of suds being swilled from a street food vendor's pitch, his raw chicken set by in buckets of water. The cook glared at me, then took to stropping his carving knife against a lamp-post.

All I could do was go on, careful of the one thing that hadn't changed with sunset: the city remained the realm of mopeds, parked across the pavements, threading through the evening crowds. I kept listening for the sound of engines beneath the music and human voices and shouting of wares, but then, cutting across it all, I heard something different.

It was music, high and wavering, discordant and strange, and yet somehow seeming more real than anything else; more welcoming than the tinny pop blaring from the T-shirt concession behind me.

All around, everyone was intent on their work or their food or their journey, on the contents of tourists' wallets, and I decided that any direction was better than none. I kept heading towards the sound, telling myself it might even be coming from the Green Farm, the restaurant Mai had chosen. We had worked together on a volunteer project in the south for a while, establishing an organic community garden in Ho Chi Minh City, and she knew that I liked to experience some of the traditional culture; a venue with music like this would have been an obvious choice.

Around the next corner, a tent had been pitched at one side of a wider street, open at the sides and bedecked with ribbons. It held a small stage where musicians played instruments I didn't recognise, along with their audience.

The rows of seats were almost full and I checked the gathered faces for Mai. I recognised no one; their eyes gleamed back light from the stage as they nodded along, none smiling, none saying a word. Then someone began to sing, their voice high and otherworldly, rising above the street's pressing humidity like a breath of clean air.

A young couple walking a tiny dog on a lead almost crashed into me. I greeted them in Vietnamese then said, 'Is this the Green Farm?'

The woman replied, 'No, not the Green Farm. Entertainment, for anyone!'

'Anyone?'

She smiled at me. 'Yes. Even you!'

Her friendliness made me feel a little better. I checked my phone again, and decided a few minutes wouldn't hurt; perhaps Mai would even find me here, similarly drawn to the music. There wasn't much choice of seats; one, in the centre of the audience, was blocked by knees and skirts and bags. It was that, or anywhere at the very front. The audience must have been shy; that row had been left entirely empty.

I slipped into one of them and knew at once that I'd made a mistake. Hissing arose behind me: the sound of disapproval in any language. Then someone rapped the back of my chair, loud, hard enough to feel through the thin plastic. Then a hand grasped my arm and I turned to see Mai.

She didn't look happy to see me. Her eyes were wide, too wide, and she didn't smile. *Entertainment, for anyone* – but not, apparently, for me. Had the woman with the dog been having a joke at my expense? Maybe I'd gate-crashed a wedding or some other family party; or worse, a funeral.

Mai pulled me away, not pausing to say hello.

'I'm sorry,' I said. 'What did I do? I thought anyone could listen.'

'They can.' Despite her assurance, she only looked more unhappy. 'It is a merry-making, for the festival. It is to honour the hungry ghosts. That is why it is so loud, you see? To reach the ears of the spirits.'

I didn't see, not at all, and so she explained.

'That chair you took – the empty ones at the front are for spirits, not for us. You took a place that belongs to the dead.'

Later, we laughed about it. We found the restaurant, which turned out to be wide and candle-lit with cosy wooden tables, and ate warming *bun cha* while we talked. She told me about the festival: the way people honoured their ancestors, but also the hungry ghosts who had no family to remember them; the ones who had died bad deaths or done evil deeds, who were left to wander, aimless, about the streets.

When the waitress cleared the table and left us, Mai leaned over to me and whispered, 'Her mother is dead.'

'Do you know her?' I asked. They hadn't appeared to be friends.

Mai tapped her collar. 'She wears a white rose. You see, today, everyone is wearing flowers. This is a day for mothers too. Red flower shows she is living. White if she is dead. And we remember.'

'You don't wear a flower?' Mai had never spoken to me about her family, and as her expression hardened, I wondered if she'd had her reasons.

'I wear nothing for that bitch,' she said. 'She wanted my money always. But she never cared for me.' After a moment she added, 'She dead, you wondering.'

Mai laughed. After a moment, we both did. She only said one more thing before we rose from our seats.

'Look like both of us make the dead angry tonight.'

The following evening, Mai insisted I come for dinner at her home. The taxi driver looked surprised when I named her district – it wasn't a usual destination for western visitors – and he set me down just before a bridge that carried the road across the river. He gestured towards some steps leading down from the carriageway. I turned to ask for clearer directions, but he was already driving off.

I could see numerous blocks of flats, each small and low rise, and each very much like the next. They crowded right up to the banks of the Red River, which despite its name flowed slow and muddy and brown. It was wide, too; the similar homes on the far bank looked tiny from where I stood.

I remembered that Mai had spoken of a balcony overlooking the river bend, so I descended the steps then took a side street that led in roughly the right direction. The street was lined with crumbling concrete walls covered in graffiti I couldn't read, with thick bundles of wiring strung between the lampposts. There were balconies too, many of them caged in with steel mesh, presumably to keep out thieves.

Then I saw a shop selling smoking paraphernalia at the corner, its placard advertising vaping half covering the balcony of the flat above, and I remembered Mai mentioning that too. I found the entrance to the building and tried the door; it wasn't locked and I tentatively stepped inside, ascending bare concrete steps. I found myself in an airless passageway, as humid as everywhere else but made more stifling still with the smells of stale cooking. The doors didn't have any numbers. I stood there, not knowing whether to go on or back, but then one of them opened; to my relief, Mai's head appeared in the gap. She looked tired, even exhausted.

'Mai, are you OK? Are you sure about tonight?'

She didn't answer, just gestured me inside. The lounge was tiny and dimly lit, and full of furniture: a fraying sofa, makeshift shelves, a clothes rail. An overhead fan paddled at the damp air, its humming interspersed with a rhythmic judder as it rocked on its fitting. To one side was a kitchen: also tiny, as was the stove, but good smells and steam poured from it. I had begun to make some comment about the feast she'd prepared when I realised we weren't alone.

Someone stood in the middle of the lounge, just a few feet away from me. I didn't know how I'd missed him; perhaps he'd been sunk into a seat in the half-dark. He was about Mai's age and slightly built, like many of his countrymen – no: on closer view, he was bone-thin. His eyes narrowed and for just a moment they caught the light, shining amber like a cat's – but when he reached out his hand, the thing that leapt to mind was a snake striking, and I flinched away.

'Linh.' Mai introduced him casually, as if I should have known he'd be here. 'My boyfriend.'

I realised I was being rude and grasped his fingers, too hard, forgetting the gentle handshake that was preferred across this part of the world. He didn't comment, only stared with half-closed eyes, no doubt making his own judgements. Before I could even summon the Vietnamese to say I was glad to meet him, Mai slipped a drink into my hand and the moment passed. I wanted to ask her about him, but how could I? I hadn't known she had a boyfriend. She'd never mentioned it in Ho Chi Minh City, nor the previous evening, and I wondered why, but she had returned to the kitchen and was busy clattering pots.

Linh sat, not looking at me, and it was then that I noticed the shrine. It had been placed against the far wall and was hung with fresh flowers; a tray of sticky rice cakes and some objects made of paper had been set there. I'd seen such votives in the temples: they were meant to be burnt, a way of transferring the thing they represented to the next life, where they would be of use to the spirits. So far, I'd spotted paper cooking utensils, houses, furniture, clothing, iPhones, televisions and even air-conditioning units, as well as hell-money, a currency of no use in any earthly shop. Mai's offering was a rather cleverly constructed paper woman. Her lips were painted red and she wore a long paper *ao dai* tunic.

With a start, I realised that Linh was standing by the shrine. I hadn't seen him move; now he too gazed upon the offerings, though his stance did not invite questions. I called through to Mai in the kitchen. 'Is this for your ancestors?'

Mai was transferring fragrant rice into a serving dish, her forehead dampened with steam or heat – or was it illness? There was a clamminess I didn't like, a pallor to her skin. She looked as if she could sleep for a month, and when she spoke, her expression didn't change.

'No,' she said. 'The offerings are for the hungry ghosts. I told you. All through the seventh lunar month, the gates of hell are open. It is the only time they may feast. They visit who they please, and cause trouble if they are not given food and other things.'

Just then, a movement drew my gaze. Linh had reached out, lightning fast, and seized a rice cake. He crammed it into his mouth, pushing it in past small white teeth. I couldn't help but stare. I had thought that such offerings were sent to the monks, or burnt like the votives, not eaten by whoever desired them.

Linh's throat pulsed as he forced the last of it down. He licked his fingers, then his lips; there was no guilt on his face at all.

We went out onto the balcony to eat, to take in the view of the river, which now, as evening fell, seemed to have no colour at all. Despite the lowering of the sun, it remained warmer out here than it had been inside. Hanoi was cooler than the south, but the humidity was intense, making the air feel thick, resistant to breathing.

We fitted ourselves around the table, its surface as crammed as the balcony itself: along with the rice, Mai had prepared *bo kho*, a huge beef stew; *cha ca* fish; a banana flower salad; spring rolls, dipping sauces and pickles. I tried everything and my spirits rose at being in this place where so few tourists came, eating not with paying visitors but with a friend.

We reminisced about our work on the city garden, falling into easy chatter. Linh sat in silence, betraying no interest or irritation whatsoever at all our talk of times he hadn't shared, people he hadn't met, things he hadn't experienced. He remained quiet even when Mai occasionally shifted to Vietnamese, and she seemed to expect nothing else. His hands, though, were busy. He reached constantly for the choicest morsels, the largest pieces of fish, pausing only to gulp Tiger beer from the bottle Mai had set before him. Soon he put down his chopsticks and grabbed pieces of beef from the stew with his fingers. He sucked them down, leaving a sliver of sauce on his lips. He didn't wipe it away and I tried not to look. I attempted to persuade myself he was only showing his appreciation to Mai, for her cooking skills.

When the dishes were empty – mainly through Linh's efforts – Mai cleared them away, lit a candle against the darkness and set it in the middle of the table. Linh showed no appreciation now, however; he pushed back his chair, stood and walked inside, without saying a word. He opened a narrow door set into one side of the living space and was gone.

I looked at Mai, expecting some comment; an excuse perhaps, or more hopefully to express an intent to ditch him, but she said nothing. I saw again that she looked ill. The candlelight that usually flattered had done the opposite; her hair appeared lank, her skin almost grey.

'When did you two meet?' I forced a cheerful tone.

'A week ago.'

A *week*? And this was how he behaved? But Mai's expression didn't change, betraying nothing of infatuation or love or even the dawning of disappointment, and I said nothing. I glanced towards the door Linh had passed through, but there was no sign of his reappearing.

'He is staying here for a while.' Mai nodded as if inviting me to nod too, to agree with her that this was perfectly normal. 'He is in some difficulty. I will sleep on the floor, of course.'

'*You* will—?' Again, my voice faded. What could I say? Whatever this was, it was her choice. I couldn't know how things stood between them, had no idea what combination of circumstance or custom or its opposite could have brought them here.

Then Mai cried out, waving her hands in front of her face; it was a moth, fluttering about the candle, but my friend's face was filled with such disgust, it might have been something poisonous.

'Mai, it's only an insect,' I said, but she went on batting at it. The moth wouldn't be banished; it wanted the flame.

When she spoke, she sounded almost afraid. 'It might not be an insect,' she said. 'It could be a spirit. They visit in different shapes at this time. Any shape. Sometimes they are moths. Sometimes they are other things. Bad things.'

I put my hand on her arm and suggested we go inside. She didn't take a seat in the living space, however, only sagged where she stood, and I said it was time for me to go. I wished her a restful night and her gaze shot towards the closed door. I had been tactless again. I'd somehow forgotten Linh, who must be sleeping in there – but the image that came to me was her boyfriend sitting upright on the bed, unmoving, unblinking; staring towards us with his eyes wide open.

'Oh, but I should go with you,' Mai said suddenly, and I half expected her to add, *To get away*, but of course she did not. She said she must find a taxi for me, but she swayed as she spoke; her eyes were beginning to close.

'Mai,' I said gently, 'Are you ill?'

'No, no. Not ill. Only tired.'

I supposed she must be, if she was sleeping on the floor. I told her to get some rest and assured her that I'd be fine. I'd go back the way I came and hail a taxi on the bridge. I stepped out into the corridor, and without saying goodbye, Mai closed the door behind me.

As I left, I glanced up at her balcony once more. It was entirely dark now, the light in the living space already extinguished, not even a candle burning there, and I thought again of Linh; sitting in her bedroom, silent and still. It only occurred to me then that I hadn't heard him utter a single word all evening.

Soon the bridge loomed above me, the shine of headlights spilling from the deck making the night seem darker by contrast. Telling myself I'd soon find a cab, I started up the steps to the carriageway, pausing only to look out across the dark blank of the river. As I did, I heard a sound. It wasn't coming from the road, nor the buildings behind me; rather, it was somewhere below.

I moved to the edge of the steps and peered down to see a dark hollow of waste land, or perhaps the dead end of an alleyway, just beneath the bridge. The sound was coming from down there: a sliding, rustling noise, distinct but furtive, like the shuffling of rats, and there was something else: a sound I couldn't quite identify, or didn't want to.

I allowed my eyes to adjust. The space down there was irregular, confusing, and it came to me that it was full of garbage. As if in confirmation, I detected the smell of rotting vegetables, mingled with that of rancid flesh. It combined with the humidity to coat my tongue, making me regret eating so heartily such a short time ago.

Something moved in the depths. I leaned over the parapet as the shadow shifted again, thinking once more of rats, or perhaps cats; but the shape that suddenly snapped into clarity was neither.

There was a man down there, and he was naked. Thin limbs sprawled in the waste, his arms moving, always moving, as he grasped after something I couldn't see. Whatever it was, he dragged it towards him and pushed it into his mouth. Then the sound came again; not the rustling, but the one I'd persuaded myself I couldn't identify.

Wet chewing. Slavering. Choking as something was gorged upon too fast, crammed down someone's throat.

I think I must have made a sound too, because as I stared, the figure beneath me froze. Then he began to twist his head – far, *too* far, farther still, until his neck was a wrung cloth; until he was looking directly up at me.

We stared at one another. We each stared as if we didn't know what we saw. It was oddly intimate. The man's neck was a rope but his naked belly was distended into a mound; impossible to tell if it was from gorging or starvation. Then he opened his mouth. He cracked his jaw wide, wider, like a child trying to show what they were chewing, but before I could make it out, the lump of matter in his mouth ignited.

I narrowed my eyes against the glare, catching a glimpse of his cheeks shining blood red as the flare shone through his flesh; then the food was gone, consumed by fire before he could begin to swallow it, and it was dark once more.

But only for a moment. Another flame lit the darkness, a fierce glint of red, and another, and more; and I saw that he was not alone. By turns, as each light flared and faded, I saw them all: men and women too, naked and writhing in a hellscape of the foul discards of everyday life. All of them were restless, all of them in constant motion, reaching for whatever they could find: old bones, decaying flesh, greedily grasping with their long fingers. And they would not stop, I realised, for their necks were so thin, the flames so quick, they could surely never eat any of it.

And then I saw a figure that wasn't moving: this one half-clothed, limbs wrenched and broken, skin covered in wounds that did not bleed. The figures were gathered most thickly where he lay, and they were gouging and biting at his flesh.

I staggered back, half stumbled up the rest of the steps, and began to run. Traffic streamed alongside me and I raised a hand in a signal for help; soon I heard a car slowing, pulling in next to me. Miraculously, it was a taxi.

I yanked the door open and hurled myself into the seat. The driver twisted to look at me, surprised, and I tried to say something about what I'd seen, but he didn't understand; he only gestured impatiently. He wanted to know where we were going. I took deep breaths of dry, cool, conditioned air, and tied to calm myself. I didn't want him to change his mind and make me step out again. I didn't want to be within reach of those... *things.*

I told him the name of my hotel. His consternation faded at once as he set about his job, nodding and pulling away from the curb. Distance opened between the car and the bridge, and I began to feel easier. I wondered if I should get him to take me to the police station, but what would I tell them? They'd assume I was high on something. An image arose of the inside of a prison cell, of being interrogated by sharp, unsmiling men who didn't believe a word, and I said nothing.

We drove on, just as if everything was normal, and we pulled up outside my hotel. I paid the driver and nodded to the doorman as I went inside. I pressed the button for the lift and rode it up to my room, let myself in and sat on the bed. I stared down at my hands. I half expected them to be shaking, but they were not.

After a while, I switched on the television and let the anodyne sound of advertising jingles wash over me. I went into the bathroom and splashed cold water on my face, brushed my teeth, then brushed them again.

Then I set about trying to persuade myself that I hadn't seen what I thought I'd seen. I told myself it was only shock at the plight of some homeless souls – no: *people,* I inwardly insisted. They were eating what they must. It couldn't have been a body; I'd only caught a glimpse, and the light had been so odd – which was surely only another illusion. They'd had candles to light their way, and nothing more.

The next morning I wandered aimlessly around Hanoi, discovering its sights by chance rather than design. I saw Hoan Kiem Lake and its ancient pagoda, Thap Rua Tower. I passed St Joseph's Cathedral and wondered if a service was in progress, stories being told, fed upon, believed. I tried not to think of anything else, though images kept intruding: Mai's expressionless face as Linh left the room. Her pallor as she batted at a moth. Most of all, those things in the alley, so close to where she lived; so close to *life*, yet seeming to have no part in it.

The day was passing into evening, the sky fading and tainted with exhaust fumes, when I found myself standing outside a temple. The festival of hungry ghosts was still going on. Supplicants came, wearing grey robes, pressing incense sticks to their foreheads before leaving them to burn in a huge metal bowl. The little specks of orange light were discomfiting, though I welcomed their strong fragrance; I wasn't altogether certain why.

Further inside, through the open doors of the inner temple, I could see a golden Buddha. He was surrounded by offerings: Buddha's fingers fruit; more rice cakes; other goods wrapped in plastic as if fresh from a supermarket, among them packets of biscuits and dried noodles. Beyond the golden figure, the wall was covered with photographs. People stared out from them, ancestors all, safely delivered to the next life – or so people hoped.

And there was something here that I hadn't seen before, set in the courtyard between the inner temple and the incense bowl. An open fire burned there, low and fitful, then flashing more greedily; someone had cast something into the flame, a votive made of paper that burned fast and bright and then was gone.

With a start, I recognised the person who had offered it.

Linh was standing just the other side of the offering pyre. He straightened, though he didn't notice me; he had closed his eyes to savour the smell of burning paper, as if it were something delicious. When he'd – *consumed* it, that was the word that came to me, he drew something else from his pocket: a wad of hell money. He peeled off the notes one by one, feeding each to the flame, transferring them to the next life.

I started walking towards him. He must have sensed my approach, though he betrayed no sign of it. He only went on staring into the fire, the vivid light making the planes of his face too harsh, reminding me of bones. I found myself thinking of something I'd read about the offering pyres: that they were said to open a doorway to the spirit world, and that to linger by them was dangerous. Anything could pass through. A spirit could slip from that world to this, and would trouble the careless; even possess whomsoever they chose. I found myself wondering if that would allow them to truly feast at last – but none of it seemed to worry Linh. He gazed on, as if the firelight held some message for him… or perhaps with longing.

He had burnt all of the money. Soon he must acknowledge me, and I wasn't sure I wanted that – but instead, he pulled something else from his pocket, plucking at the flattened paper to restore its original form.

It was a woman made of paper. She had red lips and wore a long *ao dai* tunic. It was the woman from Mai's shrine, and I somehow didn't like to see it clutched in his hand.

A quick gesture, and Linh tossed her towards the fire. This time he didn't linger, but walked straight towards me – then past me, and away, never once meeting my gaze.

But the little paper woman had not been consumed; she hadn't been transferred to the next life, where she would be – what? A dead man's servant? Wife? Cook? Instead, the votive had fallen to the edge of the pyre, and the flames had not yet caught her.

I went closer, stooped and snatched the offering from the fire. I held the little paper woman against me, and thought of Mai; not as she had been when I last saw her, but in the community garden. She'd been smiling then. Happy. Her cheeks had been healthful, her hair gleaming. On the day I recalled, she'd been wearing a silk *ao dai*. She had wanted to show me something of the traditional dress. I had been showing her some things too. I remembered the way she had taken the lipstick I held out to her; the way she had laughed as she painted her lips bright red.

I walked away from the temple, not knowing where I was heading. I was on another narrow street full of mopeds and bars and noise. A woman in a skin-tight top thrust a drinks menu in front of me and automatically, I took it; I allowed her to guide me to a plastic stool at the edge of the road. It wasn't what I wanted, not really, but I accepted the drink she placed in front of me and watched as she lit a candle and set it on a little plastic table. I realised I was still holding the paper votive and put it next to the candle. The waitress looked at it quizzically before she left.

I sat quite still and watched as the hordes filled the evening street. Soon there was a constant stream of men, women and children going past me, all intent on getting somewhere – or perhaps nowhere. Perhaps none of them was real, and they were all hungry ghosts: spirits wandering without destination or purpose, driven by nothing but the urge to consume whatever they could, whenever they could, wherever they could find it.

A shadow shifted in front of me. Something small and speckled fluttered before my eyes; I realised it was a moth.

It could be a spirit. They visit in different shapes at this time. Any shape. Sometimes they are moths. Sometimes they are other things. Bad things.

The moth was drawn inexorably to the candlelight, a hair's breadth from being burnt. I thought for a moment it had been singed already, but what I'd taken for charring was merely a pattern on its wings. When it settled on the table, two eyes opened and looked at me.

I had to remind myself that the design was only some kind of camouflage – or rather, a defence mechanism; the moth was of a type that mimicked a predator. Beneath those wide, unblinking eyes, it also appeared to possess a mouth; a snake's maw, slightly open, ready to strike.

Before I had consciously made the decision to do it, I reached out and took hold of the votive doll. I lifted her, light as air, and brought her down, trapping the moth inside her hollow body.

At once, the insect's movements became loud, wings skittering against paper. Tiny black legs appeared from beneath the votive's tunic, thrusting and retreating, methodically, as if the moth were testing the walls of its prison.

I lifted one side of the dress a fraction and peered beneath. In the shadows, the dark, squat shape under there barely appeared to be a moth at all.

Then, yet more carefully, I raised it again. As the creature darted to freedom, I brought down my hand. I felt something soft and grotesquely damp, but the residue it left behind was dry; as powdery and fine as ash. The scent of burning rose into the air and I told myself that the votive had been charred after all, but somehow, I didn't believe that was true.

Mai turned to me and smiled. It was a good smile, and she glowed with it; her hair looked glossy and strong. She passed me a drink and clinked her glass against mine. A day had passed since I'd seen Linh at the temple, though she hadn't mentioned him. When I asked how he was, she looked blank for a moment.

'It is strange,' she said, 'but he did not come back yesterday. I suppose I will hear from him.' She shrugged, as if she couldn't decide whether to be concerned, or even to care.

No matter her words, I didn't think that Mai would hear from Linh. It felt as if he had gone. Her flat seemed bigger without him, the air easier to breathe. Lighter too, despite the night that pressed in close outside.

'Do you feel better now, Mai? I was worried about you.'

It took her a little while to answer. 'I feel—' she paused. 'I feel a little strange inside. But better, yes. I do feel better.'

I nodded, relieved, certain now that she would be all right.

Then she said, 'Soon, I must eat. I am hungry. But first we should go and see the lamps.'

I didn't know what she meant, but she gestured towards the balcony and so we stepped out into the heat. The river was a blank, but then I saw it wasn't quite dark after all; tiny lights floated on the surface, pinpricks in the darkness, moving slowly outward from the bank as they were drawn by the tide.

'The festival is over,' Mai said. 'And so we float lotus lanterns. When the lights go out, that is when the hungry ghosts find their way back to hell.' She paused once more, and her voice went musing. 'Unless they can find a way to stay.'

I stared at her profile, though she didn't look at me. For a moment, in our silence, I thought I heard a sound: a skittering, fluttering noise, like wings against paper, though when I looked about I couldn't see a moth; not here, not tonight.

Sometimes they are other things, I thought. *Bad things.* And I shivered.

I watched the lights and tried not to think of glints of flame beneath a bridge. Of a pyre consuming offerings to the dead. Of a paper woman standing in a firelit doorway, or of things slipping through; things that may not want to leave again. Those things weren't real. They couldn't have been real; they only seemed close, now, because I suddenly felt so very tired, as if all I wanted to do was sleep.

We did not speak again. We only sat in silence and watched as the lotus lanterns floated away down the wide, slow river. Gradually, the lights began to wink out, disappearing one by one into darkness, until it seemed that not a trace of them remained.

|...And I'll Come to You|

~

That first night, they give us a choice: we can spend our time whittling, mending nets, writing to our wives or playing the fiddle. We laugh and spend it drinking and playing tunes downloaded from Spotify, Jez bewailing the lack of a mobile phone signal. The ship creaks and sways around us like something alive. In the half dark, when the music fades, it's easy to forget this is the twenty-first century.

'Ship's biscuit?'

Andy sticks a half-empty packet of Hobnobs under my nose. I grin at his joke and take one.

We have the passenger berths to ourselves. The proper crew, the one that isn't playing pretend, are either up top or in the captain's quarters, where the false panelling is stained the colour of mahogany and candelabra are glued to the table. Their laughter drifts through the thin wooden walls. Ours is a long, dark, low space, full of mysterious shadows. On one side, hammocks are slung from the timbers; on the other, benches are fixed to the floor. This ship, a fishing vessel converted to a square rigger, can accommodate twenty-four guests, or 'voyage crew', but most of the hammocks will be empty tonight. It seems that historical sailing adventures on the North Sea are more popular in June than November; there is only one other group, two couples currently on watch, helming the ship into the dark.

I bite into the biscuit, relishing the familiar taste and trying not to think of the mast swaying somewhere above us.

Earlier, it had been our watch. The memory turns me cold. I'd been given the chance to go aloft, up among the sails; they'd made it sound a terrific lark, and I'd leapt at it. Our watch leader, Jane, had pointed the way through the inexplicable maze of ropes and wires and said, 'You need to use the shrouds.'

She explained that shrouds were the wires holding the mast in place. I would climb the windward set, so that the ladder formed by ratlines, fixed for the purpose, would slope away from me. At first it wasn't bad, though the sea was choppy, the masts swaying, ropes and shrouds all swaying too so that nothing seemed fixed at all.

Then I secured the safety line and stepped out onto the footrope, seemingly into the air.

When I glanced down, the others were watching and grinning and the deck seemed a mile away. The motion was worse up here, exaggerated by my height as wave after wave struck the hull. It was too late to go back. My task was to free the sails from their gaskets, and I forced myself to edge out along the yard. All I could think of was the empty space around me, the miles and miles of nothing; the fragility of the link that connected me to everything I'd known, and how easily it could be torn away. I thought of the sailors who'd done this before safety harnesses or radios or the promise of help. They had committed their lives to a few spars of wood and rope and canvas, adrift on a long dark sea with only the stars for company, the splash of a breaching whale to break the silence.

Jez pulls me back from the memory, setting a new song playing. I recognise *Valerie*, and Andy digs him in the ribs. Valerie is the name of my wife, or rather, my ex. She had loved the song, had loved it when I played it for her, and for a moment I can smell her perfume.

Jez douses the sound. 'Sorry, mate.'

I shrug: *no matter*. That's the reason we're here, after all. This is my farewell trip: a divorce party, as Jez put it. A way to leave it all behind.

Now the lantern swings as we ride out a wave. It doesn't go out, doesn't even waver; there's an LED half hidden behind the ironwork. Behind the lamp, I make out the fluorescence of an exit sign; a reflective strip denoting a low beam; the bright red of a fire extinguisher. I'm not sure whether to feel disappointed by the lack of authenticity or relieved to see them there, a reminder of the life I know.

The ladder clatters against the hull, its bright white plastic incongruous against the wood. Its bottom rungs just reach the water. It is morning, and very clear. Aldeburgh is visible to the south, and further up the coast is the fantastical white edifice of the nuclear power station at Sizewell. The beach isn't far off, an enticing golden line, though there are no people to be seen.

'We're not making good time in this lull,' says Jane. 'The wind has dropped. But there's an archaeological site here, so it's a good chance to take a look, especially while the sea is calm.

'There's a preceptory almost beneath us. That's a kind of church built by the Templars, and it used to be on the shore. You could have walked to it once, but the sea's encroached a fair bit on this stretch of coast. Good for us, the sea has also exposed a lot of the ruins. They used to be covered in a layer of earth, but storms have scoured enough away that you can see the walls. Watch for a circular structure.'

I drift while she explains something of the Templar's building habits, returning my attention when she laughs. 'This one's said to be haunted, so keep your eyes peeled. There's an old story about a spirit that attached itself to someone who took something from the site, years ago. Be warned, huh?'

The whole voyage crew is assembled, awkward in wetsuits, clutching flippers and masks. I look out over the water, the cold gleaming surface opaque as far as I can see. It looks rather lonely, as though anything might be under there, moving or still, alive or dead. I shrink from the thought of the sea closing over me, sliding along my skin. I wonder where Valerie is now. It's Saturday. We would have been waking up together, lazing in bed, sharing a ridiculously strong pot of coffee. I'm suddenly grateful that the others are here, then remember that Andy just got engaged and Jez has a girlfriend. I have a sudden image of them getting married themselves, having kids even, and being marooned all over again.

I shake off the thought as I take my turn at the ladder. It swings against the ship's side, sending up rhythmic hollow rattles as I lower myself into the sea. It's as cold as it appeared but I float for a few seconds as Jane had advised, waiting as the wetsuit starts to do its work.

She tosses down my flippers and I catch them and put them on, rinse the mask that's slung around my neck and set it into place. The others are moving away, their breathing pipes bright little markers against the grey. I put my face into the water and paddle away from the ship.

At first there is nothing, only the depthless sea. Then I realise it's not water slipping by but the seabed, sand and algae all the same bleached shade, soft and formless as dust. It might have lain undisturbed for centuries. I tell myself it's a good thing there is nothing else to see. I've never been much of a swimmer and I don't know why I chose this, don't know what I'd do if I saw something bigger: a shark or a ray perhaps, or something I can't even recognise, dark and unfathomable.

Then I realise that what I'd taken to be a natural mound on the seabed is really a wall. It heads away in a straight line, pointing towards the shore. Men must have placed those stones, once; they must have walked down there in the deep.

I remember the waterproof camera I'd strapped around my arm, retrieve it and switch it on. When I look down again there's a structure beneath me, roughly circular as Jane had described – *a kind of church* – where those men whose lives I can't imagine had worshipped their god.

I hold out the camera and snap off a photo. There's a rectangular protrusion to one side of the structure which I suppose must be the altar. I picture men in pale robes kneeling before it. I wonder what brought them to this particular stretch of coast; what answers they could possibly have expected to find here.

I had thought the Templars had sailed off to the east, to convert others to their faith, or to acquire treasures they hadn't earned from a land they believed holy. I don't believe in any such things, but still, the place gives me a weird feeling. I'm not sure I want photos of it any longer, can't imagine ever wanting to look at them again. Still, I suppose I may as well take one last picture of the altar before I go after the others to take some snaps of us goofing around.

I find the shutter release with my finger, peer down and see a face looking back at me.

The water is suddenly loud, bubbling past my ears. The button depresses under my finger, an instant before the camera begins to fall. I stare past it – it's only dust down there, nothing but that; not a pale face, not a withered form standing before the altar. I gather myself in time to snatch at the camera but stirring the water only makes it dance away, out of my reach. Its colour fades, its outline softening as it sinks. A plume of sand rises from somewhere below.

I'm cold right through. I tell myself I'm seeing things that aren't there, that can't possibly be there. Humans are programmed by evolution to see faces in everything, aren't they? It was only a whorl in the sand, a half-familiar arrangement of stone.

Gradually, my heart begins to slow. I remember the first time I'd used that camera: swimming off the coast of Cuba with Val, surrounded by hundreds of colourful fish.

Now there is nothing. I can't judge the distance to the seabed. It might not be as deep as it looks; this was part of the shore once, after all. But then, maybe it is. Our ship had to be able to moor here – that takes depth, doesn't it? I imagine diving down, but for some reason what comes to me is the thought of climbing the rigging; stepping out into nothing but empty air.

I take several deep gasps before holding my breath, doubling up in the water and kicking downward. Too late, I wonder what Jane must think. Probably just that I'm a confident swimmer, that I want to take a closer look at the ruins.

As I suspected, the depth is deceptive. My hand swipes through sand before I even know I've reached it. The pressure in my lungs tells me to be quick but I can't see the camera anywhere. Something glints in the corner of my eye; something that doesn't belong. My air is gone, my chest growing hot and tight, and I snatch blindly. There's something solid under my hands so I grasp it before striking for the surface.

My head breaks the water and I wrench the mask from my face. I'm holding something but it's not what I'd sought; not my camera, nothing I recognise. Some instinct makes me turn my back to the ship so that only I can see the small metal object that's revealed when I open my fingers. It's encrusted with sand and it looks as if it might be engraved with letters, but I can't make them out.

I stow it down the front of my wetsuit and swim back towards the ship. The others are treading water, laughing and splashing, but I don't want to join them any longer. I want to be alone, so that I can investigate this thing I've found – or rather, that has found me.

～

I lie back in my hammock, alone in the ship's underbelly. The others are on deck, getting us underway, but I'd pleaded a headache. I don't know why, but I feel possessive over this thing. I want it to be mine. I've swapped a marriage for it, after all.

There's an old story about a spirit that attached itself to someone who took something from the site, years ago . . .

I let out a spurt of laughter at the thought, but it fades into the dark. I didn't take this thing; it felt more as if it meant to find me. The object appears to be a bronze whistle. It's about four inches long and I still can't read the inscription. Feeling like an archaeologist, I scrape at it with my thumbnail, crumbling away the encrusted sand. Even only partially uncovered, I can see it's a lovely thing. Ancient, too; I can feel the passing years in its surface. Somehow, I know that if I blow into it, the sound will be sweet.

When I raise it to my lips, it is cold; the metal has not warmed to my skin. There's a sour, metallic taste, but it is as I thought; even though I scarcely breathe into it, the sound is true, and soft as the air, yet so piercing I feel it in my bones. As if summoned, an image rises: the seabed passing by beneath me, but this time it is endless. It is dead and colourless, there is nothing there, nothing alive, and suddenly I don't know which would be worse: glimpsing a pale face looking back at me, or nothing at all, for ever and ever.

It takes a moment for the impression to fade – the sense of loss – but as it does, I realise that the sound must have been heard all over the ship. There's no time to think of it, because suddenly we heel hard to port, setting my hammock swaying. There's a wail, one I struggle to identify, until I realise it must be the wind howling about the ship. How had it risen so fast? I hear footsteps hammering down the ladder and shove the whistle deep into my pocket.

'Mate, you might be needed. Waterproofs, yeah?'

I yank them on and follow Jez onto the deck, expecting daylight, but there's only a lurid glow on the horizon, pushed downward by a leaden sky. The sails buffet and the captain barks orders at the watch leaders, his words snatched away as he points this way and that. I catch, 'Get the damned sail hauled in!' I don't like his expression as he stares upward at Andy, who's in the rigging, gripping the ropes for dear life. At least he's climbed to windward – but as if in spite, the wind whips around, and suddenly he's hanging from the shrouds. He's too high and yet not high enough; he hasn't reached the platform where he could have clipped his safety line.

The sail above him whips and furls and there, for an instant, a face appears, pale and yellowish. It's like a corpse louring over him, over us all, and in that moment, Andy lets go.

He grasps at the ratlines. Misses; falls.

The deck drops away beneath me as the ship heels once more and I stagger. For one sick second I think we're turning turtle, then the trim levels out and I rush to Andy's side. He just waves me away, his face deathly. He's no sailor but he can see our danger; we all can. There's no one else near and I can see what's needed so I reach for the wet rope, which bucks like a living thing under my fingers. I start to climb, realising too late that I'm not even wearing a safety harness. *Fuck it,* I think, and pull myself over the treacherous stretch of shrouds. Then I step out onto a rope that suddenly seems impossibly thin.

I hold on as the ship rocks and tilts. Everything is grey. I can no longer tell the sea from the sky; the sea is all there is, grey forever, water hanging in the air, drenching my skin, though no rain falls.

The wind sings through the rigging, its bitter message whispering cold in my bones. The ship slides down a long grey wave, seeming to stall for an instant before starting up the next, solid as a hill to be climbed. I had thought the ship was inauthentic, but this is too much reality and I close my eyes as the ship heels back. I feel myself taken down with it until salt water dashes against my face.

Still, I realise that someone below has drawn in the bulk of the canvas using the buntlines and clewlines. I start to strap it into place with numb, clumsy fingers, then I almost fall, because I see him: a pale shape amid the waves, as ragged and tattered as shreds of ripped canvas, and I tell myself that's all he is, but I know that isn't true. I *feel* that isn't true.

He appears to be standing on a raft and I tell myself he's going to die, but I know that isn't true either. He appears to be rowing with a single long oar, as if trying to reach us, and he doesn't seem to be troubled by the waves, though he isn't making any headway. He is looking at me. I can't make out his features, not really – or perhaps my mind doesn't want to – but I feel that to be so. I see once more a face glimpsed beneath the water; canvas, furling and unfurling in the wind.

He vanishes into the grey but appears again, rising out of a swell as if materialising from the waves. He's still there – *following*, that's the word that comes to me.

Dimly, I wonder if I should raise the alarm, shout *Man overboard*, but I don't think it would be any use and anyway I can't speak, can't even move. I can taste salt, feel it on my cheeks, my lips, my hands. The sea is all around me and everywhere. I can only hold on, though my arms are shuddering, my strength failing. It's that knowledge that makes me start edging my way back towards the ratlines; I know that if I stay, I'll fall.

'Voyage crew below, now.' Somehow I've reached the deck, and the captain's voice is at my ear. He sounds at once angry and relieved.

'There's someone there.' I croak out the words before I can stop myself. 'A raft.' I point, but I can't see him any longer. There is only the grey, in motion yet solid, constantly taking on new forms.

'What? No one's out there, not in this. Get below!'

I stagger to the hatch and down the steps, which are steep as a ladder. I'm still clinging to the handrail when everything falls quiet; our movement subsides. I realise the others are here, staring at me. Andy places his hand flat on the table, as if checking whether it's safe.

'Wow,' he says, all mock admiration. 'Good entrance. That's some trick.'

I open my mouth to tell him it's a coincidence the storm calmed just as I came down, but somehow I can't. It began when I blew the whistle, didn't it? My hand goes to my pocket, and I don't know whether I'm relieved or dismayed to feel its shape nestled there.

'Or maybe you're a Jonah. As soon as you got off the deck…'

'I'm a what?'

'A Jonah. An unlucky passenger. That's how he ended up in the whale, didn't you know? He brought them bad juju so they threw him overboard, and after that they did alright.'

I open my mouth to reply and instead find myself saying, 'Did you see the face in the sail? Is that why you fell?'

He looks puzzled. Still, there's something in his eyes, and I don't know if he thinks I'm barking or if he knows what I mean but doesn't want to admit it. Then he recovers himself. 'The fuck, man? If someone else was up there, that would have been good to know.' He holds out his hands, showing where the ropes have burned lines into his palms. 'I didn't see a bloody thing. Bit busy. Now, is there a bucket somewhere? 'Cos I think I'm going to puke.'

~

Later, I leave the others and go up on deck. It's almost full dark, though the sky is clear and endless, the Milky Way an impossible glittering arc. Jane is at the helm, though she doesn't seem to be looking at anything in particular. She stares out to sea, her expression blank.

She twitches as I approach – or is it a flinch? Does she think I'm a Jonah too? Probably she's been in trouble because I went aloft without a safety line. 'There's no need to keep watch tonight,' she says. 'The professional crew are taking over for a bit.'

'I just wondered if you'd seen anything out there.' I too look out across the water, half expecting to see a pale figure looking back at me; a pale figure untroubled by the cold or the waves.

There's an old story about a spirit . . .

She gives me an odd look. Perhaps the captain *has* been talking. 'You know, it's easy to imagine things at sea. But if there was anything at all, it would have showed on the radar. We're not entirely cut off from modern life here, you know. Are you guys okay?'

I hesitate. 'Fine. Andy's skinned his hands, but he thinks he'll manage.'

'I'll get the first aider to check him over. Sorry if that squall gave you a scare. It was unexpected. It wasn't forecast, though it does happen sometimes.'

I nod, and there's a long pause before she speaks again. 'While we're on it, though – did you hear something, before it started?'

I can't reply and she doesn't wait, just shakes her head. 'Just a stupid superstition. I thought I heard a whistle – really clear, though really, it could have been anything. Sound can travel oddly out here. It's just weird, though – sailors used to ban whistling at sea. They said it challenged the wind, that it raises storms. And the fact that it happened just in that spot—'

'Why?' I try for a neutral tone. 'What is it about that place?'

'Ah – nothing. It's just, I first heard of that superstition in the same story that tells about the preceptory. Of course, it doesn't mean anything. It was all made up.'

'Which story?'

'It's by M. R. James. A ghost story. It's not even supposed to be set here; it was further down the coast. Still, I do wonder if he relocated it. How many preceptories can there be? It's just a weird coincidence.'

I could only agree that it was, and move to obey her instructions; to get out of sight of that cold grey sea.

Then she says, 'Now all we need is the whistle.'

'A what?' My throat is full of dust – or perhaps salt.

'O, Whistle, and I'll Come to You, My Lad,' she says. 'That was the story. A fellow finds an old whistle at a preceptory, blows it, and he's haunted, *followed*, until he chucks it back into the sea. Or his mate does it for him; I can't remember. There's this bit – he wakes up and finds this ghost thing in the bed next to his.' She shudders, and I'm no longer sure if it's real or pretend. 'Night, then.'

Into the sea, I think. So the whistle in the story wasn't even put back in the preceptory – but perhaps the sea had carried it back again? Or that figure beneath the waves had found it, at least until I came along...

I shake my head. *It was all made up.*

Down below, the others have already turned in; we're lying in hammocks, not beds. I peer along the row of pod-like shapes, the canvas emerging palely from the dark. Most of them are empty.

I take the whistle from my pocket. I should throw this back into the sea, but the truth is, I don't want to. I turn it in my hands and run my fingertips over the inscription. I already know I can't give it back. It's the only buried treasure I'm ever likely to find; I won't give it up for nothing but a story.

I half climb, half fall into the hammock, and cradle the whistle until my eyes close. The metal is silky under my touch, though cold, and it's still cold when I awake in the dark, what must be hours later. I tighten my fingers around it and listen. I'd heard something, hadn't I? Now there is not a creak of a timber or a footstep on the deck over my head. Still, I know that someone is there.

The hammock rocks with my movement as I push myself up and turn my head to the next one, which had previously hung loose and empty. Now a shape swells its sides.

I stare, telling myself someone simply came to bed after I did. But who? The lads were asleep before me. The other couples had claimed hammocks on the other side of the ship.

So no one is sleeping there. The nearest person is Andy, and there are two empty hammocks between us. But the canvas does not subside. It doesn't sag or collapse in on itself as it rocks, gently, with the ship's movement.

Then a shape sits up in it.

Long moments. Long, long moments.

Then it turns towards me and I see that its skin is the colour of old canvas. Its clothing – robes? – are the same off-white hue, like the seabed; like death. The word that comes to me is *Filthy*. I don't or can't look away. I can't blink and I can't stop seeing him. In my mind's eye, he's turning still. He's clambering down, stepping towards me, reaching for me, touching me. If he does that, if he does it *now*, I'm going to go insane. I'll have to peel off my skin. *Filthy*.

The figure twists. I'd pictured his movements as slow, staccato, his limbs stick-like, but he is not; he is lithe and quick. A new word comes to me: *shroud*. That's what his garment is, I realise, fish-nibbled into shreds around the rough stitching. Within, I glimpse corruption: withered limbs; desiccated skin; hollow sockets where his eyes should be. Blind, yet seeing me anyway – or just knowing, somehow, that I am there.

I cover my eyes, realise I'm still clutching the whistle. I should give it to him, but still I clutch it to me, tightening my grip on the cold and unyielding bronze. I open my eyes once more and the hammock next to mine is empty. Only shadows hang between the dark beams, shifting with the movement of the ship.

The next morning there is a briefing, all crews on deck, ready to be have the holiday atmosphere restored. There are bacon sandwiches and cups of strong coffee that do little to make me feel awake. I didn't sleep again last night; I didn't dare to close my eyes.

The captain says that if we're to make berth on time we need to make good progress north, and for now, we're all on duty. The professional crew had set the sails during the night and we're moving at a fair clip. I wonder how far behind us we have left the preceptory.

I take up my role as lookout as instructed, and that's how I see the trail of footprints leading across the deck. They're wet and glistening, prints made by bare feet – or was it bone?

'All right?' Jane is at my shoulder and all I can do is point.

She watches my hand shake, catches hold of it, says again more quietly: 'Really – are you all right?'

'The raft,' I say. 'I saw it, in the storm. Someone must have boarded us. It – he – could still be here.'

She looks exasperated, then sighs. 'Come with me.'

She leads me below, to a room I've seen only once before: the captain's dining room. She goes to a cupboard built into the fake mahogany, but that is fake too; she lifts the top and it all folds back, like a bureau. Instead of quills and ink, it reveals a bank of electronic equipment. Its lights cast a sickly glow over the wood.

'Welcome to the present,' she says. 'All mod cons. If anyone had come close, we'd know. If there was a raft, we'd know. We'd even know it if a seal looked at us the wrong way.'

I stare at the incongruous lights just as the beep begins to stutter. Instead of its regular rhythm there comes a high-pitched sound, a little like feedback, but sweeter, truer. It is the sound of a whistle, soft and yet piercing and *there*.

Jane scowls, tapping the screen with the flat of her hand. When she turns back to me, there's an overly bright look on her face. 'You see? All good here.'

I nod, as if to assure her that we are.

While the others remain on deck, I sneak back down below. I have to be sure; I need to know if the sound of the whistle just came to me out of the ship's monitors. How could it have? It's only a whistle. It isn't magical; it isn't *haunted*.

Once I'm alone, I raise the metal to my lips. This time I blow strongly, though the sound that emerges is as soft as before, as if it didn't really need me at all; it still sounds as distant, and nothing at all happens, yet I cannot doubt that it is heard. I imagine everyone on the ship stopping what they are doing and turning to listen; then turning to each other to see that yes, it was real, they heard it too.

Wind blusters against the hull.

This time it is no surprise to feel the deck rocking under me, as if in protest. It isn't strange to hear the snap of canvas, followed by a cry of alarm. The storm is rising and soon we will be driven before it. We will go where we need to be.

Andy stumbles down the steep steps, looks about. When he sees me, he seems relieved. 'Batten down the hatches, mate,' he says. 'Looks like another squall.'

I raise my head to him and I smile.

I don't hold on, don't batten down any hatches. I sit at the bench with my eyes closed and listen to the wind scream. Occasionally, the rattle of boards makes me think someone is close, that they have come to me, but when I open my eyes no one is there.

I find myself standing on the deck. I am drenched through, my hair plastered to my skull. I don't need to look out across the steel-grey sea to know it is there; it always has been.

The wind's icy needles pierce my skin. Slowly, I become aware of the crew, wrestling to stow the sails. Their dark forms are dotted about the rigging like rats. One of the sails has ripped. Tatters fly loose; they look like a half-open burial shroud. Someone screams something into the wind, but the words are whipped away.

I cannot see the shore, but still, I know where we are – where we are meant to be. I look down and the whistle is clutched in my hand. It has brought us home. We are back at the preceptory, where everything began.

I walk to the rail, my steps sure despite the wash of ankle-deep water, and lean over the side into the heaving darkness. This time there is no mistaking the pale face looking back at me. When I draw back, it echoes my movement – is it only a glimpse of my own future?

I am the Jonah. I have trespassed; I've brought misfortune upon the ship. Once I am thrown overboard, the seas will calm. The others will be alright.

I climb up onto the rail, kneel precariously for a moment – a man before an altar – and then I let go.

The water welcomes me in. It is sucking and grasping, and cold; endlessly cold. Then something catches hold of my leg and drags me under. The sea closes over my head and I picture its surface becoming smooth and opaque once more, just as if it had never been broken. Then there are hands, all around; catching at my clothes, my limbs, twining into my hair. Below, I glimpse a circle – a circle made of stone.

Then another hand yanks me upward, and the surface is shattered. I heave in a breath that is as sweet as sunshine, as grateful as life. Salt clogs my throat and I cough it out of me. When I'm done choking I realise I'm back on the deck, and Jane and the captain and Andy and the others are leaning over me. I look past them, into the sails, but they are furled; there is no desiccated face in the ruined canvas. I put a hand to my pocket. The whistle I had placed there is gone.

The sky is a weak, watery blue as we pull into port, though the sun is still low in the sky. Soon it will rise and chase away the last shreds of cloud. Our journey is over.

As we near the dock, I think back to the day I'd decided to come here. I had told myself it would be an adventure, a new experience; something real. The fact was, I'd been under pressure from the lads to come up with something, so I'd flicked through the paper, seen an advert for this voyage and thought it would do. Had anything that happened in my life over the last few years been deliberate? Had it meant anything at all? And yet I *had* discovered reality of a kind, though it was nothing I'd anticipated; nothing I'd imagined.

The others stand at the rail, a short distance away. It's as if they feel my separateness and are mapping it out without a thought. I hear them laughing, becoming more themselves as they approach the shore. Andy has already sworn he's never going to sea again. He's said he'll stick to golfing holidays in future.

I run my fingers through my hair, rub my hands on my t-shirt. After they pulled me from the water, I'd stood under the shower for a long time, trying to get warm. Still, salt has permeated everything. My shirt feels stiff as a shroud. My skin scarcely feels like it belongs to a living thing.

I wish I couldn't still hear the furl and snap of sail, the creak of wood and of ropes in their pulleys, the insistent tap of water against the hull. My eyes are fixed on the land: unshifting and solid, or so we like to imagine. I try not to think of the waves etching away at the shore, stealing from it moment by moment.

There are people walking along the promenade, happy, at leisure. Behind them are brightly coloured shops, the gaudy lights of amusement arcades. Rising away from them is the town, people in their houses living their lives, oblivious to the things that lie, monstrous and unknowable, beneath the sea. A woman sits on her balcony, one hand shading her eyes as she watches the pretty ship coming into dock. Seagulls squabble for nesting places amid the chimneys. Flowers glow from the gardens. Washing flaps in the breeze, snapping like the sails over my head, and I look away as church bells begin to mark the hour. There is an unpleasant sound beneath the mellow chimes; an *after-sound*, soft and breathy and distant. I wonder if I will always hear it.

I scan the shore again and am drawn back to the garden hung with sheets. Had I glimpsed a face, momentarily, amid their creases and furls? I tell myself that it was only my fear forming shapes in my mind, and anyway, it has already gone.

Except it hasn't, has it? Because I can see it everywhere.

It stands among the people wandering the promenade. It waits by the dock, where tourists are eating ice creams. It haunts the corner of every garden, the threshold of every home. It is close. It waits, not just for me, but for all of us – all the unthinking throng, as bright and as temporary as fireflies. The fortunate ones look out at the cold and endless sea and see only the cheerful blue of holidays. One day, they will see beneath: that endless seabed, lifeless as dust; as empty as loneliness, stretching on and on for ever.

I know now that this thing is not *following*. It is not *haunting*. I did not summon it with my whistle or the breath in my lungs. It is simply there. It has always been there. And some day, it will touch. It will cling. It will look into my eyes with those hollow sockets and I will know; the face I had glimpsed beneath the water was only ever a reflection of my own.

|The Light You Can Hear|

~

It's already a blue dusk when we arrive, and I have to check my watch to assure myself it isn't yet 3 p.m. The sun was beginning to set when our plane landed on the white-over runway at Kiruna, the only airport in the world that boasts a taxi rank for dog sleds. We didn't take a sled, though. Instead we boarded the coach for Jukkasjärvi, its name a Sami word meaning *meeting place by the water*, and Jen put her hand in mine and squeezed. We were a world away from home and somehow that made it all right to smile as we passed the monochrome landscape: white roads, black trees, snow falling out of the sky in thick flakes. Only the shadows were blue: stretching, grasping for each other, growing deeper by the minute.

Now a girl in an insulated silver cape points the way to reception, in one of the warm buildings. There, we're told we've been allocated the receptionist's favourite room: it's special, she grins, though she won't tell us what's in it. That will be a surprise. There's no key, only a dull-sounding number; 215, just as if it was an ordinary room in an ordinary place. We already know that Icehotel Sweden isn't ordinary. Our fellow travellers head off to find lockers and to borrow capes and gloves, but I haven't seen such eagerness in Jen's eyes for so long that I take her hand again and we go straight off to find where we'll spend the night.

The snow that makes the land so quiet also makes people loud; we crunch-squeak down the path outside, under the first stars. The snow has thinned and specks fall through the cones of light marking our way, turning to showers of silver glitter. There's a tower in front of us. It's all blues and greens, made entirely of ice, and it glows from within. We climb the narrow spiralling steps to the top and look out over the permanent buildings, and the other: the one that only exists for four months of the year. That's where we're headed. We don't speak. Jen's smile is enough. That other look, the one that tells me we're not allowed to smile any longer, that we could never smile, not *since* – that hasn't appeared and I allow myself to relax.

Then there's a white mound like a giant igloo with an arch cut into it, and double entrance doors clothed in reindeer hide. We've seen them on TV and in brochures. Jen is the first to push them wide and peer at the wonders within.

There's a corridor made entirely of snow, formed into a catenary arch that stretches away towards a central hall. No one else is there; only glistening ice pillars, tantalising with their glister. A walkway made of ice leads down the centre and we could go around, stay on the floor of compressed snow, but instead we step onto it. It feels ceremonial, a rite of passage: *We're here*. It's as slippery as it looks and we run gloved hands along the rail, which is also made of ice, until we reach the centre: an ice platform edged by ice chairs, set beneath the icy teardrops of an impossible chandelier.

New corridors stretch away, white, tunnel-like, light gleaming through the walls to tempt us onward. It's made of magic and cleverness and the cold and I wonder that I'd once imagined all the most beautiful places in the world to be natural. Now I see that people can make something beautiful too.

We wander along the corridors to the guest rooms. We explore them all, entering through narrow openings cut into snow walls, masked with hanging curtains rather than doors. Each room is unique. Each is special; each a glistening gallery of sculptures. We marvel at a circus made of ice. We stand on the seabed, surrounded by snow-fish and snow-mermaids. White snow-lions glare at us with transparent eyes, lit with blue. Walls curve and ripple. The ice is all colours: cloudy with opaque cracks running through it; azure, bright with hidden light; the turquoise of tropical seas; the deepest blue of polar twilight; as pure and transparent as the air.

We find a room where ice-ants burst from holes cut into the snow and surround the bed, and we look at each other and laugh. We hope whoever's sleeping here isn't freaked out. All the rooms are booked, the receptionist had said so; they won't be able to swap. We wonder again what ours will be like.

Then we're outside room 215. A plaque of carved river ice tells us its name: The Light You Can Hear. We go inside and I know this whole thing was a terrible mistake.

The air is full of colour and sound. Soft greens play across one wall, a wavering glow that must represent the Northern Lights. As we watch, the light turns purple, then pink. But this room isn't just ice: it's also water. A frozen river is carved around the walls, its rippling form seeming almost to shift with the sound we can hear all around us. The noise is at once many things and unrecognisable. It's the hiss and crackle of meltwater; it's snow blowing across the hills; it's the wind in the stunted pines of the boreal forest.

The reason this trip was a mistake is standing at the edge of the river. The snow-child is life-sized, their back turned, a hood covering their head, which is tilted to gaze up at the dancing lights. I can't see their face but somehow I know they're young, about eight years old. And I know it's a boy.

Jen stands at my side, impassive. She's staring, not at the lights, but at the child, who looks as if he might at any moment walk into the river.

'We can go back,' I say, without pausing to consider my words. *Stupid. That's the one thing we can't do.* I start again. 'We can ask at reception – swap, if you don't like it? Maybe the ants.'

She closes her eyes. 'They're all full.' Her voice is distant, as if she's already moved far, far away from me in her mind. 'They said so, remember?'

She turns and smiles and she's back again. 'Anyway, it's perfect. Of course, we'll stay.'

And so we examine the room more closely. The sinuously carved river must represent the Torne, we decide, for that is what the hotel is made of: it's the stretch of water that gave Jukkasjärvi its name. When we turn, we find there's an elk jutting from the wall behind us. Its antlers spread wide, purest white, becoming spirals that reach across the heavens. A diamond of transparent ice marks his forehead and I have the odd sense that he's watching us; that he sees everything.

Then there's the bed. That too is made of ice, strewn with reindeer hides and roped off, since it isn't yet time to sleep. As I have since we booked this trip, I feel misgivings at the thought of spending the night in a room made of ice. Jen doesn't seem concerned, or to think of it at all; I'd asked her if she was cold when we stepped off the coach and she'd only shrugged. She hadn't felt it then and doesn't comment on it now and I know what she would say if the truth be told: that the cold crept into her months ago. It crept into her and didn't leave, and she didn't feel it because she can't feel anything, not any longer.

She turns and stares at the child – who doesn't respond, doesn't move; of course he doesn't. She murmurs, 'The Sami believe the land of the dead is beneath the water, did you know that? If you caught sight of it you'd be able to see everything there, just like it is in the world of the living, but in reverse. A mirror.'

I don't know what to say. I don't like the way her thoughts are tending. We came here to escape, to be somewhere else, *something* else, if only for a time.

Then she grabs my arm. 'Did you hear that?'

I realise that the sound has swelled around us, without my noticing. The static crackle has given way to a soft whistling, almost but not quite like music, and there's something else: an almost breathy undercurrent, a little like a voice. I find myself trying to make out words hidden within it.

'That's the sound the Northern Lights make.' Jen sounds excited. 'Some say the light is silent, that it's impossible for it to make a sound, but plenty have heard it. That's why the Sami call it *the light you can hear*.'

I try to smile but somehow can't.

'The land of the dead.' Jen's grip tightens on my arm. 'Sami legend says the Northern Lights are actually souls, did you know that? They bring the dead close to us. If you listen, sometimes, you're supposed to be able to hear them whispering.'

She goes back to staring at the child, his back turned, his face hidden, and I have no idea what I'm supposed to say.

The time comes to prepare for our trip and we stand at the activity desk in another of the warm buildings, equipment piled in front of us: black overalls bearing the Icehotel logo, balaclavas, gloves like oven mitts, boots fit for a Victorian diver. We're gathering it all in our arms when I think to ask about the soundscape in room 215. I'm not sure the staff member will know anything about it, but she nods.

'It was recorded outside.' Her name badge says Lucia and her accent is Spanish: people come from all over to be at this tiny village in the north of Sweden, staff and guests alike. 'They're sounds from the Arctic landscape.'

Jen turns to me with something like triumph in her eyes, which fades as I say, 'It was an interesting idea – to add the whispers.'

Jen frowns, and Lucia doesn't answer; she only gives me an odd look as we make our way to the booth we've been allocated for getting changed and storing our luggage. Jen and I shuffle around each other in the narrow space. The overalls are thick and awkward, the boots likewise. Lucia had told us to wear our own coats underneath it all and we're instantly boiling, though she'd assured us we'll be glad of them later. With relief at being in the cold again, we stomp outside to find the snowmobiles.

They're parked around the back, past the warm cabins some choose to stay in, and the stores; we spot the great metal forms used to mould the hotel's corridors, all stacked together, ready for next time. We're given helmets and instructions. I take the handlebars and we're off – juddering over compacted snow, heading into the dead cold of the Arctic Circle under the endless black of the sky. Our headlights cut into the night, showing the snow in front of us, and beyond that only the faint paleness of hills in the distance, the dark of the trees. There's no sound but the engine. No lights dance over our heads; we've already checked the Aurora forecast, been told there's no chance of seeing anything, not tonight. I think a part of me is relieved.

Pretty soon, we stop and the guide checks we're OK. He taps the ground with his foot and tells us that we're standing in the middle of the Torne River. I'd never have known it was there, though perhaps I should have; its flatness gives it away. Beyond it is only the night and the cold of almost the northernmost part of the planet and I feel how small we are, with our tiny lights and little engines and fragile beating hearts. Perhaps I feel something of what it would be like to be alone out here: to simply walk out into the whole uncaring nothing and be lost.

I picture the water flowing somewhere beneath me, as black as the sky above, and am suddenly dizzy. A picture rises: our son being dragged from the reeds, his pale skin stained with waterweed and mud and slime. I blink it away. There's nothing here to show there's even a river at all. There's no mud, no weeds. Everything is pure and white and clean, the air so cold it could cut, and I pull it deep into my lungs.

The guide tells us about the Torne. He talks about it as if it's land, something to be harvested and tended: an ice field. Each winter they clear the snow from sections of the ice to allow it to thicken and grow. In the spring, they harvest. Huge blocks of ice are cut and hauled into storage, to keep until the following winter, when they're used to construct the hotel. Then the whole thing melts, returning to the river, and the cycle begins again.

I picture my son in the water, flowing away with the current, returning to – what? But then, that's not what happened. He hadn't gone with the river but had been pulled under, caught in the weeds, and I picture the brightness of his eyes peering up through layers of water that are murky and brown. He'd gone to play with his friends. They weren't supposed to go near the river, but that hadn't stopped them. I suppose he'd felt the pull of it.

The snowmobile engine roars again in my ears. I don't recognise the point when we leave the water but we must do, because soon we're in the forest, and there's nothing but branches around us, heavy and distorted with snow.

The next time we stop, the guide gets us to switch off our engines and remove our helmets and balaclavas, and he checks us for frostbite by shining a torch in our faces. He encourages us to jump around to warm up – Lucia was right, it's fifteen below and we're glad of our coats – and then he tells us to listen.

There's nothing. There is only silence coming through the trees, silence for miles; silence for ever. I have heard such silence before, I realise. It's the same silence that came to fill the house. The silence that emerged from his room at night; the silence of air that had once moved in and out of his lungs; the silence of deep, deep water. It had settled between us, this silence that lies beneath everything, and we had listened. It came from his seat at breakfast, his absence on the sofa, in front of the TV, at dinner; everywhere.

Now it has a different quality, a new texture, as if it's changed into something almost magical. It isn't altogether empty; not altogether dead. There's a sense of waiting emerging from beneath the trees and all around us, and I half expect to see him standing among them: perfectly silent, perfectly still, a little figure with his hood raised and his back turned, his head tilted to stare up into the black and empty sky.

When we return, it's time to sleep on our bed of ice. We've swapped our overalls, gloves and boots for thick sleeping bags, together with thin liners that must save on hotel laundry. We joke that we may not have seen the Northern Lights, but at least they're in our room, though I'm still not certain I like the idea. We go to room 215 and I stand back to let Jen enter before me, the bundle in her arms almost too wide for the doorway. She shuffles in sideways and her footsteps crunch across the floor, then stop. I hear her voice; she sounds surprised.

'Hey,' she says, then I realise it was *hej*: Swedish for *hello*.

I follow her in and there is a little boy standing in front of her, wearing a bright red coat. His back is turned. He's standing right behind the snow-child, and they're both watching the same thing: the lights, which are pink now, the sound of them wavering and hissing.

Then a man's voice cuts the air. 'Lars,' he calls out, forming a little *shh* at the end of the name, and the boy grins and runs past us, returning to wherever he should be. For an instant, I envy his father; then I focus on the child carved into the ice and he is forgotten.

The boy has changed. He isn't looking up at the lights any longer, but has half turned towards us. He's still wearing his hood, though it has fallen back far enough to see the lick of hair hanging over his forehead – as familiar as home, but on the wrong side; his hair always hung over his left eye, and now it's over his right.

He looks at me through eyes made of the river.

If you caught sight of it you'd be able to see everything there, just like it is in the world of the living, but in reverse. A mirror.

Jen has dropped her sleeping bag at her feet. She goes to the boy and kneels on the frozen ground next to him. She starts to reach for him, but I don't want her to touch him and grasp her fingers. She doesn't seem conscious of my touch, just keeps on staring at the face of her son, inexplicably *here*, half emerging from the ice; or is he half submerged?

I try to tell myself the sculpture always looked like that – because it had to have, didn't it? The transparency of ice confuses the eye sometimes, that's all. I'd got it wrong, and so had Jen – who is now staring around her, at the light that constantly shifts and dances. No: she's listening. I wonder what she hears. Snow, blowing like spindrift over a hillside? Meltwater beginning to flow? Or is it the whispering coming from somewhere beyond them – or the silence that lies beneath even that?

We don't speak as I shake my head and she stirs. There's nothing we can say to each other. We spread out our sleeping bags and zip ourselves into them. There's a switch on a half -hidden panel behind the bed that says *Night Mode*. I press it and the lights slow, waver, begin to die. The sound fades with them, the quiet flooding in to take its place. The last thing I see are the boy's eyes: in the gathering dark they appear almost real, tiny lights still burning at their heart.

Sometime during the night, I wake. I have the weirdest feeling that I'm outside, lying on the frozen river, listening to the silence all around me. It seems that there is peace in it, but now and then I sense a stirring; as if someone is trying to whisper in my ear, their breath too quickly lost to the cold. Perhaps it is only some small shifting in the ice I sense: settling, cracking, breathing, as it prepares to melt back into water; as it dreams of the river.

Then I remember where I am – though of course, we are still in the river. The hotel is made of it after all; hewed from the body of the frozen Torne. Does the land of the dead lie somewhere beneath? Perhaps; but for now we're cradled within, suspended at its heart, almost but not quite hearing the secrets it whispers. Someday, perhaps we will. Everything must melt eventually.

I picture the great elk staring at us from out of the darkness, his gaze impassive, no emotion I can recognise in his eyes. I shiver, though my face is the only part of me that is cold. I pull my sleeping bag up around my head so that my breath will warm the inside, and allow myself to slip under once more.

~

We're awoken on schedule at seven in the morning by a member of staff bearing a tray of warm lingonberry juice. He grins and passes me a cup, and blearily, I thank him. I'm warm inside the sleeping bag and don't want to sit up, but I do. I look over at Jen, ready to pass her a cup, but she isn't there.

'Jen?'

I call as if she too will awake, sit up, blink the sleep from her eyes. Her sleeping bag is there, the liner pulled loose, presumably from when she stepped out of it. She isn't in the room. There's only the elk: massive, totemic, antlers stretching over everything.

The guy with the juice grins, says my wife must have been hungry and headed off for an early breakfast. He bends to the panel that controls the light and sound and starts the program running again, and then he leaves.

I push myself up. Our shoes are there, Jen's and mine, side by side next to the bed, where we left them.

I turn towards the child. The Northern Lights have begun their dance across the ice once more, but the boy is gone. He isn't watching the lights or staring at us with gleaming eyes, his hair falling across the wrong side of his face. I step towards the wall that isn't really a wall. There is no sculpture, not even a trace of where the boy had been, and suddenly I know that if I go to reception and ask about the vanishing snow-child, they'll think I'm mad. They'll tell me that there is no child in the room, there never was; not here.

I stare into the ice. Dimly, as if glimpsing a shadow far, far distant, something moves within it: a form rippling in the depths. No: there are *two* figures, flowing away side by side. One is taller than the other, and their arms are outstretched; they are holding hands.

I close my eyes and think of the river. We can take its body and give it shape, turning it into something we understand, but still it slips away from us, drop by drop. Because people can make something beautiful, they can shape it and cling to it and try so very hard to hold onto it, but it doesn't stay. And we forget they are not ours, these things; that they will leave us and return to wherever it was they came from.

They will return to the river. And all water is connected.

Jen knew it before I did. She saw everything, but then, she was frozen long before we came here. Our son had once been wrapped around her heart, had kept her warm, and without him she was exposed; she had so very quickly turned to ice.

The whispering comes from all around me. It is clear to me now; as clear as anything in this world.

I stretch out my hand towards the ice. I don't touch it, not yet, but I feel the cold on my skin, exuding from it like a breath. I no longer know what I will find under my fingertips when I reach forward. I close my eyes and realise that the whispering has ceased, but I no longer need to hear it; I never did. There is only the dark. There is only the waiting silence.

|Here Be Birds of the Air|

|Black Feathers|

~

There was a raven at the edge of the woods. It was huge – even its beak looked as long as Mia's fingers. She stared at it and Little Davey laughed at her. Mia wrinkled her nose. Little Davey was younger than her by a year, but he wasn't that little any more. He was as tall as she was and twice as loud, and he rode a bike much quicker than she could. He stood in front of her now, him and Sam Oakey and Jack Harris from down the road, and Sarah Farnham who was more like a boy than one of the boys. Mia stared at the raven. She didn't want to go into the woods, could smell its rank green warmth even from here. It was loaded with dark, with mystery, with her brother's mocking laughter as he turned his bike towards the trees.

'Come on,' he said. 'Last one in's a chicken.' He started pedalling and the others followed him one by one, Sarah giving a ring of her bicycle bell, but none of them saying a word.

Mia stared after them. Davey knew she didn't like the woods. She didn't like the way the branches closed over her head, making it impossible to know which way was in and which way was out. She knew he only went in there because of her fear; and because it was forbidden.

The thought of forbidden things reminded Mia of her fairy tales. Somewhere deep in the woods would be a castle circled by thorns that could put you to sleep with a single scratch. She reminded herself that a princess wouldn't be afraid. Princesses were never afraid, and she was much more a princess than Sarah Farnham.

With that, Mia turned her own bike towards the woods. The raven let out a dry, rasping burr, the sound a chain might make as it slipped from its sprockets. Then the bird took to wing, lifting its heavy bulk into the air. Its eyes were sharp bright points and Mia thought it eyed her as it flew, but couldn't work out what the look was meant to say. She paused, though, to pick up the thing it left for her – a single, gloss-dark feather – before following the others into the trees.

~

She heard them up ahead, shouting and laughing. Davey's laugh was loudest of all, and Mia's heart sank. For as long as she could remember, she had been wishing that Little Davey was different. Sometimes she had even tried to turn him into something else. One of her first memories was her mother pulling her off him, laughing because Mia loved her brother so very much she wouldn't stop showering him with kisses. If a frog could be turned into a prince for the simple kissing, Mia had thought, perhaps this mewling thing could be turned into a frog. It stood to reason. It was worth the sour milk smell that clung to her clothes, the feel of his faintly damp, peeling scalp on her lips.

After that, whenever Mia blew out her candles or wished upon a star, she always wished for Davey to change.

Now he stood in front of everybody, leaning out over the place where the banking fell away. They weren't supposed to come here. Mainly they didn't want to, because this was where the bigger kids played; sometimes they found cigarette butts or crushed beer cans, still with foul smells trapped inside. There were no big kids here today though; there was only the swing. The swing was a rope tied around a tree branch, with three fat knots at different heights to sit on. And there was Davey, right on the edge of the banking, the rope held in his hand.

'Don't,' said Mia, and the others laughed. But Mia saw what they didn't. The rope was too high for him. He could touch it, but he wouldn't be able to sit; even the lowest knot was barely within his reach. He'd swing wild, holding on with only his hands, and he'd let go. Mia knew what lay beneath. The banking ended. After that it was a sheer drop, nothing but mud walls and broken branches waiting in the bottom. Old leaves and slimy things, long-legged things. She swallowed. It was up to her; she was supposed to look after him. She was, after all, the eldest.

Once, Mia had made a potion out of all the nasty things she could find, dust and dirt and a hair she found next to the toilet. She mushed them all up with water and gave it to him in their father's sports bottle, so he couldn't see what was inside. Then she wished Little Davey dead.

She hadn't really wanted him dead. She knocked the bottle out of his hand before Davey could drink it. He had cried and run to Mum, and Mia got into trouble; or rather, Miranda had. Mia was always *Miranda* when someone was angry with her.

Miranda was Mia's real name. It wasn't a name fit for a princess. If anyone called Mia Miranda, she wouldn't answer, wouldn't even look at them. Even Davey called her Mia. Miranda was not the name of someone who could work magic. Mia sometimes wondered what happened to the spell she wove that day, when it missed its target and fell to the ground with the bottle.

Little Davey let go of the rope and stepped back. Then, impossibly, he launched himself out over the space. His hands reached, grasping the rope high. It moved with him and his legs followed, trying to catch up. And then he *was* sitting on it, and not even at its lowest; he was sitting on the middle knot, his face split by an enormous grin. Mia caught her breath. And she knew she had been right: the rope *was* too high for him, but Davey, with his courage, had made it fit. He had worked his own magic with his recklessness, taken a little of the world and made himself its king. She found herself grinning too, looked around at the others; but they weren't looking at Mia. Their eyes were fixed on her brother as he swung higher and higher, and they were all smiling.

Mia put her hands in her pocket and felt the smooth feather. If she stroked it one way it was like glass; if she rubbed it the other it was rough and caught in her fingers. She could feel it splitting, each thread parting from the next in a way she would never be able to put back together. She did it anyway, thinking of the raven and the way it had looked at her, its beady black eyes.

Mia had always wanted Davey to be a girl. They could have been princesses together. Of course, all the stories favoured the younger sister, but Mia wouldn't be like the older girls in tales – proud, haughty, cast aside when the prince came along. Her little sister would have looked up to her, astonished by her beauty and cleverness. The prince wouldn't have had eyes for anyone else.

After a while Davey got down from the swing and Sam Oakey had a go, and then Jack said he couldn't be bothered but Sarah tried it and so Jack did too. Each of them held onto the rope with both hands and pushed out over the drop; no one managed to get seated the way Little Davey had. None of them seemed to expect Mia to try, and she didn't care. Instead she spread herself on the grass, pretending she wore some great sparkling gown. What princess would go on a swing like that? She waited until it was time to go, and rode back with them through the woods, and the others said goodbye and headed away.

'What did you think of that?' Davey asked.

Mia scowled and turned to him. What she saw, though, wasn't Davey the pain; it almost wasn't like her little brother at all. He still had a glow that lit him up from the inside. She remembered the way he'd leapt out over nothing, the small spell he'd woven there in the woods, and she found herself smiling.

'It was pretty cool,' she said. 'Really cool.'

Davey looked surprised, and then he smiled back.

'It was like you were flying,' she said, and she fingered the feather in her pocket.

Mia went outside and headed towards the woods. She looked for the raven and he wasn't there but she saw that he had left more feathers for her. She picked them up and put them in her bag. Then she looked into the trees. She had thought she would be more afraid, but she was not. It was easy to hide when you were alone, and besides, she had the feathers. She scanned the ground for them, found one among the exposed roots of a tree. She went on, looking for the next; it led her into a bramble patch and she stepped carefully, picking the black thing out with care. She was following a trail, she realised, like Hansel and Gretel, but this time it was the birds which had left it instead of eating it up.

She found another feather beneath a curling fern, then a whole pile of them on a knoll of grass. It was as if they had been left for her to find, as though the birds knew what she needed. Mia looked up. There must be a lot of ravens living in these woods. She wondered if they were watching her now through their little black eyes. She swallowed, but forced herself to go on. It wasn't so bad. There wasn't much time to be afraid when there was something you really needed to do.

Mia's favourite story was *The Six Swans*. A maiden's brothers were bewitched and had to live their lives as birds. So the maid wove them special shirts to turn them back again, and it worked, except she hadn't time enough to make the youngest brother's sleeve and he was left with a swan's wing for an arm. The sister loved them dearly, and was dutiful and kind all her days; she married the king and lived happily ever after.

There weren't any swans near Mia's house, but there were ravens. And she knew they were good, really, that they had looked after her and Davey on that day in the woods. She knew because she had dreamed of it. In her dream, her little brother Davey leapt for the rope, and his fingers brushed by it, making it shiver. Then he started to fall.

He fell until there came a loud rasp like a chain coming free, and the raven swept in and bore Davey up. It saved him from the sharp branches and the long fall and the slimy wriggling things that waited, and carried him over the treetops and far away.

Mia took some glue and spread it on the fabric. It had been a skirt, but she had taken her mother's scissors and cut it so that it looked like a cloak. She knew her mother would be angry, but Mia had never liked the skirt, and anyway, it was black; that was good, because it wouldn't show if she missed a bit.

She pressed a feather into the glue. It shone for a moment, blue and green and white before returning to black, and she felt a throb of excitement. Davey would love this. He would be king of the air. She had always wanted to turn him into something else, but she knew by the tingle in her fingers that this time it would be different.

Mia led Davey along the path to the woods. He huffed and puffed, kicking at loose sticks. She turned and put a finger to her lips. 'It'll be great, Davey. You'll see.' She smiled at him, and it must have been a good smile because he tossed his head and half-smiled back.

She picked her way down the path, following old footprints and bicycle tracks. There weren't any feathers, she noticed that as she went, and that was a sign; the ravens had gifted the feathers just for her, and for her alone. Now they were done, and it was up to her, Mia, to do the rest.

She carried a bundle under her arm. It was bulky and Davey had cast odd glances at it as they set off, almost as though he knew.

The others hadn't been near the woods and that was another sign, a good one. This was a thing for her and her brother, the one she had been dutiful for, had thought of all the time she had been making the cloak. That was why it would work: because she'd put herself into it, all the care for him she could muster. Davey would see that. He would appreciate the time she'd spent, her caring.

She led the way towards the swing and Davey turned on her. 'Well? What is it?'

Mia ignored his words. She took the bundle and unrolled the fabric. She straightened it. And the cloak shone, but it wasn't like she'd imagined, some soft, glowing, magical thing. There were spaces between the feathers and in the bright light of day you could see the gaps, dull and glue-spotted. Feathers were falling off, or had split when she'd rolled it. At the top, where she'd tried to make a collar, you could see it was only a waistband after all.

Little Davey wrinkled his nose. 'What's that?'

'I made it for you, Davey. So you can fly. It's special.'

'It's a skirt.'

'No, Davey, it's not. I mean, it was a skirt. Now it's a cloak, and I made it for you, because...'

But Mia could no longer think why she had made it. She looked at the thing in her hands and saw it was a sorry thing, a poor thing. It wasn't something you would give to someone as a gift. Not something that could hold magic within it.

'It stinks.'

'It doesn't.' But Mia realised it did stink, a mixture of bird and glue that almost burned her nostrils. She wondered why she hadn't noticed it before. She turned the cloak, trying to make the feathers catch the light. Some of them did and she looked at Davey, hoping he'd seen. She winced when she saw his eyes. He was rolling them, as if looking at something ridiculous. He was rolling them at her and the start of something painful rose in her chest.

Davey laughed. He put his hands on his hips and leaned into it, and she heard how he forced the sound out, making it as loud as he could.

'You idiot,' he said. 'Oh, you idiot. Wait till I tell the others.'

Mia's cheeks flooded with heat. 'Davey, no.' She looked down at her work. It was already ruined. Feathers fell from it to the ground. And she heard something coming towards them through the woods: the ching, ching of a bicycle bell. She looked at Davey in alarm.

'Go on the swing,' he said.

'What?' Mia glanced at the old rope hanging down over nothing.

'Go on the swing and I won't tell.'

Davey smiled a slow smile and Mia wished, harder than she had ever wished before, that he would turn into something else: anything else.

The sound came closer. She looked down at the feathered mess at her feet. She couldn't bear the thought of the others laughing at the work of her hands, throwing it between them, scattering the birds' gifts. She picked it up and ran towards the swing. She heard Davey calling her name but she didn't stop, just went faster and faster over the ground. Then, when she was almost at the rope, she skidded to a halt and threw the cloak of feathers into the drop below. She watched it fall, spreading itself as if it were trying to take off. And then it hit a fallen tree trunk before slipping down into a gap among the earth and slime and the beer cans and spiders and the cigarette butts, and she wanted to cry.

'Hey, Davey,' a voice said. Mia didn't have to turn around to know that it was Jack. There were grunts and greetings and the laying down of bikes, but she didn't turn around. Then she heard someone at her side. She twitched when he spoke.

'Come on, sis,' Davey said in a low voice.

'Oh, are you going on the swing?' It was Sarah. 'Look everybody, Mia's going on the swing.'

'No,' said Davey. 'No, she's not.' And Mia felt his hand on her shoulder.

Sarah laughed. 'Chicken. Your sister's always a chicken, Davey. She doesn't do anything.'

'No,' echoed Sam Oakey. '*Anything.*'

'She's been on it already,' said Davey. 'It's my turn now.'

Mia turned and stared at him. He winked.

'She went really high,' he said. 'Higher than me.'

Mia felt the others staring at her, but she wouldn't look at them. She knew they wouldn't say anything, wouldn't question Davey. They never did question him, just followed him and tried to do what he did. She felt a stab of pride for her brother.

'Go on then,' said Jack.

Mia realised he was talking to Davey. She looked around as her brother backed off, then started to run. She opened her mouth to call him back and closed it again. She smiled as he raced, all boy, all freedom, towards the rope. It already felt better. He was doing that thing again, weaving his magic in the air. It was all right. It was his spell, Davey's spell, not her own; but it was all right.

He ran towards the rope and he leapt. His fingers stretched out and the rope trembled.

Then Davey began to fall.

Mia screamed. He went so fast; how could he have gone so fast? There was only his hair, floating above his head, and the weight of him, and there must have been sound, but Mia hadn't heard any sound at all because she had screamed so loud.

The others ran to the drop. The rope was hanging quite still now. Jack paced up and down in front of it. Then he turned and ran past Mia, his face white. He grabbed his bike. 'I'll get someone,' he panted, and was gone, off into the woods.

Sarah looked over her shoulder. 'Where's he gone?' she asked. Her voice wasn't like her voice. 'Where?'

All Mia could do was look at her.

'We have to go,' Sarah said to Sam Oakey. 'We can't get to him. We have to fetch help.' She went past Mia without pausing and grabbed her bike. After a moment Sam followed. He didn't look at Mia at all.

Mia stepped towards the drop and looked down.

There was the tree trunk she'd seen before; other branches, scattered about. There was an old car tyre she'd never noticed before. And Davey. Little Davey lay in the cleft, and his body was broken. She could see it in the way his back fitted to the shape of the branch on which he lay, a giant, twisted thing. His arm was bent in an unnatural way too, and Mia thought she could see blood on it. It wasn't bleeding now though.

She could tell from the look on her brother's face that little Davey was dead.

She let out a sound, something between a sob and a wail. She stared at the rope, the evil thing that Davey's spell hadn't worked upon, and wondered where spells went when they missed the thing they had been meant for. Old potions made of dust and dirt and hair. She felt sick. She bent to the ground, leaning further over the edge, trying to see into the gaps between the old wood in the hole in the ground.

Then she looked from side to side.

The ground was sheer where she was, but a little further around there were breaks in it she thought she might be able to hold onto. She remembered she wasn't supposed to – *never does anything* – as she hurried over there, threw herself onto her stomach and slithered backwards over the edge.

It was hard, but she held on tight, kicking her shoes into the dirt face to make footholds as she eased herself down. She forced herself to think it through, deciding where to step next and how to hold on. It didn't seem to take very long before she stood at the bottom, mud clumped to her shoes and smeared down her dress.

She saw the white shapes of Davey's face and arms from the corner of her eye and looked away. Instead she headed for the tree trunk, her feet sinking into the ground. It was spongy with layers of old grass and rubbish. She looked down and saw something dark and long-legged skitter over her shoe; shook it off with a little cry. She climbed over the branches and they didn't feel dry like tree bark but clammy and damp like cool skin. When she took her hands away they were tinged with green.

She could see the gap where the cloak had fallen. It was dark. She would have to lie flat against the biggest branch and reach in with her hand. She shivered but didn't hesitate, just threw herself down and let the wood dig into her belly and her knees and her chest. She put her arm down into the space and groped. Somewhere above her came the cry of a bird. She ignored it. It made her think of outside, of playing with the others, of watching Davey fly. She couldn't think about that now. She had to think of this, the darkness under her, the sudden smoothness she felt under her fingertip. She stretched down, pressing her face into cold wood; felt its clammy touch rub her cheek. She felt feathers, pinched the fabric between her fingers and pulled it towards her.

She slithered back off the branch, clutching the cloak, feeling its dry weight. She held it close, pressing it tight against her body. Davey still lay where he had fallen. Everything was motionless, everything quiet.

Mia walked towards him, trying not to see how white his face had become. His jaw was sticking out; it looked as though it was unhinged. She wondered if he had shouted anything as he had fallen. If he had, Mia hadn't heard; she had been too busy with her own scream.

She held out the cloak, turning it so that all the feathers hung downwards, like they do on birds' wings. She straightened it, trying not to see the black flakes falling to the ground. 'You're my brother, Davey,' she said. Her words seemed wrong in the empty air, too loud. *It was for them*, she thought. It was because her words were only for the two of them. She put the cloak over her brother's face. Then she turned and ran back towards the slope.

When Mia got home and looked into her mother's eyes she knew that no one had told her. The others must have run to their own homes and she felt a stab of anger. Their mothers knew, and Davey's mother didn't. It was unfair. The whole world was like that, out of kilter.

Her mother ran to Mia and knelt down and put her arms around her, and Mia wondered if she had been wrong, if her mother had known after all. Then she realised her mother was saying something, over and over: *What is it Mia, what's wrong Mia*, and she remembered the mud all down her front and the wood-slime on her face, and knew that her mother knew nothing, she'd only seen what she read in Mia's eyes, and the next thing was that Mia was going to have to tell her. And Mia started to cry.

For a moment, Mia wasn't sure what she'd been saying. Something about birds, and Davey, and the woods, and a rope. She knew her mother didn't understand. She just kept stroking Mia's hair and making shushing noises. Mia took a deep breath because she had to tell her, couldn't let her not know any longer, and she opened her mouth to say that Davey was dead and then the door opened and she saw the thing that stood there and Mia screamed.

It was Davey, but not Davey. His face was white and expressionless; only his eyes stared, dark and bright. His hair was plastered tight to his head. Mia saw that his jaw didn't stick out any more and she looked at his arms and saw that they were wings after all; pitch black, inky black, and shining so brightly they looked wet. The wings hung over his shoulders and were long and powerful all around him.

Then Davy moved and she saw it was only a cloak, her cloak, the one she had made for him. He threw it to the floor and brushed himself down, his arms shaped as they should be, moving as they should move. And he looked at her. 'I'm back,' he said, and that was all she remembered before she fell.

At first, when Mia tried to tell her mother how Davey had been hurt, her mother listened to her and stroked her head and soothed her. Later, she began to tut and brush Mia's words away; later still, she became angry. *He's fine*, she said. *Your brother's fine.*

Mia knew that Little Davey wasn't fine. He wasn't even the same. He was like Davey and yet not like him. He was too pale, his eyes too bright. He didn't smile.

The others didn't like to play with him any longer. Mia didn't really know why because they didn't tell her, and Mia knew that was because they had always been Davey's friends and not her own. They had liked his smiles and his bravado, and they were things she didn't have. Now they were things Davey didn't have either. He sat around the house, scowling at the television or staring into space. He stared at her, too, if she tried to talk to him, to ask him about the woods or the ravens. He stared at her as if he didn't really know what words meant.

One day her mother was trying to clean up around them, and she kept darting little looks towards her son. Sharp, hard little looks. At last she stopped and turned on him. 'Why don't you go out?' she said.

Davey stopped staring into space and stared at her instead.

Their mother straightened. She licked her lips. When she spoke again her tone was different: sweeter. 'Why don't you take your sister for a walk?'

Mia heard this, and thought: *I'm the eldest.* But she didn't say anything.

Her mother said, 'Why don't you take her to the woods?' and Mia knew then how much their mother wanted them to go because she never told them to go to the woods; it was somewhere they weren't supposed to be.

Her brother turned his head. 'Do you want to come to the woods, Miranda?' he asked.

She looked at him and saw that he hadn't called her that to be funny or mean. He hadn't meant it in any way at all, he'd just said it, and they were only words, things that didn't seem to mean anything to him.

Mia, she mouthed. She was Mia. Even Little Davey had always called her Mia. But she didn't say it out loud.

He got up and put on his coat and so did she. When he went out of the front door she followed him. She didn't try to talk; she knew it would be easier that way. Instead she walked at his heels until they reached the woods. The raven wasn't there but Davey stopped and stared for a moment, at something only he could see.

'What is it?' asked Mia, and he just started walking again and so did she.

They went into the woods and Mia wasn't afraid, not really. She had learned there were other things to be afraid of; things that came into your home and slept in the room next to yours; things you weren't really sure were the people you had known or the ones you had loved, in spite of yourself, all the time you were wishing they were something else.

She followed Davey until they reached the swing. He walked over to it, leaned out and grasped the rope with his fingers. He didn't jump for it, though, or do anything else. He just stood there with it clasped in his hand, looking down into the drop.

'You died,' said Mia.

When he turned, she wasn't sure that he had heard her. She saw his eyes, though, and they were dark, and small, and bright. She couldn't look away from them. Then Davey smiled, and although it was something Mia had wished for, she suddenly knew it wasn't a thing she wanted to see. It wasn't Davey's smile. It wasn't a good smile.

Davey opened his mouth and spoke to her in the voice she'd known was inside him. His voice was the sound a raven made and she knew then that the birds hadn't been good, after all; they hadn't meant well. They had taken her brother just as she had dreamed, and the birds had brought him back; except, when they did, they left a part of him behind, in whatever dark place they had been.

Mia shuddered. She felt stinging at her eyes. She closed them and felt the tears come, no use now. So many times she had wished, and she wished again, but she knew it wasn't any good. The magic had gone. It had gone with Davey, and he had known that. He had looked at her and called her by her name.

So many times she had wanted her brother to be something else, some strange and magical thing. Now she clenched her fists, still feeling Davey's stare, and wished harder than anything to have her brother back. To have Little Davey come home, just the same as he had always been.

|White Feathers|

~

There was a feather lying on the rocks at the base of the mountain. At first Alma thought it was white but then she saw it wasn't, not really; its tip was banded with the palest of greys. She sighed with disappointment, but then she hadn't expected it to be so easy, had she? Nothing worthwhile ever was. That's what her mother always told her, usually when they were dusting or sweeping snow from the paths or doing something else that was dull and everyday and had no magic in it.

Alma and her mother lived away from anyone and everything, not at the edge of the village but beyond it, where the little paths and tracks ended and the crags began. Alma wished it wasn't so. The village was pretty and sheltered by trees. Up where they lived, no trees grew. There was only the grey rock and the harsh wind. The girls at school laughed at Alma. They said the wind would redden her cheeks and make her ugly.

It was blowing now. She pulled her hood further around her face, but it wasn't any use. It wasn't yet winter but up here, winter's breath was always in the air. Alma's fingertips felt numb and soon her face would be too, the warmth being stolen from her bit by bit. *But she was a heroine*, she reminded herself. This time, the story was about her. And when she succeeded, when she found her feather, she wouldn't be red-cheeked and ugly at all.

She clambered over an outcrop of stone, scanning the ground, but there were no more feathers.

She frowned. Little birds of all colours nested in the trees in the village and in the rooftops and the chimneys: pink, yellow, grey, brown. Her friends' mothers hung strings of nuts for them outside their windows. Alma wished they could do the same from their own eaves, which were steep to let the snow slide off, and once she did, but no birds came. There were only the white doves that flew high overhead, their soft cooing drifting down to where Alma craned her neck after them.

Now there were no doves either, and it occurred to her for the first time that it might have been a trick. But somehow it wasn't the schoolgirls' voices she heard in her mind, but her mother's: *There's no use staring at the sky and wishing.*

She shook the words away. Her mother wasn't one for dreaming and telling stories, no matter how Alma begged for them. Still, her mother couldn't keep them from her: stories of beautiful princesses bedecked in finery, of paupers winning the prince's hand in marriage, of girls with skin as white as snow and lips as red as blood...

Girls with their heads stuffed full of fairy stories. No good ever came of it.

Her mother didn't know Alma was here. If she did, it probably wouldn't even work.

She closed her eyes against another blast of the north wind and remembered what her friend Leonora had told her: that if she only found one perfect feather, up where the wind blows coldest and the white birds fly, she would receive the gift that only the doves could give. She remembered the look in Leonora's eyes when she said the word, *Beauty*, and the way she cast a glance at Christian Rollinson, the handsomest boy in school, the one with wild yellow hair and green eyes. The one who had smiled at Alma but never at Leonora. The one she hoped would ask her to go with him to the end of term ball.

Christian Rollinson. It almost sounded like *royal son*; that was the kind of name that might belong to a prince. Alma wrinkled her nose. She sometimes wondered if her mother had chosen her name to spite her. 'Alma' didn't sound like a princess. Even her mother's name, Miranda, was more like the name a princess might have.

Leonora had looked a little bit jealous, but then she'd smiled and her eyes shone, and that was good, because some of the time, Alma wasn't even sure that Leonora was really her friend at all.

But she would be. Leonora had said so. When Alma had the feather, she would have lots of friends.

She stumbled and put out a hand to save herself, cutting her palm on the side of a bluff. The mountain's grey rock was like that, splintered and sharp. It didn't look sharp, but it had drawn a neat line of blood on her skin and she smeared it across her skirt. She couldn't afford to have blood on her fingers. When she found the feather, it had to be perfect; it couldn't be stained. She didn't know what that might mean.

Ahead of her was a flake of white. She hurried towards it and saw one of the tiny flowers that clung to cracks in the rock and bent and nodded in the wind. Her heart beat a little faster. In spring, white butterflies came to visit them. She must be getting closer. Sure enough, there was a feather on the ground ahead of her.

She reached for it just as it flew out of her grasp, lifted by the breeze, swooping from the edge of a drop. Alma let out a cry of disappointment. She leaned out, but it was too late; it had already gone.

She sat back, sure that must have been the one, *her* feather, and she choked back her disappointment. It wouldn't happen. There was no magic in the world, not for her, and she had known that already, had known it even before she set out. It was why they lived here, where there weren't any trees and there weren't any stories. She had heard her mother wish it so, back when she was small, and now it had come true.

Her mother had once found a book of fairy stories hidden under her pillow. Alma still remembered the way her eyes had narrowed in horror, as if it was something terrible. And she had shrieked at Alma about how something bad happened to her brother when he was small, something that could never be undone; that the ravens had taken him away. Then she said they were leaving, and they had come to the mountain.

Alma shivered. She couldn't remember being cold when she was small, but she did remember being frightened. She had met her mother's brother once. It was at her grandmother's funeral. She remembered a silent man with a pale, bloodless face and tight lips, and in his black coat he had resembled nothing more than a raven himself: a tall, stern raven. She was sure he could never have been a little boy. Then he was gone, never having said goodbye or even having spoken. And it came to Alma then, when she saw the sadness in her mother's eyes, that the bad thing hadn't just happened to him. It had happened to her mother too.

Alma had never seen a raven. From what she'd heard, not many people had. They weren't everyday birds. They were bigger for a start, and blacker, and their harsh call was said to contain nothing but the word *Corpse! Corpse!*. They could smell death and feasted on carrion and their gathering was called an unkindness. She pulled a face. How on earth could her mother think she would ever seek them out?

No, it was the white birds she sought, not the black ones of which her mother was so afraid. What harm could come of that? They were all goodness and purity and beauty. She could see it in their white feathers when she squinted up at the bluest skies. Surely they could spare one for her now? They weren't evil. They were like the birds in stories. She remembered the ones she had read about: the bewitched brothers to a princess; the ugly duckling that became a swan; a kindly duck that carried Hansel and Gretel across a lake to safety. Briefly, she thought of the birds that had pecked away their trail of breadcrumbs through the forest, and she pushed them from her mind. It wasn't like that. Anyway, here there was no forest, no danger, no wolves…

She turned around and saw the fog below her, its creeping whiteness blanking out her house and the village and the world beyond it. She caught her breath in dismay. When had it ever come in so fast? But she couldn't go back now. She hadn't finished. The highest peaks were above her still and if she didn't try, if she didn't do something, why should the birds repay her?

If the mist had come in quickly, the cold had come quicker still. It found its way beneath her coat and nestled in close to her heart. Her throat burned with the ice of it. Ahead of her, another feather lay on the ground. She reached for it eagerly, only to draw back her hand. The barbs had separated; it was a torn and ragged thing. She turned it over with her foot and saw a fat black grub clinging to its underside.

She stumbled away. The fog was all around her. It was because she had gone wrong, she knew that. She had seen her feather and it had been snatched from her by the wind, the cruel wind that howled over the crags. She stopped, looking towards the edge. Then she walked towards it, crouching against that cruel wind, and peered down.

There was only the white boil of mist. She scanned the crag, its fissures and outcrops. She thought there was a way down, but it would not be easy. And if she fell…

She couldn't see the bottom.

She edged out over the drop and began to feel her way from one handhold to the next, her breath pluming in front of her and rising into the cold air.

~

Alma couldn't stop shivering. The cold was bone deep, had put out its claws inside her and was gripping so hard that it hurt. Her hands shook, even while she eased the white feather from her sleeve. She had protected it from the cold and the damp while she stumbled down from the mountain.

She held it in front of her face and smiled in spite of the chill that ran its thin fingers along her spine. It was perfect. Pure white and beautifully curved, its edges sharp as a blade, angled for flight. At its base was a tuft of soft down that made Alma think of babies, new and clean-smelling.

She had found it at the base of the cliff, waiting for her. She had known it was hers.

Her smile grew wider. She knew what she must do, though Leonora hadn't told her. She touched the feather to her cheek, just once, then placed it under her pillow.

Perhaps she would dream of her future husband. Perhaps he would wear Christian Rollinson's face.

She was still shivering when she slipped beneath the sheets.

~

On the first day, Alma got up and dressed and went downstairs as usual, the smell of her mother's porridge already drifting up to meet her. She went to the table and pulled out a chair, sat down and greeted her mother, who turned and dropped the bowl she held. Porridge spattered across the floor. Her mother didn't notice. She rushed to Alma, whirled her around and put a hand to her forehead. Alma, puzzled, pulled away.

'You're not hot,' her mother said. 'Do you have a fever? Do you feel ill?'

Alma frowned. She did not feel ill, not exactly. A part of her mind felt as if the mist was in it, that roiling mountain fog, but she didn't mention that.

'You should stay at home. Go back to bed.'

A memory of Christian Rollinson's face rose to the surface and was gone; it was enough. 'Mother, I have to go to school.'

'But you look…'

Alma pushed herself up from the table. She walked out of the room and towards the mirror that hung by the door in the hall. She stared into it. She did look pale. Ill; yes, she looked ill. Her cheeks were wan, almost waxy. She bit her lip and leaned in closer. The whites of her eyes were very white indeed; she did not think they had ever looked that way before. Her forehead was high and clear and – *royal*. Her lip, under her small white teeth, was bloodless, but inside her mouth the skin was a bright rich crimson.

She pulled away. *White as snow*, she thought. *As red as blood.*

'Alma? Are you all right?'

She barely made out the words. Yes, she was all right. She leaned in closer to the mirror. Her hair, a lustrous brown, hung about her face, making her skin appear paler still. There, sprouting from her forehead where it had not been before, was a single thread of white. She reached out, separated it from the rest and pulled it from her head.

She stared at her reflection. She did not recognise what she saw. And then she realised: she couldn't remember her dreams of the night before at all.

'No. No, I'm not ill.' Alma forced herself to smile at Leonora. Her friend's face was creased. Christian was sitting on the other side of the room, but he kept casting little glances in their direction. Mostly he looked at Alma. It was as if he was fascinated.

Leonora hadn't noticed the boy, and Alma was glad of that. But she didn't like the look in her friend's eyes.

'It was climbing the mountain, that's all. I perhaps caught a little chill.' Alma wanted to tell Leonora about the magic, but found she couldn't. She wanted to tell her about the *beauty*. But here, with her friend standing in front of her, not understanding a thing, she could no longer find the words.

She had looked in a mirror at lunchtime. She had continued to fade: hair, lips, face, eyes, the colour draining from them all. What remained looked almost ghostly. She was ethereal, like a girl in a story.

She smiled at Leonora, but her friend still didn't see. Leonora couldn't meet her eyes; she looked away, gathering her books together as if she wanted to leave as quickly as she could. Then she glanced at Alma once more, still with that concern on her face, and Alma saw something else written there: guilt.

Alma's smile faded. What on earth had she said? She couldn't seem to think. Then she had it. *It was climbing the mountain. I perhaps just caught a little chill.*

She knew, then, that was what her friend had wanted for her all along. Not beauty. Not her single perfect feather. Just a nasty trick with a nasty end. She had wanted Alma to be ill for the end of year ball, so that she couldn't go. So that Christian Rollinson would have to ask someone else.

She looked for Leonora again, her eyes narrowing, but she wasn't there. Or rather she was, but hidden among a group of her kind: her *unkind*, a bunch of them all opening and closing their mouths at once, words spilling from them that Alma couldn't make out and didn't try to understand. She let them drift over her, *Kaa! Kaa! Kaaah!*, the noise becoming like the sound the birds made when they roosted in the village trees at nightfall, and she did not utter a word.

Alma sat close by the fire, staring into the flame. She almost didn't like it, but her mother had insisted. She still felt cold but found she didn't mind it any longer. At least, through the closed window, she could still hear the wind sweeping across the mountain, going who knew where.

There were colours in the fire she hadn't seen before. It sang to her of dark, wild places, so that she almost didn't notice her mother when she set tea by her side and then just as silently retreated.

She roused herself, looked around, and saw that her mother was watching her. She had seen that same careful blankness on her face before, but not for a long time. Alma closed her eyes. *Words*. Her mother had been talking to her when she last looked that way. She had been saying something about magic, hadn't she? *Head full of stories*, that was it. Warning stories, about little girls who went chasing after fairy tales.

But what was childhood without magic? Wasn't that what all little girls wanted?

Alma shook her head. Her hair swung before her eyes, a shining curtain holding pale lights within it.

It was a long time before Alma noticed that her mother had gone to bed. The fire was dying. She went upstairs without troubling to switch on the light. When she looked under her pillow, she found the white feather had gone.

On the second day, Alma's mother set her porridge down in front of her without speaking. She retreated to the other side of the room and leaned against the dresser, watching while her daughter ate. She did not cry over her appearance or insist that she stay at home and Alma thought that was probably because her mother wished her gone.

She found words crowding into her mind, but they eddied and whirled and would not stand still. She remembered certain images: her mother taking her hand when she was frightened of the dark. Her mother laughing and tickling her when she tucked her in. Her mother snatching a book from her hands, the look on her face one of dismay; almost of fear.

There was fear on her face now. It wasn't easy to see but Alma knew it was there, hiding beneath the surface. She could sense the rapid pounding of her mother's heart. On the surface, though, there were other things, more complicated things: the recognition that something had happened. The uncertainty about who it had happened to.

Alma could remember the feeling of being alone, though she did not feel it now. She acknowledged it, as if she were seeing it from a great height. She had not thought that aloneness was a thing of degrees: she had been alone or not alone. Now she saw it was possible to be more lonely still.

She finished her breakfast, tipping her head back to swallow the last of it, and picked up her bag and went to the door. She stopped and looked in the mirror and observed her own pure and brittle beauty. Then she went outside.

Colours crowded in on her as she walked down the slope towards the village. Red berries were like drops of blood in the hedges. Yellow flowers sang from the lawns. Green dragonflies, almost the same emerald as the grass but not quite, darted and flashed. The world was full of such burning brilliance and Alma wondered that she had never seen or even imagined it before.

When she reached the school she pushed open the door and caught sight of her own reflection in the glass, there for a moment and then gone: her white hair; her skin, colourless and new as paper. Then she was inside with the warm meat smells of her classmates, their endless noise, their slow, clumsy movements.

She did not realise that Christian Rollinson was at her side until he caught hold of her arm. She pulled away, wanting to be free, and then saw the way he stared at her, his eyes running over her features, her skin, his expression one of wonder. And she realised that he had spoken, something about the ball, about going to the ball with *him*.

She shot a look across the room to where Leonora stood watching. And she turned back to Christian and smiled.

He did not seem altogether happy with that smile, but he nodded and smiled back and he let her go as the bell rang for lessons and they all moved to go to class.

Alma sat at her desk, nursing her own satisfaction. What she felt wasn't joy, not exactly. What she felt wasn't love. She wasn't sure what it was. Her feelings seemed to have faded along with the colour in her cheeks and the blue of her eyes.

She felt cold. She felt the north wind in her bones.

On the third day, Alma awoke early. She wasn't sure if she had been dreaming or if it had come to her as she left sleep behind, but for a while, a thought had circled in her mind. It was about fairy tales, or more specifically, about stepmothers. The way Snow White's queen wished for the huntsman to cut out her heart. The way Gretel's parents abandoned her in the forest. And she couldn't shake from her head what someone had told her once: that in the original tales, they weren't stepmothers at all. They were real mothers, mothers of flesh and blood and bone.

She did not look in the mirror. It did not matter what she saw. She went instead to the window and gazed out at the mountain. Its grey peak was waiting, and it was full of colour after all, shattered prisms of light calling out to her.

She pushed the window open and stepped up onto the sill. A moment later, she was surrounded by the clear air.

It bore her up. She felt it holding her, at once steady and treacherous, and she soared, awkward and new. She banked, swooping about the rooftop, once, twice, three times, and feathers fell from her, foamy and white and beautiful.

She watched them fall, perfect and whole, drifting slowly to the tiny garden. Then she saw the door open and her mother came running out. Her mouth was open, her head tilted to the sky. Alma did not know if she saw her but she saw the things she had let fall, the gifts she had left behind, and her mother screeched and threw herself upon them.

Alma circled the house once more before she flew away. Her mother was on her knees, holding a single white feather to her breast. She was crying. Tears shone on her cheeks, as perfect and pure as the thing she held, clutching it so tightly she must surely crush the quill; so tightly she might never let it go.

Alma flew higher and she felt joy at last: a cold, airy, endless joy. The sky went on for ever. Why had she never seen it that way before? She felt each variation in flow and temperature and direction of the air and she adjusted the angle of her feathers and it took her higher, soaring up into the mountain. A mouse nosed through the grass far, far below. She left it; there was always time. And then she saw the place she sought, higher than she had ever been before.

The white birds were strewn across a clearing, sitting amid their white flowers. Alma's heart leapt to see them. She landed among them and heard their voices, words she could understand. They did not greet her. Why would they, when she was one of them? She didn't look quite like the birds, not yet, but they knew her still. They had been waiting for her. Now they rose together into the sky.

They flew as one down from the mountain, moving with the north wind, and Alma flew with them. Soon she would see past the edge of the world she had always known. There would always be more of it, more and more.

First, way below her, she saw the school.

A lovely girl was holding a young boy's hand. His yellow hair shone brightly, as did the girl's eyes. His teeth shone too as he let out a trilling laugh.

Alma flew lower, and as she did, things began to come back to her. *Beauty*, she thought. *You will be beautiful, and you will have all the friends you want.*

Alma's sisters flew all around her. And they were beautiful; the girls of the village had been right. She could see them now, clucking and gossiping, the girls who teased and the boy who laughed.

Lower still, she could see the way he patted Leonora's hand. She sensed the heated blood in his veins. She swooped lower, but still they did not notice her. She let no feathers fall; there would be no gifts. Instead she stretched out her sharp grey claws and with a harsh cry, she caught him up.

He struggled as she flew. He called out but his words meant nothing and he weighed nothing at all. Alma rejoiced in the touch of him: his beating blood, his soft skin pierced by her claws, the fragile bones beneath. She tucked her head into her chest and looked deeply into his eyes before she let him fall.

She was curious. She wanted to see if he would shatter like an egg. Eventually, he did.

|Swanskin|

~

Later, it is not so much the attack that I see, again and again, in my mind, but what came after it.

The two of them were walking along the shore at evening, a distance ahead of me. The sky and sea were as grey as each other, and the air still had winter's cold nip, carrying now and then a scouring of sand into my face. The town was behind me, a pretty little spill of houses built into the side of a cliff, nothing but the sea in front of it and miles of flat brown land behind. Across the dunes, just ahead of the couple, was a quiet little river mouth, where swans gathered and dabbled for pondweed, no doubt dreaming their strange avian dreams of the north.

I couldn't make out their features, but I knew who they were. Horrocks, his very name meaning 'part of a ship', owns the largest fishing boat in the fleet; and next to him was Syl, his young wife, a little taller than he. If I hadn't recognised her form I would have known her by her hair, more golden than the evening sun, rippling finer than the sea.

Horrocks was hunch-shouldered under the weight of a pack, his head turned to the sand, while Syl gazed upward, into the sky. And yet both of them stopped when a clamour arose, seemingly from nowhere, a sound I couldn't place. It echoed from the dunes and at first I thought of machinery, coming from the town perhaps, though I'd never heard such a thing before; then the wings appeared, as if from out of the ground.

Suddenly they were everywhere, surrounding the two of them, flocking above their heads. The birds were dark against the sky, yet I knew them to be white, for I recognised their cruciform shapes, their chiselled heads, the long, graceful arch of their necks.

Horrocks stumbled. He raised one arm to fend them off as the swans fell upon him, beating and stabbing. Each one of them was wider than Syl was tall. I rubbed my eyes, wondering if it was some illusion formed of the sand – swans, I knew, did not attack men, not like this, not all together. One at a time perhaps, if he strayed too close to its nest, and even then, I was certain the stories must be lies: that a swan's wing could break a man's leg; that they had once drowned a man at the edge of the sea.

Horrocks fell to his knees. The birds shrieked in a kind of blood lust, the beating of their wings a tumult. I couldn't tell if Horrocks cried out; I couldn't see his face. He *was* in the edge of the sea, I realised, though hidden by the chaos of feathers and flight.

I began to run towards them, even as I realised that his wife had not moved at all. Syl stood by, no doubt shocked into stillness, horrified; fear-frozen.

Horrocks pushed himself up from the water, roaring and choking salt from his lungs. One moment the air was thick with plumage; and the next the swans were gone, beating and creaking their way back towards the river.

All was suddenly quiet. I slowed a little, the sand making hard work of it, but they hadn't seen me; they hadn't looked at me all the time it was happening. I'm not sure they ever knew I was there.

After the attack, Horrocks got to his knees and then his feet. His trousers were darkened with seawater, but he didn't trouble about that. He didn't pause to retrieve his pack from the waves. He half walked, half stumbled to where his wife stood, tall and motionless, and he stepped in front of her, then struck her, hard, across her lips.

Unnatural, they say later, ensconced in their booths, pints frothing across the upturned barrels that pass for tables in the Anchor. *Uncanny. A freak.*

It is the same every night, at least when they are not at sea. The men of the town sail and fish and go home to hot meals and warm beds, but before they sleep they retire to the alehouse, spinning their yarns about the women who are trying to trap them. And yet tonight it is not the same, not quite. There is unease in their words and in their sidelong glances, which meet and slide away from each other.

Their words are cutting. They speak of the chatter of women, meaningless as the gabble of geese. They speak of the one thing they *are* good for, and spurt laughter before falling silent again, staring into their tankards.

They haven't yet said the word *witch*, but it isn't far behind *unnatural*. The air is thick with it, the echo of a thought that is louder than their obscenities, their laughter.

Soon I will go to sea. I shall be one of them – sitting at their table, talking as they do, flushed with drink and laughter. I was intended for a farmer, but the death of my parents ended that; now I live with a distant and ancient relative, a dry husk of a woman, in a tiny cottage nestled halfway up the cliff. The soft ploughed land of my childhood has become rock; the air I breathe has turned to salt.

I leave them, ducking out of the tavern in time to see a bevy of the town's women walking by, arm in arm. I stop and watch them go. Syl is at their centre, the tallest, though I can see little of her face; it is almost concealed by a dark hood. When she sees me, she passes a hand across her mouth, as if to conceal her swollen lips.

Contrary to the men's talk, they do not gabble. Indeed, they do not say a word. One of Syl's companions looks at me sidelong. She is softer made than Syl, though still tall, still elegant. I think I make out, as she goes, a single white feather caught in the soft curls of her hair.

At evening, we sit before the fire, my ageing relative and I. She rocks in her chair, staring into the flames while my gaze is drawn, over and over, to the window. There is nothing out there but the dark. It is parcelled into tiny diamonds by the leaded glass.

"You begin to see, then," she says.

I turn to her. Each crease on her face bears its own deep shadow. Her eyes look rheumy, as if damp with tears.

"See what, Aunt?" For Aunt I call her, though she is more distant than that in relation. Still, she has never blamed me for burdening her; she never reminds me of the thinness of our bond, that I am a stranger here.

She takes the pipe from between her lips, freeing a skein of mist scented of sandalwood and cloves.

"You'll know the truth soon enough." She gestures towards the window with the pipe's stem, just as a pale shape passes across the sky.

"The swans," she says. "They winter here. But here is not their home. That is what you sense, boy, when you look at them." She silences me with another wave of her pipe.

"Sometimes, a swan may shed her feathery skin. She casts it off and becomes a lovely maiden. And if a man should steal her skin – why, then she will stay, and keep her human shape, and be his wife, as long as her skin is kept from her. But sometimes, a whole flight of her sisters will come. They will try to free their sister and her swanskin."

Her eyes reflect the fire's gleam. "You should beware," she says. "Find a nice girl. A good girl. Not—" She spits, mutters something about *unnatural forms*.

I do not answer, am not certain how, and she takes to gazing once more, before nodding in her chair. I do not wake her; I wish to keep to my own thoughts. Somehow, I never once doubt the truth of her words. I half close my eyes, picturing the massing of the swans, the way they had swooped on Horrocks as he walked with his wife along the shore. I remember the way he struck her; I see again her grace as she touched her fingers to her lips.

Unnatural forms, my aunt had said, echoing the gossip at the Anchor. She never did tell me which of their forms was unnatural: whether it was their human or bird shape that was to be so feared.

The fishermen have sailed, the town left to the women, and to me. I wander the little streets between tall white houses, each set on their own angle, and try not to stare in at the windows. When I reach the largest, though, I cannot resist. I pass by it often and see Syl pacing the rooms, back and forth, restless, and I wonder: is she searching for her skin?

All know it when the boats return. The streets fill with bootsteps and chatter, and I too throw on my coat and head down to the dock to help offload the catch. This time, they have been absent four days. One more sailing and the eldest sea dog from Horrocks's boat, a fellow with half closed eyes and leathern skin, will be done. I am promised his place.

I heft crate after crate of still-squirming silver to the quayside, where the women wait with their curved knives, their trestle tables set out ready. Gulls circle overhead, wailing, ready to snatch whatever they can with bladed beaks. Most of the town is here, I realise: the grizzled men, the soft-skinned maids, though few children, unless it is only that I do not see them.

The women's movements are quick and sure as they grasp the slippery fish. Syl is among the rest. She guts them one by one, her hands gored and shining, and she cuts slivers from the edge of their flesh and swallows them whole. She catches me watching, freezes for a moment, gives a small nod in return for my smile.

Unnatural, they had said. My cheeks colour with shame at the memory of their words; the way they condemn her, forgetting, as perhaps her husband had himself, how he must have stolen her skin, kept it from her, made her what she is.

When the catch is done, the menfolk head up the narrow cobbled lane to the Anchor, but the women walk away, down to the shore. After a moment, I follow them. The sea has by now retreated, smudging the line where the earth meets the sky, and the beach seems a vast stretch of mud. They do not walk towards the brine, however, but to where the river meets the sea. They do not turn and I stand behind them as they look at the swans out on the water, gliding, their necks bent into hooks.

I cannot see the women's faces. I do not know if they are remembering or dreaming, or perhaps both.

After a time the swans beat their wings and skim along the surface, forming a noisy trailing procession before they lift from the water. Their flight is hard-won and the sound of their wings is like applause, as if they are glad to be in the air, rejoicing at their freedom. I wonder if they tell their own tales to each other – stories without words, warning of the wiles of man.

The swans circle around once more. The women exchange not a word, only watching them, tilting back their heads; then they hold out their hands. As I watch, the swans let fall their feathers: gifts for their skinless sisters.

∿

The Anchor smells of burning. The air is acrid and dense and I almost don't go inside but through the haze I hear the rumble of the men. I step across the threshold, blinking against the sting of it. I collect a tankard and the ale is mercifully cold at the back of my throat, though I still want to cough. No one else does, however, and I swallow it down.

They are seated in their accustomed places, Horrocks at the centre, his eyes already glazed with liquor – or perhaps that too is from the smoke, which rises in front of him, obscuring his features. He tips a little of his ale onto the table, which extinguishes something with a hiss. He holds up what remains – a blackened quill, the filaments burned away, not a trace of white left.

They all laugh, turning to look at me, this newcomer in their midst, not yet certain if I will be a subject for further laughter or if I will swell its volume. I force a grin, wave my tankard in their direction.

"Sit, boy." Horrocks surprises me with his words, which fly from his mouth in a cloud of spittle. They move aside for me, scraping their stools across the floor. I sit between their bulky warm bodies.

"See this?" he throws down the quill onto the upturned barrel between us. Other burned feathers are scattered there, scarcely recognisable, the source of the stink. "Know what that means, boy?"

I don't know what I'm expected to say, so I simply shrug, then nod.

"You will." Horrocks grasps his crotch and makes a thrusting motion, and guffaws rise into the air.

I gulp at my drink. Then, buoyed by the ale or their sudden silence, I say, "Where is it you keep the skins?"

Horrocks is suddenly motionless. All traces of humour are gone; his eyes are tiny points of light. They pierce the gloom – pierce me. "Be careful, boy."

The quiet stretches out. I'm not certain what it will become, but then the fellow at my side nudges me in the ribs. "I take mine to sea," he says. "Use it to line my hammock. Keeps me warm."

Glances flit around the group. They still aren't sure, but Horrocks's shoulders relax and amusement ripples between them.

"Feel this, lad." Another offers the edge of his jerkin to my fingers. I notice that its surface is pocked with little dimples. "Plucked and tanned," he says, and they roar. Strike their tankards against each other. Drink spills across the table.

"Buried," another mutters.

"Burned."

My smile fades. I sit in the midst of their noise, their movement. I have no words. I think of them sullying the pure white skins, the things they must have craved, once; loving and yet fearing them, coveting them even as they tear them to pieces. I stare down at the scorched feathers, abandoned now; in them the wrecked hopes of the women who had stood on the shore and snatched them from the sky.

Horrocks suddenly leans across the table, grasps my arm. His grip is hardened by years of working the wet ropes, hauling in the nets, the constant scrape of salt. "We saves 'em, boy," he says. "Never forget that. Not if you want to stay."

The others watch, intent on his words.

"We save them from the spell," he says. "Enchantment. The trap they're in. It's against nature. Remember that."

He waits for my nod before he releases me. I refrain from rubbing at my arm. I can still feel the bone beneath the skin, as if his fingers remain wrapped around it. Does he really believe he has freed them – saved them from what they are – from magic? Does he think he has remade them, shaped them as they could and should have been? And yet how he must value the memory of that magic: the grace of her, the sinuous form, her loveliness beneath the skin.

My thoughts are lost in their mirth, released once more in gulps of amber and guffaws. The volume of it gathers, a rising tide that carries everything with it, so that I only dimly hear it as he says, "A feather bed. I had it stitched inside, right at the centre. We sleep on it every night."

They are gathered in the street, just back from the quay, not far from where the Anchor hangs its old painted sign. It is not the day for market, or for sailing, or even for church, which anyway, few here trouble about. They are bending over an object made of wood. I cannot see or guess what it is but a great rustling and struggling comes from within, and they step back, snorting with laughter or mockery.

At last, I can see. The object is a wooden cage made of old crates and lobster pots, and inside is a folded, cramped, crushed creature. A golden beak, tipped with black, stabs at the bars. Momentarily it opens its mouth, revealing a long thin tongue as it hisses. Its feathers no longer appear white. They are damp, soiled, stained. I cannot make out its eyes against the dark sides of its skull.

Another ripple runs through the gathering as someone pokes a stick into the cage. The action is that of a child, but it is Horrocks; he turns, scans the crowd, and I see that Syl is standing there, at the back, looking on; seeing everything.

He nods, as if with satisfaction. Then he calls out, loud, so that everyone can hear.

"A witch." The word, spoken at last, cannot be contained. It runs about the street, touching all, lingering on their lips as they echo it.

"This creature would have beguiled a man. Inflamed his senses. Trapped him." He slaps his hand down on the top of the cage. "But we trapped it first, hey?"

They cheer. Fists assault the air. Someone kicks the cage. They are grinning, slapping backs, congratulating each other. The women stand by, watching, silent. They are cowled in their hoods, perhaps to cover their dangerous forms, their sinuous curves, lest they inflame a man; lest they bewitch him.

The swan in the cage does not make a sound. I do not know what they will do to her, but I cannot help her now; no one can. At least it will soon end, I think, and then Horrocks's voice rises again.

"A cull."

Now they have purpose. Now they know what to do. They gather behind him. Some are carrying guns, I realise, or sticks, or cudgels. They were ready for this. Primed. Someone releases the door of the cage and the swan stumbles out, clumsy on land, webbed feet sliding on the cobblestones.

"A head start," Horrocks jokes, and they give chase. The swan never did have a chance. She vainly spreads her wings but there is no room for her to take flight. She goes to the ground and one of the men sets his boot on her long and shapely neck.

They begin to chant, others taking it up so that the words become something different and strange. "A cull, a cull."

I try to interject, grasping shoulders, calling out that such a thing is not lawful, that they cannot take it upon themselves. It is no use; my words are lost. They brandish their weapons, pounding the ground with their sticks as they go, stamping their feet. *A cull* – as if it is something scientific they do, something necessary.

They march away towards the river. The women follow, able to do nothing else. Will they fight? They have nothing but the clothes they wear. They trail behind, their gaze fixed not upon the sky but the earth the men have trodden; upon their duty; their destination. Will they watch as their sisters are torn and trampled, their feathers broken and ruined? Will they witness the snapped necks of their sons and daughters? Perhaps it would be worse, after all, to turn their faces away.

Still, as Syl passes me at the back of the crowd, I reach out and grasp her hand.

We run, away from the others, unseen, towards her house. She unlocks it using a key kept on a string about her neck and we go inside. I stride ahead of her, as if it is my own. I pass through the living space, not cramped and crammed with nick-nacks and scrimshaw like my aunt's cottage but airy and neat. I go to the stairs. Syl does not protest at this intrusion in her home, only watches, her dark eyes the only brightness.

"A knife," I say, and run up the steps, not worrying about the noise I make. He will be gone a while yet; there is time. There *must* be time. I wonder for a moment if his boasting words at the Anchor were really the truth as I pull back the embroidered sheet of their bed, wondering if she made it by her own hand. I wonder if the knife she passes to me is the one I saw her wielding by the quay, sliding in and out of the belly of a fish. It is slender and sharp and I plunge it into the mattress.

Feathers: white feathers, downy and soft and choking. They fly into the air, floating down once more, and at first she grabs at them – whether to conceal them or take them back I do not know, but I do not think these are a swan's. I thrust my hand into the rip I have made and feel inward to the centre, trying not to imagine Horrocks on this bed, sweating on top of her.

Then I touch something that does not give, does not slip through my fingers like the other feathers; something that is as soft as they, yet supple, pliant as the finest leather.

I grasp hold of it and pull it towards me. She gives a harsh, choking cry – the first sound she has made – and snatches it from me. It is almost liquid, that brush of feathers against my skin; then it is gone, though I turn and see the glow of it, pure and shining, spilling from her hands.

I almost expect her to throw it over her shoulders at once, but she does not. She turns and runs for the stairs. But of course, there would be no room here for her to fly. The space she leaves behind feels cold and empty and the thought rises; I had imagined she might have spared a word for me.

When I step out of the door she is standing there, staring down the steep little street towards the glimmer of the sea. The swanskin is still in her hands. A muscle twitches in her cheek – it is as if she is tasting the air, a savour she had almost forgotten. She half closes her eyes, then whirls the feathers around her and she runs.

She moves away from me, fast, faster – and I see the stretch and curve of her wings, spreading wide, finding the air, finding their rhythm, feathertips spreading as she casts it all behind her. She is flying, I realise, her feet lifting from the ground, and still she does not look behind her, and still she has no word for me. An image: all the beautiful swans, her sisters, gliding upon the water, and yet separate from it; their feathers, with a simple flick, always remaining entirely dry.

But her transformation is not complete. Beneath the white is the merest suggestion of an arm, a hand, of weight, of darkness. Then a single shot rings out.

At first, her movement does not change. Then she begins to fall.

I cannot do what she would have done; I cannot watch, though I hear her bones shatter on the stone, the sound of her body breaking. Then they are there, the men, blooded and blood-hungry, the red light of it in their eyes, and it is not enough, will never be enough. They are all around and still they do not stop but raise and lower their cudgels and their sticks and they go on and on stamping with their feet.

Then they turn to me.

When the boats have sailed, there is time to mend. My arm is still in a sling, and I walk with a limp that I suspect will always be with me. I shall not now go to sea. No one has told me this; they do not have to. The knowledge does not lie in the way they look at me, but in the way they do not.

The women say nothing of what has passed. They clean and they cook and they wait for their men. They sit by the shore, dutifully mending nets and sails, always busy with their needles.

I stay with my aunt, doing whatever tasks she requires of me. Mostly she requires nothing; she sits in her rocking chair, smoking her pipe, staring into space and saying nothing of my failure.

After she fell, the thing that Syl had become was given to the fire. No one wished to look upon it too closely, that mangled and twisted form: fingers, beak, feathers, hair.

Outside the window, I hear the pattering of steps. I look out to see hooded shapes hurrying by, heading down the hillside towards the quay. This time there is little conversation, no excited calls ringing into the air, but still I know what it means.

The men have returned from the sea.

At a glance from my aunt, I don my coat and slip out of the door. The cold air in my lungs feels like a relief after the closed rooms and I limp along in the wake of the women, scarcely knowing why.

The tables are set out along the quay, shining knives waiting there like smiles. Waves gently tap the hulls of the boats, lined up against the harbour wall. There is a stink of bladderwrack and brine; the sky is not grey but a fresh clear blue scudded with white, and a firm breeze is blowing from the north. I realise something strange. There are no gulls, not today; no wailing cries ringing across the water.

The women are not seated at their tables, are not waiting for the catch. They stand a short distance away, together, still wearing their hoods. I can barely see their faces beneath them; I cannot see their hands. Then, as one, they cast them off.

Beneath their capes, they are naked. They do not wear the clothes their men have given them. Their hair is loose, rippling down their backs. They stand tall. They are unashamed of their bodies, of their bruises, the useless stubs of their wings.

Each is holding a mass of white feathers. They have made new skins, I realise, though not of swan feathers; the men have burned or broken too many for that. I peer into the air once more, cold suddenly, searching again for the gulls, listening for their rapacious cries. The sky is empty.

The women's faces are solemn. I cannot tell by their expressions what they are thinking. It only strikes me then that swans do not cry. They keep the brine inside them; the salt permeates their bones, their blood. It changes them. They, too, can adapt; after all, the river always has flowed into the sea.

The women are ready. And when they take their new forms, red of eye, sharp of beak, gulls sinuous and quick, feathers slick and shining, it is plain for anyone to see that they are also very, very hungry.

|Here Be Mysteries and Wickedness|

|The Adventure of the Avid Pupil|

~

1

I have long found it to the credit of my friend Sherlock Holmes that he has always clung to what he sees as right, regardless of any desire for personal vainglory. Indeed, he often insisted that I forebear from making my little accounts of his cases, particularly as his fame grew; he even came to disdain the approbation of the public. Unlike other men, he did not require the approval of the world, but trod his own path within it. Thus it chafed upon my senses all the more painfully when it appeared that another might turn Holmes's talents to the purpose of furthering his own reputation.

I brought the matter to Holmes's attention as we sat one evening perusing the papers. Only a brief time had lapsed since he had agreed to pass on his skills in observation and deduction in a new school of detection, and to mentor some of its students; and such was the subject upon which I opened.

'That fellow, Simon Smedley,' I said. 'Is he not one of your apprentices?'

'He is,' Holmes replied. 'A young police officer under Inspector Lestrade's tutelage, and very keen to find improvement, though I do believe his mind to be fixed upon still greater things.'

'Indeed! For I find I must warn you, Holmes, of what I heard from his own lips this very afternoon.'

Holmes did not react to my tone. He raised his rather expressive eyebrows and tilted his head for me to continue, and I did so with alacrity. 'I heard him boasting at my club – indeed, to all who would listen! He said he was not only learning all the master knew, but that as any pupil should, he would soon surpass him; upon which time he would begin his own academy, one which would not only improve upon your own, but usurp its ripest fees.'

My cheeks flushed with indignation, yet Holmes sat undisturbed. He drew on his pipe and let out a cloud of blue smoke so that for a moment, I saw him through a fog.

'Well, Holmes – what do you think?'

He set down his pipe, leaned back and closed his eyes. 'I think,' he said, 'I may have a little nap, Watson, if you have no objection. I find the demands of the academy, along with my own cases, have left me somewhat enervated this evening.'

'But Holmes, something must surely be done! For I carried out some detection of my own, and it took little time to discover that the fellow has been repeating his boasts all over the city. He is claiming to all who will hear that he shall soon be a detective the like of which London has never seen. You should write to Lestrade – tell him, indeed, that you will no longer assist the man in his endeavours to take your place.'

To this, he made a low sort of grunt.

'Holmes? Is the man's boast so empty, then, that you intend to do nothing?'

His eyes remained closed. 'Not at all, Watson. No, he is a rather intelligent fellow, and keener than mustard, as you have so ably recounted.'

'Why, then—'

'I apologise, Watson. I am in somewhat low spirits, I admit. But there can be no harm in the increase of knowledge and the improvement of skill, can there? I should think there cannot, at any rate. And if we were to dismiss every man of whose manner we did not approve, we would become lonely individuals indeed.' He sighed. 'Perhaps the pupil *should* one day outflank the master.'

'But he is nought but a swaggerer, Holmes!'

Another tilt of the head informed me that Holmes concurred with my judgment, and yet he could not be prevailed upon to denounce the man. Instead it was I that was forced to subside, trying to focus once again upon the newspaper; though I soon found myself staring into the fire, listening to its hiss and spit, occasionally interjecting with my own impatient sigh. It was but a short time later that I deduced, from my own observations, that the reigning master detective, Sherlock Holmes, was fast asleep.

2

The next morning I professed to Holmes that I should very much like to observe a little at the school of detection, in order to broaden the scope of my memoirs and witness any new side to his character the endeavour might have brought to the fore. I did not imagine him a natural tutor. He was too impatient of others' slowness for that, and a little too inclined to enjoy baffling those around him with his own peculiar genius; but in reality I wished to discover a little more about our friend Simon Smedley. In short, I found myself seated in an almost circular, steeply-banked lecture theatre, watching Holmes standing in the pit below, next to an object which, despite its covering sheet, I could have little doubt was a human cadaver.

Naturally this was no new sight to me, although its presence in this room, surrounded by eager students leaning over the heads of their fellows to better absorb the sight, made it somewhat difficult to tear my gaze away. However, I wished to make a closer study of Simon Smedley. The day was made gloomy by the constant assault of rain against glass somewhere above me, but even allowing for the shifting light, I must say that I found him wanting. His black hair lay flat and lank and without life in it; his forehead was a little too smooth; his snub nose was like a child's; his wide-set blue eyes stared unpleasantly; and to finish the impression, he possessed a receding chin and a flattish skull that nobody would covet.

I could not fault his rapt attention, however, as Holmes began to speak.

'To discover the story of what happened to a body,' he said in stentorian tones, 'one must see its wounds. We must know who he was; what tool was employed to stop his breath; the place in which the deed occurred. We must understand his life, in order to understand his death. Only by making close examination – the most minute observation – can we hope to succeed. It would be a remarkable man indeed who expects to solve a crime without leaving his rooms.'

He swept the sheet from the table and a stir went about the galleried seats, for what lay beneath was indeed a corpse, but what a corpse! It was that of a man of middle years, and it was torn and mutilated and stabbed with a dozen injuries.

'I shall ask each of you to step down,' he said, 'and demonstrate your aptitude in making out the cause of a wound. Tranmer!' He pointed to a callow youth in the first row, who glanced around before leaving his seat. A moment later he was at Holmes's side, who, despite the lad's gangling build, stood a head taller.

Holmes pointed. 'Left leg. Double puncture marks, small and close-set. What do you suppose to be the origin? Pray, do not tell me a vampire did it.'

A titter went about the room, subsiding into the shifting of feet as Tranmer bent to the body then started back, his hand pressed to his bloodless face.

'Come now, no squeamishness,' Holmes said, 'for many of your fellows are officers, and they will mock you. We must not be deterred by the small matter of odiferous unpleasantness, for it is in examining the first effects of the crime that our best clues may be found.'

Tranmer cleared his throat. 'He – he has tripped, perhaps—'

'Nonsense!' Holmes dismissed him with a wave. 'Can anybody enlighten our young friend?'

I heard someone rise to their feet; I knew, before I turned, that it was Smedley. 'It is a snakebite,' he said, 'as encountered in your own case of the speckled band.'

'Exactly,' Holmes said. 'Of course, I possessed certain advantages. Enquiring into the life of Dr Roylott informed me that he was accustomed to travelling throughout the tropics and that he possessed several Indian animals. An examination of the room revealed a dummy bell-rope and ventilator, allowing his swamp adder to reach his intended victim. A deduction as to the cause of death provided the key to preventing the lethal bite.'

'Yet there *was* a bite,' said Smedley. 'You frightened the creature into turning on its master; it took his life in seconds.'

Holmes bowed. 'You have made a study of me.'

I stirred uncomfortably. I had written an account of the case myself. Had I done my part in fuelling this upstart's pretentions?

But Holmes had moved on. 'You see the importance,' he declaimed, 'of knowing who a man is; his habits; his enemies; where he came from; the circumstances in which he was struck down. Only then may we form a complete picture. This very week, the body of a finely-dressed man – a gentleman, no doubt – was found at the Thames embankment, having been cast into a sewer as if less than worthless. It has perplexed the police, and I dare say will continue to do so a while yet – particularly as no one appears to be searching for him.'

'The victim of a cut-purse.' Smedley had not yet retaken his seat.

'The lack of injury to his person would suggest otherwise.'

'But you will solve it, will you not?' a voice called from the back of the room.

Holmes's lip twitched. 'Contrary to expectations,' he said drily, 'I cannot take upon my shoulders *every* case in London.'

The lecture theatre was reduced to silence. Holmes paused for a moment, leaning against the table whereupon lay the much-maligned cadaver. The pattering of rain seemed suddenly loud; the light shifted and flowed across my friend's face. He appeared exhausted, his complexion grey. Smedley was seated once more, leaning forward, his pale eyes a-gleam in the shadows. He reminded me of nothing so much as a snake himself, poised and watching and waiting to strike.

The rest of the lecture brought a repeat of the same performance, though with different actors and examples of the detective's art. Holmes revealed his knowledge of stab-wounds; their width, angle and positioning, whether made by sword, ice pick or stiletto; the numerous effects of strangulation; and some insight into how a bullet may be matched to a weapon. None of his listeners proved as well-informed as Smedley, who asked several pertinent questions, pressing his instructor until the hour grew late and Holmes looked quite spent.

Then Smedley said, 'Are we to apply these theorems in the actual realm of reality at any juncture?'

The question was impertinent, but Holmes merely inclined his head. 'When you are ready,' he said, and turned to leave the room.

Smedley's face darkened. I remembered he was a practising officer prior to taking up his place in the school, and must have encountered several real cases before now.

'However.' Sherlock paused without turning. 'A little sojourn about the streets of London would not harm any of you, I am sure. Tomorrow!'

With that, he swept from the room. I did not see him again until we boarded a hansom cab to return to our lodgings at 221b Baker

Street. He was little inclined to speak, and I was scarcely more so; anyway, it was an effort to raise our voices above the sound of the rain, which lashed the cab roof and the driver's oilskin, and hissed about the streets. I could not prevent my outburst, however, when Holmes asked how I found his lecture.

'It was informative, Holmes – too informative! Why, the fellow drained you of knowledge – and you told him everything!

'Of course, dear fellow. Is that not the purpose of a teacher?'

'But perhaps it would be better to hold a little in reserve, would it not? Why should you—'

'I am mortally tired, Watson.' Sherlock settled into his seat and tipped his hat over his eyes. 'Pray, let us discuss it another time.'

I blustered, I admit, but subsided, valuing the peace of my friend above my own indignation. I did not like his appearance; his cheeks were quite bloodless, as if he had been drained of more than knowledge. And I told myself there was little to be done, if Holmes really was set on giving up every last one of his secrets.

3

I had not intended to spend another day at the school for detection, but Holmes's proclamation about the streets had piqued my interest and so I found myself once more surrounded by the eagerness of youth. We all watched as Holmes unpacked a series of boxes, rags and other items spilling across a table. I smelled old fustian, spied the rusted black of a clerk's jacket, an indifferently clean apron, various hats and caps. From another box he removed pairs of spectacles; next, he produced face-pastes, paints and powders, and several rather unpleasant wigs.

He smiled and gestured about him. 'A lesson in disguise.'

Holmes was a master of such things. During the course of his investigations he had taken on the appearance of everyone from a clergyman to a groom to an opium addict. I had before now looked him square in the eye and entirely failed to recognise him. He could mimic to uncanny degree the way of standing or walking of other men, and further, he could control the musculature of his face so well that his visage almost appeared to change with his apparel.

'We shall each adopt the dress, expression, posture and habits of our chosen character, before proceeding into the streets,' he said. 'But it shall not be so simple; for sometimes, you may find it necessary to throw off pursuit. How useful, then, if your disguise may be adapted or exchanged – a moustached clerk becoming a bearded fellow with a stoop. Such is your challenge. You will go in pairs: one to flee, one to follow. When one is caught, the game is up and your positions are reversed. Half an hour, I think, will suffice to affect your transformations.' He gave a rare smile.

A shuffling ran about the lecture theatre. Without looking up, Holmes said, 'Yes, Smedley?' There was no trace of irritation in his voice.

'Thank you. I merely wish to point out that there is an irregular number of students in the room.'

'Is there? Then *I* thank *you*. In that case, I shall myself take on a disguise, and I shall be your pursuer – at least until such time as you give me the slip.'

Smedley barely concealed his eagerness as he made his way with the rest to the items on the table. All seized their choice of attire; some began stepping into voluminous skirts where they stood, whilst others concealed their finds and retired to try them in privacy. There were muted guffaws and excited murmurs as they blackened teeth and tried various wigs. Holmes, though, turned his back on it all and left by a side door.

A short time afterwards, the students began to return, wearing an outlandish array of costumes. There was a beggar, his beard too well-trimmed and his cheeks too well-fed; a costermonger with straggling locks; and a grinning hawker of penny bloods, a bundle of pamphlets clutched before him. A passable clerk there was too, and a clergyman who gave me pause. His round eye-glasses sparkled in the light and some mild arrogance in the tilt of his head, under his low-crowned hat, was so fitting I found myself wondering if he was genuine. Then I realised it was Smedley.

'Good-day, sir.' I turned towards the wavering voice and saw a woman in mourning weeds making her way towards me. The widow's beringed hands shook around the handle of her cane, but I saw through the guise at once.

'Holmes,' I said in a low voice, 'good heavens! I had expected better.'

For it was plainly him, his features merely half covered by a veil rather than changed. I supposed that would be easy to cast off if he were pursued, but the skirts would scarcely be so simple.

'Did you, Watson?' he asked mildly. He surveyed his students at the bottom of the amphitheatre. 'Perhaps you are right. This dye is nasty stuff – pah! There is little wonder that widows complain of their eyes. Still, I'll warrant the irritation must provide the appropriate tears, even if they have no genuine ones to shed.'

'But Holmes – it is more of a pity not to lead by example. I know that no one could recognise you, if you really did not wish them to do so.'

He stared into space for a moment and his hand went to the rather intricate jet brooch at his neck. I peered through the veil at his fine nose, his wan cheeks, and realised that any casual observer *could* imagine him a woman, her sharp features hollowed with sorrow.

Holmes drew a deep sigh. 'Strange to think, Watson, of the gentleman cast into the sewer. He had no disguise, yet no one knows him. How he must wish, if he could cry out from the ground, that someone would recognise him!'

'And you really have no interest in the case?'

'A little interest, though very little time. And half of London is fascinated with that particular matter. Such is the way, when death is tempered with mystery, and indeed with horror. It is a pity that no direct examination was made of the circumstances...'

A low cough at our backs made me start. I turned and saw that Smedley had crept around the gathering to stand directly behind us; I wondered at once how much he had heard, then felt only shame at the judgement I had passed on Holmes's guise.

Holmes appeared not in the least perturbed. 'Capital! You have apprehended me already. Then it is my turn. Let us proceed at once.' He raised his voice to the rest. 'Do not forget: be artful! Evade, dodge, melt into the very walls! We reconvene at two, to consider what we have learned. For now: London!'

'London!' came an echoing cry, as the motley gathering of every class and occupation tried to spill all at once from the door.

I was left alone in the room. I glanced around at the shadowy ranks of seats, seeing again the eager faces that had filled them. I smiled to think of Smedley, trying to shake off Holmes in the streets he surely knew better than anyone, and I decided to step out and enjoy luncheon at my club. Today, at least, I would not have to listen to the young buck's boasting as I ate.

Outside, the sky was lowering, the clouds swollen and heavy with yet unfallen rain. It was not so dank as yesterday, and for now, there was no downpour; only an ever-present dampness hanging in the air, the humidity turning everything grey with mist. I wondered if that would help Holmes's students make their various escapes, then banished them all from my mind.

As I walked, I realised I could smell not only the damp, but the river. There was a taint of ordure in it; the sewers must be overflowing into the Thames once more. At least the system had been much improved since the time of the Great Stink, when they had to hang blankets soaked in chloride of lime at the windows of the Houses of Parliament to keep out the stench.

A pleasant repast of cutlets and kidneys made me forget such matters, and when I returned, the day, as well as my mood, was brighter. The latter was not to last, however; although I returned well short of two o'clock, I heard the exulting tones of a familiar voice in the passage.

'That's right!' Smedley crowed. 'Less than twenty minutes! I swear it upon my life. I slipped into an emporium, and dashed away – he was hindered by his skirts, ha! From thence it was a simple matter to make my escape, by the doors into the opposite street.'

There came the scornful laugh of one of his fellows.

'I required no great trickery, though I was prepared for it. I did not even have to change my disguise. He is losing his sharpness – he is worn down! – unless his skills were only ever exaggerated by his buffoon of a friend.'

That was too much. I strode around the corner – his eyes were alight with mirth and triumph, though at the sight of me, he lowered them at once. He gave a shallow bow and stole away; his callow friend followed likewise.

I was glad to have routed them, though I should have liked to give vent to my anger. How dare he? And yet it would not have rankled so deeply, if his boasting had not carried a point. Holmes's disguise had been simple. He could do better – I had seen better!

I was still glaring at the space where Smedley had stood when a small sound made me turn. There, framed in the doorway, was Holmes himself. He was stooping; for a moment he leaned against the door jamb, before throwing back his veil to reveal a waxen countenance.

'There you are, Watson.' He spoke gruffly, as if it were I who'd been off chasing wild geese around the alleys and by-ways of London.

'Yes indeed, though I did not expect you for a while yet, Holmes.'

'Ah – no. That is true.'

'What on earth happened, dear fellow? Are you well?'

'I am, to answer one of your questions, Watson. As to the other – hmm.'

'The fellow is boasting that he threw you off within minutes, Holmes. How can that be so?'

'Ah – the luck of youth, Watson, or perhaps the legs. Curse this veil!' Holmes rubbed his eyes, which were by now quite red.

'You are ill.'

'No: it is simple. He gave me the slip. I could not even find him again to reverse our roles.'

'He is making much of it, Holmes. He will do so again when the others return, I have no doubt.'

'Then, pray, accompany me to my office. It would not do to be mocked whilst wearing a dress, even if it is one of such sombre colour.'

His skirts rustled against the wall as he passed me, and I followed along seemingly endless corridors to his office. He did not at once remove his outer vestments, only throwing off the veil before slumping into a chair and slipping his pipe into his mouth. He did not light it, but stared contemplatively into space. I opened my mouth to question him further, but there came a sudden sharp rap at the door.

A moment later, it opened to reveal a police officer. He started in surprise at Holmes's attire, then shuffled over the threshold as if not quite certain how to proceed. Holmes merely raised his head and waited. The scene struck upon me as somewhat comical, though I could not laugh.

The constable's next words made such an impression evaporate into the air. 'Sir, I wonder if you are able to accompany me to the

Embankment? There's been a body found. A woman, this time. We would very much appreciate your eye at the scene.'

Sherlock stood, his manner dignified, despite the rustling of his crape. 'Of course. I shall join you forthwith. Just allow me a moment.'

The constable raised one sly eyebrow. 'To remove your gown, sir?' he said.

'Quite so,' was Holmes's colourless reply.

4

A dismal sight met our eyes when we stepped from the hansom near the bank of the Thames. It was almost a pity that the skies had begun to lighten, delineating the scene so clearly. The constable led us towards the swollen river until we saw a narrow platform, just above water level. There lay the woman, foully begrimed and soiled. Her dress must once have been white, though was now greyed with water and discoloured with abhorrent matter. Her face was as grey as her dress had become, and her hair likewise; it was loose, tangled and matted, flowing like water-weed about her shoulders. She had not the dignity of a cap or bonnet; perhaps that had been lost.

Holmes did not hesitate, but jumped down to join an officer at the woman's side. He leaned over the corpse with neither repugnance nor compassion. Then he peered around, seeming to stare at the river wall.

Rapid steps announced a new arrival, and I turned. My spirits fell as I made out Simon Smedley. He stopped at my side and he too gazed down at the body, not with pity but the same rapt eagerness he had shown in the lecture theatre. The similarity of the scene struck me, and yet here were no banks of seats or plinth or respectfully covering cloth: there were only the lighters out on the river, the blank rushing water, the glare of the sun spearing through broken clouds.

'Smedley.' Holmes had seen him, and I was pleased to hear his peremptory tone.

The upstart's expression changed at once, replacing his fervency with something more apologetic. 'Forgive me, Mr Holmes,' he said. 'I thought I caught a glimpse of you outside the school, and felt I had better take my turn in pursuing you. I am quite sure you had caught up with me at the emporium, after all.'

I stared. The fellow spoke as if I'd never overheard his boasting – but Holmes spoke before I could.

'This is a pressing case. You must return at once.'

Smedley's eyes flashed with something other than apology. 'Ah – if you wish it, of course. I am your most humble servant. But – I am here, am I not? Perhaps I would not be entirely in the way, if I could observe the master at work?'

Sherlock stared at him a long moment. I waited for him to dismiss the fellow, but Holmes did not; he gestured for Smedley to jump down to the platform. He did so, his lip curling, and I decided I should go too; I could perhaps offer some insight as a medical man. And so we crowded into the little space around the body, which gave rise to a noisome stench. Then I realised that it alone was not the source; behind us was a large, brick-lined sewer outflow, dripping with foetid matter and clots of loathsome origin.

'The body came from in there.' The constable's explanation was scarcely necessary. 'The rainfall overflowed the system, and carried her here. If she hadn't been snagged on the platform—'

I wondered how long the pitiable remains had been in the sewer before being expelled in such an undignified fashion. Perhaps she had been cast into it some time before – it struck me then she might have drowned in it, and grimaced.

'A trawlerman spotted her,' the constable went on. 'He came in a skiff to examine her. Lucky he did – if the water rose higher, it would have carried her off.'

'Then,' said Holmes, half under his breath, 'we might never have discovered where she came from, or what her life was. Her gown is expensive, is it not? The embroidery is very fine. Have the police received any enquiries after a missing woman, constable?'

He gave it that they had not.

'Like the other.' Holmes spoke under his breath, though not so low that Smedley couldn't hear. He leaned in, missing nothing.

'Her attire is stained with ordure, but there is no blood, no visible injury. Her gown is not otherwise damaged.' Holmes turned to the outflow, staring into its dark emptiness. His olfactory powers were legendary; I saw his nostrils twitch. The miasma came from it in waves, damp and cloying, more putrid than any quantity of fresh air could efface.

'Well,' he said, 'it is a pity.'

'A pity?' Smedley edged as close as he could without actually stepping on Holmes's shoes.

Holmes suddenly sagged. 'Constable,' he said, 'do you possess such a thing as a lantern?'

'Holmes, you cannot mean it!' I said. I looked at the black tunnel mouth in horror. A man could not even stand straight within it; he'd have to stoop, balancing himself by running his hand along those filthy bricks—

No. He was ill; he could not do it. But the constable nodded, calling to his colleague to bring a light, and the relief in his voice was such that I knew this was what he'd intended; that Holmes, not he, would have to enter that dreadful conduit, until he found – what?

'It leads north, I take it?' Holmes said.

'It does. The tunnel lets onto the main passage, which is both taller and wider than this opening. By following it against the flow, one might find the source.'

'Indeed.' The lantern was put into Holmes's hand and he held it high, revealing more clearly the stained brick. The light wavered; his hand was shaking.

'*Holmes.*' I stepped towards him, reaching for his shoulder. There was something wrong, I knew that now.

'If I may, Mr Holmes.' It was Simon Smedley. 'Perhaps I might be of assistance.'

'Yes,' I said. 'Perhaps he could. Please, do listen.' It was infuriating to say the words, but my friend's health was more important than any amount of irritation.

'You do not look well, Mr Holmes.'

'Nonsense. I have some little irritation of the eye, that is all. The veil, you know.'

'Pray, allow me to help.' Smedley spoke eagerly. 'I have listened to your lectures most assiduously, Mr Holmes. I have studied your ways. I am quite sure, if I can discover where this woman came from, I can solve it all.'

Holmes gazed at him, new respect dawning on his features. 'I almost believe you could, at that.'

'Of course I could! And after all, Mr Holmes, you cannot take *every* case in London.'

'I cannot.'

'I shall make my report to you with all haste.'

Holmes turned to the constable. 'I take it that you have spoken to a representative of the sewer company,' he said. 'It is safe to pass – it will not flood again today?'

'We have, sir, and it will not. Levels have been falling throughout the fore-noon. It will be unpleasant, to be sure, but it will be safe.'

Holmes stared out over the murky river. After a moment, and without looking at Smedley, he held out the lantern. Smedley reached out; his fingers closed around the handle.

'There is just one thing I should like to ask before I embark on my adventure,' Smedley said.

'You do not need to name it.' Sherlock raised his head and met his eye. 'Should you solve it, I assure you, the triumph shall be yours alone.'

5

We made a taciturn party during the ride back to Baker Street, accompanied only by the constant rumble of the wheels of the hansom cab. I kept opening my mouth to speak, but really, I had nothing to say. I could not approve of what had passed; nor could I wish my friend within the dark and malodorous tunnels beneath London. Yet I could not but wonder: was this to be the future, then? Would others take his place, one after the next, whilst Holmes retreated into his lectures and quiet rooms?

We stepped out into the early evening. I paused to look into the fading sky, which matched my melancholy, only for Holmes to reach the door before me. I heard him striding up the stairs, two at a time.

I hurried to catch up and found Holmes already ensconced in his chair, just lighting his pipe. A blue-grey haze rose before him, obscuring his features. Its spiced scent was a relief after the awful vapours that had emerged from the tunnel.

'Really, Holmes.' In that moment, safely inside, and with my friend so suddenly recovered, I couldn't help remembering what he'd said about enduring a little odiferous unpleasantness. 'He is set upon stealing your cases away, beginning with this. Are you not even concerned that he will solve it before you?'

I saw the white flash of his teeth through the smoke. 'I very much doubt that, Watson. I solved it myself this morning.'

I started; he laughed at my astonishment.

'Just so. Inspector Lestrade will be calling upon us shortly, to discuss my conclusions. I think he shall find them satisfactory.'

'But who – what—'

He settled into his seat, with relish rather than exhaustion. 'It was quite elementary,' he said. 'Did you not wonder why nobody sought these unfortunate souls?

'Of, course, but—'

'Or why they should be found in such a place, yet with no marks of unnatural death upon them?'

I sighed. 'Pray, do explain it to me. For I find I am once more at a disadvantage, and somewhat out of sorts at that.'

'I thank you for it, Watson. You have ever been a dear friend to me, and I am indebted to you for guarding my interests so zealously.'

'You are teasing me, Holmes.'

'I am; and yet I am sincere.'

I could only bow in answer.

Holmes went on. 'Did you happen to notice a small piece in the newspaper about Saint Michael's Chapel? It has long been used as a place of worship, and yet its congregation is much depressed in these godless times.'

'I did not,' I replied. 'Are they dissenters?'

'They are not. But there have been some strange occurrences at the chapel. Children going into fits, woman fainting, men vomiting and so forth.'

'And the cause?' I spoke impatiently, for I could not possibly see how the two things could be connected.

'Foul air,' he said, 'emerging through the floorboards from the burial pit below. It was closed some years ago, naturally; the Burial Laws have seen to that. Yet people continue to complain of a dreadful odour, and of biting insects – *body-bugs*, they call them – coming from beneath their feet. The vault has never been sealed, you see. It remains packed to the rafters with coffins and festering bodies, and there is no lath or plaster, only floorboards that have warped over time to let the miasma out.'

I frowned.

'It has happened before, Watson. You have heard of Enon Chapel? It was constructed before we were born, in 1823, but it remains quite notorious. Over twelve thousand bodies were interred in the burial pit beneath, making some of its congregants terribly ill. It was Enon Chapel that spurred on the Burial Laws, and the establishment of new cemeteries outside the city.'

'I never heard of it.'

'Have you not? It is a fine story. Before the bodies were removed, the place was turned into a dancing salon. It was quite the morbid attraction. Wait!' Holmes sprung to his feet, returning with an ageing handbill, curling and yellowed. I read:

ENON CHAPEL – DANCING ON THE DEAD – ADMISSION THREEPENCE. NO LADY OR GENTLEMAN ADMITTED UNLESS WEARING SHOES AND STOCKINGS.

'Shoes and stockings!' I exclaimed. 'But Holmes, what does this have to do with – it does not make sense! Old bodies would not emit the sort of stench you describe. And there would be no insects, so long after interment.'

'Ah.' Holmes was suddenly grave and I realised that he was waiting.

'Oh,' I said.

'You see – you have hit upon it. There would only be such a fetor if the vault had been re-opened and was being used again for burials.'

'But that would be illegal!'

He smiled. 'So it would. And yet such is the case. The vault is full, of course. The only way it could accommodate further occupants is by finding some additional room. In this instance, it was an easy matter, since the church is situated above an open sewer.'

I grimaced. 'You have investigated the tunnels already, then?'

'Not so. Do you think me a fool? I sent for a map of the system; I am already well equipped with a map of the city. It was simplicity itself to compare the two.'

'So our victims—'

'Are not victims at all, in the sense you mean. They were buried, in the full knowledge of their families, in a grave the like of which can scarcely today be found in London: within the sanctified walls of the church. That is why no one looked for them. Their relatives were not to know that their loved ones had actually been thrown into the sewer. If it were not for the recent rains, they might never have known it.'

'How terrible. But Holmes – how on earth can you be so sure of it?'

'Why, did you not wonder about my choice of a widow's guise this morning? I had all the facts before me, and so I paid a little visit to the chapel. I made certain enquiries about the cost of such a burial, for my husband, you know. I found the curate to be a rather grasping fellow, and somewhat down on his luck. He was most sympathetic to my plight, particularly when he saw what a fine brooch I wore. Did you notice that little touch? I was rather proud of it. He imagined I must have a not inconsiderable sum set by.'

I stared at him. 'But Holmes – Smedley! He was meant to be pursuing you, was he not?' And then I understood how neatly he had worked it, and a smile spread across my features.

'You see it all, Watson,' he said warmly. 'Smedley has been my constant shadow; waiting, I am certain, for just such an opportunity as he found today. And yet I struck upon the very means to shake him off when it was needed, did I not?'

'By having him do that very thing to you. Why, Holmes, you are a genius.'

'Not at all. I simply know that there is little use in observation, if you do not trouble to read the papers.'

I thought of Smedley, his pale eyes penetrating the shadows of the lecture theatre, so intent upon Holmes's words; and it returned to me where he had gone. 'And now?' I spluttered.

'He is, at this very moment, immersed in the foulest underbelly of London. There, I fancy, he may discover for himself the source of the body. I have no doubt he is equal to the task.'

I imagined Smedley stumbling through the dark, filled with its cloying mephitic vapours, only his little light for company. I imagined the shadows that would shift and dance about him; the rats; the foulness of what he must wade through. And where would his journey end? He would discover the vault full of corpses, coffins stacked one upon the next until they burst, revealing the skeletons in their cerements. What horrors would come to him then? I almost pitied him.

'You might simply have dismissed him, Holmes.'

He gave a grin that was almost wolfish. 'Ah,' he said, 'I could.' He chuckled.

'But perhaps he may still claim the credit.'

'Hm. Well, Watson, I have a confession to make. I have broken with my usual reticence; you may read everything about the case, if you wish, and very soon. It shall be in the evening edition. I don't doubt that Smedley will see it too, when he emerges. A burial pit discovered beneath London – it will have created quite the stir by then, I imagine.'

I let out my breath. 'Why, Holmes! I do believe you have done it all without heeding your own lessons. What of all your advice about observing the body and the place it came from, of understanding the life to perceive the death? Were you not incorrect on that, at least?'

He met my gaze, his eyes glinting. 'Not at all, Watson. For did I not also say that it would be a remarkable man indeed who could expect to solve a crime without leaving his rooms?'

I stared at him. After a long moment, he drew on his pipe and breathed out, slowly and with evident satisfaction, and I could not help it; I began to laugh. In a moment, Holmes was laughing with me; and for once we allowed ourselves to be lost to a veritable contagion of mirth.

|The Flowering|

~

Afterwards, I cannot help thinking of her. I am supposed to be setting down in my notes a description of some new cultivars, which my master, Mr Petherton, shall put into his catalogue. It is easy work in comparison to digging the flowerbeds and the constant vigilance against weeds, and I am grateful to be entrusted with it. And yet I read again what I have written: *Growing to a height of about two feet, with clusters of small flowers, white, pink, or violet, and pale fronds about the eyes...*

My pen has run on with my memories, and I strike out the last word, an unaccustomed blot on my work. I do not write the things that continue to run through my mind: *Hair of gold gathered into fantastical gleaming twists, skin of blameless white, and yes, those eyelashes, appearing like white fronds in the morning sun; the dress, simple and blameless likewise, all the graceful adornment she requires, and in her hands...*

I remember what happened yesterday and frown. My master and I had dressed so carefully, Mr Petherton donning his fur-trimmed gown and chains before calling for a carriage to take us to St Giles Without Cripplegate, that ancient church so beloved of the Worshipful Company of Gardeners. I had helped him alight and stood by as the Company processed towards the altar in pairs, carrying their ceremonial silver spade, before we took our places for the Fairchild Sermon.

A glory of light set the windows ablaze in brilliant reds and blues. The pews were full, the choir in good voice, and there was only the faintest smell of dust, which must have arisen from the church, since I had thoroughly scrubbed the soil from under my nails.

Then I twisted in my seat and saw her: Millicent Ashton, the luxuriant fronds of her eyelashes resting on her cheek, since her face was demurely downcast. I could still see their loveliness, however, as the priest stepped to his lectern and any last shuffling and whispering ceased.

The priest spoke of creation. He spoke of the third day, when God called forth every single herb and grass and fruit-bearing tree, fixed and unchanging, for ever and ever, amen. He spoke of the wondrous variety that was then called into being, the fecundity which Adam would have the pleasure of naming. He spoke, in short, of the wonderful works of God in His creation, which was no surprise, since that was what he'd been paid to do. And all throughout his droning twaddle I could not help but glance towards Millicent Ashton and finger the little flowering plant I held in my hand: the one that proved the Company hypocrites and the priest an oaf; the one that gave the lie to it all.

Thomas Fairchild, the patron of this sermon, was also the originator of the first man-made hybrid flower. He was the nurseryman who birthed a flood of new creation, new life and new colour, blooms of which the Creator never dreamed. I turned the flowers in my hand, white and pink, pink and white. I pictured Fairchild labouring over its parent plants, first drawing a feather across the stamen of a sweet William, back and forth, before setting it to the stigma of a carnation, up and down, and sitting back, satisfied, leaving the rest to nature. Waiting as the pollen impregnated the ovule, creating a seed hitherto never seen; as it grew, becoming something new under the sun; as it unfurled, living proof of the sexual reproduction of plants.

Then, shocked at his own audacity, he declared to the Royal Society that it was created by 'serendipity'. Chastened by his blasphemy, he bequeathed the sum of £25 for this sermon to be preached and droned and rattled out annually forever, God bless his fearful little soul, if indeed he possessed such a thing; if do we all.

And the wondrous title of this wonderful specimen? Why, nothing grander than Fairchild's Mule, the same flower I held in my somewhat damp fingers in these latter days of the nineteenth century, over a hundred and fifty years later.

I smirked at the sight of Millicent Ashton's father, that rich old bearded Billy goat, sitting next to his daughter, a ramrod up his back. He could scarcely decline such a specimen on her behalf, not on such an occasion. It was surely of too great an interest to a botanist such as he, albeit he pursues that interest in a respectably amateur way.

I pictured her wearing my little gift, taking it to her room, turning it in her hands. I had made it a habit to present her with little samples for her flower press, on her visits to the nursery; she follows her father in his interest, in an even more amateur way, naturally, and I liked to think of it – her fingers wrapped around their seed heads, tasting their nectar, touching their fruit to her lips.

I shifted in my seat at the image, fixing my eyes on the cadaverous face of the priest, surely enough to cool anyone's ardour. Then I followed my master, filing outside into a day bright with sunlight, holding the Mule – only a little marred with moisture from my hands – to see Millicent Ashton talking and laughing with a fellow I had never seen before.

My consternation was in no way alleviated when my master, upon seeing him, called out a greeting, his hoarse old voice suddenly bright. 'Mr Andrew Nicholls, as I live and breathe! How splendid!'

The young man turned.

'And such a pleasure to see that you are making the acquaintance of the daughter of my most esteemed patron.'

It was neither a pleasure nor especially splendid to see the fellow turn and smile. I would have wished him to have teeth rotting in his head, skin ravaged by the pox, or indeed his whole self to the Devil, rather than in the company of Miss Ashton; but I gave a stiff-jawed smile and followed Mr Petherton, who went towards him and, rather than shaking his hand, enfolded him in his arms.

After more earnest declarations of pleasure, and oddly, apologies on behalf of the young man for not being able to come sooner, my master remembered my presence.

'Do meet my faithful assistant, he said. 'Simon Smith.'

Damn the man, I had to shake his hand, only then remembering the Mule, which had slipped from my fingers. How could I present it to her now? It was sullied; it was ruined. I could not even lift my eyes to her face. I did not wish to see the glow in hers, or how those fronds had been set all a-flutter by this fresh young breeze. I simply placed one foot over the fallen hybrid, as coy as Fairchild himself when he requested this sermon to be preached, as I heard Petherton say the words that put a chill into my heart.

'This is my second cousin's boy,' he said. 'A great surprise for you, I think, Simon! Though it could hardly be otherwise, as I am certain anyone could predict. He is soon to be coming to work with us.'

He clapped the youth on the shoulder. If it were not too obvious to state, too simple to *predict*, I was utterly wordless.

~

All I remember of my mother was walking through Regent's Park, so long ago, holding her hand as she told me of the trees interlacing over our heads and the occasional wild flower that had somehow managed to thrive amid the grass. I remember her gentle looks as she taught me of them all. My mother loved me. She adored me. She would have given me the world; little wonder, then, if her last act in this life was to apprentice me to a man who grew every kind of flower within it.

Perhaps I exaggerate, but so Mr Petherton's nursery had appeared to my young eyes, and if he had not yet obtained every single flower, he was at least avid in trying to fill the deficiency.

Now he wandered with me between the raised beds and trays and pots, demonstrating all the means by which man could overcome nature. He showed me the glass- and hothouses that could give rise to new flowers, both in their season and without, as was required. He offered up all the plants and gave me their names: not those devised by Adam, but the binomial names given by Carl Linnaeus, that great systematiser and scientist of the last century, who categorised plants according to their number of stamens and pistils.

Mr Petherton did not hold my hand, but he had often said he valued me as a son, and stood as a father to me, and he was besides old and without an heir, and who in my place would not imagine…?

For Petherton, too, has flirted with hybrids. The place is seething with their unnatural colours and fantastical forms. And it seemed by no means out of the question that he might one day wish to see a baser scion grafted to a nobler stock – to mangle the words of Shakespeare – for the pleasure of seeing what would become of that.

Now there is this interloper, this popinjay, this distant cousin's son, blue of eye, blonde of hair, bright of smile, hideous; hideous. As I watch, he gestures across the geraniums as if he birthed them all himself, and Miss Ashton, who walks at his side, simpers at his wisdom.

I curse to see him so, strutting about the place like a coxcomb, as if he already owns it all, while I, who reared so many of these jewels from seed, am entirely forgotten. Mr Petherton walks behind them, talking with Mr Ashton, who nods along as sage as Solomon. In their full view, Adam in his Paradise stoops and selects a flower here, a herb there, and snip, snip, gathers them for her. I cannot prevent a snort of laughter. A herb, a twig of evergreen? She has seen them all, many times. Even Linnaeus knew that botany was not opaque to the gentler sex; his system was so simple, he had declared it could even be understood by a woman.

Why, then, does the fool imagine that these commonplaces will fascinate her? Yet she lowers her head as he presents his gift, the better to breathe it in, and looks up at him through those eyelashes.

They take a turn about the rose bushes until they are close by, walking past me without a word.

'Ah, yes,' Petherton is saying to her father, 'I dare say that should be of interest. It is in my special hothouse – it is not, as you know, for everyone. The scent is quite – overwhelming.'

I know at once that they are speaking of one of his special rarities, now in its finest hour: the stinkhorn, or as Linnaeus had proudly named it, the *phallus impudicus*. It could be said that that gentleman was, on occasion, a little injudicious when it came to his naming; one more reason, I suppose, why his publications were somewhat gloriously placed on the Vatican's list of forbidden books.

Still, I wonder that Mr Petherton should mention it within his patron's daughter's hearing. I suggested only a week ago that we should enter the smallest of the hothouses and observe its growth, only for Mr Petherton to answer, in scandalised tones, that perhaps it was a little inappropriate.

I picture it: not a flower or a tree, but a fungus of splendid proportions. The stinkhorn begins its life as an egg. As it develops, the fertile part is thrust upward on a single fleshy stalk of prodigious girth. The deliquescent, gelatinous mass containing its spores, known as the gleba, is enclosed by a membranous cap. The characteristic foul smell is designed to attract *hymenoptera*, the insects which are the instrument for the spores' dispersal.

Now, together, they make their way to gaze upon the *phallus*. Millicent still has her head lowered as she lifts her white skirts, to avoid soiling them on a bed of fine tilth. The father makes no demur. It seems that what was objectionable to look upon with me as their guide is no obstacle with young Master Nicholls at their side.

They emerge a little later, Miss Ashton flushed and pressing Andrew's posy to her nose, as if he had presented it to her for just such a purpose; Mr Petherton smiling at his – *my* – expertise in raising such a beast; Mr Ashton, smiling over his daughter's blushes; and the popinjay, who holds out his arm for her to take. As he does, I notice a book tucked into his pocket.

It does nothing to improve my temper to see, as they take their leave, its title: *Flower Lore: the Teachings of Flowers, Historical, Legendary, Poetical and Symbolic*, by Miss Carruthers of Inverness, where I should very much prefer her silly notions had remained. It is a floral dictionary, wherein, among other nonsense, is to be found a key to the language of flowers, those secret messages passed between lovers, encapsulated in the form of various blooms. He tilts it towards her as she leaves, and I see the nod of understanding she gives him in return.

I think again of the posy he presented to her. Lily-of-the-valley: that, I believe, in the terms of his floriography, is for sweetness and purity. There is lavender, for devotion. Marjoram is for happiness and finally, pricking or not, there is holly: for hope.

In his slovenly, imprecise, girlish breed of language, he speaks to her of love.

I am gathering the flora that Mr Ashton has ordered to be sent to his home in the country: great shrubs and saplings, carefully planted and tended and watered by my hand, are now uprooted by my spade. I am digging, in fact, like a peasant, of no more notice than the seagulls with clipped wings that Petherton keeps to peck at snails before they can damage his leaves.

I wipe sweat from my forehead before wrapping a root ball in linen and placing it carefully into a box so that not a hair shall be crushed. In the glasshouse, I can see Andrew – or Adam as I prefer to think of him, this man who seemed to spring into being as suddenly as his namesake, who enjoys this Paradise of another's making. Indeed, he is harvesting the work of my hands. He has no spade, not even a trowel.

He snip-snips with a little pair of silver scissors, tilting his head this way and that.

I think of Millicent Ashton: the way she has been tended, watched over, nurtured. She has no siblings, no rival in her blooming. She is lovely; magnificent. Furthermore, she is a perennial, for she alone is to inherit her father's fortune.

I had thought, once I had the nursery, I would have the girl too. Now, like a sunflower, she has turned her face towards a brighter light, as do we all. I watch as Adam arranges the second order placed by the Ashtons, this one of blooms intended to adorn their townhouse, where they currently reside, this being the correct season for the City.

He pauses, bows his head, considers. Then he begins on an arrangement they did not order: a womanish little nosegay wrapped in a paper doily. But of course it is womanish, I realise, as he makes his choice. White jasmine: that's for sweet love. A white rose: purity. And chamomile for patience. He wraps it about with honeysuckle for the bonds of affection, ties it with a silken ribbon and slips it into the case intended for her drawing room. I do not suppose it will reach so far. I imagine her pressing it to her bosom, slipping away with it to her chamber, where it will fragrance the air with the thought of him.

I close my hands into fists. The popinjay sends her such chaste blooms: surely his bed will be every bit as cold.

The father, perhaps I mentioned, is an Enthusiast. He relishes new specimens, the finest examples of which he uses to adorn his carriageway, so that the world may see and admire. His country residence is his hobby; the townhouse, for now, is his home, and cut flowers are essential. They are born and die to decorate his halls, to freshen the air he breathes, to provide a frame for his daughter's loveliness. I wonder if he is something of a Quaker? There is certainly a touch of it about him. The plain way of dressing, the upright stance… I imagine him standing back from my arrangements in sublime contemplation, glorying in God's creation; flowers as a path to the Almighty.

And there they shall be, an extravagant efflorescence. Even Adam nods with admiration when he sees what I have gathered for them today, but he cannot read my language, not yet. For mine is that of true botany – a language that any could understand, if they should only look.

Linnaeus categorised them all by their lascivious nature. The lilies, he said, each frolic with six husbands. The tulips – late bloomers these, but I have coaxed them – are pleasured by upwards of twenty males in a single marriage. And there are marigolds, profligate fellows who dwell not only with numerous wives but concubines too.

I picture Mr Ashton running his hands over my exotic blooms, each displaying their flamboyant wares like a harlot on a street corner, raising their skirts to exhibit their parts; every flower a beautifully curtained and scented bed.

Well, was Linnaeus made of stone? Not for nothing was his taxonomy known as a Sexual System. Plants were arranged into classes and orders by the number of male and female genitalia, while other parts were compared to the labia minora and majora. Little wonder if his obsession spilled over into his descriptions; the language of flowers is not coy, not something to be found between Miss Carruthers' pages but rather between her legs. This is the man who termed the calyx the lips of the cunt; the one who named the impudent phallus. Rousseau once declared that the study of nature could help prevent the tumults of passion; I say Rousseau was a donkey.

And here comes Adam, the innocent fool, dreaming of his Eden. He is holding something in his hands: ah, his little message for his sweet dove. His posy has mint, for virtue; I smell that at once. The red salvia means forever mine, a little florid in its hue, that, but no matter. Likewise the carnations, which signify admiration. The white clover is a mere fodder plant, but its meaning? Think of me.

I stand back and pretend not to notice as he slips it into the box with the rest, and he stands back, though I am certain he listens as I clatter the lid into place and secure the straps. He is already picturing it in her hands, I am certain. It is good that his back is turned, for I cannot entirely conceal a smile.

Later, I open the box again. I remove the popinjay's tussie-mussie, rip away its ribbon, scatter his sighed-over gifts across the floor. And I take out the choices I have made, arrange them, touch them, tease them, and bind them with his ribbon.

First there is bladder senna, a plant first grown on these shores by Fairchild himself, the swollen pink fruit of which resembles pursed and ready lips. Then there is the arum lily, a rarity: this specimen is known as red desire, a shapely, maidenly white bloom, its sweet cup enclosing a thrusting crimson spadix. Then, in case the message is not sufficiently clear, there is the *clitoria ternatea*, another name sprung from the salacious mind of our revered mentor, the term so obviously suggested by the soft, sensuous folds of flesh-like petals, leading inward to a secret, blushing centre.

I stare at it and reconsider. I look down at the flowers scattered on the floor. I have trampled on Adam's mint; its sharp stink hangs in the air. But there should be a little something of him in this gift, should there not? I stoop, pick up the salvia, strip some of the petals and scatter them among the rest like bright drops of blood.

Still, I am not finished. Before I seal the box again, and ready the sixpence that will ensure my delivery does not arrive until after Mr Ashton returns home from his business, I perfect my arrangement. I straighten the little posy, ensuring that my final touches are positioned at the very front: camellia, representing a gift that has been given to a man; and sweet pea, for pleasures taken, for deepest gratitude; for goodbye.

Outrage. Horror. Success! Ashton could not have failed to detect something of my meaning, but it proceeded better than I had hoped. He was so scandalised I ought to have heard the outcry all the way to the glasshouses, though of course I did not. Still, it was enough to hear Mr Petherton's words to Adam, albeit so spluttered and full of spittle and wind he could scarcely get them out.

The bags are packed; the invasive seed is ousted; the innocent corrupted – and I used God's own creation to do it.

I can barely keep from laughing as Adam's conveyance pulls away from the door. He will go back to his second, third or whatever cousin, I suppose, in disgrace and shame. He will benefit from being a little chastened, I think. I can already picture his eyes growing dull over his recollections, his thwarted joys, his disappointed ambitions, but

I straighten my face for Mr Petherton is coming down the path, leaning on his stick more heavily than hitherto. He is aimless, now; meandering. *It will not be long,* I think.

Still, I wonder if this expulsion of the upstart weed will be enough to salve Ashton's wound? Indeed, that is something I am long in pondering.

'Twould be a pity if word of his daughter's ruin were to spread, would it not? And he so proud, so very upstanding, such a pillar of the community. I suppose, with the suspicion cast about that his little bloom is already spoiled, he may be rather less averse to an alternative suit. He could scarcely object any longer to the prospect of infecting his family's fine roots with a little wilder stock.

After the marriage: bruised stems. Crushed calyx. Torn petals, dampened fronds. Purpled and broken lips.

A pluck'd flower so very quickly begins to wilt.

I throw back my head and straighten my spine and walk ahead of Mr Nicholls along the path. There is nothing for him to do but follow, since I am more learned in his business than himself; and he cannot cross so great a patron.

Ah, there was a time when I had hoped that my Adam would be disinherited as well as cast out, but it seems that Petherton could not go so far. And so he has come back again; still, being wrong can bring some fine compensations. I throw open the door to the hothouse and step into the hot stink of overblown flesh. I can tell at once that it is ripe once more; I hear the lazy buzz of flies somewhere among the leaves. However, it is not the shrubs I seek. I step forward until I am standing before the stinkhorn and, with little choice, Adam waits at my side. We contemplate its thrusting glory, its fecund cap. I find I am smiling, though more at the memory of my own restraint than the view. I had been so very tempted to place it at the centre of my rather dramatically effective bouquet; now I am glad I did not. Petherton would almost certainly have dismissed Adam altogether if I had taken his pride and joy as well as his respectability.

Now I savour Adam's discomfort. I am sorely tempted to bid him cut it off himself, by his own hand – to have it wrapped and sent to the townhouse along with the rest. Instead I smile and I wait. That pleasure shall be saved, perhaps, for a future day, and besides, the smell really would be terrible. I have a position to maintain after all, particularly now that Mr Ashton is dead – of shame, some would say – and everything has fallen to me.

Anyway, I scarcely need go so far. I tap the floor sharply with my cane, the silver-tipped one that had belonged to Millicent's father, and lead the way from the hothouse. This time I go directly to the flowers and shout out my orders, not so very different from those I request every week. Mostly, they are yellow: cyclamen for resignation. Marigolds for cruelty, for grief. A pity it is too late in the year for hyacinths or carnations, though I make a point of asking for them: jealousy, rejection, disappointment, disdain. There is rosemary for simple remembrance – one should have something green – and this time, feeling a little mischievous, I add tiger lilies for wealth and pride. I find I have become somewhat adept at this language that was once his own possession; I rather enjoy slipping in and out of it now and then.

I order everything to be sent to the townhouse, for the pleasure of my wife – he already knows the direction. As he nods and makes some note on a scrap of dirty paper, we both know that it is I who shall enjoy them the most.

And she? Ah, but I have taught Millicent a more direct language. Indeed, she has found little use for words as the days of our marriage have worn into weeks; she does not need to tell me what she feels.

Now she is bent over her sewing, engaged as I am, I suppose, on sublime contemplation of this life we have made between us.

I sit back in my armchair with the sigh of a satisfied man. The fire crackles. It shines from the floral arrangement I have placed in the centre of the table – a little strident in its colours, but I like that it cannot be missed, wherever one might sit. My choices arrived prompt to their time, and at my bidding, she unpacked and arranged them in their vase. What were her thoughts, I wonder? But I know what they were. I always know. Adam's messages were obscure, coded, simpering and trite; it is I who taught her the true language of flowers.

Now I breathe in deep and savour their scent and enjoy this, my favourite way to pass an idle hour. I admire Adam's ruin. I look upon Adam's sorrow. I breathe in the scent of Adam's pain.

Suddenly, my dear little wife stands. She looks tired; she looks unhappy. She blinks those luxuriant eyelashes – is there a bead of moisture clinging there? – and she walks from the room, without putting away her sewing, without finishing her tea, without once looking at me or bidding me goodnight.

I reflect that I shall need to teach her better manners.

For now, I push myself from my chair and go to hers and examine her work. She is sewing a patterned border with not a flower or a leaf to be seen. I smile and set it down and sit, for a moment, in her accustomed place. Here she must have rested as a child; here she must have learned at her father's knee, and I suppose her mother's, and listened as they spun tales of what her future would be.

I think of my own mother. I smile fondly. She would have liked my wife, I decide, especially so when she begins to bear fruit. Such a thing can surely not be long in the making. Such a rose! She has lived all her life under a dome of glass and now she lives as in the finest hothouse. Soon, she will begin to bloom.

The fire spits and crackles. It is already as warm as a hothouse, and I reach out for her abandoned cup. The tisane she has made smells faintly of rosemary and I smile before draining it. I drink of her bitterness, and it *is* bitter, and I relish it.

When I stand, I know at once that something is wrong. My lips tingle; my body sways. Perhaps I have taken some chill from my visit to the nursery – that would please her, no doubt. I remain motionless, licking my lips, my senses searching for something – and my gaze rests upon the flowers, for resignation; for grief; for goodbye.

I smile and step towards them, suddenly remembering another bloom on another day: the little pink hybrid I had prepared for her so carefully, ready to present it to her like a page before a queen, only to see it trampled underfoot. That was before she had learned to admire another – but I find myself wondering, for a moment, if we could find a way to be so again. We could be tender; we could put out new shoots, find our way back to each other, twine like stems about one another's hearts.

I shake my head and my vision blurs. I move back, meaning to sit once more, and find myself sprawling full length on the carpet. My head spins and the room with it. Something is *very* wrong.

The teacup has fallen from the table – I must have caught at it with my hand. I stare at the bone china and suddenly wonder: was the teacup full when I drank from it? Had Millicent touched it at all?

I try to call out but only an inarticulate sound emerges, nothing like language, and a cramp doubles me up. I moan; I feel spittle dripping from my lips – or is it foam? There is a great pressure in my chest. I am crying, I realise, like a child. There is something very, *very* wrong, and pain racks me again, rooted in my stomach, something I have eaten perhaps – or something I drank, something close by; something left there on purpose, intended, perhaps, for me.

I open my mouth and thrust my fingers into my throat but instead my jaw clenches and I bite down on them. I cannot make myself vomit; it is inside me, poisonous and deep and very much too late.

I hear little steps, a light foot, the brush of a gown against my leg. I try to focus and make out Millicent standing over me, her posture straight, her countenance calm. As I watch, as if she had come to arrange the *flowers*, for God's sake, she takes hold of the heavy vase and slowly spins it around, though her gaze remains fixed on me, her head tilted as if to better make out my reaction.

And I see it: among the marigolds is something that isn't yellow, that doesn't belong, that I didn't order. I recognise it at once, of course. Not for nothing the years of labour at Petherton's direction, of hanging upon Mr Ashton's coattails. An herbaceous perennial, often cultivated as an ornamental plant, prized for its loveliness, with dark blue flowers that curl like a friar's cowl.

It is monkshood, and it is deadly.

I stare up at her and she stands there and watches me. Soon she is a blur; her eyelashes, her hair, her gown, are nothing but pale fronds, everything curling and swaying beyond my reach. Why did I never suspect that it was she who would teach me a new tongue – a new language of flowers? Perhaps it was always Millicent who understood their meaning better than any of us.

My body is turning entirely numb. I cannot banish the mist drifting over my vision, cannot move my lips, cannot make my feelings heard. But as I stare up at her, I know what it is she means to tell me: that silence is the most perfect language of all.

|The Entertainment Arrives|

~

The Professor drove slowly down the rain-lashed promenade, passing sign after dispirited sign that marked the boarding houses still clinging to whatever sorry living this place could afford. Westingsea in early May, and the angry sky flung handfuls of rain at its houses and pavements and the battered old black Wolseley he drove, drowning out any other sound. He could see the sea, dark and heaving to his right, shifting in as surly a fashion as it always did, but only the rain was listening to any murmur it made. He knew without looking that the belligerent clouds, fierce as he'd ever seen them, were indifferent to whatever lay beneath. Of humanity there was no sign, unless it was the mean slivers of light trying to escape the windows of the blank-faced, three storey properties along the front.

None of it mattered to the Professor. In fact, it was probably better this way; there was no one to see him arrive and no one to see him leave. He required no witnesses, no applause; there would be enough of that later. He knew where he was going and he knew what he would find when he got there, since it was always the same. The jaded, the worn out and the mad; that was who he had come for. Momentarily, he closed his eyes. *After the strife*, he thought, *after the rain, the entertainment*. He could almost smell their clothes, redolent of over-boiled potatoes and their own unloved skin. He could almost feel the texture of it on his hands, and his fingers, resting on the steering wheel, twitched – though sometimes it seemed to him that the car responded to his thoughts, or someone else's, rather than his touch.

He suddenly wanted to look over his shoulder at the things on the old and clawed back seat, but he didn't need to look. He could feel them, as if their eyes were fixed on his shoulder blades, boring into him. Punch had awoken, then. He must be nearly there; he saw the spark of irritation from a neon sign to his left, *HO EL*, it said, the 'T' too spent to play its part any longer, and he spun the wheel, or it spun under his hands; he wasn't sure which. The even movement of wheels on road gave way to the jolt and judder of potholes and the car drew to a halt facing a crumbling brick wall, drenched and rain-darkened. He stared at it. He still didn't want to turn around, though he never eluded what he did; it was his – what? Duty? That seemed too mild a word, for duty could be shirked. It's who he *was*. He was the entertainment, and he was here to entertain, and entertain he would. *After the rain*…

But for now the rain showed no sign of ceasing. It hammered on the roof and spat at the windows, and he switched off the engine and the wipers, and the deluge blurred the world entirely. He realised he hadn't even looked for the name of the hotel, but he had no need to do so; it had called him here and he had answered, just as he always did, even when the day wasn't special, as this one was.

He pushed open the car door, his right sleeve soaked through at once, but that didn't give him pause. Rain seemed to follow him even in the height of summer, and at least this smelled right: of ozone and tarmac and, peculiarly, of dust. He stepped out, retrieving the heavy duffel bag from the back seat before heading for the hotel entrance. He heard the cackle of the neon sign and turned to see that the 'O' had also given up the ghost. A matching spurt of electricity ran down his spine, and he savoured it; he hadn't felt anything like it for a long time. It was a special night indeed. The shadow of an echo of a smile tried and failed to touch his lips, and he reflected that such a thing hadn't happened for a long time either.

The glass doors slid aside at his approach – unusual for the establishments he frequented – and the rain was suddenly cut off and other sounds, human sounds, returned. From an opening to one side came the clink of glasses. Somewhere someone was vacuuming, which made him frown, and he stared down at the dust-free carpet. His shoes were as wet as if he'd emerged from the sea and he shifted them, watching the moisture darken the floor with something like satisfaction. Then a voice, a cheery voice, said, 'Can I help you, sir?'

A young woman with sleek hair pulled back against her head was seated behind a reception desk, smiling at him with reddened lips. The desk was grey, as was her uniform, and the wall behind her, and indeed that too-clean carpet. It looked anonymous; the hotels he frequented were often shabby and dirty, but they were never anonymous. The Professor frowned in answer, but he felt a sudden jolt of – what? Hunger? Eagerness? – from within his bag, and the contents shifted as if they were settling, or perhaps its opposite. He walked towards the girl and simply said, 'Snell?'

His voice was dry and cracked. In truth he was unused to using it; his real voice, anyway. Sometimes he used his clown voice, or his jolly comedian voice, but not today. Generally, until it was time, he didn't need to; he certainly didn't like to.

'Welcome, Mr Snell. One night, is it?' She wrinkled her nose as if she could smell something unpleasant, then covered her expression by parting those red-painted lips once more. It wasn't quite a smile.

'No.' He leaned in closer until he could sense her wanting to recoil, *needing* to recoil, and he stared at her and he did not blink. "The manager. Snell. Booked the entertainment. Snell.'

Her forehead folded into wrinkles. 'Our manager – Miss Smith – she's not on tonight, I'm afraid sir, but I don't—'

'Snell.'

His voice was implacable, and she knew it was implacable, he could see it in the way her eyes struggled to focus when she raised them to meet his. 'Of course. I'll get someone for you, sir. I'll only be a moment.'

She was as good as her word, trotting into the room from whence he'd heard the sound of glasses and returning a few seconds later with a gangling lad in dark, ill-fitting trousers and a waistcoat with grey panels down the front. He looked puzzled, was muttering something to her, but he fell silent when he stood in front of the Professor, who stared at the pock-marks in his skin until he was forced to look away.

'I'm sorry,' the lad began, but suddenly another voice rang out behind him, so bright and full of excitement and somehow *pure* that they all turned to look.

'Punch!' the voice cried. It belonged to a small boy of maybe six or seven, his hair curling and golden, and he grinned and pointed at the Professor's bag.

The Professor looked, though as soon as he saw the shadow of a hand reaching across the carpet towards the child he knew what he would see. The crimson sugarloaf hat with its jolly green tassel had escaped the fastening and was poking from the top of the bag, along with the beaked nose, the hooked chin, the single avaricious eye, staring and endlessly blue.

'Mr Punch!' the boy said again, his voice disturbing the air, which seemed to reconfigure itself around them. 'Is there a show? Is Judy in there? Can we go, Mummy, can we?'

The child looked up at the slender woman with the fond gaze who was holding his hand, and she smiled back at him. 'We'll see.'

'We will,' the Professor said, but it was like being in the car; that odd feeling that he wasn't always the one steering, the one forming his lips into words. It was better when he had the swazzle in his mouth. Everything he said felt right then, even though the sound emerged as a series of shrieks and rasps and vibrations, words that no one else could understand. He realised he didn't know if Judy was in the bag, as the boy had asked. Sometimes it was the earlier one, the older one: Joan. Sometimes it was the newer one, the one he never quite knew where she came from: Old Ruthless.

The waistcoated lad who'd only managed to say *I'm sorry* drew a sigh. 'I suppose we could – in a corner of the bar, if it's just a booth.'

The Professor answered him with a look.

'Just the one show, is it? Just one? Because we're kind of busy.'

'And dinner.'

The boy looked puzzled. 'I'm afraid service just finished. Chef might be able to plate something up for you, before he goes.'

The Professor scowled. 'I'll be fed.'

The lad nodded in relief. 'Our manager – she left no information about paying you—'

'I'll be paid.' The Professor started to walk across that grey, too smooth carpet, leaving the youth to follow in his wake. A special night, and nothing was ready: he did not suppose his theatre would be set up waiting for him, as it usually was, nor his watery soup turning tepid upon the table. It was lucky he always carried his booth; and his puppets – his special puppets – were always at hand, as they should be, or he wouldn't deserve the name Professor, or Punchman, or, as some were wont to call the entertainment, Beach Uncle. And without such a name, what would he be? He supposed, once, he had borne some other moniker, but if he had, he could no longer remember it.

The space opened around him, larger than he had expected. The walls were painted a slightly paler grey, too bright, but it was flaking in the corners and the edges of the sofas were scuffed. The bar was grey too, and the high ceiling, lost to the dim lighting, was a deeper shade. He saw at once where he would set up his booth. There was a little nook off to one side, too small to be of use for anything else, where he knew the floors would not have been swept and the dim corners would have been abandoned to the spiders or whatever else cared to take up residence there. Yes: that was the way to do it.

He did not look at the faces of the occupants of the room, not yet. It wasn't time. But his gaze went towards the wall of windows, which were dark, reflecting back the interior of the bar and the deeper shadow where he stood. He nodded with satisfaction. The rain, finally, had stopped.

In the long pause, in the silence and the darkness, the Professor waited. He was on his knees, his back bent; the bag was at his feet with Mr Punch still supine, half in and half out of the opening. Above the Professor's head was the little waiting stage and beyond that was the bar, entirely stilled, its patrons gathered in to a row of chairs hastily brought forward by the lad who'd said *I'm sorry*.

Outside the booth nobody spoke, but he could picture their faces, all turned expectantly to the little rectangular opening draped in fabric that had once been brightly striped in red and white. Without looking, the Professor slipped the swazzle from his pocket and into his mouth, tasting the old, cold bone, and he held it in position with his tongue. He could still sense the excitement creeping from the bag and towards his hands. It was *the* night. Early in May on the seafront, and not just any day in May: it was the 9th, the evening that was recognised throughout the land as Mr Punch's birthday.

In answer to that thought a faint wheezing, a little like a laugh, emerged into the quiet. He was not sure if it came from his own breath passing through the swazzle or the bag on the floor or from the air around him. It didn't matter. Soon they would begin and everything else would end. It was almost time. He reached down, his fingers seeking out Mr Punch's hat, passing over the soft nap of its fabric and finding the opening into which he would slip his fingers. He couldn't see it but he pictured the soft brown substance; its touch felt like skin against his hand as he pulled it home.

He closed his eyes. *That's the way to do it.*

He pictured the little boy's face. *Is Judy in there?* He knew, despite his excitement, the child would not be watching. He was too new, too fresh for any of this. The show wasn't meant for the likes of him. He knew who would make up his little audience: ladies in voluminous chintzy skirts, their face powder clogging the wrinkles beneath; old men, tired from years of stale marriages and disappointing jobs, disillusioned and spent. The worn out, the mad and the lost. That's who would be waiting for him, who was always waiting for him.

In the next moment, he had poked Mr Punch's head up over the stage and an odd sort of sigh rose from the audience. With his other hand he stretched down and rummaged in the bag, finding another soft, leathery opening. As Mr Punch began to shout for his wife, he slipped it on. It wasn't Judy, he felt that at once. It was the original: it was Joan, though he knew the people watching wouldn't know the difference. Sure enough he heard a call of 'Judy, Judy!' as he used her little hands to grab her baby from within the bag's innards and sent her up to join her irascible husband.

He spoke through the swazzle, every word and gesture coming as if from somewhere miles distant, the show drifting over him as if he wasn't the one in control at all, and yet it was the same as always; a sense of being in the very right place at the very right moment, though he felt discomfited at that, and an image of that hotel sign rose before him, flashing its maimed sign as a woman's voice said: *Mr Snell. Mr Snell…*

As he thought of it, Mr Punch dropped the baby, Joan screamed, and the couple set to, she beating him with her hands, he fighting back with his stick until the sound the swazzle made rose to a scream. Joan fell, though within reach, as she always did; he pulled her into the dark with the tip of his shoe. He knew that she was waiting; she was only ever waiting. And then he realised that no one had yet laughed.

He listened, hearing only silence on the other side of the booth, and felt the stillness creeping from that side of the grimy fabric and into the dark, and the little twist of discomfiture inside him grew a little. But of course all was still; nothing was happening, and he grasped in the bag for the policeman and sent him up to make his arrest until Mr Punch beat him too and flung him into the void.

At last there came a titter, too high and too clear, but there was no time to think of it. The words were forming, the next puppet fitting itself slick and snug onto his hand.

'It's dinnertime.' The words were clear, even swazzle-distorted as they were, but as he said them the Professor thought, *No, it's not, I haven't had my dinner*, and he knew something was wrong even as Joey the Clown entered stage right and waved his string of sausages at the onlookers. Punch descended once more into the dark and nestled in close. He didn't speak in words, not exactly, but the Professor heard him anyway: *Hungry*.

I know. I know you are.

It's my birthday. I want cake.

The Professor swallowed, carefully, around his swazzle. Punchmen had been known to die that way, choking on the thing that made them what they were; when their time was up. He felt suddenly very tired. His time would never be up, he knew that. The characters were all there, in his bag, waiting: Scaramouche and the skeleton; the hangman; the ghost; the lawyer; Jim Crow; the blind man; the crocodile, who would soon go up and wrestle the clown for his sausages. All had made their appearance in his show, always appearing in the very right place at the very right time. Old words ran through his mind:

With the girls he's a rogue and a rover
He lives, while he can, upon clover
When he dies – only then it's all over
And there Punch's comedy ends.

As if in answer, laughter finally came from the other side of the curtain, as the sausages and then the clown went to join Mr Punch's wife in the nothingness beyond the booth. It wasn't the right kind of laughter though, he knew that, *felt* that, and he found himself wondering if tonight was the night and an odd kind of hope rose within him. Tonight, the devil might come, the one character from the show who never did; the devil might come and take them all.

That's the way to do it, he thought but didn't say, because it wasn't yet time: he always knew when it was time. First Punch went back to dispose of the crocodile and then the doctor tried to treat him, only for Punch to beat him with his slapstick – 'Take that!' said the swazzle – and he too was thrown into space, emptied and wrinkled without the enlivening force of the Professor's hand, nothing but an empty skin.

Another delve into the bag and a jolt of that same electricity he'd felt earlier crackled through him. Jack Ketch, the Hangman, was soft yet cold against his hand. Suddenly, he knew he had to look. He didn't know why but he felt almost sick with the need to do it, and he used Ketch's arm to draw the awning back, just a slit.

The breath seized in his throat. The golden haired boy he'd seen earlier was there after all, sitting in the front row, his smiling mother on one side and a man who must be his father on the other, each of them smiling, not used up, not worn out, not *ready*. It wasn't right. None of it was right, and he realised he'd known it when the steering wheel had turned in his hands and he'd felt the greed rising from the back seat where Mr Punch lay, watching with his blank blue eyes and hungering, always hungering, but especially today.

I want cake.

The Professor closed his eyes. He knew suddenly it was not the right time; it wasn't the right time and it wasn't the right place. It never had been. Snell was waiting, he knew that too. Mr Snell had called him and booked him, the entertainment to follow the strife, to follow the rain, but Mr Snell wasn't here.

The Professor opened his eyes and saw Punch's blue orbs staring back.

'I don't know how to do it,' he said, except it came out in a series of wheezing growls, the words lost, because this was what he did: a duty that could not be shirked. Mr Punch whipped his head back up onto the stage and Jack Ketch chased him with his noose, Punch pointing at it, condemned but not ready to go quietly, not yet. 'I don't know how to do it.' The words, this time, were clear.

Here, the Professor knew, was where the hangman would put his own head in the noose to show Punch how to do it, only to be kicked off the stage and hung himself. That's what was supposed to happen. It wasn't what happened in his show, however, because Joan was back, taking Ketch's place, holding the noose herself and looking about, shading her painted eyes with one hand.

'I need a volunteer,' she said, every word crystal-sharp despite the swazzle, the old bone that was cold in the Professor's mouth. He recalled that it was sometimes called a *strega*. The word meant *witch*. He had never known why, not properly, and yet somehow he had always understood and had felt strangely proud of the fact, because it showed that he belonged: he was the Professor, the Punchman, the Beach Uncle.

He realised the boy was staring directly at the slit in the curtain, looking straight at him. He nudged it back into place even as the child pushed himself to his feet.

'A volunteer!' Joan shrieked, waving her little hands in excitement, jangling the noose, beckoning him on, and the Professor heard footsteps approaching, too soft and light.

For a moment there was silence. Then Joan made prompting noises, little wheezy nudging sounds, and she waved the noose, and he heard:

'I don't like it,' spoken softly and with a little breathy laugh at the end, and the same footsteps retreated, and Joan shrieked more loudly than she had ever shrieked, so loudly that it hurt the Professor's ears.

Then came another voice, a louder, smoother voice, which said 'Don't worry, it's fine, I'll show you,' and louder, more tappy footsteps approached, and the Professor knew without looking that the child's mother was coming forwards; that she was going to show him the way to do it.

Joan showed her the noose. She slipped it over the woman's head. And then there was a pause because Mr Punch wanted a souvenir; he always wanted a souvenir. He bobbed down and reached his camera from the bag – an old, heavy, Polaroid camera, and he bobbed up again and had her pose, trying this angle and that before there was a loud bang and a flash drowned the world in light, just for an instant, and the woman's son caught his breath.

The camera whirred and spat its picture onto the floor. The Professor could just see it, below the old tangled fringe that ran around the bottom of the booth. Faintly, like a ghost, the woman's grin was appearing in the photograph: only that, her lips parted in the strained semblance of a smile, revealing teeth a little less white than the paper.

Then Mr Punch stepped forward and hit her with his slapstick. There was another bang, this time so loud that everyone would be forced to close their eyes, just for a moment, just as long as it took, and the woman was hung, her body limp and falling, emptied of enlivening force; nothing but an empty skin.

'I don't know how to do it,' said Mr Punch.

'I need a volunteer,' said Joan.

A rough shout came from the other side of the booth, of mingled surprise and awe, followed by applause, albeit from a single pair of hands. The Professor peeked out to see the woman's husband looking impressed, grinning and clapping. They always grinned and clapped. And he realised that the child and his father were the only ones watching the show. There were no worn-out old ladies, no tired and ancient men. The boy wasn't grinning and clapping, however. He was peering to left and right of the booth at the blank grey walls and the grey floor, no doubt wondering when his mother was going to appear again.

But his mother didn't appear. Instead his father was coming forward, his smooth-soled shoes making hardly any sound on the carpet. Joan placed the noose over his head. There came a *bang – flash – whirr*, and a photograph drifted to the floor, the ghost of another fixed smile already beginning to form.

'Dad,' the boy said from his place in the front row. 'I don't like it.'

'Come on, son!' his dad replied, his voice full of humour. 'It's all jolly good fun!'

The words didn't sound right, even to the Professor who didn't know the man, who should never even have seen him, and yet Joan tightened the noose about his neck and held him steady for Mr Punch, who grasped his slapstick in both little hands and spun, and the man slid to the floor, as empty and used up as his wife.

This time there was no laughter; there was no applause. There was only a pensive little boy looking up at the stage, waiting for his mum and dad to come back.

'I need a volunteer!' said Joan.

The boy shook his head. The Professor peeked once more through the curtain and thought he saw, in the dim light, the glisten of a tear on his cheek. *Don't*, he thought, *don't you do it, that's not the way*, and something in the child sagged and he pushed himself to his feet, as weary as any old lady in chintzy skirts, as any old man waiting to live out his retirement, and he stepped forward.

The Professor felt his hands carry out the motions as Joan slipped the noose over the boy's golden head. He felt it as she tightened the rope. He heard the bang and the whirr but he didn't see the flash because his eyes were already pressed tightly closed. He realised he hadn't felt much at all in a very long time. He wasn't certain he ever wished to again. There was only darkness behind his eyes and then Mr Punch said, 'That's the way to do it!' and it was so full of excitement, so full of triumph, and the Professor opened his eyes to see another little square of white, a photograph of a child's clean smile. He knew the boy hadn't been smiling, that he would never smile again, but Mr Punch's camera had caught it anyway, just as it always did.

He lowered his hands, feeling the strain in his elbows and shoulders, feeling suddenly very old. He caught only disjointed words as he started to thrust the puppets, without looking at them, back into their bag. Soon he would be on the road again. He would be driving somewhere else, anywhere, and he knew that it would be raining, and that the rain would smell inexplicably of dust.

Dinnertime, said Joey the Clown.

Birthday, said Joan.

Cake, said Mr Punch, and his voice was the most contented of all. *Cake.*

The Professor slipped his hands under the booth's fringe and felt for the puppets that had fallen. He grabbed Joey and the crocodile and the doctor, feeling the old, cold skin, and then he grabbed the new ones, those who had fallen. He paused when he felt their touch on his hands.

Their skin was still warm, and it was supple, and smooth, and soft. He drew them towards him and picked them up, holding them to his chest, then stroking them against his cheek. Their warmth went into him. It awakened parts of him he had rather hadn't awoken, because it was wonderful; conditioned by their love, seasoned by their life. They weren't used up and they weren't jaded. They weren't mad or spent or lost. They were fresh and new and something inside him stirred in response.

Cake, Punch murmured again, and the hard unyielding surface of his face pressed up close to the Professor's. *Cake*.

The Professor squeezed his eyes closed, though he could see everything anyway. There were beaches outside, not just rain-tossed promenades. There were hotels limned in sunlight. There were roads he had not yet taken. All he had to do was see where the Wolseley wished to go, then grip the wheel tight, and force it to go somewhere else.

The entertainment would arrive, and he did not suppose they would welcome him in. He had a sudden image of Mr Snell, thin and bent and grey, twitching the dingy curtains of a faded boarding house and waiting, fruitlessly waiting. The Professor decided he did not care. He had tasted cake, the only kind he wanted, but he had not had his dinner; and he found he was very, very hungry indeed.

One day, he supposed the devil might come and take them all. Until then, he would find them: the golden little boys and girls who did not laugh and did not clap. He would find every one of them. He whispered under his breath as he emerged from the booth into the empty and quiet bar. He began to dismantle the stage, his whisper sounding different as he slipped the swazzle into his pocket, speaking in his own voice at last the words that were always waiting there for him. *That's the way to do it.*

|The View from the Basement|

~

The Hyde Hotel looked like the sort of place a travelling salesman might use, and Leslie Baines should know, for a travelling salesman he was. For now, though, he was on holiday, and he set his bag down next to his feet and ran his grey eyes over the grey exterior. It was the first time he'd been on holiday to a city, and the first time without his wife.

The sign saying 'Hyde Hotel' gave a dispirited flash, as if electricity had sparked through it before giving up the ghost. Leslie took it as an invitation. He picked up his bag and went inside. The reception desk looked much the same as those in all the other hotels he'd ever stayed in. Behind it was a bored looking lad, probably not yet out of his teens. His head was shaved at the back and long on top and a silver stud shone in his eyebrow. He wore a name badge, but his name wasn't on it. Instead it said *Assistant Manager*. Leslie imagined that if he came back in a year, someone else would be sitting there, wearing that same badge and the same expression.

It seemed to pain the boy to lift his head from the magazine he was reading, which was about fast cars. He didn't say anything and his expression didn't change. Leslie found himself thinking he looked like the kind of kid who'd have lusted from afar over all the prettiest girls in school, but had never once dared speak to them. If he had, they wouldn't have known his name. He was the kind of kid Leslie understood all too well.

He realised now that no one had spoken for a little bit too long. 'This *is* the Hyde Hotel?' he asked.

'Oh, yes *sir*. You've most definitely come to the right place.'

Leslie frowned. Now he thought this was probably the kind of kid who'd fantasised, all through his final year, about murdering his classmates. He might even have written stories about it; stories that weren't very good.

The boy held something out. It was a key-card, but with a hole in the corner attached to a loop of twine as if it was a regular key, a mingling of the past and present. Attached to the loop was a rough wooden block that looked as if it could conceivably have been used to brain somebody.

Leslie took it. He didn't say thank you. He just shuffled away towards a sign that said, *LIFT*.

~

There was a picture in the lift. It looked like one of those motivational things, the sort that should have writing underneath designed to cheer people up or spur them on, but instead left them feeling mildly depressed. 'Bless all our tomorrows' or 'Love is forever' or some such thing. This one was of sunset over water, except, when Leslie looked again, it wasn't quite like that. The sky was red and bloody but he couldn't see the sun. The water was purple and dark. *Sunless*, he thought. That's what it was: *sunless*, like in that Coleridge poem.

Then he saw there was writing on the poster after all, right at the bottom. *LESURE CLUB* it said, like that, with one letter missing. *There's no I in club*, he thought, smothering a giggle.

'Floor?'

Leslie let out a yelp. He hadn't realised there was someone in the lift with him; now he turned to see a fellow wearing a dark suit and a mild expression. He looked a little like a travelling salesman. Of course, Leslie must have seen *something* when he'd stepped inside – perhaps he'd assumed the figure to be his own reflection, except there was no mirror in the lift, and Leslie wasn't wearing his suit; he was on holiday.

He consulted the number on his wooden block. 'Second,' he said, and the man pressed the button and they clanked and whirred their way upward.

~

The room wasn't all that a hotel room could be. Leslie remembered the last holiday that his wife, Carol, had arranged. She knew how to organise a holiday, did Carol. She'd have telephoned in advance and got them a better view than they'd paid for. There'd have been a pool, maybe even a spa. She'd have got extras. There would have been a banana sitting in the cracked fruit-bowl on the coffee-stained table, maybe even an orange. Leslie shrugged. He never usually troubled about such things when he travelled alone, but generally, his trips were planned by the office. This one was his.

He tried to open the window for some air, but an old paint job had sealed it shut. He let the yellowing net curtain fall back across the view of the rear yard and its collection of metal bins. The cracked concrete out there was strewn with cigarette butts, though no one was smoking there now. He went into the tiny bathroom. There was a bar of soap by the sink, unboxed and wrinkled, its centre fractured with deep grey cracks. There were no extras, unless he counted the nailbrush sitting on the ledge by the bath, its remaining bristles resembling the curled legs of dead flies. He found himself placing his toiletries bag on the floor under the sink, where his wife would have liked it; then he straightened and put it on the shelf instead.

Carol, he thought, would have liked the kind of poster he'd seen in the lift. Or rather, she'd have liked *him* to like it. She always wanted him to conform, to fit in; to succeed.

He shook his head as if to clear it of the echo of her nagging voice, and went to take a look around the city he'd pitched up in. He was, he reminded himself, on holiday.

Leslie bought a map. He wandered around the things that tourists were supposed to be interested in. He stood and looked at the pigeons breeding on the north face of the cathedral. He saw the statue of the city's founding father, looking fat and pompous in the square. He ate a dry scone in the museum cafe, staring out of the window at a teacher trying to herd her recalcitrant pupils onto a coach.

Then he went back to the hotel.

As he entered reception, thinking, *She would have known how to get the best room*, he was hailed by a voice. 'Mr Baines.'

His insides froze. Leslie felt as if he'd done something wrong and now he'd been caught and everything was at an end. For a moment he couldn't turn around; then the same lad he'd seen before poked his metal stud into his face.

'Been trying to tell you. Double booked. Had to move you.'

Leslie started to breathe again. How odd, that he should react in such a way. He reminded himself that he was the guest here, and should be spoken to in a manner befitting—

The lad pushed something into his hand. It was a key, much like the first, except that the numbers were different. *She would have known how to get the best room*, he thought, and started to smile.

In the lift, when he consulted the numbers again, his smile faded. He thought he'd have been moved upward, onto the dizzy heights of the third floor perhaps, maybe even higher, but he had not. The first number on the key was a minus. He scanned the row of buttons until he found the one with a B for Basement, and pressed it, and began to descend.

The lift opened onto a long corridor that had once, long ago, been painted white. Fluorescent lights flickered and buzzed. Leslie was unsurprised to see that his room lay in the direction of the hotel's rear yard. The back of the hotel must be lower than the side that faced the street, because he could see daylight through the door at the end of the passage; he could just see the bins, distorted through its glass panes.

He started to walk down the corridor. There was a ringing sound in his ears. No: a squeaking, regular and rhythmic, that made him think of the tricycle in *The Shining*. When he entered his room, which was much like the first except smaller and hotter and without any windows, he found that his possessions had been moved for him. His bag was there at his side of the bed. His toiletries bag had been placed on the floor, next to the sink. There was nothing on the shelf at all.

Leslie had married his wife because she was a prize he coveted. Once he had her, he found she bored him after all. Later, it was more than that.

His wife thought he was selfish. 'Leslie,' she'd say, 'you're selfish.' That was how he knew. She'd say he should try harder at work so he could buy her things. She told Leslie he wasn't very good at anything. She said that he should notice her, which was odd, because he couldn't avoid noticing her. He had wished he could, many times.

Leslie closed his eyes. A picture came to him of his hands; more specifically, his fingernails. They were filthy with compressed earth trapped beneath them and he thought of the nailbrush that had been in his original room, its dead-fly bristles, and he grimaced.

Then he reminded himself that he was on *holiday*. He would go down – no, up – for dinner. He changed his shirt and straightened his hair in the mirror. His skin looked grey in its reflection, his eyes pouchy, and he thought about ordering something really fattening – *with too many numbers*, as Carol would have put it – followed by something else really fattening.

He smiled as the lift ascended. He tried a whistle. It mingled with the discordant groans of the lift cables, and he stopped. He looked at the buttons and noticed that they had changed. LESURE CLUB, one of them said now, though it hadn't been there before, had it? Or perhaps the button had, and only the label was new.

He peered at it. It didn't look new. The writing was faded and pink against a dull purple background that reminded him of something. Then the door opened and he forgot about it and headed towards the dining room.

There weren't many tables left. One in the corner was free, next to someone who looked like a travelling salesman. Another was adjacent to an old woman seated by the far wall, focused on her knitting. He sat at the table next to hers. A girl came and took his order and he waited. He couldn't hear any conversation, only the *clack-clack, clack-clack* of knitting needles. Leslie made sure not to catch anyone's eye. Polite chit-chat would have felt too much like work. Instead he examined the ceiling, then the mismatched chairs, then the floor.

It was only when the clacking stopped that he glanced at the woman seated next to him. She had turned in her seat and was watching him. Her stare was intense, her face more lined than any face should be, her grey hair diaphanous around it. She leaned towards him and opened her mouth. There was a smell. He tried not to recoil.

'You're selfish, Leslie,' she said, and Leslie rocked back in his own seat, his mouth falling open.

'What?' he said. 'What did you say?' But the woman had gone back to her knitting. She didn't even look at him, just kept moving her hands, the needles flying, *clack-clack, clackety-clack*, the knitting spilling from her table and pooling at her feet, the wool as grey and fine as cobwebs.

A plate banged onto the table in front of him and Leslie jumped. He looked down. He opened his mouth to tell the waitress *No, that's not my order*, but she had already gone. He sighed. He didn't have his curry; he didn't have any chips. Instead there was a small piece of grilled fish on a few limp lettuce leaves and thin slices of watery-looking potato. He realised, dismally, that it's what Carol would have ordered.

He picked up a fork and poked at the fish. The outside was coated with black crumbs. He wasn't sure if they were supposed to be there or if they were something the fish had picked up from an unclean pan. Inside, the flesh looked wet, almost raw. *Still wriggling*, he thought, and that reminded him of something and he pushed the idea away before it could take form. His head was beginning to ache. He no longer felt hungry.

He put a piece of potato in his mouth anyway and began to chew. Almost at once he spat it onto the plate. It was green inside, and hard, and had a funny taste; a bad taste. He looked up to see the waitress watching him, contempt written across her features.

'It's rotten,' he said.

She leaned in and looked at it. 'Looks fine to me,' she said, though it clearly wasn't fine, it was half-chewed food spat onto the plate. 'Nothing wrong with it.' And then: 'She'd have made sure it was perfect.'

'*What* did you say?'

'I said there's nothing wrong with it. Want it, or not?'

Leslie looked at the plate. Something about it made him shudder and he decided that 'not' was the better option. He glanced at the table next to his as he stood, but at some point during his dinner, the old woman had left.

Descending to his room in the lift, he noticed that the LESURE CLUB label had gone. Maybe it kept falling off; maybe, later, the bored lad from reception would come along and stick it back on again.

~

Leslie had forgotten to bring toothpaste. He ran his tongue over his teeth. Something was sticking to them, probably that awful stuff he'd put into his mouth earlier. He should go and complain. He should demand they provide toothpaste, free and with their bloody compliments, and they shouldn't expect him to pay for dinner.

He pushed himself up, feeling sick. He couldn't purge the taste of dead things from his mouth. When he got to the lift, though, he found it was blocked; a maid was trying to manoeuvre a laundry trolley into it. Still, he squeezed in after her. The laundry gave off a stink that belied the hotel's claim of *Fresh sheets every day*. It mingled with the taste in his mouth. He felt suddenly faint and leaned against the wall, squeezing his eyes closed. When he opened them again, the maid's face was up close to his.

'You're no good, Leslie,' she said. 'You don't try. You go to work but you don't get anywhere. You don't like the posters, Leslie.'

He swallowed hard against the sour taste. The words went on, and on some more. He felt they were sticking to him, surrounding him like cobwebby wool, like a cloud of floating hair. He couldn't breathe. He was being smothered. No: he was drowning, drowning in words, drowning in her disgust, her contempt, her *hate*.

Love is forever, he thought, which made him want to laugh, and that was better. He straightened. The maid wasn't looking at him. She was gazing into the air, busy chewing gum. No: she was looking into a dismal looking poster, which showed a dark and sunless sea. Leslie might not even have been there at all.

It came to him then that Carol had once told him, on a holiday that was a little but not quite like this one, that she would hate to be drowned. *That would be awful*, she'd said, *just awful*, and for some reason Leslie wished he could remind her of that now; he thought, somehow, that it would make her happy.

He shook his head. What on earth was wrong with him? It wasn't as if—

He felt sicker than he had before. The lift doors slid open and he staggered out, into a corridor. He was back in the basement. The lights flickered and buzzed. Through the glass panels in the doors at the end, he saw a faint purple glow.

He forced himself to walk, as steadily as he could, back to his room. Food poisoning; that might be it. *She'd never have allowed that*, he thought, as he fell in through the door and pushed it closed behind him.

~

Leslie couldn't recall going upstairs. He could remember crossing reception, the way he'd weaved in and out of all the people who suddenly seemed to be thronging the hotel; he remembered wondering if there was a convention, perhaps one intended for travelling salesmen.

'You should try harder,' a woman with big dangly earrings said before he ducked out of her way, into the course of a mother with a young boy.

The mother said, 'If only you weren't so selfish.'

A cleaner said, 'Just bloody eat it, it's healthy, I made it for you.'

An old man said, 'You don't notice me any more.'

Leslie stumbled into the dining room, which was now the breakfast room, and he spooned cornflakes into his mouth. When he'd done, the man who took his dish away said, 'Your name's not Baines. You only told us that.'

Leslie stared after him. He felt cold, all over. He felt frozen, like the ground: the hard, unforgiving ground. He looked down at his hands. For a moment he saw dark earth embedded under his fingernails; then it was gone.

'She's not dead,' said the old woman with the knitting. She gave a soft laugh, each spurt of it like a last breath: *uh–uh–uh*. 'Of course she's not *dead!*'

'I'm on holiday,' said Leslie, his voice a little too loud. 'Holiday!'

His vision cleared. A face was looking at him, full of wariness and not a little contempt. It was a man in a suit. He looked a bit like someone who would work in sales.

'My name's Baines,' Leslie said. 'If they ask. Baines!'

The man backed away. He couldn't seem to move fast enough.

Leslie put his hand to his head. He pushed himself up to leave the table and went in search of the lift. When he reached it, the button that said LESURE CLUB was back. The doors closed. The lift clanked and began to descend.

As soon as Leslie stepped into the basement corridor, he felt better. The lights still flickered but the air was cooler and his headache dissipated at once. He didn't feel like going back into his room yet; he suddenly hated the thought of shutting himself into that tiny box. Instead, he passed his door and kept on going, the lights buzzing louder than ever as he approached the door at the end of the corridor, the one with the glass panels. He couldn't see through them very clearly; the windows were of textured glass backed by wire mesh. He put out his hand to the push bar, half expecting an alarm to shriek when he pressed on it, but there was no sound, none at all. Even the buzzing of the lights was cut off, as if he'd already stepped outside and closed the door behind him.

She'd have had a pool, he thought, and he wanted to laugh because a pool was there. He must have pressed the wrong button; he was at the LESURE CLUB, except wasn't this where the bins should be? He must have got off at the wrong floor, got turned around somehow.

But he saw that the water wasn't a pool. He didn't know how it was possible, but this was a sea. It stretched all the way to the horizon and the surface was dull and purple-grey and shifted in an uneasy rhythm. Leslie instinctively knew that there were dead things in it, if indeed anything could ever have lived in such a dreary place. But it was definitely the sea; a sea where no sea should be.

He turned and looked back into the corridor. It was a perfectly ordinary corridor, but now there were people standing in it. They were staring at him, peering over one another's shoulders to see him better. For a moment he thought his wife was among them; then he blinked and all of them were gone.

He turned back to the sea and the sunless sky. He felt better when he was looking at the water. It wasn't that it made him happy; more that he didn't feel anything at all. It filled his vision with its emptiness. Its surface was completely opaque. *Anything could be in there*, he thought. *It could be covering anything, and they'd never be found again.*

They'd never be dug up.

He shook his head and smiled. He was on holiday, wasn't he? He was on holiday and here was the LESURE CLUB, and he should be taking advantage. Availing himself of the facilities. He slipped the jacket from his shoulders and let it fall. Then he didn't move. He stood there for a long time, and he heard a sound and looked behind him.

There were people in the corridor once more. First, there was the man who looked a little like a travelling salesman. Behind him was a policeman. The salesman pointed towards Leslie, mouthing something he couldn't hear.

Leslie slammed the door between them. Instantly, the corridor went dark; he could no longer see anything through the glass at all.

He turned and waded into the water.

At first, it was cold. Then it wasn't cold any longer. It was the exact same temperature as his skin, and it opened, and it accepted him. The ground beneath was made of cracked concrete. It sloped downward, a ramp not steps, and then it felt as if there were tiles but he began to sink into them and realised there was mud sucking at his feet. He stepped on one heel and pulled his shoe off, then prised the other free with his muddy sock. He knew he wouldn't find his shoes again, but it didn't seem to matter now. He kept on moving, the water lapping up to his knees and then his thighs. He didn't trouble to look back at the things he was leaving behind. Before long, he was up to his neck.

That would be awful, he thought, *just awful*. But somehow, it wasn't. It was unreal, like a postcard, or a poster; one that would have made Carol happy. And Leslie found he could bring himself to like it after all.

|The Same as the Air|

~

Three days ago, when I went to the Ebersole house, I didn't peek through the window or call out or try the door handle before I turned the key in the lock and walked in. I just watered the aspidistra, sprayed the orchid and sprinkled fish-food into the bowl, where Goldie rose to the surface, opening and closing his – or her – mouth.

This time, I peek through a window into the empty snug and then through another, from which I can see that the hallway is still clean and bare, before I take out Edda's fluffy owl key-ring and open up.

I call out when I'm standing inside and I wait for the answer but it's already clear that the house is empty. It still has that closed-up, gone-away feel. Their shoes aren't on the rug; their jackets aren't thrown over the newel post. It's absolutely quiet and still and I don't want to move, though I call for them a second time when I go into the kitchen to check that Goldie's still swimming, and again when I tiptoe upstairs to their bedroom, where the bedspread doesn't have a crease in it.

I stare at the door across the landing, but I don't go in.

A little later I'm walking through my own front door, trying to release the stiffness in my shoulders, or maybe shake off the dust that's settling in the Ebersole house.

'Marni?' I glance into my own kitchen, at the postcards on the pin-board, the trail of Edda and Dick's travels mapped out in pictures. I don't like the silence that comes back and I hurry up the stairs, throw open the door to my daughter's room – but that's quiet too. She's left the Everly Brothers on the turntable but it's switched off.

Through the window, I see the corner of the pool; two feet, close together in the water.

'Marni!' I run down the stairs again, almost falling down the last few, then rush to the back door, and stand there while my pulse thrums in my ears.

She's drifting in the pool, only that. She's on her back, her arms crossed behind her head as if on an inflatable, but she's simply floating; her eyes gaze up into the sky, which is story-book blue and scattered with fluffy clouds.

It takes her a moment to stir, as if her name had to pass through layers of deep water to reach her, and she suddenly flails as if my voice has robbed her of the ability to float. Splashes darken the Mexican tile.

'Mom! You startled me.'

'I see that.' I try to smile, hiding how she startled me too, though it's not easy with our friends so present in my mind, and the thing they'd written: *Say hello to Ada.*

'So, are they back?' she asks, and my smile fades.

Dick and Edda were supposed to be back two days ago. That's when their vacation ended; when Edda should have dropped in to collect her keys, when Dick should have gone back to the cider mill that fills one side of Maplewood with the scent of fermenting apples.

I shake my head, thinking of that empty house, and have no idea what to tell her.

What's really weird is, the next day, when the police arrive, I already have the postcard in my hand.

I've been looking at it more closely, examining the postmark, the picture they selected, their every word; and of course, that extra line – the one that gave me a chill even when I first saw it. But I had told myself then that everything was fine; the cold trickle that ran down my back was only the air-conditioning, fighting back the humidity a little too hard.

It had begun with my name, written neatly over our address: Margret. I had put the misspelling of Margaret down to the Florida heat, but then Edda had gone back and carefully written 'Miss' over the top of it, rather than 'Mrs' – as if she'd forgotten my husband, Paul, altogether. Was that a joke, or something else? Was it because the postcard held some message meant only for me?

When I had read the block of text, nothing else was strange, not really:

Dick and I having a wonderful time. Weather is beautiful. Today we went swimming for a couple of hours. The water is wonderful warm, 84 degrees the same as the air. On Thursday we leaving for the East-Coast. Love Dick + Edda.

PS. Hi Marni! Next card we send is going to be for you again.

I had put that grammatical lapse, 'we leaving', down to her rushing; that, and the way she'd crossed out the word 'water' and scribbled another word over the top. It had still given me a strange feeling though, mainly because I couldn't read the word she'd added – what else could they have been swimming in? – but then I realised it said *gulf*. Of course it did, and that was perfectly normal too, except the idea of Dick and Edda going swimming was just so odd, not like something they'd do at all. Why had the word 'water' not been enough? And why was her description so entirely different from the image they'd chosen – the Ringling Residence, a mock Venetian-Gothic mansion with its marble fireplace and arches and balconies and chandeliers? That was more their kind of thing, the sort of place Dick would admire while smoking a cigarette, without having to dirty his neat leather shoes.

It had all just seemed a little off, though it was nothing more than that – until I saw the line she must have appended last of all, written in a space at the very top of the card but upside down, as if floating there.

Say hello to Ada.

I had stared at that for a long time, as a darker feeling took hold somewhere inside me: dread, perhaps. The first inkling that something was very deeply wrong.

I had tried to put the postcard out of sight, but Marni had seen it. She'd snatched it from my hand, read it quickly then stuck it on the pin-board and left. I had no idea if she'd noticed that extra line and I didn't point it out to her. I figured if she hadn't, it was best hidden right where it was, in plain view: the picture outward, revealing nothing but that opulent, mannered, but *normal* red and gold interior.

Say hello to Ada.

Ada had been their daughter, not mine. And she had been dead for two years.

I show the line to the policeman, though, when he calls to see if I know where the Ebersole family have gone. He frowns and gives it back to me. 'So you think their state of mind was disturbed?'

'I have no idea.' Do I think that? *Having a wonderful time.* They were on vacation. They had seemed fine when they drove off, Edda waving out of the window of their Studebaker until they passed out of sight. I look down at the tightly slanting letters she had written. It pains me to think of her forming the words and not being able to ask her why.

He tilts his head and takes the postcard back, peers at it. 'Says here they're going to the East Coast.' He glares over the top of it. 'And you really have no idea where they went?'

'No. I'd have told you. I supposed Fort Lauderdale or Cocoa Beach or one of those places.'

'You've heard nothing from them since?'

'Like I said.'

He yields up the postcard again, a last communication from – where? An absence, now. A mystery. I have a sudden image of Dick and Edda floating in deep water – or perhaps it's the sky, or perhaps it's all one: *84 degrees the same as the air.*

'It's just strange,' he says, 'because that's not where they went.'

I think of that picture of the Ringling Residence, combined with the information that they'd been swimming in the gulf.

He goes on. 'Their last known location was only a few miles inland from Sarasota. They were at a cabin at Myakka River, at the state park.'

If he has any suspicion I know more than I'm saying it must be allayed by the expression on my face. A state park – Dick and Edda? It seems as likely as them going swimming. Less likely, even. I have an image of Dick tiptoeing through a swamp in his smart shoes, grimacing up at wild birds flying overhead.

'Well, Ma'am, you'll keep us informed if you hear anything.'

I agree that of course I will and close the door after him, only then realising that Marni has been listening from the top of the stairs. I hear the bang as she shuts herself in her room and a moment later *All I Have to Do is Dream* floats into the air.

Marni doesn't come down, not even when I call her for dinner. I walk up the stairs, wondering when she'd stopped playing her records. I hadn't noticed the silence creeping back into the house.

When I go into her room she has the same sightless expression in her eyes as when she was floating in the pool, but instead she's gazing down at a book held in her lap. It's illustrated, meant for a younger child, and my misgivings don't subside when I see that it's *her* book – the one Edda gave to her when Ada died. The girls used to love it when they were small, and it was always Marni's favourite.

It's a book of Swedish fairy tales. Edda was of Scandinavian origin, her family having travelled the ocean to settle in New Sweden, further north on the Delaware. Dick was Pennsylvania Swiss; my husband was of English extraction, and I was born in the old country. Maplewood always had been a melting-pot.

Edda told us once that her name, in ancient Scandinavian, meant 'great-grandmother'. It was the perfect name for a story-teller, and she'd spread her book of fairy tales before her and read them aloud, enchanting us all.

I knew which story Marni would be reading before I looked at the page. There was the picture they used to love: a little princess sitting at the edge of a dark pool, staring down into the water.

Her name was Cottongrass, and she lived contentedly at her castle until she saw an elk, a thing of the wild, and begged him to take her to see the world. He warned her there was danger in it, but of course she wouldn't listen. She flung herself onto his back and off she went, encountering wicked elves and the witch of the forest with tangled hair and reaching arms. Eventually, they found a dark pool amid the trees. Cottongrass leaned over the water and saw there another forest, one she couldn't reach; and the golden heart she wore about her neck slipped into its depths.

She stared after it, caught in some spell, until no one could tell she had ever been a princess. There was only a tall plant tipped with cotton leaning over the water, and there she remained, always looking after her lost heart.

The way Marni was staring at that picture now discomfited me, and I called her name, hearing the echo of another voice, another time:

'Marni comes from the word *Marina*,' Edda had once said. 'It means *of the sea*. And Margaret is from the Greek *Margarites*. That means *pearl*. A secret and underwater thing.'

I reach out and take the book from Marni's hands, closing it against that image of the dark pool. It is only then that she shifts, only then that she seems to realise I'm standing in front of her. There are tears in her eyes, salt water, and I want to brush them away, but her smile is so confused that I don't touch her.

'What did they mean?' she asks.

'Who, sweetie?'

'They said the next postcard they sent was going to be for me.'

An unpleasant jolt passes through me. 'Nothing. Only that they'd address it to you, like they used to – remember?' Even as I speak, I wonder if there was more to it. Had it been another way of saying that this card was meant just for me?

She frowns, as if she doesn't understand. 'Yes,' she says, 'but what did they *mean*?'

I just look at her. And all I can think is, why doesn't she ask about the other line – the one about Ada? If she hadn't seen it before, she must have heard the policeman talking about it. Why isn't she wondering about that?

But we don't mention it. We remain quiet and a little dull all through dinner, although her father is home early. Paul keeps looking from one of us to the other as if to puzzle us out, but he doesn't say much either. He tries to start a conversation about where we should go this summer, what we should do, but he soon gives up.

After she helps clear the dishes, Marni goes outside into a golden evening full of the hum of insects. Somewhere close by, some boys are shooting baskets; the noise they make doesn't seem to trouble her. She's quite motionless, sitting by the side of the pool, staring down into the clear and lovely water.

We hadn't used to vacation apart. We used to go with the Ebersoles every year, having met through the girls, who were the same age. We'd grown close – had barbecues together at their peach-painted colonial, pool picnics at our place, hung out together at the block parties which were a regular feature of life in Maplewood. So when it came to the summer it seemed natural to choose a rental together too, to decide between us where to go and what to see.

On the last trip we took together, Dick had wanted to visit some old country house. It had sounded dull even to us adults but we said we'd go too, and so did Marni; only Ada hadn't. She'd just turned thirteen, though she was sensible, we all said so, and when she insisted she was old enough to take care of herself for a couple of hours, we'd agreed. And we hadn't worried, not really; not until we got back and walked through the empty rooms, hearing no reply when we called her name.

I can still remember, with absolute clarity, looking out of the French doors and seeing two feet floating in the pool, though I hadn't recognised what they were, not all at once; not with the toes pointing downward.

She was just as she had been in that line on the postcard: at the top and upside down, though she would never say hello to anybody ever again.

I look out of the window now at Marni's downturned face. Her hair is hanging over her eyes so that I can't see her expression and something about the scene makes me shudder – the similarity, perhaps, to an illustration in a book. Is it the water itself that so draws her attention, or something else? It almost seems as if the word 'water' should be crossed out and replaced by something more mysterious: not a thing, but an empty space; an absence; a gulf.

I jump when Paul comes and puts his head on my shoulder, wraps his arms around my waist. 'About the summer,' he murmurs.

'Myakka,' I hear myself say. 'The state park, Paul. I want to go to Myakka River.'

We're gone later that same week – school is out, Paul is due the time off, and there's no point in waiting. I only go to the Ebersole house once more, to retrieve Goldie – I leave him with a neighbour, likewise the orchid. The aspidistra's too heavy; it will have to fend for itself.

I called ahead, managed to reserve the same palm-log cabin that Edda and Dick last stayed in, but when we walk in the door I can't sense anything of them. Of course, there's no sign they've ever been here, which is to be expected. The park ranger told me they'd left their luggage behind, still unpacked in the various drawers and closets, but it's all been cleared away. The police came by and looked at it, he said, but haven't been back since.

The cabin was built in the thirties by the Civilian Conservation Corps along with the picnic pavilions and visitor centre. It's pretty comfortable, but too big; it was designed to sleep six and I can't help thinking that's how many we would once have been.

The park, too, is huge. It hadn't occurred to me before how very extensive it is; how impossible to follow where they have gone. Myakka River flows for mile upon mile through wetland, prairie and pineland. We saw the prairie from the road, dry and empty with treacherous sugar sand interspersed with grasses and palmetto, and I don't feel drawn to it at all. But there are two lakes as well as the river, and thousands of wetland areas scattered across the park.

We don't go far on our first day. It's getting late and we pause only to watch the sun spreading itself over the Myakka, Venus shining low in the sky. Marni scowls and slaps at the mosquitoes biting her arms. The banks of the river are hidden in reeds, and it takes me a while to see the night-heron standing at the edge, staring fixedly into the water until its head darts down. It straightens, its catch lost, and takes to wing.

It was the Seminoles who called the river 'Myakka'. If there was ever a translation, it has long since been lost.

The water is wonderful warm, 84 degrees the same as the air.

It's so humid that night I don't think I'll be able to sleep. Paul's a twitching weight next to me and it's too hot to bear touching his skin. I must sleep, however, because I awake at some unknown time of the night, thrashing the single sheet away from me, feeling like I'm drowning in its folds. *Wonderful warm*, I think, and open my eyes to see shifting veils of cloth and think of Dick and Edda immersed in some liquid too warm to be the sea; viscous and dark, like amniotic fluid. They're waving their arms, though not to me. Their eyes don't see me and I wonder what it is they're focused upon. Have they found a pool they can stare into for ever? Or is it the faces of the dead they see all around them – have they found Ada at last?

I lie there listening to the lonely cries of shorebirds coming out of the night until I sleep again. When I wake, Paul and Marni are making pancakes, and the smell is of home and Maplewood, somewhere safe and known, and I smile.

We eat at the table in one corner of the big empty room. The sun is low but it's already warm, and I sense the heat of deep green water coming from somewhere beyond the window.

'I want to go swimming,' Marni says, but that's not what we do. It had come as an indefinable relief to me to know that she couldn't, not here; the water isn't fit for swimming. The river is wide and deep and wild. It's a nature reserve. There are rare birds: roseate spoonbills as pink as flamingos, bald eagles, caracaras, sandhill cranes, black vultures. There are raccoons and opossums and whitetail deer, and alligators too, hidden in the reeds at the edge of the wetlands.

And yet I know why my daughter longs for the water; the heat will be unbearable by midday. Is that why Dick and Edda had overcome their aversion and gone swimming, wherever they were? Had they simply wanted to cool off – something as ordinary as that?

We spend the morning following the park drive, then trying to spot wildlife from the boardwalk by Upper Myakka Lake. We don't see much; a couple of noisy families keep the birds at bay. Marni says little and I can see she's bored already, unless it's her innermost thoughts that are keeping her lips pursed. And suddenly I know what will happen. We'll spend a day or so here, then the two of them will want to leave. They'll want the cooler breezes of the coast; they'll crave the sea. We'll head west rather than east, having learned nothing. We'll go home and eventually the Ebersole house will be sold and Ada and Edda and Dick will be nothing but a memory that occasionally surfaces, like a fish in a lake, there and then gone.

When Marni clamours to go on the airboat lake tour, I plead a headache. Someone has to look for our friends; they can't be altogether forgotten.

I go back to the cabin first, searching the place as if Edda could have left some clue for me – a postcard perhaps, stuck to a pinboard – but there's nothing, only plain log walls, not even a picture hanging there. I rummage through the field guides and nature books and information about the park but they're all printed glossy pictures; there's no way to reach beneath the surface. But it's not in here that I'll find them, I know that. They're gone – vanished into water that feels like air, or perhaps into the soupy air that feels like water.

I step outside again, not sure where I'm going to go. No one else is around; I'm surrounded by trees, though I can see other cabins through the trunks. The place seems empty. Any other guests must be out sightseeing, and there's no reason for anyone else to wander here. A narrow track leads back to the road and a dirt path, narrower still, winds into the woods. I imagine Edda and Dick walking away between the trees, her blonde head next to his dark one, until they pass out of sight. But in that direction they'd only reach the lake – it's where everyone goes, all the families with matching shirts and hats and sunburned noses.

Instead, on a whim, I walk into the trees. There's no trail here, no wooden signs to point the way. A straight line is impossible and I wind around their trunks, duck beneath low branches. Hard-packed dirt soon gives way to softer earth that stifles the sound of my steps. The wind turns the leaves this way and that, sighing like waves on the seashore. It feels almost as if they're talking to me and I keep going, wandering until my feet begin to sink. Patches of reeds are showing beyond the trees; the purple of wild iris marks the edge of a marsh.

I take another step and my sneaker is soaked. I draw back as a bird starts up from the reeds – black body, long legs, some kind of wader. I watch it go, then I'm startled again by the fleeting brilliance of a monarch butterfly.

It's beautiful, but I can't continue, not this way. This is real wilderness. Surely no one could have come here. There's no path and it's half flooded and I suddenly realise I've wandered at random – how will I find my way back with no markers, no map, no compass? But a leap of hope comes: the ground's so soft I can surely follow my own footprints, and I turn and see a deer standing in front of me.

It's a whitetail, delicately boned, its hide softly dappled. Its nostrils are flared, twitching after my scent; its eyes are wide and fixed and looking straight at me. For a moment we regard each other. I wonder if there's knowledge in its eyes, but all I can see is fear; it must be reflected in my own.

The deer bounds off, crossing my path in one huge leap, and away. Where it pushes the undergrowth aside I glimpse a new trail, hollowed into the earth and overgrown, canopied with twisting branches dripping with moss. Even the light is green.

When the twigs spring back over it, it's like the closing of a door. The energy drains from me. I could wander here for days. There are miles and miles of trees and swamp, all of it appearing exactly the same.

I hurry to retrace my steps, but everything looks different. How could I have been so stupid? I picture Paul's face when he realises I'm lost, his annoyance passing into disbelief. I imagine what he'd say to me if he could: *But it was you who wanted to come*, as if that should have protected me from this – the wilderness around me, the miles and miles of nothing.

But there's a twisted oak I recognise, and I duck under it, and then there's a footprint after all. I keep walking, winding around the trunks, and eventually I catch a glimpse of hewn logs: the side of a cabin. It's only then that my pulse ratchets, as if I hadn't dared admit the possibility of truly being lost until I was safe.

I don't want to return to the cabin though, not yet; I'll only sit there, dwelling on the empty spaces and my own futility. Instead, I go to meet Marni and Paul from the boat. I arrive just as it's coming in to dock and I see Marni leaning over the side, her hair stretching down towards the water. When she lifts her head and waves, she doesn't look entranced; she only looks like what she is, a girl on vacation, saying something to her father and laughing, not thinking about anything else. Then she points. I'm just in time to catch the smooth slide of an alligator entering the lake.

They're all exclamations and laughter. Paul bought some gator jerky on board and we share it, though I grimace at the salty taste. Marni doesn't. She pulls a piece of it away with her back teeth then tells me they've done a deal; Paul is taking her kayaking tomorrow, if she'll try some freshwater fishing. But she'd rather go fish in the sea.

∿

That evening the dark drops over the land before I even notice it's there, and we settle down to read our various books. There's no television in the cabin, but we can hear birds calling to each other, their eerie cries coming out of the tangle of trees that quickly fade out of sight. We close the curtains against them and I take out the volume I borrowed from Marni before we came away. It's her book of fairy tales, and I read again about the girl's encounter with the wilderness.

For the first time, the similarity to another tale strikes me: the one about Narcissus of Greek myth. He was out hunting stags in the forest when he was followed by the nymph, Echo, who tried to embrace him with her reaching arms. When he rejected her, she faded away amid the lonely glens until only her voice remained. Narcissus, though, was punished by Nemesis. He discovered a deep pool hidden in the trees, and when he glimpsed his own reflection there, he fell in love. He gazed down at it until he died, when a flower grew in his stead.

I suppose Edda too had been cursed with a love that could not be returned, that would always now be out of reach.

Of course, it hadn't been a stag I'd seen in the forest, nor an elk, but the image still comes to me of a deer's fathomless eyes; its twitching ears and wide nostrils; the strength in its slender legs as it left me in a few brisk leaps. It had possessed no name, the thing I saw. I wonder what it sensed when it looked at me. Was it fleeing from the scent of something *other*? Or was it running towards something – had it caught the scent of the wild itself, and heeded its call, going ever deeper without looking back?

I go to the window and peer through the curtains. I wonder if Edda had once stood in this very spot, doing the same thing. What had she heard, calling to her from out of the wilderness?

I try to reach out to her with my senses, but see only the reflected light from the room behind me. She isn't altogether gone, though. I can almost hear the echo of her voice as she said my name, giving to me its meaning like some kind of gift: *Pearl. A secret and underwater thing.*

The next morning, when Marni and Paul prepare to set out for the boat ramp, I tell them I'll join them later. They don't seem especially surprised. I hug and kiss them and tell Marni to be careful around the water and she rolls her eyes. When they're gone, I pull on my hiking boots and a hat to keep the sun off – though when I think of those canopied trees stretching to meet each other, I don't suppose I'll need it.

I'm going off the trail again. That is where Edda and Dick must have gone – I feel sure of it, though I don't know why; it could be nothing but a story I'm telling myself, in the absence of anything else. I have no reason to be certain, but then, I don't think reason will help me now. I can almost scent the wilderness in my nostrils and I mean to heed its call. I think that's what they must have done. They went into the forest, immersing themselves in its warm humidity, the water and the air like a single element.

I think of the deer that paused to look at me under the trees. Was she trying to warn me that there is danger in it? But I turned back once; I won't again.

I try to follow the same route I took yesterday. Almost immediately, I feel a presence tracking my footsteps, though when I look around there's nothing to see; only moss hanging from the trees like tangled hair, branches reaching towards me like pale arms. I imagine a witch, or perhaps it's only an echo; my own thoughts, maybe. The words that come to me are *great-grandmother*.

After a time, I realise I'm standing in the same place where I saw the deer. She isn't here now but I think I catch a trace of her scent, musky and vibrantly alive. I lean under the trees and push the undergrowth aside and see that narrow path, barely wide enough for a deer or a human to pass. The thick canopy makes it appear almost like a tunnel. Sunlight filters through the leaves; the air is redolent of green and living things.

I duck under a trailing strand of Spanish moss and sink into the path to my ankles – I'm not sure if it's made of earth or water. The liquid is warm, making me think of leeches, of black and wriggling and slimy things.

Marni's face flashes before me and I suddenly have no idea what I'm doing here. The certainty I felt earlier evaporates. I know nothing about this place, or about my old friends, not really. I don't know where they went or what happened to them. How could I? Possibly they're still lost in some corner of the Ringling Residence, surrounded by its red and gold opulence. If I looked hard at their postcard, I might even see their faces peering from behind an archway or between the pillars of the balcony. I might see their eyes reflected in the crystals of the chandelier or a golden statue.

I look up, with that civilised, normal, *safe* interior filling my mind, and am fixed by the sight of a hawk perched on a branch not far above my head. It challenges me with its yellow eyes. A snake dangles from its talons.

Something inside me goes still. *Here*, I think.

I don't call out for Dick and Edda. What would be the use? But I step forward, brushing hair-like moss away from my face, ducking beneath the branches, stepping from root to root. I know I'm growing close when I see little clouds floating past me: the cotton-like seed of a water-loving plant. There is something ahead of me, not yet seen, but I feel its presence anyway. It's shadowy under the trees and difficult to make out, but it appears to be black water.

I hear the sudden loud buzzing of flies. With another step comes the trace of something on the air: a terrible sweetness. There is knowledge in the constant sound, in that scent.

It surprises me not at all when I see the pool beneath the trees. I knew it would be there, waiting for me. I peer between the branches, trying to see its surface. The water isn't black after all. It is every colour: brown and blue and darkly green, flecked with shining gold. And I see another forest growing within its depths. I wonder if I will be able to reach it, to learn the secrets it has kept all these long days.

The buzzing grows louder. I brush a fly away from my face – it has grown fat on whatever bounty it discovered here. I take another step. I want to look into the pool. What will I see – something beautiful? Will I find a nymph – a great-grandmother – a witch? Or only my own reflection: a secret and underwater thing?

Whatever it is, it will be like a story that has already been told. I will never again be able to discover its ending – or forget what it is that I have learned.

I take in a long breath and walk towards the pool. I gaze down, down, and deeper; then gaze deeper still.

|Words|

The day my father tells me about the wedding, I'm happy. As his only daughter, I think he expects me to weep and wail, to cling to his shirt sleeves, but the truth is that my mother died a long time ago and I'm tired of being raised by maids. I'm really too old to need a mother anyway, but I'll be leaving him soon and the thought of my father having a companion, to sit with by the fire after his day's work at Shapley's mill, makes me smile. I take his hand, dry and a little wrinkled, and press it, thinking of another hand I held so recently: one with long, white fingers, almost feminine, curled around mine.

'That's not all,' he says.

I have to shake my head to bring myself back to the room – this little room, not half so grand as *his* – and I can only look puzzled when he says, 'This is something of a fairy tale, after all.'

I remember the stories I learned at my mother's knee: wishes granted, splendid weddings and glittering gowns, the prince, all the happily-ever-afters. What else could there be?

'It's only right you should gain a stepsister too,' he says. 'Even if it is an ugly one!' He pulls his hand away, slaps his thigh, throws back his head and laughs.

On the day of the wedding, I'm in the glen behind our cottage, and I'm trying not to think of my father. Still, I wonder if this is the moment when he's saying his vows; perhaps he's kissing her, or smiling kindly upon her poor daughter, whom I have learned is called Mathilde – such a doll of a name for one so unfortunate in looks. My father did not want fanfare and fuss, and I didn't protest the decision to hold the ceremony in her town, nor that he would go alone. He's not a showy man; he dislikes such occasions. It is the homecoming he was looking forward to, the day we truly become a family.

The reason I am trying not to think of my father is wrapped around my waist, is stroking my arm, is kissing my lips so hard it feels like they might bruise. I push him off, laughing, and catch hold of his white fingers. My father's dear smiling face rises before me again and I blink. Have they served the wedding breakfast? Are they stepping into the carriage – have they started along the road?

What would my father *say* if he could see us now?

He would be shocked, I know, yet perhaps there would be pride too, and relief in the knowledge that I will be safe, that I need never fear about having food for the table or clothes on my back. What will his fairy tale be, next to mine? Only a shadow, and he will be so glad—

I remember my first sight of Dominick Shapley. It was at the mill, on a day of feasting held for all the workers and their families to welcome the owner's nephew to the fold. Everyone was merry, wearing their finest clothes. Old Shapley was so proud when he beckoned in his special guest, his only relative, come to clerk for him and learn the feel of the place before he inherits.

When I saw his face, I'd been glad of wearing my prettiest white dress. Dominick was a little older than me, and taller, a beanpole of a man, accustomed to working with his brain not his hands. There were no airs about him, though; he had a haphazard, slightly distracted manner, his lower lip still bearing the traces of blue from moistening the nib of his pen with his tongue. He'd looked at me and rubbed his cheek with his thumbnail, as I would learn was his habit when feeling uncertain.

Then he scanned the miscellaneous humanity in front of him and gave a hesitant smile. He lowered his eyes and looked at his feet; when he raised them again, it was only me he looked at.

Now he stretches out one long, thin finger and strokes my cheek, my neck, and down, lower...

I giggle. 'Stop it. We can't, not today. They'll be home soon, and I can't get dirty.'

I see the obvious joke rise to his lips, but he bites it back as too crass, too common for me, and a blossom of love unfurls in my chest. I lift my hand – my left hand, ringless as yet, but not for ever; he has given me his word.

He sees the direction of my gaze and his smile fades. 'Don't worry.' His voice is low, full of meaning. 'I'll speak to my uncle soon enough.'

I open my mouth to tell him that it needs to be soon, it *must* be soon, before too long there won't be any choice – just as his forehead creases into a frown; one that says his uncle will not necessarily be happy, that things will be said, there will be more *words*. I close my lips against the news I have for him, just once more. For this is a happy day, a perfect day, and it will wait a little longer; there's time enough for him to bury his kisses in my neck.

But he pulls away, suddenly decisive. 'Come on,' he says. 'They'll be home now, won't they? Let's go and have a look at her.'

I know it's not the bride he means from the laughter in his eyes. 'Dominick, you can't!' I say. 'You mustn't laugh.' Though I'm laughing too, even as I say the words. I told him all about my father's wedding, of course. I also told him about my ugly stepsister. He knew just what to say then; he always knows what to say. *No one could be prettier than you anyway. So what else should she be?*

'I have to pay my respects to the new couple! It's the only decent thing.' He stands tall above me, stretching down his hand to pull me upward. 'Come! I'll say I met with you in the lane.'

Dominick is right, the carriage is at the door when we arrive, and suddenly I'm nervous. I've never met this woman who is to share my home – who is she? Will she be kind? Impatient? Domineering? I push my concerns away. My father is a sensible man; surely he will have chosen well. Anyway, we won't be sharing a house for long. I feel Dominick at my side, the height of him, and slip my hand into the crook of his arm, and find myself smiling.

They are gathered in the drawing room, which seems rather crowded, even with such a small party. No one seems to find it odd that Dominick and I arrive together and I take that as a sign of things to come, that it will soon become quite ordinary, and then all thought of it is lost in the bringing of tea and sherry and clasped hands and professions of welcome and pleasure in everyone being together at last.

Then my father and stepmother – a plain, unremarkable woman, but with warmth in her brown eyes – step aside and for the first time I see my new sister, standing quietly in the corner of the room.

I blink. It cannot be. This isn't the dowdy creature I've come to expect: the twisted form, the hooked nose, the straggly hair.

She is golden.

She stands there self-contained and lovely, with fine blonde hair teased into perfect curls, porcelain skin, prettily blushing cheeks, luxuriantly curved lips. Her dress is gleaming silk, clinging to her slight little figure as if desperate to never let her go. She smiles and I am suddenly certain that if I was to strike her, she would chime like crystal.

I'm vaguely aware of my father's roar of laughter at his fine joke about her ugliness; my stepmother's wry shake of her head. Mostly, though, I am conscious of Dominick as he steps in front of me, reaching out a hand to take hers; hearing him say, in hesitant tones, 'Charmed.'

For a moment she is hidden behind his form. Their voices are a low murmur, exchanging pleasantries I can't make out, and then he steps back and a little away from me. I sense the movement as he rubs at his cheek with his thumbnail.

I see Mathilde again. Her cheeks are roses; her eyes are full of glitter.

She rushes to my side and clasps my hand. She tells me that she loves me already.

～

Mirror, mirror…

I lean in towards the glass and frown at what I see. *The loveliest of all*, I think. That's who I am; that's what I'm supposed to be. I am younger than Mathilde, if only by a month. Everyone is supposed to desire the younger sister, aren't they? They're always the best, the cleverest, the most beautiful; the most deserving.

No one could be prettier than you anyway. So what else should she be?

But Mathilde is prettier than I am. And if she's the fairest of them all, what does that make me?

I scowl. My skin is pallid and my hair lank, my eyes dulled with worry. I wrap my arms around my waist; is it thickening already? If it isn't, it soon will be.

I close my eyes and go into the dark. Images arise: Dominick chatting to Mathilde outside church on Sunday, her silver laughter tinkling into the air; his eyes, never looking away from hers; his uncle smiling on, as if *this* face, so pretty, would lighten his household so much he wouldn't mind if she failed to lend weight to his coffers.

But it is my father's face that I see most clearly, his eyes looking steadily, softly, into mine. How can I tell him my shame? And what can he do? There's no way Dominick will have me now.

Then I know what it is I need, what any fairy tale needs. I have to find my fairy godmother.

The wise woman lives at the edge of the woods. She's been there as long as anyone can remember and will no doubt be there when they've gone. No one knows how old she is or where she came from. They speak of her in whispers. They say she gets her power from the little folk who live beneath the hollow hills, that she sticks an iron knife into the earth in order to converse with them and share their secrets.

I hack my way through thick thorns to get to her, low branches clutching at my hair. It feels like the quest before the prize, or perhaps a penance given before the deed is done, paid for by the blood running from the scratches on my arms and legs.

When I reach her hut, the light is fading and the ramshackle structure is barely distinguishable from the mass of reaching twigs and thrusting roots that frame it. I hesitate a moment, gazing into the lowering sun. It will be dark soon. Perhaps that is fitting.

Be bold, I think, and I take a deep breath before I walk up to the door and knock.

'Mother,' she tells me. 'That's my name.'

I try not to notice the smell of her unwashed clothes, the animal must of her skin and hair. Her voice is cracked from lack of use. I hide my disgust and bow my head in assent. Why not? The name's as good as any other.

'You have coin?'

I nod. I sold my mother's necklace for this. It was the one thing she had left me. I told myself it's what she would have wanted. What is a bauble, compared with the heart's desire?

She gestures towards some rough wooden shelves, which are laden with dusty bottles filled with liquids or seeds or pastes; jars turned opaque with grime; leathern skins of creatures no longer recognisable; bundles of dried herbs.

I wonder what they are. Am I supposed to choose? There is such a number and none are labelled. So many charms a woman needs, to gain a man or lose one, to heighten passion or rid her belly of his seed. I suspect that many are meant to inspire love. Yet I doubt there is anything here a man would want; they never seem to need such things.

I recognise a sprig of yew. Then nightshade, a mandrake root, the blue of monkshood. And there are plants for the unwanted, for bringing down the flowers, as the squeamish might put it: pennyroyal and rue.

I turn to Mother. I give her an earnest smile, one that I hope will persuade her to help me, and explain what it is I need. She doesn't comment or question, merely snatches with clawed hands at this herb or that preparation. She places them on a wooden board balanced on two stones, all she has for a table, and shakes drops into a bottle, adds a pinch of something dry that smells like old pepper. The grey rags of her hair hang over her face as she wraps my purchase in a scrap of fabric. I cannot tell if she is frowning or smiling or if her expression is blank.

My hand goes to my belly, stroking it as my gaze roams the shelves once more. 'Wait,' I say. 'I may need something else too. Just in case it doesn't work.'

'Doesn't work?' She grins at last, revealing sparse yellow teeth like pegs in her mouth. 'Aye, well, it might not. If you don't have the fairies' favour, there's nothing that will help you.'

She reaches once more for the shelves.

I hear a low wail. I bite my lip and glance at my father and stepmother, though they remain motionless, standing by the fire.

The doctor is in the next room with Mathilde. I wonder what he is doing. Perhaps he is blistering her fine skin to see if she can feel it. Perhaps he's sticking silver pins into her limbs to see how she twitches.

I cover a smirk. I hadn't quite imagined this when I went to the wise woman, looking for a spell; seeking a miracle.

My stepsister's golden hair is darkened now, plastered to her skull with sweat. Her skin is clammy and taut, distorted by her pain. Muscular spasms wrack her body so hard her bones are almost breaking.

I can scarcely hide my pleasure.

My success is a shock; I must have the fairies' favour after all. My wish has been granted. My stepsister is ugly at last.

The first time the fit came upon her, they excused it. They claimed it was mere delicacy, that her nerves were disordered for a time and would not be so again. Or perhaps she had eaten something that disagreed with her – if they only knew! But it happened again, and again, her lovely form thrown into hideous convulsions. And so the doctor had to be summoned, though he was a man of *fixed views*, as my father put it, and those of the most old-fashioned kind.

Now the doctor speaks quietly to my father and stepmother. His countenance is solemn and there are few words required; if we are to do what we must, he says, better it should be done at once.

He leaves my father staring into the fire and my stepmother shedding bewildered tears. I comfort them as best I can. Anyway, it will be over soon. The doctor has gone to summon the closed carriage that will take Mathilde away. She has been classified with the deficients, and she will be taken where they are: a foreboding building in the next town with bars at the windows and locks on the gate, where strange cries pierce the air, not from without but from within.

It is the kind of establishment not mentioned in fairy tales. Or perhaps it is only that the occupants of such places do not return to tell their stories.

And there she will sleep for what may as well be a hundred years.

'It's your child,' I tell my prince, but he will not look at me.

I had waited for Dominick outside the mill. It took three days before I could catch him alone. I smooth my frock over the slight swell of my belly, but still he turns his face away.

I stare at his features, remembering kissing those lips, those cheeks. Clutching at his hair while he worked at me. He wanted me badly enough then. He had grasped my body, clinging to me even after he was spent. He'd laughed with me. He'd laughed at *her*.

Now I see the pain of her absence in his eyes. They are hazy, and I realise he isn't here at all, not really; he's still with her, or lost in grief at the loss of her. I cannot reach him, though I try, catching hold of his white hands and pressing them to my cheeks.

He snatches them back as if my touch burns. With a wordless cry, he rushes away.

The next time I see him, at first, I think it is an apparition.

He is walking up the path to our door, and a little arm is tucked into his. I catch a flash of golden hair, a white-toothed smile, a blushing cheek. I blink. It isn't real, I know it can't be real, but my stepmother shrieks in my ear and I know that it is.

I came back, she simpers in a weak little voice, and everyone thrills over her words. I put my hand to my forehead, which is damp; it is damp with sweat from the layers I am forced to wear to conceal my pregnancy.

I see Dominick's face and forget how to breathe. His words are like a new language in my ear.

'Yes, she is quite restored,' I catch. 'Almost as soon as she arrived there! Can you imagine? No, there can be very little wrong with her, indeed.'

I think of the tiny bottle concealed at the bottom of my trunk. There is not a drop of the wise woman's tincture left. There is only the other: a potion wrapped in a filthy scrap of cloth, still bearing the stink of her hands.

My own hand goes, unconsciously, to my belly, concealed beneath a loose shawl. My gaze returns to the happy couple, glowing with their joy. It spills from them. Everyone feels it. Everyone smiles. Dominick tells us that they are engaged to be married.

And so here is the fairy tale. Prince Charming, claiming his bride – what was her name, in the stories? There were several, weren't there? I cannot remember it, and I wonder that she was so interchangeable. But then, the only name she ever needed was *Beauty*.

I grimace at the bouquet I carry: all white for a wedding, roses and lilies. The smell of the latter makes me nauseous, though I had insisted on large blooms to help conceal my shame. For this is a happy day, a perfect day, and that will wait a little longer. Who, after all, would wish to spoil such an occasion?

The traditional music plays and we stand for the bride. Brides are always radiant, the fairest of them all even when they're not, but in this case everyone is thoroughly bewitched. How could they not be? Such loveliness, peeping modestly through her veil, dressed in dazzling white and glittering with jewels. Of course; the groom can afford it, after all. He is waiting by the altar, and he has eyes for no one else.

The church is full. I had thought the doctor's decision would be a stain she'd never wash off, but everyone found themselves so happy to forget; to receive once more my blonde and shining sister, the princess of us all.

The prince takes her hand in his. He places a golden ring upon her finger.

Don't worry, he'd once said to me. *I'll speak to my uncle soon enough.* Nothing but words; nothing but air.

They kiss and a murmur passes about the room. Everyone can see how perfect they are, this man and his wife. Soon they will walk from the church, under an arch made by everyone's hands. Their guests will shower them in white petals.

First, they go to the table where they will sign the register. He pulls out the chair for her, then leans in close, takes up the quill and pulls the parchment towards him. He dips the nib in the silver inkwell.

But the pen blots. He dabs the white page with blotting paper, inspects the nib more closely. Then, delicately, he touches it to his tongue, always and ever a clerk, just as he was to me; just as he always did. When he resumes his signature, there is a little blue smudge on his lip.

Mathilde's laughter is a chiming bell. She reaches out with a snowy handkerchief, to wipe the ink away. He shakes his head, as if to say *This is who I am*, and instead he leans in and their laughter is smothered in their kiss. She takes the quill and signs her own name, and when they stand, laughter spreads through the gathering; the bride and groom are not quite so perfect now, nor so lovely. Both of their lips bear traces of blue – a stain they can't so easily cast off.

The two of them stand shoulder to shoulder, bound into one before us all.

It's then that Dominick begins to choke.

I cannot help it; I smile. We all lean forward as Mathilde too starts to clutch at her throat – as they both fall to the floor, gasping for air. Old Shapley bends over them, calling Dominick's name, patting at his shoulders, as if that will save him.

Of course, nothing will. He signed his life away the moment he signed his pledge to *her*.

My stepmother's shrieking hurts my ears. I suppose she thinks her child has been taken by another fit, but she must see that this is different when froth starts to gush from Mathilde's lovely mouth.

I alone am motionless. Everyone else crowds in, wanting to know what they can do, there must be something, are they all right?

They are not all right. The spell is working. It is taking hold of their souls, and it will not give them back again. I made sure of that.

Then someone picks up the pot of ink. They sniff; they peer into its black depths.

Poison. The word is taken up, passing from mouth to mouth, like a promise; like a kiss. It stops when it reaches me and I stir, then see that the man holding the ink is my father. He is staring at me. His gaze alone is quiet, and so soft; so steady. I realise that I have let my bouquet fall, revealing the mound of my belly.

Everyone begins to shuffle back. The happy couple are lying side by side, their eyes wide and staring and sightless. They are at peace now, and no one wants to be near them any longer.

Then, one by one, my gathered neighbours begin to turn and look at me.

And I understand at last: I do not have the fairies' favour. I never did. I was never the fairest of them all, was never going to have the happy ending. I am not even a sister any longer.

There is only one thing left for me to be, and they know it. I glance from face to face and see my future in their eyes. They will rip my baby from my arms. They will take my firstborn in return for just a little more life and then they will fall on me like wolves. They will make me dance in shoes of red hot iron or at the end of a rope. And they will tell stories of me, but not by name: I will only be the bad fairy at the wedding, the wicked witch at the feast.

But the fairy tale is *mine*. It belongs to me. I stride forward and snatch the pot of ink from my father's hand. It contains all the words that could ever be needed. Here is the ink that wrote their names as they declared their love. Here is the story of their lives that was yet to be written. And here are the only words I require, now: here is THE END. I tilt the bottle and see the wise woman's herbs floating amid the dark liquid. When I touch it to my lips, I make certain to drain it to the very last drop.

|A Journey|

~

It's often said that life's a journey, but writing is one too, marked with striving and effort and lessons learned, milestones reached and new ones sighted, not to mention a few trips and spills, and right at the start of it all, that necessary thing: the will to begin.

I started out with a lot of dreaming before I set pen to paper. I was a child who loved books, and it's not a big step from there to imagine writing one, but it was a dream I kept quiet and close and safely untested. At some point, though, it began to seem like it was time to try, or to put the dream away.

This took until I was in my thirties. (It wasn't particularly quick, this journey of mine.) Spurred along by the encouraging words in Stephen King's *On Writing*, I finally joined a local writing class. That was in 2003, and it didn't carry me all that far; I didn't write what I'd call a complete short story until six months afterwards. And yet it took me from uncapping my pen and putting it to paper, which was a pretty giant leap. I wrote poetry, and snippets, and oddities, and showed the first signs of having an imagination that was, let's say, just a little dark.

I would point out that it's for all our good that I left poetry behind me, but just this once, and since you're getting a glimpse behind the curtain, here is something else that happened during that course: my first foray into horror, albeit in the form of some fairly ropey verse. Don't say I didn't warn you…

The Mighty Sostris

The Mighty Sostris casts aside his cape
And heaves a sigh of black despair.
Down go his wand and silken hat
He stands: a stooping man with thinning hair.

An all-too seasoned act in a second-rate club
An unsurprising rabbit. A flea-bitten dove
A besequinned blonde with mouse-brown roots
The scant applause. The derisory hoots.

Later, he sits with drink in hand
Staring at naught, thinking no more
Is startled into answering
A knocking at the door

A small, fearless girl with Bible clutched
She wants to talk, she feels his plight
She senses his yearning to be touched
She prays with him. He sees the light.

Loaves and fishes, water to wine
The greatest magician of all time!
No trial for Him – these magic shows.
The Lord will help him. That, he knows.

The crowd is muttering, supine, bored
As the sequinned assistant lies down to be bound.
As he fastens and gags her with silken cord
A moment of doubt enters her mind.

Her eyes open wide as Sostris stands forth.
The chainsaw screams, but his face is like stone;
The blade splashes through flesh
And grinds on the bone.

A flash of light. A woman's shriek.
People rising to their feet.
'I think she's dead!' comes the call.
This isn't what they came to see, at all.

Then, 'Alakazam!' Great Sostris cries.
'God's own grace won't be denied.
This woman will stand whole again.
A miracle is now made plain!'

A silence falls, as though by force.
'Show them, Lord,' he whispers, hoarse.
The woman lies still. Her blood still seeps.
The Mighty Sostris falls onto his knees and weeps.

Moving swiftly onwards, after that came more milestones. There was my first published story, a piece of life writing called 'The Day I Drew God', written for the *Toowrite* website and picked up by *The Lincolnshire Echo*. Then came my first genre story to be accepted for a website; a magazine; an anthology. My first reading, at Waterstones Liverpool ONE, a *Black Static* showcase alongside Joel Lane and Conrad Williams, and with the great Ramsey Campbell in attendance (no pressure, then). My first convention, FantasyCon 2011, where I made some very dear friends. My first story to appear in translation. The first picked for a *Best Of* anthology, and then the next. Winning the Shirley Jackson Award for short fiction. And of course, in January 2012, the publication of *A Cold Season*, my first novel, which was somewhat astoundingly selected for the Richard and Judy Book Club. Six more novels with Jo Fletcher Books followed, then two with Titan, published under the pseudonym A. J. Elwood: *The Cottingley Cuckoo* and *The Other Lives of Miss Emily White*.

But the short stories have continued. I started writing them for the sheer love of the thing, and I hope that never stops. They act as charge for the batteries, refuelling stations along the road. Writing novels can be arduous, but short stories are complete little adventures in their own right. They're inspirational. I couldn't have written my novel *Path of Needles* without first writing 'Black Feathers'. I couldn't have embarked on my neo-Victorian books without working on stories like 'The Adventure of the Avid Pupil', for Sherlock Holmes themed anthologies.

My earlier tales were collected in 2016 in *Quieter Paths*, a limited edition from PS Publishing, now out of print. A bird themed mini collection, *Five Feathered Tales*, followed from SST. That one grew out of my very first FantasyCon, where I met talented genre illustrator, Daniele Serra. I still remember him saying to me, 'Aliiiii! How do we work together?!' It was a very limited edition and a beautiful thing, full of Dani's gorgeous artwork, and is also now out of print. Two of its stories are included here.

Then came another fortuitous meeting at a con, with Steve Shaw of Black Shuck. I'd contributed short stories to his anthologies previously, but this time he asked if I was interested in submitting work for a *Shadows* micro collection. I promptly revealed some ideas for themes I'd brought along to the event, all ready to pitch to him. That's how *The Flowering*, my collection of Victorian tales, came about; two of its stories are included here too.

Yet most of the stories in *A Curious Cartography* have not been previously collected. They've been written for a wide range of anthology submissions or magazines or simply for my own pleasure, or because they kept up an insistent knocking at the back of my mind. And, appropriately for a collection that sets out to map part of a writing journey, many of them arose from their settings. Travel is itself inspirational. New places come with folklore, myths and legends, and give rise to new tales all their own. They can also be unsettling; sensory impressions strike all the more vividly when they're unfamiliar. The stories included here range from Vietnam to Sweden, from London to New York, from the east coast of Yorkshire and over the border into Lancashire. Of course, some also hail from a land far, far away, where yet more stories lurk…

But then, writing is always a case of picking up a pen and stepping off the edge of the map. Here be monsters. Here be spirits. Here be birds of the air. Here be mysteries and wickedness, and long may there be so, as long as the ink holds out and the mind wonders, 'What if?'.

That's the thing with writing though, isn't it? You never know where it will lead. I certainly didn't, when I sat there, terrified, in my first ever writing class. It's been an adventure, and indeed a privilege. There are always new journeys to be had; thank you for joining me along this part of mine.

Alison Littlewood, South Yorkshire, June 2023.

|Acknowledgements|

~

A huge and heartfelt thank you to Steve Shaw, not only the editor and publisher of this volume, but also a genuinely lovely person.

Thank you too to the many editors and publishers who have helped inspire these stories with anthology invitations, ironed out the creases and shepherded them into print, including Mark Morris, Marie O'Regan, Paul Kane, Ellen Datlow, Stephen Jones, Paula Guran, Ian Whates, Dan Coxon, Michael Kelly, Mark Beech, Andy Cox, Sean Wallace, Simon Clark, Scott David Aniolowski, Joseph S. Pulver, James Everington, Dan Howarth, Tim Lebbon, Christopher Golden and John Joseph Adams.

Special thanks to Ramsey Campbell for allowing me to play in his toybox with my tribute tale, 'The Entertainment Arrives'. My story '…And I'll Come To You' is another tribute, this time to that great writer of ghostly fiction, M. R. James.

Thanks go to all the publishers, editors, fellow writers, booksellers, librarians, reviewers, bloggers, event organisers and supporters who champion the short story in all its forms. And of course, as ever, to the readers.

Love and thanks always to my partner, Fergus, and my parents, Ann and Trevor.

Milton Keynes UK
Ingram Content Group UK Ltd.
UKHW040626120424
441048UK00001B/63